A Note from an Old
Acquaintance

A Note from an Old Acquaintance

Bill Walker

New York   Bloomington

iUniverse
1663 Liberty Drive
Bloomington, IN 47403
www.iUniverse.com
1-800-Authors (1-800-288-4677)

ISBN-13: 978-1-4401-3335-0 (hardcover)
ISBN-13: 978-1-4401-3333-6 (pbk)
ISBN-13: 978-1-4401-3334-3 (ebk)
ISBN-10: 1-4401-3335-2 (hardcover)
ISBN-10: 1-4401-3333-6 (pbk)
ISBN-10: 1-440-13334-4 (ebk)
Printed in the United States of America

Five copies of the book and cover of
A Note From An Old Acquaintance were printed
in just one minute using print-on-demand digital technology.

To All Loves Lost...And Found.

And to my Muse,
who continues to inspire me
in the profoundest of ways.

2006

It is said that something as small as the flap of a butterfly's wings can cause a typhoon on the other side of the world—that every action, no matter how insignificant, affects everything else in incalculable ways. And therein lies the irony.

—Anonymous

1

"Please tell me why you're doing this, Brian! Please!"

He tried opening his mouth, tried to tell her the truth, but the words he'd always wielded with such effortless aplomb, failed him, slipping away like smoke on a windy day. His throat felt as if it were gripped in a vise, his mind a flat, cracked slab of flyblown desert; and her muted sobs echoing through the phone's earpiece made him want to take it all back. Every word. But how could he do that, now?

"I—I'm sorry, Joanna...for everything...."

"BRIANNNN!"

THE PHONE JANGLED, RIPPING Brian Weller out of the dream. He sat up, gasping, sounds and images jumbling in his groggy brain until none of it made any sense.

The phone rang again, startling him.

He grabbed it, his eyes struggling against the darkness in the room.

What time was it?

Jesus, it was only 6:00. It felt even earlier due to the late night he'd spent at the computer.

He cleared his throat. "Brian Weller."

"Is this a good time?"

Brian's body stiffened. It was Armen Surabian, Penny's neurologist. "What's wrong? Is everything—"

The voice on the phone softened. "Hold on, Hoss, everything's fine. Her vitals are stable, but we need to talk."

Brian sagged back against his pillows, his heart rate dropping. "I keep dreading that phone call, Armen."

"And this one isn't it, but we still need to talk."

"What about? And why couldn't it wait until a decent hour?"

"I'd rather not discuss it on the phone."

"Now, you're making me nervous again, Doc."

"I'm sorry, I don't mean to, but it's been awhile since we've assessed the situation, and I think it's time we did. And don't call me Doc."

Brian grinned. "And don't call *me* Hoss."

It was an old gag between them, a sure sign that things were status quo...for the moment.

"All right," Brian said. "What time?"

"How about we do lunch? Meet me at the Bistro. I'll buy."

"Now, that's an occasion. You're on."

Brian hung up, then padded into the bathroom and threw cold water on his face. Might as well get up and see if he could get any more writing done. Donning his bathrobe, he trudged downstairs, turned on his MAC G5 then entered the kitchen to brew up some much-needed java. How much sleep had he gotten? Four hours? And Armen's phone call coming at this ungodly hour didn't make it any better. Brian shook his head and laughed. Did the guy ever sleep? He was always calling at weird hours and never seemed to realize that he might be inconveniencing someone. Still, he was the best doctor in Los Angeles, and Penny deserved the best.

A Note from an Old Acquaintance

When the coffee finished brewing, Brian filled his mug, went back into his study and sat down in front of the computer. The familiar image he'd put up as wallpaper on the screen stared back at him. It was a picture of Penny and their son, Joey, taken on a postcard-perfect summer day at Roxbury Park two years before. They'd both mugged for the camera, looking silly. It wasn't the best photo. It was just the last one...before the accident.

"Miss you, Little Guy," Brian said, to the image of the towheaded boy grinning back at him.

He took a sip of his coffee and grimaced. When would he ever learn to make it right? It was something Penny always did, and she'd always chided him that he should learn.

"Guess, I never will, Pen."

Looking down, he turned the mug in his hands, the one she'd given him after his first book sold, its once stark white glaze now chipped and yellowed. He read the stenciled words for the millionth time.

GENIUS AT WORK!

He sure as hell didn't feel like a genius. Not now, anyway, no matter what the *L.A. Times* or any of those other rags spouted. They'd called his latest, *A Nest of Vipers*, "a towering landmark of suspense." It still sat in the top ten after twenty-five weeks. No small feat. And to tell the truth, he was proud of it. But because of the mess his life had become, it had taken every ounce of will and discipline to finish that book. Now, after six months of beating his head against the wall, it was time to acknowledge that the well had run dry; and the thought of *that* scared him to the core.

He brought up the previous night's work and read through it, hating every word.

"Who are you kidding, Weller?" he said, shaking his head. He reached for the DELETE key, and noticed the little mailbox icon in the upper right-hand corner of the screen was flashing, indicating fresh mail.

Well, at least *someone* loves me, he thought, grabbing the mouse. He opened his AOL account, ignoring the headlines shouting about the latest North Korean saber rattling and the newest fad diets.

Thirty e-mails. Thirty since last night.

Most of them were the usual spam for hot stocks and hotter singles, as well as those from the ubiquitous pharmaceutical touts. He deleted them with the practiced motions of one who'd done it a thousand times.

That left four. Two were from his agent. He smiled, knowing Doris would be falling all over herself to apologize for her caustic humor during their last phone call. He'd read them later. The third was from his college alumni association with the usual pitch for money.

Not today.

He stared at the subject line of the last one, frowning.

A Note From An Old Acquaintance....

Odd. A part of him wanted to delete it, feeling it was just another spammer with a crafty come on. But another, deeper part of him *knew* it wasn't.

"The hell with it," he said, clicking the READ button with a jab of his index finger. The e-mail flashed onto the screen. The font resembled feminine handwriting, almost as if someone had scanned an actual letter.

August 19, 2006

Dear Brian:

I know it's been almost fifteen years since we last saw or spoke with one another, and I'm not at all sure if I'll be able to put my feelings into the proper words as eloquently as I know you can, so I'll just muddle through.

A Note from an Old Acquaintance

I often think about the night you and I met at that private party Nick Simon threw at the Metropolis Club back in '91. And I still remember the feelings that went through me when you asked me to dance and how we spent the evening together. I wanted you to know that night, and all the days and nights that followed, were magical ones for me, as I've always hoped they were for you.

Ever since I saw your interview on the Today Show *last month, I've wanted to contact you and tell you this—to see if I could find out why things turned out the way they did. I have so many unanswered questions, Brian. You see, you really made an impression on me, one I've carried with me all these years. What's really silly to me is why I've waited so long. Guess I was afraid of how you might feel.... And maybe how I'd feel, too. Truth is I've never stopped wondering if I deserved to meet someone as wonderful as you. Maybe I didn't. Does any of this make sense? Maybe you'll just laugh at this e-mail or...maybe you've forgotten. I hope not.*

Anyway, please tell your agent that I'm sorry for my little deception. I told her I was your cousin, so she'd give me your e-mail. She wouldn't budge on the phone number. Boy, you must REALLY think I'm nuts!

I'm now the head of the Fine Arts department at The Boston Art School. You can reach me at 617-555-8795 on Mondays, Tuesdays and Fridays when I hold office hours.

I'd love to hear from you.

Sincerely,

Joanna Richman

PS—I've read all your books. They're terrific!

He stared at the screen, his mind spinning.

"It couldn't be...."

Joanna Richman.

Brian shook his head, his emotions warring. He remembered her, all right. Her *and* that night in the minutest detail, his nascent writer's mind recording everything: the shadowy modernist interior of the club, the moment their eyes met, falling madly in love with her in the span of a heartbeat, and the one other not-so-insignificant thing that hung over that night and its aftermath like a pall: *she was engaged to another man.* And as far as how he might feel, he wasn't at all sure *how* he felt.

And the dream he'd just had.... It was more than a little uncanny.

"Why now, Joanna? Why the hell now?"

2

FOR YET ANOTHER LONG and fretful night, Brian had haunted Joanna: his sweet handsome face...his velvety voice...the breathless memory of his touch...even the smell of him! Every memory of him more vivid than ever. And despite her determined attempts to meditate, to put those thoughts into their proper perspective, the calming effects she sought had eluded her, along with much-needed sleep and blessed forgetfulness, however fleeting. Instead, she'd again lain awake for half the night, her stomach twisted into guilty knots.

What's happened to my life?

Lying there, with tear-clotted eyes, on her thousand dollar silk sheets in her multi-million dollar home, with every luxury her husband's money could buy, she felt helpless and adrift, as if she'd somehow lost herself. That was the sum total of her life.

Lost.

She'd lost the one man who'd truly loved and understood her, for reasons that still remained a mystery, and spent the best years of her life living with a man who put her on a pedestal and worshipped her as if she were a goddess; and yet he was so obsessed with his ambitions, and the power and the money that followed, she'd become just another trapping of his life, another half-forgotten trophy.

Why did she let that happen? Why had she stayed with him for all these years? Was it a stubborn refusal to admit she'd made the wrong choice? Perhaps. Her Buddhist faith gave her comfort, but she was far from attaining its lofty goal of surrendering her ego.

Was it the money? As tempting as all of it was, if it weren't for her son, Zack, she knew she could leave it all behind without a second thought. So, it wasn't that.

What about love, then? Yes, there *had* been love...once, but of a far different sort than the passion she'd felt for Brian. With Brian it felt as if they were two halves of a greater whole. Funny thing was, a part of her still loved Erik; she couldn't deny that, but her feelings for him now were like a faded photograph pressed into a dusty shopworn album.

And she was no goddess.

She was gawky little Joanna Richman from the wrong side of West-bury, New York, who'd worn braces all through her teens, and didn't have a date to her senior prom, but who loved creating her sculptures, teaching her students about life and art, and being the best mother she could be to Zack. The only other thing she wanted—and needed—was someone who would understand her and appreciate her for her virtues and her flaws—someone like...Brian. Was that so much to ask? Was her life over at forty? Maybe it was, and she was just too stupid and stubborn to accept it.

If that's the case, then why on earth did I send that e-mail?

That question roiled in her mind, as well, much like the dust motes dancing in the bright August sun streaming through the cracks in the blinds. She watched them, momentarily distracted and enthralled by their acrobatic grace, and tried to find the hidden meaning in their swirling patterns. But they were as mute as the smiling statue of Buddha sitting atop her dresser across the room.

A Note from an Old Acquaintance

Why had she stirred up something perhaps best left in the past? After all, Brian had a life, now, didn't he—a different life? Who was she to intrude upon it? Was it just because she couldn't get him out of her head?

No. The truth ran deeper than that. Nature abhorred a vacuum... and so did her heart.

He'd looked so dashing during that *Today Show* interview, so assured, so funny, so...Brian.... Yet she still couldn't make that suave televised image jibe with the news stories she'd read about his wife and son.

And there it was.....

How could she send him e-mails raking up another part of his past, a past he'd no doubt forgotten—or wanted to forget—when he was doing all he could to put on a brave face to the world? How could she be so selfish...and so cruel?

Tears stung her large green eyes for perhaps the hundredth time that morning. She sat up in bed, reached for the tissue box, and dabbed them. God, her eyes felt as if they'd been rubbed with sandpaper.

She squinted at the clock. It was after seven.

If she didn't get going now she would be late getting Zack to school and her first student meeting. A glance toward Erik's side of the bed, the covers neatly remade, told her the usual story. With his new building nearly completed, he would be manic, consumed by the myriad details, his family an afterthought. It was almost as if she were a widow herself.

Climbing from the bed, she took a quick shower and dressed in a simple black silk blouse and wool skirt, then sat in front of her vanity. Though the soft lights ringing the mirror cast an even glow designed to flatter, they failed to hide the dark circles under her eyes and the crow's feet standing out like the stark lines on a roadmap. And was that another worry line at the edge of her brow? She sighed and began applying her makeup. It would take a bit more of her artistic flair than usual, and the irony of that made her sigh again. What would Brian think of his "favorite artist" now?

A movement in the mirror drew her attention.

"Hi, Mom," Zack said, moving up behind her.

Joanna smiled, her son's auburn curls a mirror of her own. "Hi, baby, you ready?"

The boy rolled his eyes. "Mom, please."

Joanna chuckled. How he hated it when she called him "baby." Or at least he pretended to hate it, judging by the twinkle in his eyes. "You get something to eat?

Zack nodded. "Just some toast."

"You need more than that, honey. You're a growing boy."

"I had wheat germ, too."

"Okay, fine," she said, knowing it was useless to argue with her teenager. "I'll meet you downstairs. We're heading out in five minutes."

The boy turned to leave the bathroom then stopped. "Did Dad read my new story yet?"

The hopeful look on his face tugged at her heart. "I'm not sure. You know he's been pretty busy."

"Yeah, I know."

"I'll talk to him about it tonight, okay?"

Zack gave his mother a sweet grin. "Okay."

After dropping her son at school and braving the bumper-to-bumper snarl on the Mass Pike, Joanna made it into her office with three minutes to spare. She'd promised herself that she wasn't going to check her e-mail—wasn't even going to turn on the computer—but she'd known it was a hollow vow when she'd made it.

A Note from an Old Acquaintance

There was nothing from Brian.

"Well, what did you expect?" she muttered.

"Excuse me, Professor?"

Joanna turned, seeing her first appointment of the day standing in the doorway, an elfin freshman with soulful eyes right out of a Walter Keane painting. Joanna smiled warmly. "Come on in, Erin."

The girl sat down on the edge of the hardwood chair, fumbling with her portfolio. "Oh, Professor Richman, I don't know how I'm going to pass drawing, I just can't get it, I just can't—"

Joanna reached out and grasped the young girl's hand. It trembled like a frightened animal. "Hey, it's okay, relax. No one's failing, here."

The young woman took a deep breath. "You make it look so easy, Professor. And I feel like such a klutz."

Joanna reached over to her bookshelf and pulled out a sketchpad and opened it to a blank page, then picked up a pencil off her desk. "It wasn't always easy for me, either. The first thing you have to have is the desire, then the talent. You have both, Erin. Now all you need is the confidence that comes with practice." Joanna handed the pad to the girl, who took it, then looked at her questioningly.

"Do you see anything in this room that compels you to sketch it?"

The girl studied the room, frowning. After a moment, her eyes stopped moving and she nodded. "That white rose in the vase."

Joanna smiled. "Good. Now, go on and draw it."

Erin began sketching lines on the page, her attention shifting back and forth between the rose and the paper.

"It's a beautiful rose, Professor."

Joanna felt her eyes grow misty again. "Yes, it is."

3

THE BISTRO, AN ELEGANT little restaurant nestled into a one-story building erected in 1890, sat in the shadow of the sprawling new wing of Saint John's Hospital in Santa Monica, where Armen had privileges.

Brian edged his Dodge Viper through the noontime traffic and found a space in the lot behind the restaurant. The valet smiled, remembering him. Throughout the drive, it had taken all his efforts to keep his mind from speculating about what the good doctor wanted to talk about. The trouble was, when he avoided thinking about that, his mind kept returning to Joanna's e-mail. He'd left it on the screen, as if by shutting it down he might somehow lose it. He just wasn't sure what bothered him more: the thought of losing it or the fact that he was concerned about losing it.

Locking the car door, he wondered if he should have taken the Expedition, instead. The Viper stuck out like a sore thumb, parked between a battered VW Passat and a dusty Toyota Forerunner. He'd loved it's sleek metallic-blue exterior and dual white racing stripes when he'd bought it some years back; but now, even though it was still fun to drive, it seemed ostentatious somehow, almost decadent, not to mention expensive as hell with gas prices the way they were. He pocketed his keys, wiped a beading of sweat from his brow, and walked toward the restaurant, his sand-colored hair already plastering itself to his skull.

The coolness of the Bistro's darkened interior wrapped its arms around him in a grateful embrace, the air redolent with a heady mix of continental spices. Even though it was just past noon, only a few tables were filled. Silverware and lead crystal glassware gleamed atop starched white tablecloths, and potted palms dotted the floor in strategic locations designed to give each group of tables the illusion of privacy. He spotted Armen toward the rear sitting at his usual table. Brian waved, and stepped past the upright piano, already feeling the midday heat leeching from his body.

"Hiya, Doc," Brian said, sliding into the plush chair across from his friend.

Armen Surabian was a study in contrasts to Brian. Where Armen was stocky and developing a paunch, Brian was tall and lean. Where Armen had thick black hair that fell over bushy brows and dark penetrating eyes, Brian's baby-fine locks were brushed straight back, cornflower blue eyes cool and steady.

Armen smiled, full lips parting to reveal white, even teeth. "We've already done that for the day," he replied, laughing.

"And we've only been whipping that horse for ten years, old friend, why stop now?"

A waitress approached and the two of them ordered drinks. A Samuel Adams Light for Armen, chilled Evian with no ice for Brian. They kept to small talk until after the drinks arrived. Brian sensed his friend's mood turning somber.

"Okay, out with it, why all the cloak and dagger? You said she's stable."

"And she is, that's the problem."

Brian frowned. "What the hell does that mean?"

23

Armen took a swig of his beer and shook his head. "Penny's been in a coma for almost two years—"

"Two years next month."

"Her muscles have atrophied, despite our best efforts to keep them limber, and her brain waves show the same low levels they've maintained for all that time. She's not brain-dead, but she's not showing any improvements, either."

"You're not telling me anything new."

Armen nodded. "I know, and I'm sorry, it's—"

Brian leaned towards his friend. "What are you trying to say, that she isn't going to get better, that she'll never wake up?"

Armen's eyes stayed focused on the table.

"Look at me, for Christ's sake."

The neurologist looked up, his expression tightening. "I'm sorry.... I'm just plain lousy at this bedside manner crap. Should have become a researcher. The truth is I no longer think the prognosis for recovery is viable."

"Please do me a favor and cut the doctor talk. How many times do we read or see stories on the news about people waking up after decades? And how many times did you tell me things were going to get better?"

"Yes, that's true, but—"

"I'm not finished. Why are you giving up, Armen?"

A dark cloud passed over his friend's face. "I'm not giving up," he said, leaning forward. "I never give up. I just hate to see you sitting there in her room every night...waiting. You need to get on with your life."

"Penny *is* my life!"

The couple at the next table turned. Brian felt the hot flash of a blush rising up his neck to his cheeks.

"Sorry," he mumbled, shaking his head. He signaled the waitress.

"Give me one of those." He pointed to Armen's beer. The waitress nodded and moved toward the bar. A moment later she reappeared, setting the beer down with a soft thud. Brian waved the proffered glass away and took a deep swig from the icy bottle, then sighed.

"Now I remember why I stopped drinking these. I liked 'em too damn much."

"You okay?" Armen asked, placing a hand on his friend's arm.

Brian shrugged and pulled away, gazing through the tinted glass at the traffic stopped at the 23rd Street light. "As okay as anyone can be with his wife in a coma and his little boy rotting in a grave."

Armen looked stricken.

"I still can't believe it, you know? I still can't believe my little Joey isn't going to come bounding into my study yelling at the top of his lungs, 'Daddy, Daddy, play toys, play toys!' He was only three, Armen, only three goddamn years old."

"I really wish I could be more of a comfort to you about all this," Armen said, "I really do. But the fact remains that you need to face the issue of long-term care. A special facility. Keeping her at Saint John's is going to bankrupt you."

"Money's not a problem."

"Still, these facilities are top-notch and are better equipped to deal with the issues of those who are chronically comatose. I know one in Westwood that would be perfect."

"No."

"Please, Brian."

"I want her here...under your care."

Armen sighed and leaned back in his chair. "I appreciate that, but I've done all I can."

Brian turned his gaze from the window. "You *are* giving up, Armen. Face it. And you want me to give up, too."

"I told you, I—"

Brian lifted his hand, cutting off his friend. "I'm not blaming you. I guess I'm just feeling that I'm at the end of my rope. You know the new book I keep telling you about? Well, there isn't one. I can't get the damned words out anymore. Nothing sounds right—nothing. I should be in that hole next to Joey or lying in that bed instead of Penny, for all the good I am. She'd handle all this a lot better than I have."

"You're selling yourself short," Armen said.

"Am I? I'm not so sure."

Armen stared back at his friend. "I am. Losing Joey would have devastated Penny, as much as it has you. And having you lying in that bed would be as much a torment for her as it is for you. Don't kid yourself. You were her rock. And you still are. She needs you as much now as she ever did. Maybe more so."

Brian blinked back tears, shaking his head. "I know that. I just don't know if I can keep going like this. At least when I was writing, I could lose myself in the story with the characters. But I don't even have that."

"You will."

"Please, tell my agent that," Brian said, a grim smile turning up the corners of his mouth.

"Nothing has to be decided now. I just wanted to give you the heads up. Of course, she can be here as long as you wish, and I'll be honored to help with her care. And we'll both pray for a miracle. Like you say, people are known to beat the odds all the time."

Brian nodded, staring at the remnants of his beer. "Some people say I beat the odds when it came to my career.... Maybe so." He raised his head and leveled his gaze at Armen. "But I'd give it all up in a New York minute just to have them back for one more day."

"I know," Armen said.

For the rest of their meal, they talked of other things: the Red Sox and whether or not they would repeat their miracle, as well as the fine art prints that were Armen's passion. An hour later, Brian drove the Viper into the garage of his Beverly Hills home, and sat listening to the ticking of the cooling engine.

Maybe it was time to think about getting on with his life, maybe a change of some kind would spur his writing. Lord knew he needed that. But what did that really mean? Dating? How could he do that? After all, just as Armen had said, she wasn't brain-dead, but in the shape she was in that might even be a blessing. If she woke now, with her twisted limbs—

Brian pushed that image from his mind and climbed out of the car and headed into the house. After a quick workout on his treadmill and the requisite bench-presses, he showered, dressed and returned to the computer for another round of pointless auto-flagellation. However, when he brought the computer out of sleep mode, instead of finding the familiar blank page for his novel, there was Joanna's e-mail staring him in the face. He read through it again—twice. It still elicited a disturbing mix of emotions: a quickening of the pulse, a quiver of joy, an overlay of guilt...and anger....

...I have so many unanswered questions, Brian.

"You don't know the half of it, Joanna."

He stared at her words for a moment longer, reaching a decision, then picked up the phone and punched in a series of numbers with a rapid staccato. It was picked up on the second ring.

"Romano Public Relations," a silken feminine voice intoned.

"Hi, Evie, how's tricks? You're sounding more like a radio announcer every day."

The voice giggled and abruptly changed, rising in pitch and taking on the familiar Flatbush accent. "I'm doing better, aren't I, Mr. Weller?"

"You certainly are. I think you're ready for Prime Time."

"And lose this cushy job? Forget about it." She laughed. "Mr. Romano's on a call. You want me to have him return?"

"I'll wait, if that's okay."

"Okay, by me."

Evie clicked off, her voice replaced by a local New York radio station playing classic rock. Brian recognized the song. Boston's "More Than A Feeling." Even though he was only ten years old in 1976, when it was originally released, he felt a jab of poignant nostalgia. A perfect mirror of his present mood. Sometimes life was weird that way.

The music cut off.

"Hey, Brian, how's it hangin'?"

Brian smiled. "About as well as one might expect, Kevin."

He heard the other man sigh. "Sometimes I'm just an asshole," Kevin said. "Too much hypola and you start thinkin' it's all true. You do sound good. You really okay?"

Kevin Romano was one of those rare types in the Public Relations field who actually gave a damn about his clients and his integrity, a quality Brian cherished. "I'm fine, really."

"Good. So, what can I do to you today?"

Brian shook his head, his grin widening. The man was incorrigible.

"I need to get out of L.A. for a bit, shake out the cobwebs. You think any of the bookstores in Boston would be interested in hosting some signings for *Vipers*? I know it's old news—"

"Old news! Are you kidding? Your book's been in the top-frigging-ten practically forever! They'll fall all over themselves. You wanna little tour? I'm your man. But why Boston, why not somethin' a little closer?"

"Got a personal matter to deal with there, so I thought I'd combine it with a little business."

"Smart boy. You should've been a publicity agent."

"Then I wouldn't need you."

"Got me there." He laughed. "Anyway, give me a couple of days and I'll let you know what I come up with."

"One thing, though," Brian said. "I want a mix of stores, some Mom and Pops, as well as the chains. It gives a boost to those little stores, and it's the least I can do. Besides, those big places make me feel like I'm in a Wal-Mart."

"I can get you Target, too." Kevin said, chuckling.

Brian laughed. "Shut up, you mook."

"Hey, that's why I love you, you put up with my lousy jokes."

"And I'm beginning to wonder why."

"All right, all right. Call me in a couple of days."

After a few more moments of small talk, they hung up and Brian faced his computer once again. He clicked on the REPLY button and a new e-mail window appeared with Joanna's address. He started typing, surprised the words came so easily.

August 20, 2006

Dear Joanna:

I must say I was surprised to hear from you after all this time. Pleasantly so. I've often thought about you over the years, wondering what you were doing at a given moment, and if you were happy. You see, you made quite an impression on me, too....

Anyway, you know what I've been up to, so I won't bore you with a recitation of my career highlights, but I may be in Boston in the near future for some book signings. I'd love to see you, maybe take you out for dinner, if that's okay.

I apologize for Doris, my agent. She's a real watchdog, where I'm concerned. I'm surprised she even gave you the e-mail address. Then again, the cousin gambit was a clever one, as she knows I have a gaggle of those scattered across the country.

Brian paused, wondering if he should put in his phone number and decided against it. He wasn't sure why, perhaps a part of him felt the need for a little caution, or maybe he didn't want to burst the bubble, whatever the hell *that* meant. He resumed typing.

I'll let you know when the dates firm up for my little tour and hopefully we can get together.

All my best,
Brian-
PS—Please give my best to Nick

❀　❀　❀

Erik Ruby eyed the two oafs struggling to hang Joanna's life-size photo, and felt the heat rising in his cheeks. In his mind, he saw the younger one with the low-rider trousers and backwards baseball cap tripping over the laces of his tatty Air Jordans and—

"Careful with that," he snapped.

The two men froze, their expressions a mixture of fear, exasperation and weariness. The older of the two, a graying heavyset man with pale-blue eyes and a bulbous nose full of burst capillaries, signaled to his younger co-worker to put the photo down, then mopped the sweat from his brow with a soiled blue bandana.

"Are you sure you want the lady hung here, Mr. Ruby? She'll be in the afternoon sun for a good portion of the day, that way. Bad for the complexion, if you get my drift."

Ruby's dark eyes narrowed. "There's a UV coating on the glass."

The heavyset man nodded. "Right. Well, then we'd best get to it. Ready, Mike?"

The younger man nodded and the two of them bent down and, with a grunt, lifted the photo and hung it from the two fifty-pound hooks embedded in the wall over the wet bar. The heavyset man stood back, stared at it a moment, head cocked, meaty fists on his hips, then reached out and straightened the ornate Victorian frame with a gentle shove.

"There you go, Mr. Ruby. She's right as rain. And a pretty one, too, if I do say so."

Ruby's gaze shifted from the photo to the older man, his expression stony. "Yes, she is. But I'm not paying you for your opinions."

"Uh, sorry, Mr. Ruby. No offense intended," the older man mumbled, embarrassed.

Ruby came from around the desk, handed the heavyset man a wad of cash and watched while the two workers gathered their tools and exited the office, leaving Ruby to his thoughts.

He stared up at his wife's image, drinking her in. Joanna was still as adorable as the day the photo was taken, fifteen years before. She hardly looked a day older, but as of late she'd been restless and distracted. And while the cause could be anything, a difficult client with one of her commissions, one of her students on the edge of failing, their son, Zack, it was her evasiveness—her unwillingness to speak of the problem—that rankled him. He hated it when anything caused her pain.

The phone on his glass-topped desk buzzed. He walked over and glanced at the blinking light.

His private line.

At least the idiots from the phone company had finally gotten the lines working. He reached over and jabbed the speaker button.

"Yes?"

"Mr. Ruby, it's Dean Meltzer, from IT."

"Ah, Meltzer, what can I do for you? I trust everything's on schedule for the move to Ruby Plaza?"

"Yes, yes, of course. Can't wait 'til December. Everyone's sick and tired of tripping over one another."

"It won't be long now. So, what do you need?"

"I have your weekly report, sir."

Ruby smiled and shook his head. Too many damned details with this new building. He was forgetting things he shouldn't. Then again, he wasn't getting any younger.

Still shaking his head, he said. "So what's my boy been up to?"

"It would seem that Zack has quite a few female admirers. I really had to stop reading them after awhile."

Ruby chuckled. "Well, if that's his only problem, then his mother and I will have one less thing to worry about. Can't be too sure with all these predators on the Internet, you know."

"Yes, sir, you're right about that."

"Is there anything else?"

"You did say to monitor *all* your home accounts."

"Yes...." Already bored with the conversation, Ruby picked up his Blackberry and began checking his calendar.

"Well, your wife's e-mail account was fairly inactive until the other day, when she sent a message to a man in California."

Ruby frowned. *California?*

"What was the address?"

Meltzer told him.

"Doesn't ring a bell. Did he reply?"

"Yes, sir, he did."

"Forward everything to me and I'll check it out."

A Note from an Old Acquaintance

"Already done, sir."

"Thank you, Meltzer. And be sure to let me know if my son makes any conquests."

Meltzer laughed. "Will do, Mr. Ruby."

Ruby ended the call and reached for his Blackberry.

4

THE HEELS OF BRIAN'S dark red Lucchese boots struck a hollow cadence on the shiny linoleum of Saint John's new wing when he made his way toward Penny's room at the end of the hall. Open only for the last few months, the paint still smelled fresh, though now it was mixed with the familiar odor of hospitals: rubbing alcohol, pine-scented disinfectant, the rot of disease and the sickly sweetness of death. It was an odor he'd grown to detest.

Reaching the room, he strode through the door and stopped short, as he always did, struck by the quiet horror of all the monitors and tubes. So many damned tubes snaking into and around what was left of his wife. The respirator breathed, inhaling and exhaling with robotic precision, making a sound that almost qualified as a sigh.

Wssssshhhhh. Haaaaaaaaah.

Wssssshhhhh. Haaaaaaaaah.

A nurse stood near the monitors making adjustments and marking down updates on Penny's chart.

"Any changes?" Brian asked.

The nurse looked up, startled. "Oh, I'm sorry, Mr. Weller. No, nothing's changed."

A Note from an Old Acquaintance

He nodded and made his way over to Penny's bedside.

It was just past four, the sun a fiery ball above the Pacific, casting a reddish glow into the room and reminding Brian of a scene out of an old horror film. It made him shiver. The nurse misinterpreted this.

"If you're cold, Mr. Weller, I can turn down the air. We keep it cool for your wife. She seems to do better with it this way, but I can—"

"No, it's fine. Thank you."

He wished she would finish her rounds and leave them alone. It was clear she was a fan, and felt awkward seeing her literary hero in such surroundings. Perhaps reading his mind, she wrapped up her duties and left the room a few minutes later, a tentative smile on her face.

Brian gazed down at Penny. Armen had not been exaggerating. Both arms and legs were curled in on themselves in impossible angles that would have been painful for a normal, healthy person. And she'd lost weight over time. How much he couldn't tell, but her athletic body had become a shell, with deep hollows and crevasses where gentle curves and taut sinew had existed before. Her face, even in repose looked gaunt, with deep almost black shadows under her eyes, as if someone had decided she would look better made up as a Goth.

The hair was the worst. What were once long, silky blonde tresses reflecting the sunlight like a hundred thousand tiny mirrors were now drab, lifeless husks. The hospital kept it cropped close to her scalp, making her look even more skeletal and reminding him of a painting of Joan of Arc he'd seen in a museum as a child. Joan stared out of the painting, the flames licking around her, her eyes beseeching heaven— for what?

Wssssshhhhh. Haaaaaaaaah.

Wssssshhhhh. Haaaaaaaaah.

Penny's chest rose and fell, swelling to a point each time where he thought her fragile bones would break, then subsiding only to repeat, over and over and over.

"Hi, Pen," he said in a soft mumble barely audible above the machinery. "I went and saw Joey yesterday, just thought you'd like to know. Believe it, or not, the flowers I placed there last week still looked fresh. I'll have to remember what variety they were, for next time."

One of the monitors attached to his wife gave a quiet *beep* in response.

"I sure could use your help with this latest book. Nothing I do seems to work anymore. You always had a way of shaking things up—making me think. And you never let me take myself too seriously...."

He closed his eyes, feeling the ghosts of her arms wrapping around him, the haunting aroma of her Chanel perfume teasing his nostrils, her sweet breath tickling his earlobe.

"What's doing, Big Guy? My sexy genius run out of words?"

"Never.... But, can I buy some from you, if I do?" he asked, caressing the soft, downy flesh on the backs of her hands. She chuckled, running her fingers through his hair. "Oooh...I don't know, they're pretty pricey these days. They'll cost you an arm, a leg...and a couple of family jewels."

The memory of her laughter nearly drowned out the sound of...

...Wssssshhhhh. Haaaaaaaaah.

Wssssshhhhh. Haaaaaaaaah.

Brian's lips trembled and he turned from the bed, anger tightening his chest. He wanted to put his fist through the window. For a moment he even considered the stout metal chair the nurses occupied after visitor's hours, but thought better of it. It was the kind of publicity Kevin could live without. Not that Brian gave a rat's ass about that anymore. Maybe it meant there was a sliver of hope if he still cared enough about other people's feelings, even a publicity agent's.

A Note from an Old Acquaintance

Sighing, he sat down at the desk and moved aside a vase with a single flower in it, then opened the MacBook he'd brought with him and turned it on. It was a ritual he repeated every night. Like so many in his life it helped him retain what little sanity remained.

The hospital provided a wireless Internet hookup in every private room, which allowed him to access his AOL account.

More spam in his "New Mail" box.

And a reply...from Joanna.

His throat ran dry, making him cough when he tried to swallow and his hand trembled when he touched the track-pad. He forced himself to dispose of the junk e-mails first, then placed the cursor over her e-mail. But he hesitated in pushing the ENTER key.

"Come on, Weller, what the hell's the matter with you? It's just a lousy e-mail."

Wssssshhhhh. Haaaaaaaaah.

Wssssshhhhh. Haaaaaaaaah.

Penny's presence intruded into his thoughts, flooding him with shame. He started to drag the e-mail over to trash. His finger hovered over the ENTER key. One push and this nonsense was over. Another long moment passed; his finger began to cramp. And then he knew it wasn't over—not by a long shot.

He sat back, took a deep breath and pushed the READ button.

Dear Brian:

I'm so glad to hear from you. I must admit that seeing your reply gave me mixed emotions. Anyway, I'd love to have dinner with you. I'm prepping a gallery show over the next couple of weeks, my son, Zack, is gearing up for his Sophomore year in high school (I still can't believe he's a teenager), and Erik is immersed in his latest building downtown, so things are a bit busy. But once you know when you're coming, we'll work

37

out the logistics. You pick the place, but I'll warn you, I'm a diehard vegetarian. Bet you don't remember that. Anyway, please call me, if you get the chance, I'd love to chat with you.

Best,

Joanna

PS—I'm so sorry to tell you this, but Nick passed away about five years ago. Lung cancer.

Brian turned from the computer, blinking back bitter tears. Though the news came as a shock, it was no surprise. He'd half-expected something like this for years, as Nick was never in the best of health. Still, his friend deserved better than to end his days in such a dreadful way.

They'd lost touch not long after Brian left Boston, their phone calls less and less frequent. And of course, whenever they did speak, Brian always inquired after Joanna. Nick never said much in reply, his answers invariably a mumbled "She's fine," or "Haven't talked to her in a while," blah, blah, blah.

It was understandable—all things considered.

The last time they'd seen each other all those years ago was over an impromptu lunch in a little book-lined café on Newbury Street. During that lunch Nick bared his soul, revealing something that astounded Brian even now, all in an effort to keep him from making what Nick considered to be a grievous error. He'd never forgotten it...and the promise he'd made to his old friend.

"I know you meant well, Nick. And Lord knows I probably should have listened to you," he said, with a sigh. "But I just couldn't help myself, as you well know. I kept my word to you, though. I kept my word...."

And then there was Erik Ruby, Joanna's husband.

He'd nearly forgotten the bastard's name.

A Note from an Old Acquaintance

Memories of that last fateful night pushed Nick from Brian's mind in a torrent of sounds, images and emotions. His head throbbed in time to the pounding of his heart, and his chest felt as if someone were tightening a steel band around it.

"Oh, God...Joanna," he said, his brain reeling. For the briefest of moments he felt as if he might be sick. It was then the flower sitting in the vase next to his laptop caught his eye. It was then he realized just what kind of flower it was.

A rose—a single white rose.

Nausea turned to blind fury.

With a strangled cry, he swept the vase off the desk. It shattered on the linoleum floor, spraying shards of cobalt-blue glass and rank smelling water in every direction. He stared at the mess, blinking, as if not quite believing what he'd just done. Then he rose to his feet and shambled into the cramped bathroom, his hands trembling. The light snapped on automatically, a dead-white fluorescent that reflected off the gleaming ice-white tile, its faulty ballast humming like an angry insect. He stared at himself in the mirror, feeling a mixture of rage and humiliation. His pale, blotchy reflection reminded him of something out of a George Romero zombie movie.

"What the hell is happening to me?" he said, knowing the answer before he'd asked the question.

He shook his head, turned on the cold water and splashed it against his face, taking deep calming breaths. After toweling dry, he returned to the room, grateful for the hiss of cool air flowing from the vent over Penny's bed.

Wsssssshhhhh. Haaaaaaaaah.

Wsssssshhhhh. Haaaaaaaaah.

Nothing had changed with Penny, not that he'd expected any. But it seemed as if the world looked and felt entirely different. He looked

toward the desk where the computer sat. Its glowing screen beck-
oned.

His head still aching, Brian eased himself back into the chair and typed
in: *www.google.com*. When it loaded, he then typed in "Erik Ruby."

Two seconds later the screen flashed up with the first ten results out
of a total of 3,990. He spent the next half an hour poring over dozens
of web sites, most of them civic or charitable, and every one of them
featuring at least one page with a picture of Ruby's smug smiling face,
glad-handing dignitaries of every stripe. There he was, his arm around
His Honor, the Mayor, both men grinning like love-struck schoolboys.
And there he was again handing over giant photocopied checks, the
amounts on them obscenely large, and the recipients of which looking
as if they might explode with joy. Still others showed him breaking
ground on building after building, juxtaposed with shots of a ribbon
cutting ceremony in front of the completed edifice.

The photos he lingered on, however, were the ones showing Joanna
standing off to his side. He lingered on them, not only because she
looked beautiful and elegant in her formal attire, but because in nearly
every photo, there was an ineffable sadness in her eyes, as if she knew
she was there mainly as Ruby's ornament, his trophy wife, and nothing
more. Brian's anger mounted. He switched back to Google's main
screen and typed in: "Joanna Richman."

The very first entry struck pay dirt:

Harvest Gallery
... Gallery Artists: Joanna Richman. Joanna is a sculptor who builds
apparatus that prompts the viewer to question his or her relationship
with their world.
www.harvestgallery.com/artists/aRichman.html - 10k - Cached -
Similar pages

There were other web pages from different galleries and shows, all with these wonderfully arcane descriptions of her work, accompanied by pictures of the works themselves. And every piece bore the unmistakable stamp of her distinctive style, though that style had grown and matured since he'd first seen examples of it years before. Brian stared, mesmerized by a piece entitled *Corpus #5*, which depicted a white human form lying on a bed with all manner of tubes, sinewy fibrous forms and fiber optic strands—all colored in the same perfect white— entering the "body" and emanating from it. The entire piece glowed with a preternatural light, reminding Brian of Huxley's *Brave New World*. It also reminded him of something else—

Wsssssshhhhh. Haaaaaaaaah.

Wsssssshhhhh. Haaaaaaaaah.

"Jesus Christ," he said, folding the laptop closed.

The form in *Corpus #5* had been female.

A knock at the door made Brian look up, startled. Armen stood in the doorway. "You look as if you've seen a ghost," he said.

Brian shook his head and rose from the chair. "Just tired, I think." He looked over at Penny. "I've been thinking about what you said, Armen. Maybe I *should* consider moving her. It's so damned sterile in here."

Armen moved into the room and stood opposite his friend, with Penny's bed between them. "Well, it is a hospital."

"Right." Brian continued staring at his wife.

Armen checked all the gauges and glanced at the chart before speaking. "I asked you this already, but are you sure you're okay?"

"I've been wondering that myself. To tell you the truth, I've also been thinking about taking a little trip, doing some signings. Just not sure I should."

"I think it's a *great* idea."

41

Brian looked up from his wife's bed. "You do?"

"Absolutely. I know what I said at the restaurant sounded a little harsh—oh, hell, I sounded like a jerk—but I really do think you need to change your routine. Anything's better than seeing you like this."

"But, Penny—"

"—will be fine. I'm worried about *your* health, too."

Brian nodded, his eyes returning to his wife's prostrate form.

"Are you staying the night?" Armen asked. "I can have the cot brought back in. No trouble."

Brian looked over at his wife, a gentle frown creasing his brow. "Thanks, I think I'll take you up on that."

"Sure, no problem. And like I said, Penny will be fine, as always. I'll talk to you in a couple of days, when I've had a chance to get some more information about that facility in Westwood, if you're still interested."

Brian stared out the window. The sun had set and the lights of Santa Monica twinkled in the dark. The ocean loomed like a black hole. "Yeah, why don't you look into it? Can't hurt."

Armen looked past his friend, a puzzled frown creasing his brow. Brian followed his gaze to the broken vase on the floor. "Sorry, I got a little carried away with something I was trying to write."

The doctor smiled. "At least you're trying." He came around the bed and grasped Brian by his shoulders. "Do yourself the favor and *take* that trip. It'll do you a world of good."

"I'm not so sure about that."

"I am. Go. Doc's orders, Hoss."

Brian cracked a grin in spite of his dour mood. "Okay," he said. "If you're putting it that way."

Armen left a few moments later and Brian went back to his computer, his eyes straying to the white rose on the floor, the delicate petals torn and crushed by his fit of anger. He felt guilty about lying to his friend, but Armen was right. He turned and looked over at his wife. "I'm sorry, Pen, but I think I really need to do this."

Wsssshhhhh. Haaaaaaaaah.

Wsssshhhhh. Haaaaaaaaah...

...was her only reply.

Pulling out his cell phone, he put in a call to his publicist, but only succeeded in reaching his voice mail. He ended the call without leaving a message. Kevin would get in touch when everything was set. He'd just have to be patient, which was not his strong suit at the moment.

Sighing, he turned off his MacBook, gave Penny a tender kiss on her forehead, and walked down to the hospital's commissary, where he had a chef salad and an iced tea laced with too much lemon.

Back in the room, the cot in which he'd slept for so many nights had returned, the white cotton sheets taut and crisp, the pillows plumped. He also noticed they'd cleaned up the broken vase and the waterlogged mess he'd left behind. An identical vase stood in its place containing an arrangement of red & white carnations. It was as if the rose had never existed.

All during his solitary meal, he kept seeing those photos of Joanna in his mind and that look of sorrow and loneliness in her eyes. That look tore at his soul. It was never there all those years ago, and he blamed Erik Ruby for that.

The problem was, in his heart of hearts, Brian knew he was just as guilty....

❀   ❀   ❀

"Please tell me why you're doing this, Brian! Please!"

Brian started awake, squinting against the harsh fluorescent light

43

dazzling his eyes. It took a moment for his vision to clear and to realize he and Penny were not alone. A team of nurses and doctors huddled around her bed, their voices low and urgent. One of them was Armen.

Brian bolted from the cot and staggered to his feet, his eyes darting to the monitors. They were silent—flatlined.

"What's going on?" he asked, throat croaky from sleep.

Armen turned and met his gaze with tear-glistened eyes.

"Are you going to call it, doctor?" a nurse asked.

Armen glanced at the clock and sighed. "Time of death...3:05 AM."

"No...." Brian whispered, his lips trembling.

He turned and faced the wall, so the nurses wouldn't see his tears.

Penny was gone, and even though he'd been expecting this—God, he'd even prayed for it during those times of deepest pain and grief— the reality of that thought knocked out the underpinnings of his life, casting him adrift on a dark and foreboding sea.

Why hadn't Armen awakened him?

Brian already knew the answer, of course, though his heart rejected it. Armen wanted to spare him the agony of watching them work on Penny. He knew they'd done their best, could see the floor littered with the detritus of their valiant though fruitless efforts.

He sighed and wiped the tears from his face with a swipe of his sleeve, then turned and approached the bed. His legs still resisted normal movement, feeling stiff and mechanical. A part of him hoped this was all a dream, an elaborate construct of his subconscious mind designed to prepare him for the worst, and from which he would awaken into a sundrenched morning, the quiet horror of it fading from his mind. In his heart he knew better.

When Brian reached the bed the nurses drew aside. Armen hovered nearby, his swarthy face etched with grief and concern.

A Note from an Old Acquaintance

Now that Penny's face held no life, it appeared as though it were a replica fashioned from mottled gray wax. Her chest no longer rose and fell with that terrible robotic precision and his mind, rejecting that stillness, provided the illusion that it moved as before, but that hollow metallic sigh, the sound that had provided the accompaniment to their lives for the past two years was gone.

Armen grasped his shoulder and spoke gently into his ear. "We did everything we could, Brian. We think it was either a blood clot or an aneurysm. We won't know for sure until we perform an autopsy."

Brian nodded and remained silent, his puffy, red-rimmed eyes still riveted on her face. He reached out and took hold of one of her hands, caressing the soft roadmap of veins and feeling the delicate bones shifting beneath the cool, dry flesh. Tears threatened to overwhelm him again. A moment later he leaned over and placed a gentle kiss on her forehead.

"Goodbye, Sweetheart.... Please give a kiss to Joey for me and tell him his daddy loves and misses him so very much."

5

August 21, 2006

Dearest Brian:

I've been sitting here for the last hour, typing and retyping this e-mail, trying to figure out how to express the inexpressible. I'm so, so sorry about your wife, Brian. Please know that. When I read your e-mail, and then heard the news reports, I felt as if I'd lost a dear friend, and we've never even met. The only thing I can be sure of is that if she loved you, she must have been a wonderful person, too. And, of course, I understand that you need to postpone your trip. You need to take care of you. I wish I could be there to help you through this, but you know I'm here any time you want to talk or if you prefer e-mailing, that's fine, too. I'm saying a prayer for you...and Penny.

All my best,

Joanna

September 2, 2006

Dear Joanna:

Thank you so much for your condolences. They meant a great deal to me. And please forgive me for not writing you sooner. There was so much to do, arrangements to make, the memorial service, etc. What was so amazing is how many people attended, people from all over the country, some who knew her from childhood and hadn't seen her for over twenty years! The media was low-key, for once, something for which I'm very grateful. It was her wish to have her ashes scattered from a favorite hilltop in Malibu. The sunset was breathtaking that night. I take solace that she and Joey are finally together.

Thanks again for keeping me in your thoughts.

Brian

September 19, 2006

Dear Brian:

Now it's my turn to ask your forgiveness. Ever since we instituted a Summer Session last year, it gives us basically no time to prepare for the Fall. It's nuts! Student evaluations, new student orientations, faculty meetings, fire and hazmat inspections, blah, blah, blah. It seems the older I get, the busier I get with bureaucratic nonsense. Less and less time for the creative things I love. But you don't want to hear me complain, do you?

The one bright spot is a prospective student I interviewed this week. Her portfolio was stunning and she shows so much promise. Without sounding like an ego-maniac, she reminds me of me when I was that age, so eager to take the art world by storm. I think she could really do it—go all the way. To have a student like this is something every teacher dreams about.

What's happening with your work? Are you writing anything new? Got to go, someone just stuck their head in my office and told me there's yet another faculty meeting. Yuck. Talk to you soon.

Best,

Joanna

October 3, 2006

Dear Joanna:

I really love reading your e-mails. They make me realize how normal life can be. Mine's anything but normal; but I suppose it's not too shabby having two studios fighting over you. It's almost embarrassing, except for the money they keep offering.

The writing's slogging along. It's hard not having Penny as a sounding board. She was always great at telling me that I was too full of myself and then showing me the perfect solution to my literary conundrum. Now, there's a ten-dollar word for you free of charge.

Oh, before I forget, I spoke to my publicist this morning and he's bugging me to reschedule my little tour, he says that even though A Nest of Vipers *is still hot, the flames won't burn forever. He's right, of course. So, I'm thinking of early November. Will that work for you? Let me know.*

Brian

October 7, 2006

Dear Brian:

Early November would be perfect. Even though I'll be in the midst of evaluations again, I should be able to break away for that dinner we talked about. You up for Tandoori again?

Seriously, I'm so looking forward to seeing you, though I have to confess I'm more than just a little bit nervous. You nervous, too?

As for your writing, I have every confidence you'll be able to get through any momentary dry spells. You're too good not to. Everything I've read of yours confirms that. And I would absolutely have no apologies concerning those two studios. Let them fight over you. So much the better for you.

A Note from an Old Acquaintance

Oh, by the way, just got word that I'm up for a "genius grant." You know, those foundations that give out big fat checks with no strings attached, just because they think you're cool? Well, I think I've finally got them all fooled. Hah! All kidding aside, it's a great honor, and I still have you to thank for it, even after all these years.

Anyway, sorry for my blather. Let me know when you've firmed up your plans and we'll do this mad thing.

Yours always,

Joanna

October 8, 2006

Dear Joanna:

CONGRATULATIONS! Wow, a genius grant? That's something I'll never have to worry about. Seriously, I always knew you had it in you. I'll bet your family is very proud.

Oh, not to toot my own horn too much, but I'm going to be on Jay Leno tomorrow night. Should be fun, as they want me to sit in with the band and trade licks with Kevin Eubanks. Should be more interesting than listening to me try to one-up Jay.

Congratulations again. Now you can treat me to that Tandoori!

Brian

October 11, 2006

Dear Brian:

It's all your fault! I stayed up and watched you on Leno the other night and ended up not falling asleep until one o'clock. You're bad! No, actually you were terrific, especially with the band. I really love that old Cream tune and you and Kevin really "cut heads."

49

And thank you for your kind words about my grant. My son, Zack, is about as proud for his mom as a boy can be, though he tends to be rather quiet about it. But isn't that typical of teenagers? As for Erik...well, he was certainly happy to hear about the money, though it's not as if we need it. When I told him I was thinking of donating it to charity, he just about blew a gasket, until I asked him why he was allowed to be the only philanthropist in the family. We seem to be at odds all the time, Brian. But there I go complaining again. Anyway, I can't wait to see you. And you're on for that Tandoori.

Fondly,

Joanna

BRIAN STARED AT HIS bedroom ceiling, waves of emotion racing through him. Memories were such precious, fragile things, remaining hidden in the recesses of one's brain for years until a troubled night's sleep and a wandering mind coaxed them back into conscious light. Lying there, in the dark, he clearly recalled sights and sounds comprising moments both heartbreaking and sublime.

One such image nearly brought him to tears, and yet there was nothing about it that connoted sadness. It was simply the memory of Joanna smiling at him while they sat together at a sidewalk café one unseasonably warm day, the sun shining through her fiery curls and her eyes shining with love—a Kodak moment frozen forever in the crenellations of his brain.

He'd loved Joanna, deeply and without reservation, and he'd wanted to remain in her arms forever.

What about now? What did he feel now with everything that had happened?

A part of him didn't want to give substance to that thought, though it would seem his subconscious had other ideas. Brian sat up and shook off the last remaining tendrils of slumber's grip from his mind, not wanting to ponder that question either.

Downstairs beside the front door, the alarm pad gave up its hourly "beep." That told him it was now 5:00 AM. He'd been awake for over two hours, and there wasn't a prayer of him going back to sleep, now. Might as well face the day. He staggered into the bathroom and showered, grateful for the hot spiky spray sluicing down his body.

Fifteen minutes later he sat at his desk holding a steaming mug of Starbucks French Roast, re-reading Joanna's e-mails. The warmth and contentment he'd felt from his earlier reminiscence spread through him once again, warmth far greater than the coffee could provide.

There were no new e-mails from her, but he hadn't really expected anything, since the ball was in his court.

So, why was he afraid to call her? After all, she'd been the one to contact him out of the blue after fifteen years, and they'd been corresponding now for nearly three months.

She's given you her phone number, you dope! Why don't you use it?

If there had been any bad feelings on her part it was obvious from the tone of her e-mails they were long gone. As for *his* feelings, that was another story. All that remained were regrets.

Too damned many of those.

So, what the hell was he waiting for? It was just after eight on the East Coast, she'd be there in her office—right now—getting ready for her first class. *Call her now, Weller, before it's too late—before you chicken out again!*

Shaking his head, he picked up the phone and dialed, fumbling the number twice, his stomach fluttering. "Jesus Christ, you'd think I was a teenager calling a girl for a first date," he mumbled.

"Good morning, Boston Art School."

"Yes. Professor Richman, please."

"Please hold."

The phone switched to bland hold music for a few agonizing moments then someone picked up.

"This is Joanna."

Brian swallowed the lump in his throat.

"Hello? Anyone there?"

"So...how's my favorite Professor?" he said, managing to keep his voice smooth and steady.

"What? W—who *is* this?" she said, annoyed.

"Hi, Joanna, it's Brian."

He heard a sharp intake of breath. "Oh, my God, I'm sorry. How *are* you?"

"I'm fine. How are you?"

"Feeling like a ditz, for one thing. I thought you were some kind of weirdo making a crank call. I can't believe I didn't recognize your voice. Forgive me?"

"Of course, I do. Besides, I've been called a lot worse, especially by some of the critics."

They both laughed.

"Got to tell you, though," he said, "your first e-mail really caught me by surprise."

"I can imagine." She laughed again. "It's so *great* to finally speak to you."

In spite of his vivid memories of her, he'd forgotten the unique timbre of her voice: a soft huskiness with a hint of her Long Island roots. The sound of it sent a delicious shiver up his spine.

"It's my pleasure," he said, swallowing that lump again. "I've wanted to call you a few dozen times. Guess I was just chicken 'til now."

Joanna laughed. "That makes two of us."

It was funny. He'd thought about Joanna every now and then for years, imagining a moment just like this, and all the things he'd say—needed to say. And now, when that moment had arrived he was turning into a tongue-tied schoolboy.

"There's so much I want to say to you—" Brian began.

"I know, me too."

He wanted to say something witty right then, something that would make her laugh. He'd forgotten that, too, how musical it sounded, and how much he'd adored it.

"So, are we still on for November?" she asked, breaking yet another uncomfortable silence.

"I should know more in a day, or so. My publicist is working out the details. What's your schedule like?"

"I'm pretty free in the evenings. Erik's still busy with his building, Zack is doing set design for his school play, and I've got another show opening in a week. I'm ready, but to tell you the truth, I'm a little bit nervous about it."

"You shouldn't be. They don't give genius grants for nothing, you know. And I have to confess I couldn't resist *Googling* you. Your art's wonderful, Joanna, even better than I remember. You've grown."

There was another silence, but Brian sensed this one was different, that she was absorbing the tenor of his words, measuring them. "Coming from you that means a lot," she said, finally.

"Well, I'm not exactly an art connoisseur—"

"And that's exactly why it means so much. You're not trying to read anything into my work, like some of the critics and the phonies do. You were never a phony."

Now it was his turn to measure her words. They sent an electric charge through him.

"Listen," she said, her voice pitching lower, "you actually caught me right before a meeting with one of my students."

"Jeez, I'm sorry."

"Don't be. You've made my day. Give me a call when you know what you're doing and we'll set something up. It'll be so good to see you."

He hung up a moment later, feeling aglow. "You've made my day, too, Joanna."

❀   ❀   ❀

The next several days were a whirlwind of activity. There were two print interviews, one with *Writer's Digest* and another for *Esquire*. He'd enjoyed doing them both, but while the *Esquire* article would reach a wider audience, it was the *WD* piece that had fired him up, the young journalist reminding him of his own enthusiasm in wanting to become a writer. It also made him feel guilty as hell.

Then there were the mundane aspects of being a published writer, such as poring over cryptic royalty statements and checking through the galleys on a new paperback edition for one of his earlier books, a little potboiler called, *Extreme Makeover*. There'd been a minor legal flap over the title with the producers of the popular TV shows. Their trademark attorney wanted Brian to change the title, claiming that re-publication of such an old title was an obvious, transparent ploy to capitalize on the show's popularity; but his publisher was adamant. No way.

Clearly, since he'd written the book nearly ten years ago, and had been published under that title, the issue of prior use was moot, at least that's what his own lawyer had said. They were in the clear. But Brian felt the producers had a point. In his opinion, it *was* a transparent ploy, albeit a clever one. Deciding to take the proactive approach, he called the executive producer and smoothed everything over. It helped that the man was a fan of his books, and Brian was able to persuade him that keeping the present title was good for both of them, although he did promise to have his publisher avoid using a similar typeface.

Once that was out of the way, he gave the new introduction a quick look, found no errors, and initialed the pages with his okay. He placed them into the outgoing pile for his messenger service.

After a quick lunch, he picked up the phone and called Kevin.

"Anything new with the Boston trip?" he asked.

"You're cookin'," Kevin said. "I've got five stores lined up, and it looks like another two will come on board in the next few days. Good mix, too, like you asked for. You were right about those little Mom and Pops, they practically crapped themselves."

Brian grinned. "When are the dates?"

"Your first signing is at eleven AM on November 11th at the Pruden-tial Center Barnes & Noble. How long did you want to stay in the area, anyway? Looks like I can keep you busy for a bit." He laughed.

Brian chewed his lip, mulling this over. Realistically, he couldn't stay there for longer than a week, maybe two if he really stretched it. He needed to be back in L.A. for a meeting with a producer looking to purchase *A Nest of Vipers* out from under the current option hold-ers, when it came up for renewal next month. He stood to make a small fortune, and his agent had insisted he be present. And what about Joanna? What did he really expect when he saw her again? Pleasant conversation over an intimate meal—nothing more. Did he really *want* anything more than that? And what if their little reunion went badly (in spite of their friendly correspondence), descending into awkward silences peppered with agonizing realizations that they had nothing in common? How awful that would be. Then again, what if it *didn't* go badly?

Get a grip, Weller. Make the trip short and sweet.

"You know, Kev, maybe we should keep it to the five you've got. I do too many of those and every Tom, Dick and Harry will be hawking autographed copies of *Vipers* on the street for pennies on the dollar."

Kevin's goofy laughter exploded from the phone's earpiece. "I told you, you should have been a freaking publicist! Hah! When you're right, you're right. Okay, you got the Barnes & Noble on the eleventh, two Mom and Pops, one in Cambridge and another in Arlington, plus the B. Dalton in Chestnut Hill. I can't remember the last one." He coughed. "'scuse me, getting a cold, I think. Anyway, I'll spread 'em over the course of a week. How's that?"

"Perfect."

"All right, Captain, keep your powder dry."

They hung up and Brian checked the clock. Nearly two hours before he needed to head over to The Polo Lounge for breakfast with his agent. Might as well try and get some writing done, for all the good it would do.

In the study, Brian took the MAC out of sleep mode and spotted the blinking mailbox icon. Only one e-mail, this time, from someone called *RedJewel@hotmail.com*. The subject line read: A WORD OF ADVICE.

What the hell, he thought. I could use some of that. Clicking the READ button, he stared at the screen, his hands curling into fists, knuckles whitening. A dry, dead taste formed in his mouth, and his guts felt as if they were falling through the floor.

There were only seven words, the last three written in bold seventy-two point caps, forcing him to scroll down to read them all:

WE HAD A DEAL. LEAVE HER ALONE!

Ruby.

Anger flared, washing away the guilt and focusing his mind into razor-sharp clarity.

"Not this time, you son-of-a-bitch. Not this time."

1991

6

"CAN WE TRY IT the way we did it a few minutes ago?" the client asked, her voice taking on an exasperated edge. She glanced at her watch, shaking her head.

Brian nodded. "Sure, no problem. Just give me a minute." He knew how the woman felt. The lines on her freckled brow had deepened. They'd been editing the spot for the last five hours and had become stuck on one short, maddening five-second sequence, going back and forth between two versions of it over and over again. He knew exactly how she felt. For that matter he wasn't at all sure how much of his own patience was left. Then there was the master tape itself. If they went on much longer, the wear and tear caused by her indecision would render it useless. Checking his time code log, he typed in a set of commands, his fingers flying over the keys. Two of the three Sony U-Matic 3/4" decks containing the selected shots rewound to the beginning of the sequence. The third deck, with the master edit, stood poised.

The client leaned forward peering over her wire-framed glasses, and squinted at the monitor, her frizzy shoulder-length brown hair falling into her angular face. She brushed it back with an annoyed flick of her hand, and began chewing on her nails. Brian noted they were already gnawed to the quick.

A Note from an Old Acquaintance

"Ready?" Brian asked.

She sighed and nodded. He pressed the ENTER button. The Sony decks whirred and the sequence played itself out, the computer previewing the edits.

The thirty-second spot featured the elderly CEO of a local chain of convenience stores making a surprise visit to a store and finding it in a shambles. The punch line was the revelation that the store belonged to one of his competitors, prompting the old man's last immortal line: "Oh...keep up the *good* work."

It was a cute, but flawed concept that only served to point out that perhaps the old guy really wasn't as on-the-ball as he first appeared. Thank God the photography was great, at least.

The woman nodded. "You know, I think that's the best we're going to do. Old Henry's not exactly Clio Award material, is he?"

Brian laughed. "No, but I think that's a part of his charm."

The woman grinned back, just as the door to the edit suite flew open with a quiet whoosh. Brian's partner, Bob Nolan strolled in. He wore his typical lopsided grin, his boyish face belying a keen intelligence and a sharp eye for framing the perfect shot.

"How's my ace editor treating you, Helen?" he said, flopping himself down into one of the black director's chairs scattered about the suite.

"Very well, in spite of my demanding ways," she said, shooting an amused glance at Brian.

Bob's thick eyebrows shot up. "Oh, really? Does that mean we get to double his rate?"

"Not on your life. My budget won't allow it."

They all laughed. Bob turned to Brian. "Everything work out?"

"Everything cuts great. It's just that Henry...." Brian left the rest unspoken. Bob rolled his eyes, no doubt recalling the nightmare on the set with the old CEO forgetting his lines for nearly every take, prompting Bob to order the dialogue placed on cue cards. The problem was, unlike professionals, the old duffer couldn't mask the fact that he was reading the lines, making him appear stiff and wooden.

They all watched a preview of the final edit and everyone agreed that it was the best that could be done. The client left fifteen minutes later with a VHS copy of the spot stuffed into her scuffed Louis Vuitton bag, promising to let them know if her client, the CEO, wanted any changes.

Brian turned to his partner when the front door slammed shut. "You weren't joking about doubling my rate, were you?" he asked.

"Hell, no. That woman's been busting my chops since day one about her budget." He sighed in disgust. "That spot should have been cut in half the time. I shot it so it would go together like a paint-by-numbers picture for a four-year-old. And what does she do? Wastes your time going over the same shots for three hours!"

"It wasn't her fault, Bob. Henry—"

"Forget Henry. She couldn't make up her mind. That's *our* money she's wasting."

The phone rang and Bob snatched up the earpiece, his jaw clenching.

"Newbury Productions...." He listened, slouching back in the chair. "Hey, man, how's it going? I'm glad to hear that. Here? Everything's great, just great.... What's that? No kidding? Sure, Debbie and I would love to come. Wouldn't miss it.... All right, you too."

Bob held out the phone.

"Who is it?" Brian mouthed silently.

"Nick Simon."

Brian smiled and took the phone. Nick was an old friend, a graphic designer who'd helped Bob and Brian establish their business right after they'd graduated from film school. In fact, they now inhabited the very office space once occupied by Nick's company, Wunderkind Graphics, before he moved to larger, more prestigious digs.

"Hiya, Nick, long time no speak. What's up?"

The voice on the other end coughed. "My balls—from the highest yardarm," he wheezed. Nick suffered from chronic asthma and always sounded as if he were on the verge of a coughing jag. "But that's beside the point. Cassie and I are renting out the Metropolis for a little shindig on Valentine's Day, seven PM; and we want you to come."

"That's in two days!"

"I know it's a little last minute, but what can I tell you, I'm a spontaneous guy. What do you say? You up for a little partying? From what I've heard, you guys could use it."

As always, Nick's gossip was deadly accurate. Since the first of the year, Newbury Productions had been cranking full tilt. Now, nearly six weeks later, the juggernaut had picked up steam, promising a year that could be their most profitable yet.

"I'd love to Nick, but...I don't know. I'm not much of a party guy, if you know what I mean. And I've got a real backlog of work, here."

Bob rolled his eyes again, his lopsided grin returning.

"Bullshit," Nick said. "I want to see you there, or I'm gonna send Rocco and Freddie to persuade youse." His hoarse laugh turned into a wheeze. This was an in-joke between the three of them, the mythical Rocco and Freddie being two Mafioso characters from an aborted feature film Bob and Brian shot while still in college.

"Okay, okay," Brian said, "I'll come."

"That's the ticket," Nick said. "Besides you never know, you might meet a real babe, for a change."

"Just what I need."

Nick ignored the sarcasm, turning serious. "Listen, Brian. You know

I've always liked you. You're like a little brother to me. Just give me the word and I'll set you up with a real sweetie-pie. Least I can do."

"I appreciate that."

"Forget about it. I'll see you mugs at the club day after tomorrow. And by the way, the drinks are on me. Hah!"

Brian hung up the phone and shook his head. "The man's incorrigible."

"He try to set you up again?" Bob asked, grinning.

"Yeah."

"He's got a point. You've turned yourself into a hermit."

"And I suppose you and Debbie have someone in mind?"

"I don't, but Debbie might. I can ask her—"

Brian held up his hand. "Please...don't. Look, I know it's been over a year since Julie turned me inside out, but I'd rather things just happen as they will. Is that okay?"

Bob shrugged. "Okay by me. As far as Thursday, how about Deb and I swing by and pick you up?"

"That's fine."

Bob left the suite and Brian spent the next hour cleaning the heads on the Sony decks and prepping the suite for the next day's session: a music video by a hot local rock band. At least that would be fun. He'd seen the band a couple of times and liked their music.

Outside, the traffic on Newbury Street stood gridlocked, horns blaring, exhaust fumes sending thick white plumes skyward. The temperature had plummeted to twenty degrees and a freezing wind blew in off the Charles, cutting through Brian's thin leather jacket like a razor. Shivering, he locked the front door and crossed the street to Bauer Wines, where he picked up a six-pack of Samuel Adams, gossiped a moment with Howie, one of the owners, then hurried the half mile to his apartment at the corner of Fairfield and Beacon Streets.

A Note from an Old Acquaintance

Housed in what was once the basement kitchen of a French-style mansion built in the late 1880s, it boasted floor space of just under a thousand square feet, with ten-foot ceilings, two seven-foot windows facing the carriage house, a walk-in closet, a delightfully archaic bathroom with a claw-foot tub and a kitchen larger than some of the places he'd lived in while a student.

It felt like home the moment he'd first walked into it.

The mail was the usual mix of bills and throw-aways, except for the envelope marked: *The Hendricks Agency*. He opened it, feeling the usual mix of excitement and dread.

Dear Mr. Weller:
Thank you so much for sending us your novel, The Normandy Conspiracy. *We thought it was tautly written and shows a great eye for detail. Unfortunately, we do not feel we have enough enthusiasm for the material to sell it in today's very competitive market. We wish you the best of luck in your writing career.*
Sincerely,
Jan Hendricks

Except for a few alternate word choices, the letter could have stood in for countless others. He knew, because he'd kept them all. And while it bothered him on a gut level, his search for an agent had gone on far too long to let one more rejection get him down. He had the book out to five other agents, and would send it out to five more if those didn't pan out. One day, one of them would bite. If not with this book, then with the one he'd just started.

Later, while he ate a quick spaghetti dinner, along with his third beer, his mind wandered back to Nick and his offer to set him up on a date. On one level it repelled him, on another...well...he *was* a healthy

male. And to be honest, Nick had really good taste; and dating someone with no strings attached might be refreshing. No complications,
just good hot, sweaty sex.

Julie, his last serious relationship, had driven him crazy with her
neuroses. One minute she was a temptress, wanting all sorts of kinky
things in bed, the next she acted as if he were the plague. He'd been
madly in love with her and thought she'd felt the same way. It came
like a hammer-blow when she'd dumped him for another man, a man
he viewed as nothing more than a milquetoast. After months of intro-
spection and a few sessions with a sympathetic therapist, he'd come to
realize that Julie was afraid of true intimacy. Scared to death of it, in
fact. The irony was that she was a therapy-junky, loved to air her dirty
laundry for all to hear; yet when push came to shove she ran for the
cover of a "safe" man she could control.

The one amusing thing about all this was that every time he ran into
Julie and her new boyfriend (far more frequently than he wanted), she
went out of her way to let Brian know that she and "Chip" had "not
made love yet." Poor Chip must have been embarrassed as hell, though
he pretended not to show it. But one thing Brian knew without a shred
of doubt: Chip was over the moon for her, and as soon as she realized
this she would break his heart—like so much cheap dishware.

After cleaning up from dinner, he decided to put in some time on
the new book. He chugged the last of the six Sam Adams and placed
the bottles into the growing pyramid of empty six-packs in the corner
of the kitchen. Next came the inevitable pot of coffee and his old Royal
typewriter from out of the closet. It was going to be a *long* night...and
he knew he was going to love every moment of it.

7

THE INTERCOM BUZZER RANG at 6:30. Brian struggled into his plain white t-shirt, while pressing the talk button. "Just finishing up. I'll be right out."

"No sweat, we found a space right in front." Bob said, his voice sounding robotic through the tiny speaker.

Turning away from his front door, Brian scrambled to pull on his pants. Nick had called the office earlier in the day to let them know that the party had a "Grease" theme: leather jackets, chains, jeans, and lots of hair pomade. It was another last-minute "masterstroke" that had Bob rolling his eyes.

Typical Nick.

The only thing Brian owned that fit the bill was a pair of tight-legged black jeans he'd never worn, some Western style boots and a newly-purchased black leather motorcycle jacket, the same style as worn by Marlon Brando in *The Wild Ones*. Shiny and stiff, it squeaked whenever he made a move in it.

Zipping up the jacket, he turned up the collar and glanced at his image in the mirror. He had to admit it did make him look a bit dangerous. The hair was where he drew the line, however. His was so baby-fine, he would have looked like a wet Pekingese if he'd tried to pomade it. He gave himself a thumbs-up, a final spritz of Halston Z-14 and was out the door.

Bob's car, a three-year-old gray Honda Accord, idled at the curb. Brian slipped into the back seat, grateful to be out of the biting cold. The motorcycle jacket squeaked loudly and Bob eyed him in the rearview. With a sinking sensation Brian saw that neither Bob nor his wife, Debbie, were dressed in anything resembling Fifties attire.

"Oh, great, I'm probably going to be the only one dressed like this. I'll look like a fool."

"No more than you usually do," Debbie said, giggling.

"Thanks," he said, grimacing. The jacket squeaked again.

"Actually," she said, "I think you look kind of cute. Doesn't he look, cute, Sweetie?"

"Very cute," Bob said, smirking.

They pulled out into traffic a moment later. The ride to the Metropolis Club was a little less than a mile straight down Beacon Street, through Kenmore Square now choked with crowds of restless college students hitting the clubs and bars, up Brookline Avenue and over the Pike, with an immediate left onto Lansdowne.

The club occupied a long two-story cinderblock building crouched in the shadow of Fenway Park's titanic green carcass. The only indicator the building housed anything other than non-descript industrial space was the large blue neon "M" mounted above the thick polished stainless-steel doors.

Amazingly, they found a space near the other end of the street and walked back to the club, joining a small crowd poised outside the vault-like doors. A tall muscular bouncer dressed in black, holding a stainless steel clipboard, turned some of the people away as they approached.

A Note from an Old Acquaintance

"Private party, ladies and gents. Invitation only," the bouncer said, moving to bar the door. "You can't enter, if you're not on the list."

Several couples groaned their displeasure and left.

A moment later, when the three of them reached the head of the line, the bouncer eyed them, his thick brows arching inquisitively.

"Bob Nolan and guest," Bob said.

The bouncer consulted the list on his clipboard and nodded toward the door.

Brian gave his name and watched the big man flip through several pages. Brian did some quick math in his head. At roughly fifty names per page, that meant at least three hundred invitees. Nick had to be spending a bloody fortune. *I'm in the wrong business,* Brian mused.

"You're cool. Go on in," the bouncer said finally.

Brian eased through the steel door and found his friends standing in an impromptu receiving line in the reception area. The room was easily twenty by twenty feet with black walls, charcoal-gray carpeting, and stainless-steel sconces shooting white-hot beams of light upward toward the fifteen-foot ceiling. Watching over all of this was a twice life-size replica of "Maria" the sexy Metropolis robotrix, her metallic curves gleaming. He could hear music thumping through the walls, the beat shaking the floor.

Nick and his partner, Cassie Bailey, stood at the head of the line greeting their guests. To Brian's relief, both Nick and Cassie wore clothing similar to his own. In fact, except for the cowboy boots Brian wore, Nick could have been his clone. The similarity ended there, however. Nick stood a hair over five-foot-seven, had dark unruly hair poised like a crag over a lean face that bore more than a passing resemblance to Matthew Broderick.

Cassie, taller by a good two inches, wore a battered russet-brown bomber jacket two sizes too small—which did little to hide her ample figure—and skin-tight jeans rolled to just below the knees, exposing shapely calves and sockless feet shod in bright-red high-top sneakers. Her dark brown hair, always in disarray when working, was now sleeked back into a greasy pompadour, completing the haughty biker moll look.

She sidled up to Brian and enveloped him a hug that lasted a little too long.

"You gonna save a dance for me, Honey?" She spoke this into his ear in a breathless whisper.

She pulled away, her black eyes flashing. It was obvious she'd had a few too many already, though she'd made it crystal clear in past encounters that she had a thing for him. And while Brian was flattered, she just wasn't his type. It wasn't anything physical he could put his finger on, either, as she was fairly attractive. She certainly filled out her jeans well enough. No, it was more her overt predatory nature—fueled by an undercurrent of desperation—that made him uneasy.

Brian managed a smile and was about to answer when she slunk away, distracted by another guest. He breathed an inward sigh of relief and moved over to Nick, who was hugging a tall brunette dressed in a poodle skirt and matching sweater.

Nick spotted him and grabbed his hand in a vise-like grip, a toothy grin creasing his gaunt face. "Hey, kiddo, you made it. I was laying money down that you were gonna chump out on me."

"Sorry you lost the bet," Brian said, returning the grin.

"You kidding? It was worth it. You're gonna have a blast—or else." He raised his fist, laughed, and slapped Brian on the back. "Go on in. Bar's open."

Brian rejoined Bob and Debbie and entered the club proper. The motif from the foyer was carried over into the main room on a grand scale. More duplicates of "Maria" were placed at strategic points, like sentinels. Lights flashed and spun, reflecting off a mirrored ball, making for an eye-dazzling display. The bar was even more impressive: an amalgam of polished steel and Lucite, the Lucite pieces seeming to vibrate with an unearthly blue glow. The sunken dance floor, a seamless sheet of obsidian, was deserted in spite of the pounding music. The sheer volume of it made it impossible to ignore. The bass frequencies shook the room hitting him in the gut at the relentless rate of 120 beats per minute.

Bob pointed toward the bar and made drinking motions.

"Get me a Sam Adams!" Brian shouted.

Debbie held up two fingers indicating that she wanted the same, and Bob left to get the drinks. Brian and Debbie found a table near the dance floor and sat down in two of the plush chairs. Brian studied the room then turned to find Debbie studying him, an amused expression on her Botticelli face.

"You okay?" she said, leaning closer.

Brian nodded.

"Seems like you've got your work cut out for you tonight."

"How's that?"

"Cassie. I'm not blind."

"Yeah," Brian said, chuckling. "I can handle her."

"Oh, I'm sure you can," Debbie said, her deep brown eyes twinkling.

"Wait a minute, that's not what I meant. I'm not interested in her."

"I kind of figured that." She paused, glancing toward the bar. Bob stood in a crush of partygoers, trying to get the bartender's attention and looking peeved. Her expression softened when she turned back to Brian. "How long have we known each other?"

"Six years. Since junior year."

"And in all that time, have I ever tried to set you up with anyone?"

"Thankfully, no."

Debbie laughed then turned serious. "Well, I've thought about it—a lot, especially after you broke up with Julie. But to be honest, I hesitated because I didn't think any of my girlfriends were good enough for you."

Brian looked down at the table, not sure how to take that. "I appreciate that...very much."

"But I think I've finally figured out your type."

Brian looked up, puzzled.

Debbie nodded toward the dance floor. Two women were dancing—the *only* two people dancing, at the moment.

"The curly redhead on the left in the sequined cocktail dress."

Brian stared, watching the woman dance, her lithe body moving with a fluid grace. A moment later her friend leaned in and said something, making the redhead convulse with laughter. Her smile was so carefree and natural, so ineffably sublime; it lit up her entire face.

"So what do you think?"

"Uhh, Deb, she's dancing with another woman."

Debbie glared at him. "She's not—"

"How do you know?"

"Women know these things. She's available."

"And what makes you think she's my type? You know her?"

"No, of course not."

"Then what?"

Debbie turned and watched the redhead, her expression turning thoughtful. "There's just something about her...."

Bob returned with the drinks, setting them on the table. "What's going on?" he asked, sipping his gin and tonic. Brian was grateful for the interruption, taking a swig of his beer. It tasted especially sweet.

"I was just telling Brian that he should go ask that redhead to dance."

Bob looked over at the two women and shrugged. "Hmm. Not bad."

Debbie scowled. "*Not bad?* She's adorable, you dope."

"Not as adorable as you," Bob said, blowing her a kiss.

"Flattery will get you everywhere...later," she said, turning back to Brian. "I think you should go for it. I've really got a feeling about her. She's ripe for the plucking."

He nodded, only half listening, his attention now drawn back to the redhead. From where he sat, she appeared to be about five-eight in her high heels, an effect accentuated by the mass of loose auburn curls piled atop her head. The cocktail dress she wore was a simple, flattering design, but it hid whatever curves she possessed, making her appear slim, almost lanky. Brian usually liked his women with more meat on them; however, something about this one stirred his emotions. Maybe a part of it was because she was having so much fun out there.

And then there was that luminous smile.

Even from thirty feet away, it made his heart pound and his throat go dry. He slugged back his beer, draining it.

The woman and her friend stayed on the dance floor through two more songs then took a break. By that time the floor was packed with undulating dancers, and Brian craned his neck, watching the two of them snake through the crowd toward the bar. He lost them behind one of the "Marias."

"What are you waiting for?" Debbie said into his ear.

"The right moment."

"The right moment is now, you schnook. You wait too long and some dickhead's going to grab her."

71

Brian held up his hand. "All right, all right, you win. I just need another beer."

"Liquid courage?"

"You could say that."

Debbie laughed. "Get the beer, then go get *her*."

Brian wormed his way through the crush of people. It appeared his original estimation of the guest list was a bit shy of reality. There had to be more than four hundred people crammed into the club. About half of them seemed to have congregated at the bar. Pushing his way to the front, Brian caught the eye of one of the bartenders and held up his empty Sam Adams bottle. The man nodded, grabbed one from out of a cooler, twisted off the top and handed it to him. Brian tipped back the beer, letting the cool hops-heavy liquid glide down his throat. Out of the corner of his eye, he spotted the redhead talking with her friend at a small table a few yards away. Butterflies swam in his stomach and his head felt as if it were swathed in cotton.

Oh, Christ, I can't do this.

Yes, you can, you schmuck. Do it. Do it, now!

He started to move, stopping when he felt a hand on his arm. He turned to find Cassie Bailey staring at him, a carnivorous grin on her pink-frosted lips.

"Where do you think you're going?" she purred in his ear.

Caught off-guard, Brian was left without a snappy comeback. Cassie tugged him toward the dance floor. He placed his beer on a nearby ledge and went reluctantly, his eyes darting between the redhead and the direction Cassie was leading him. They reached the dance floor and she immediately began gyrating suggestively, making sure to bump and grind against him at every opportunity. Brian did his best to appear enthusiastic, without encouraging her, a delicate balance if there ever was one. He also tried not to look like an idiot on the dance floor.

A Note from an Old Acquaintance

Dancing had never interested him. The old cliché about two left feet definitely applied to his, at least he'd come to believe that after years of torturous dancing lessons as a pre-teen. His mind returned to the redhead and how uninhibited she'd been on the dance floor. Cassie was uninhibited, too, but in a far less innocent way. And then it hit him. *That* was what intrigued him about the redhead, the innocence of youth—a freedom of spirit—that few people, beaten down by life, ever managed to hold onto.

Brian glanced toward the table where the redhead and her friend sat, relieved to see her still sitting there. A moment later, disaster loomed. A man approached with a confident swagger, his garish polyester shirt opened to the navel, gold chains clanking.

Great, here comes the dickhead.

Brian watched the pantomime unfold between the man and the redhead with morbid fascination. Wait a minute! What was this? The redhead was shaking her head, a frown creasing her smooth brow. Her friend had turned away, looking as if she wanted to melt through the floor. The man shrugged and turned away, his swagger gone.

Brian felt another tug on his arm and he turned back to Cassie, who wagged a finger at him.

"Naughty, naughty," she mouthed, bumping and grinding against him once again. His patience left him then. He leaned closer, feeling her body melt against his, her breath a hot murmur in his ear.

"Excuse me, but there's someone I need to talk to."

He walked off the floor, leaving her fuming. He had no doubt that if her eyes had been twin lasers, he'd have been instant toast. The music changed, the beat becoming more primal. Drums and bass thundered, matching the pace of his gait. Every step toward that small table where the redhead sat vibrated through his entire body.

Come on, Weller, just a few more steps.

Twenty feet away, he saw her stand up and move toward the bar. He halted in his tracks—unsure about what to do next—then followed her. His beer had disappeared from the ledge where he'd placed it, so a trip to the bar was now called for. A moment later he stood right behind her, watching her order a glass of chilled Chablis.

Now, you dimwit!

"Would you like to dance?"

God, he sounded like such a pencil-necked dweeb.

She turned, and Brian braced himself, praying she would treat him with more kindness than she'd treated Mr. Polyester.

When her gaze found him, her impossibly green eyes widened, jolting every molecule in his body, leaving him reeling and tingling, as if struck by some mystical static discharge. He swallowed hard and stared back at her, feet rooted to the floor, blood roaring in his ears. He could barely breathe.

The redhead edged a step closer and tilted her head, her stunned expression turning inquisitive. He felt those gentle eyes probe and caress him, searching the very deepest regions of his soul. They made him feel naked and humbled and ecstatic, all at once. And he couldn't look away—didn't *want* to look away.

Standing there, adrift in his timeless enchantment, the music faded into a subliminal drone and the crowds surrounding them became nothing more than fleeting shadows. He was aware of nothing—and no one—but her.

A heartbeat later the redhead spoke, breaking the spell.

"I—I'm sorry," she said, in a voice like velvet. "Did you say something?"

"Do you...." Brian trembled. "Do you want to dance?"

She reached over and touched the sleeve of his leather jacket. "How about we just talk for awhile?"

"Sure...." The word nearly caught in his throat.

"You want something?"

"W—What?"

Her ruby-red lips parted in a wry grin, revealing white even teeth. "To drink," she added.

"Oh, right, sure, that would be great."

Relax, Weller, relax!

Brian's paralysis ended and he slipped into a space next to her at the bar, signaling the bartender once again. He felt the redhead watching him and his pulse raced. The Sam Adams arrived moments later.

She nodded then led the way toward the other end of the room. The crowd pressed in on them, yet Brian felt as if his feet were lighting on cushions of air. And though he was on his third beer, alcohol *never* made him feel like this.

They came to another sunken area behind a wall of Plexiglas dotted with candlelit tables and more plush chairs. Here, the music lost its thunderous power, making for a tranquil and intimate atmosphere—a sonic oasis. Except for half a dozen other couples, they were alone. The redhead sat down at a table hidden in the shadow of one of the "Marias" and Brian took the seat opposite her.

Those eyes found him again, so large and round and green, brimming with a vitality and intelligence that exhilarated and scared him witless. He just wished he could think of something funny and brilliant to say, something that wouldn't make him sound like a bloody fool.

"My name's Brian, by the way. Brian Weller."

"Joanna Richman." She extended her hand. Brian took it, marveling at the long, graceful fingers and their silken softness. Yet her grip was firm, resolute, surprising him. She held his hand a moment longer than he expected then released it and picked up her wine glass.

Brian's hand tingled where her skin had touched his.

"I have to be honest," Brian began, "I'm kind of off-balance, here."

"Me, too," she said, laughing.

A loose strand of curls fell over her eyes. She pushed it back then took a sip of her wine.

"So, who are you, Joanna Richman?"

"You don't mince words, do you?"

"That's because I'm a writer—at least I'm trying to be."

Her wine glass paused halfway to her mouth. She set it back on the table.

"Tell me about it."

"Wait a minute, I asked you first."

Joanna's eyes sparkled in the candlelight. "A woman's prerogative," she said.

Brian smiled. "Fair enough." He tasted his beer, putting his thoughts in order. "I suppose I've always had a talent for words, ever since I was a little kid. And I've always loved telling stories, creating worlds that never existed. Yet they existed for me. I'd spend hours scribbling all sorts of fantasies, seeing them unfold in my mind like movies. Now..." he paused. "Now, I've got four manuscripts in my dresser drawers, the fifth making the rounds with agents, a sixth I've just started, and an antique file cabinet crammed to the gunwales with rejection letters."

"You were a lonely boy, weren't you?"

Brian stared at her, stunned. "How did you know?"

"I—I saw it in your eyes," she said, looking down into her glass. The same curly strand escaped again. She left it dangling this time. "For me it was my art. Like you, I'd lose all track of time when I worked on a piece. Nothing else mattered. Drove my poor mother crazy." Joanna sighed, shaking her head. "She'd always tell me the world was passing me by. She never understood my sculptures were the way I saw the world."

"Nothing passes you by, does it?"

She gave him an enigmatic smile and sipped her wine.

"What about now?" he asked.

"When I'm not working in my studio, I teach fine arts at The Boston Art School on Newbury Street. I want to give something back—give those kids the support and encouragement I didn't get."

"I really admire that. But I don't know if I'd have the patience to deal with all those sleepy apathetic faces every morning."

"It's not that bad—except for Mondays." She laughed. "I really love it, though. There's nothing like seeing that flash of enlightenment in their eyes when they've made those same connections I made. It's better than sex."

Brian arched a brow. "Oh, really?"

"We'll...maybe not...."

They both laughed.

"I'd like to see your art," he said, after a moment of awkward silence.

She brightened. "Would you?"

Brian nodded. "I'll bet it's amazing."

"I don't know about that, but it's definitely me."

"Are they abstract or realistic?"

"A little of both, actually. I guess you could say they're like machinery. I find it hard to describe. Words fail me that way. They don't for you, though, do they?"

"Only when I'm sitting with a pretty woman."

She looked back down at her drink, a wistful smile turning up the corners of her mouth.

"What's the matter, did I say something wrong?"

She shook her head. "Just thinking...."

He'd hit a nerve, damn it. He'd tried to pay her a compliment, a genuine one, and it backfired.

Brian leaned over the table, catching a whiff of her perfume. It made him dizzy. "I'm sorry if I offended you, Joanna. That was the *last* thing I wanted to do."

"I know...and you didn't offend me—far from it. It's just that I...." She stopped, looking off toward the bar. "It's just that I haven't heard that kind of thing in a long while...and it's so nice to hear it from you."

Brian swallowed, feeling as if someone had just turned up the heat. Maybe it was time to switch gears.

"So, how was it for you growing up on Long Island?"

"How did you know I was from Long Island?"

"Your voice. You've lost most of your accent, but I can still hear it."

"You're very perceptive. But, believe me, my childhood was very boring. I'd rather hear about you, anyway. What kind of books do you write?"

Brian sat back in his chair. Clearly, Joanna was uncomfortable talking about herself. Perhaps it was the combination of modesty and meeting someone new. Or maybe, in spite of what she'd just said, her childhood had been hard. Kids could be so mean, especially for a sensitive young girl who had not yet become the swan she was destined to be. Painful memories like those died hard, if ever. He decided not to press it. There was time enough for that later.

"I write thrillers, mostly," he replied. "A couple of them have been the international type, like Robert Ludlum. It's what I love to read." He took a moment to describe his latest novel, a story about a little-known aspect of the Normandy Invasion. What impressed Brian most was that Joanna really seemed to be listening.

A Note from an Old Acquaintance

"How intriguing," she said, when he'd finished. "I especially like the fact that you've woven in a personal story with the two brothers against the bigger canvas. But I'm wondering if maybe it's too much of a man's book."

Brian frowned. "How so?"

"Well, for better or worse, most of the book buyers are women, and I think they find it harder to relate to a macho point of view."

"I think I've heard that once or twice," he said, picturing that over-stuffed file cabinet.

"So, maybe that's why your books aren't selling. Maybe you need to change your direction, try something new."

"Such as romantic thrillers?"

"Why not?"

She picked up her glass, clinked it against his beer bottle and drained it.

The funny thing was Brian had begun to think these very same thoughts. It sure as hell was no fun banging one's head against the wall year after year, knowing you've got talent, but meeting the same unyielding resistance over and over again. Somehow this amazing woman had seen this right off the bat. What was more amazing was that he could accept the wisdom in her words.

"Sage advice for one so young," he said.

"I think you're better than you're giving yourself credit for."

"I appreciate that, but you've never read a word I've written."

Brian felt her hand on his. "I don't have to," she said, her smile finally returning.

He was about to reply when a cocktail waitress approached. "You guys need anything?" she asked.

"Uh, not for me." He turned to Joanna. "You?"

"No, I'm fine."

The waitress left and Brian realized that all the tables around them had filled up. "How about that dance, now? You game?"

"I'd love to," she said.

They stood, leaving their drinks. Brian took her hand and led the way back up to the dance floor. It seemed less crowded than it had been a while before. The music changed. Brian recognized it as "Night Fever" by the Bee Gees. Joanna started moving, and Brian did his best to keep up. And even though he despised Disco and everything it signified, he found himself getting lost in the rhythm, his body making moves he'd never thought himself capable. And watching Joanna was like watching music incarnate.

He moved closer to her and she reciprocated. They each aped the other's movements, unconsciously synchronizing their choreography. Suddenly feeling overheated, Brian removed the motorcycle jacket and began using it as an impromptu dance partner. Joanna threw back her head, laughing. Brian grinned, knowing he looked silly and not giving a damn whatsoever. All he knew was that he wanted to get to know this terrific woman better.

No time like the present, Weller, no time like the present.

"Would you like to go out sometime?" he yelled, hoping she could hear him over the crushing din.

"Sure, but I'll have to get rid of my fiancé first."

Brian missed a step, nearly tripping himself. He studied her face, trying to discern if she'd been joking. Fiancé? She was freaking engaged? It figured he'd meet someone wonderful like her and she'd be taken. But where was her ring? When they were talking at the table he'd noticed her left hand was devoid of any jewelry. Christ, Weller, maybe the guy hadn't sprung for the rock yet. But even as all this rushed through his mind, she continued smiling at him and Brian realized it didn't matter. He wanted Joanna—wanted her as he'd never wanted anyone or anything else in his life. If she wanted to be with him, too, so be it. After all, she wasn't married yet. Let her worry about her fiancé.

❀   ❀   ❀

"Who's that dancing with Joanna?" Ruby said, draining his martini. He lounged next to Nick on a long black leather sofa to the right of the bar, a quiet, desperate anger smoldering in his gut like the embers of a dying fire. He hated parties like these, tolerating them only because he knew they were good for business; but he should have left Joanna at home. That way, he'd at least be able to relax and enjoy himself—wouldn't have to worry about every two-bit lothario who made eyes at her. Problem was he could never refuse her. And she so loved to dance, which was fine, as long as it was with Marcia, her best friend. Now, though, it was a different story.... "Did you hear me, Nick?"

Nick sipped his drink and shrugged. "He's just a friend. Nobody special."

Erik Ruby gazed across the dance floor, his dark eyes narrowing, and watched his young bride-to-be laughing at this "nobody special" swinging his leather jacket around like some bargain basement Fred Astaire.

A cocktail waitress approached, placing a fresh martini on the low table in front of the sofa. She was a tall busty blonde with all the right curves, and made it plain with her knowing look that more than drinks were available. She was certainly easy on the eye.

He reached into his Armani jacket and pulled out his wallet, handing the girl a crisp fifty. Her eyes bugged out. "Thank you, Mr. Ruby."

Ruby's mouth split into an indulgent grin, capped teeth gleaming. "You deserve it, Honey. Just don't spend it all in one place."

He waited until the girl moved away then turned back to Nick, placing a manicured hand on his shoulder. "You're my friend, too, Nick. And we've known each other far too long to bullshit one another. I just want to know Joanna's safe. So, come on, tell me about your friend."

Nick tossed back the rest of his drink and chuckled. "All right, all right, I know when I'm licked." He lifted his empty glass, signaling the busty blonde for a refill. "It's really no big deal; he's a nice guy. His name's Brian Weller...."

While Nick spoke, Ruby watched Joanna; watched her dance and laugh and do all the things he'd seen her do a thousand times before at countless charity balls and posh parties with countless forgettable men.

This time it was different.

This time *she* was different.

And for the first time in his life, Erik Ruby knew he stood to lose the one thing he valued most. For the first time in his storied existence, Erik Ruby knew the true meaning of fear.

8

HE WAS LATE.

It didn't matter that he'd set his alarm, double- and triple- and quadruple-checked it—it had failed to go off at the appointed time. Either that or the previous night had exhausted him so thoroughly he'd never even heard its familiar, annoying clamor.

It didn't matter. Only the client's time and money did. There was barely time to shower, throw on some clothes, microwave some tasteless instant coffee and rush out the door.

Brian sat up with a tired groan, and the phone rang. Damn. Should he grab it, or let the machine take it? The ringing became more insistent, or was it simply his throbbing headache making it sound that way? He glanced at the clock and sighed. What difference would another couple of minutes make, anyway?

Swearing under his breath, he snatched the cordless handset from its cradle before the machine took over.

"Hello," he said, scowling at the brackish taste in his mouth.

"Brian? That you, Honey?"

"Hey, Mom, how are you?"

"I woke you up, didn't I?"

"No, you didn't. I was already up. Got a busy day."

"Your father and I were just wondering how you were doing. We hadn't heard from you in a while."

It had only been a week, if that. He wasn't in the mood for her usual litany about what he did for a living—didn't have time for it. And it didn't even matter that he and Bob were finally starting to make good money. To his parents, any career in the entertainment business, no matter how far removed from Hollywood, was "unreliable."

"I'm fine, Mom, business is great. But I do really have to go—"

"That's not why I called."

A weary grin creased his face. There was no deterring Mom when she had something on her mind. Brian heaved himself up and threw off the down comforter, shivering in the cool air. The heater must have quit during the night, or the oil delivery was late again.

"What's up? Dad okay?"

"He's fine. He had to go into the store early today, something about inventory, and I didn't want to wait for him to get home before I called you."

Brian went to his closet and pulled out a brown terry-cloth robe—an old Christmas present from his parents—and slipped it on. It resembled a monk's habit, replete with a hood, and was deliciously warm, if a little threadbare.

"I'm worried about you, Brian."

Brian chuckled. "I'm sorry, I don't mean to laugh, but isn't that what parents are supposed to do?"

"Of course, but I meant more than usual." There was a pause and Brian heard a faint buzzing on the line. "I never liked Julie, you know," she said, breaking the silence. "I always thought she was a bit of a flake."

Ah, so this was where things were going.

A Note from an Old Acquaintance

"You're right, Mom, she was. And I'm well rid of her. So, stop worrying. I'm fine. In fact, better than fine."

"Oh?"

Brian glanced at the top of his dresser, spying the business card. Before he'd left the Metropolis Club with Bob and Debbie, he'd asked Joanna for her number. She'd written it on the back of a business card—her fiancé's business card.

Now there was irony for you, in its purest form.

"It's my studio number," she'd said, the implication clear. "I'm there most evenings from seven 'til eleven, or so."

The card stock was translucent vellum, the logo and text embossed in black and gold. It stated simply:

Erik Ruby

President/CEO

Ruby & Associates

Architectural Design and Property Development

7 Newbury Street, Boston, MA 02116

Phone: 617-555-4530 / Fax: 617-555-4531

"Honey, you there?"

"Sorry, Mom, lost my train of thought."

"You were saying that you were 'better than fine.'"

"Yeah.... I've met someone."

"That's wonderful, dear," she said, sounding relieved. "What's her name?"

"Mom, if it's okay, can we talk about this later? I really have to get going. I've got a long day ahead of me."

"That's fine. I really just wanted to hear your voice. I'm so glad you're feeling better about things."

"Me, too. I'll talk to you later, promise."

He hung up the phone, feeling like a bit of a heel. It was not as if he'd lied to her, or anything, it was just...superstition, silly superstition. Over the last few months after his break up with Julie, he'd thought long and hard about all his girlfriends since high school. And the odd thing was that every time he'd mentioned the girl's name to his mother early in the relationship, it had gone sour. It was weird.

Now he knew, as any rational man would, that this was all a bunch of bull, but it had popped into his mind again, as soon as his mother had asked for Joanna's name. And he'd almost said it before stopping himself. He just didn't want to tempt fate again, not this time.

Shivering again, Brian went into the kitchen, put on the coffee and jumped into the shower. At least the water was hot. That meant there was plenty of heating oil, so perhaps someone had tripped the breaker on the furnace. It had happened a few times when his upstairs neighbor had fired up his foreign-made all vacuum-tube stereo, which ran on the same 220-volt circuit as the heating system.

Old wiring. In a house this ancient, it was bound to be an issue, that is, until the homeowners association was forced to spend the money to fix it. Or the place burned down. The biggest problem was Brian only rented his unit from the absentee owner, who lived in Europe year-round. Still, he made a mental note to call one of the board members that afternoon and try and make him do something.

After drying off and tossing on jeans and a flannel shirt, Brian filled his spill-proof mug with coffee, grabbed his leather jacket and hit the street. He struck across Beacon when the traffic broke and headed up Fairfield.

The sidewalk had a light cover of snow that came down sometime during the night. It crunched under his feet, sounding like the gravel driveway he'd grown up with as a kid in Ohio. It was another cloudy, windswept day with a temperature he guessed to be somewhere in the mid-twenties.

He took a sip of his coffee. Creamy and sweet, it made a delicious burn down his throat, warming him. He patted the pocket of his jacket where he'd slipped the business card, as if to reassure himself that it all was real. And even though he knew it was, the previous evening's memories already possessed a dreamlike quality. The question was when to call her. Every fiber of his being demanded that he do it that very night, but how often did he hear that a man shouldn't be too eager, that it would scare a woman off. He didn't think Joanna was the type of woman who played games, and the uniqueness of the situation made the usual rules seem pointless. So why was his stomach already doing somersaults? Why did he still feel as if he were drunk from the night before? The wonderful thing was that he'd had less to drink last night than he usually did on a typical weeknight. Any intoxication or its aftermath was due to a more esoteric cause.

When he approached the front door of his office, he spotted the band and their manager waiting outside, stamping their feet, breath billowing in the frigid air. All of them looked as if they'd been dragged out of bed about four hours too early.

"I hope you guys haven't been waiting too long," Brian called out.

"It's okay," the manager said, coughing into his fist. "We need to get this done today, so I figured the earlier the better."

Brian smiled. He hadn't expected them for another hour, wanting the extra time to get things ship-shape. "That's fine by me."

The manager grinned back. "I got some more great ideas for this video, man. Can't wait."

Brian unlocked the door and tried to hide his reaction. Whenever any client said that, it really meant they wanted to start over, taking everything that had been assembled and throwing it into the proverbial trash. He'd have to be tactful, but firm. There would be no radical changes from what they'd spent the last two days creating, unless the band would like to spend *lots* more money. Sometimes, all it took to get everything back on track was a little financial wake-up call.

Ushering them all inside, he climbed the stairs to the second floor and steeled himself for another day at the circus.

❋ ❋ ❋

Erik Ruby stared out the plate-glass window of his fourth-floor office watching the snarl of traffic on Newbury Street. The window took up the entire wall from floor to ceiling, affording him a panoramic view, with the Public Garden to one side and the rest of Newbury Street, up to where it ended at Massachusetts Avenue and the entrance to the Mass Pike.

It was just after 9:00 AM, and he'd been at his desk for at least two hours, readying a presentation for a new client. The models were wrong, and he'd spent the last ten minutes castigating the modeler for putting the new Wrightson Building on the *wrong* side of Boylston Street. Even now, the sorry bastard was scrambling to get it fixed before Wrightson and his entourage showed up. It didn't help that he and Joanna had fought on the way home from the Metropolis Club, either. They'd left just after 1:00 AM, far later than he'd wanted. What made it worse was that Marcia, her best friend, was in the car for most of the ride back to their home in Newton, making for strained and oblique conversation. He hated to be oblique about anything, especially where Joanna was concerned.

"So, you had a good time?" he'd said, keeping his eyes glued to the road, knuckles white on the wheel.

"A wonderful time," she'd replied.

A Note from an Old Acquaintance

"Meet anyone new?"

"A couple of people."

Yeah, right. Now *there* was a wealth of information. He'd certainly reaped a bushel where Nick was concerned, though. The problem was he wasn't sure what to do with it, at this point. He needed to sort through it. More important: he needed to see what would happen next....

"I spoke with Nick and he said he's almost done with the mailer for your first show."

She turned to him, anger flaring in her eyes. "I told you I didn't want you to do that, Erik."

"Why not, he's done a bang-up job and it'll go out to the crème de la crème of Boston."

"That's not the point. I don't know why you keep bringing this up. I don't want you to *buy* me a show. I want to earn it. I'm not ready."

"Sure you are. Your stuff is great."

She chewed her lip. "I appreciate that, but I just don't think—"

"Honey," he said, "Sometimes you've got to go in and sell these people. It's as much *you* as the art."

She sighed. "No, it isn't. *I'm* not the show. It's the art. That's the only thing that matters. And there are so many worthy artists out there who can't get a show. To just write them a check—"

"It's done every day."

"Not by me."

Erik shook his head. She was so beautiful and so damned stubborn; sometimes he just wanted to ram the Jag right into a wall. He mentally checked himself, easing his foot off the gas. No sense in getting a ticket.

"You know I'd do anything for you, don't you?" he said.

"Yes," she replied, staring out the windshield.

"Then I wish you'd let me help."

"Can we talk about this tomorrow? I'm really tired."

Well, maybe you wouldn't be so freaking tired if you weren't flirting with jerks in black leather jackets, he thought.

"All right, but at least let me show you what Nick's done. He's worked real hard on it."

"Okay," she said, heaving a heavy sigh.

A moment of silence fell between them.

"Are you going to the studio tomorrow night?"

She nodded. "I've got to get this one piece done, and it's really frustrating me."

She didn't know the half of it. While he didn't pretend to have any artistic sense, wouldn't know a Whistler from a Warhol, he knew how the business world worked. And all these high and mighty gallery owners were no different. They were running businesses. And if he wanted to foot the bill for a two-week show, he'd bet they'd let him hang dried dog crap on the walls. And they'd be only too happy to describe it as: *a deeply moving portrait of modern life.*

Everybody had his price; and his pretty, idealistic fiancée had no fucking clue.

9

"I THINK IT'S KILLER, man, just killer," the manager said, beaming. "What do you think, guys?"

The members of *The Musical Threats*, four lanky lads all dressed in black, gave a collective nod, still dazed and dazzled from viewing their video performance for the umpteenth time. Brian smiled and hit the rewind button on the deck containing the master edit and watched the tape roll back.

"So, it's a wrap?" Brian asked.

"Absolutely, man, you did great. Wouldn't change a thing. And I really appreciate your reining me in, too." The manager laughed.

Brian nodded. Just as he'd predicted, the manager had wanted to start over from scratch. That's when he'd hit them with his financial trump card: starting over now would double their bill. Suddenly, all those great new ideas didn't seem so great anymore.

"I've got a half-inch dub for you guys, so you can show the record company. The three-quarter duplicating master will be ready and waiting for you, once they've paid."

"No problemo, man, no problemo. I know how to get those blood-suckers to fork over. You'll get your dough by the end of the week."

"Great," Brian said, pulling the VHS copy out of the deck and pasting on the preprinted labels. He handed it to the manager who took it with a surprising amount of reverence.

"This is gonna put you guys on the map, mark my words," the older man said.

The four band members grinned and stood up, looking eager to go out and hit the clubs. Brian saw them out, locked the front door and returned to the suite to clean up. He glanced at the clock. It was nearly 8:00 PM. Christ, he'd been there for almost twelve hours. God only knew what that would have turned into had he let the band's manager walk all over him. But the man had turned out to be a reasonable sort, which was a rare commodity in the music business. Brian silently wished *The Musical Threats* the best of luck and set about cleaning the suite.

For perhaps the zillionth time that day, his thoughts turned to Joanna and the phone number burning a hole in his pocket. Should he call...or not? Even now, she might be at her studio....

Stop it, Weller, cool your jets.

He forced himself to tend to the tasks at hand and fifteen minutes later the tape heads were cleaned, the system was powered down and all the logs were updated, printed and filed. But instead of rushing out the door for his usual six-pack from Bauer's, he sat down and pulled the business card out of his pocket.

Joanna's handwriting was a series of precise graceful loops, and while it looked distinctly feminine, it had authority, avoiding the usual clichéd flourishes and curlicues.

Oh, Jesus, now you're analyzing handwriting? You know you're going to call her, you putz, so just get it the hell over with!

Before he could change his mind, he grabbed the phone and punched in the numbers. It rang three times.

"Hello?"

"So, how's my favorite artist?"

"W-what? Who *is* this...?" she paused. "Brian?"

"Guilty as charged. How are you?"

She laughed. "Oh, my God, you really had me worried there for a second. I didn't recognize your voice without a hundred and twenty decibels of music behind it."

"People tell me I sound different on the phone."

"You do. Like you're on the radio. It's kind of sexy."

Brian's nerves, already humming, ratcheted up a notch.

"I've embarrassed you, haven't I?" she said after a moment of awkward silence.

"No, no, not at all. I'm just not used to hearing that. I like it." He paused, gathering his thoughts. "Anyway, I just wanted to call and tell you how much I enjoyed spending the evening with you last night. I really needed the distraction, believe me."

"You're welcome. I had a great time, too. You're a wonderful dancer."

"Are you sure you have the right guy?"

"Hmm, I don't know.... Weren't you that silly man dancing with his leather jacket?"

"No, that was my evil twin. He's always trying to make me look bad."

Joanna laughed. "Oh, God, that was so funny. I couldn't believe it when you started doing that."

"I do aim to please," he replied, cracking a smile.

"You did, you really did." She giggled. The sound of it caressed his ears. He wanted to hear more of it.

"Listen, I won't keep you, but I wanted to know if you'd like to meet for coffee or a drink sometime?"

"I'd love to," she said. "I'm just finishing up at my studio. How about we meet at Charley's? Is that anywhere near your office?"

"About a block and a half."

"Great. I'll see you there in say...half an hour?"

"Looking forward to it."

They hung up a moment later and Brian pumped his fist into the air. "YES!"

He spent the next twenty minutes puttering around the office, jotting himself a reminder to write the payroll checks the next day, then threw on his black leather jacket, locked the front door and hit the street.

He tried to recall the last time he'd been to Charley's and realized he hadn't been near the place since the restaurant had moved from their old location right next door. Charley's Eating & Drinking Saloon now occupied the entire building on the southwest corner of Gloucester and Newbury, boasting a basement sports bar, fine dining on the parlor level, and private function rooms and offices on the upper floors. Whoever did the interior design had striven to keep the same upscale neighborhood bar atmosphere and had largely succeeded.

The only downside to the place, on this particular evening, was that they had the heat cranked up too high; it made for a stark contrast with the twenty-degree weather outside. At least the reception area was relatively clear of waiting patrons, though the downstairs bar seemed to be hopping. He heard the thump of the sound system and the chatter of the crowd through the floor.

"Good evening, sir, and welcome to Charley's," the young hostess said. "How many in your party?"

"Just two of us." He glanced at his watch. "She should be along in a few minutes."

"Will you be dining?"

"I don't think so, but we'd like someplace quiet."

"I do have a table in the front. Would that be okay?"

Brian nodded.

"Right this way, sir."

The young woman led him through an archway into the dining room that looked out over Newbury Street, seating him at a table for two near the bay window. Still feeling the heat, Brian stripped off his leather jacket and hung it from the back of his chair.

A waiter dressed in a starched green apron embroidered with the Charley's logo approached. He handed Brian a menu. "Can I get you anything from the bar, sir?"

"I'm waiting for someone."

"Very good, sir, I'll check back shortly."

He was about to call the waiter back, having decided to get something after all, when Joanna appeared in the archway. She scanned the room, spotted him and smiled. Brian rose when she approached. She was dressed all in black with the exception of a pair of fuzzy gray earmuffs that gave her an appealing childlike appearance. On anyone else they would have looked silly.

Brian held out the chair for her.

"Thank you," she said, sitting down. "Such a gentleman."

"My mother taught me well."

"I agree." She removed her earmuffs, pulled off her leather gloves, and slid her fur-trimmed coat off her shoulders and onto the chair behind her. Her cheeks were flushed from the cold and her lips a ruby red from freshly applied lipstick. "So, how are you?"

"I'm fine. Had a really long day, though."

Joanna rolled her eyes. "Me, too.... I had all these student meetings, taught three classes, and then I worked all afternoon on a piece at my studio. I'm bushed."

"Well, you certainly don't look it. In fact, I think you look terrific."

Her smile widened and her face flushed even more. "I could say the same for you."

Brian returned her smile, and was about to offer a cheeky reply when the waiter reappeared.

"Hi, I'm Aaron, and I'll be your waiter. Can I get you something from the bar?"

Brian gestured to Joanna. She frowned in thought then said: "I'll have an Irish Coffee made with Bushmills."

"You know, that actually sounds pretty good," Brian said. "Make it two."

The waiter departed and Joanna leaned forward. "I don't normally drink things like that, but it's so cold out, I thought it would be a nice change of pace."

"Like being here with you."

She gave him a shy smile and fiddled with her gloves. Her hands were even more beautiful than he'd remembered from the night before. Not a vein or a blemish in sight.

A few moments later the waiter reappeared with two tall glasses topped with whipped cream and two straws apiece. He placed them in front of Joanna and Brian.

"Will you be dining with us tonight?"

"No, thank you," Joanna said.

Brian shook his head.

"Very good. Please let me know, if you change your minds."

The waiter moved to another table and began taking an order.

"I'm curious about something," Joanna said. "How do you know Nick?"

"He did some work for my production company. My day job. We became friendly."

Joanna nodded. "So, you do your writing at night?"

"Often until the wee hours of the morning, but only if I don't have an edit session the next day. It's tough because once I get going it's hard to stop. And when I do, I'm wired for half the night."

"I know what you mean." She sipped her Irish coffee. "Ooh, that's good."

Brian took a sip of his own, surprised to find the taste appealing. He'd never liked whiskey, but it blended well with the coffee and the whipped cream, making for a wonderfully warming drink.

"I think I owe you an apology," she said.

"Oh? What for?"

"When you told me about your book, last night, I think I was overly harsh with you about it."

"No, you weren't. Nothing you said was anything that I hadn't mulled over myself. Truth is you have a valid point. I think a new direction is something I need to consider. Not sure what that is, though."

"Tell me about your other books."

"You sure you want to know?"

"Absolutely," she said, smiling.

For the next twenty minutes, Brian gave Joanna the cook's tour of his four other manuscripts, trying to keep the descriptions of the plots succinct and to the point. As she had the night before, she listened attentively. When he finished, she remained silent for a moment, then said: "I think you have a remarkable imagination."

"I'm glad you think so, though sometimes I feel like I'm beating my head against the wall to get some of that stuff out."

"Silly question?"

"No such thing," he said.

"Where do you get your ideas from?"

"Oops, I take that back. That *was* a silly question."

"What!" she said, laughing.

"Sorry, couldn't resist," he said, chuckling. "You had such a price-less look on your face just now. Forgive me?"

"You're forgiven.... But I really want to know."

"Not going to let me off the hook, are you?"

Joanna's grin turned sly. "Nope."

"Okay.... Well, the obvious and disingenuous answer is that they come from me, but that's not entirely true. Sometimes, I'll read some-thing in the paper or hear something on the news that'll spark an idea. Other times, I'll come up with just a title and the ideas will flow from that. In the rarest instances, and this is the spooky thing, I'll have a dream and get an entire story 'beamed' to me from my subconscious. When I get one of those it's a race against time to get it written down before I forget the fine details."

Joanna's eyes widened. "Oh, my God, I get that, too, with my art."

"So I'm not losing my mind?"

She took another sip of her drink, licking a dollop of whipped cream from her upper lip with an endearing flick of her tongue. "No, you're at least as sane as I am."

"That bad, huh?"

"Absolutely. You're hopeless."

They both laughed.

"I think this coffee is going to my head a bit," she said, taking another sip. "Seriously, though, you understand what it means to cre-ate and the dedication it takes. What's it like for you when you know you've finished something? Do you miss your characters?"

Brian started to take another sip of his drink then stopped himself. What a *great* question. He'd never given it much thought, but she had a point.

"I guess it *is* a bit like the 'empty nest syndrome.' I live with them for so long that I really feel as if I know them, as people. So, yeah, I do miss them when it's done. The only saving grace is that I can always pick up my book and read it and visit them all over again. The thing is I *love* the process. So many people want to have written a book, but they hate having to write it. I've never understood people like that. Anything I hated to do I always found a way to stop doing it. Is it like that for you?"

"Definitely. Every piece for me is like giving birth. When it's done, I have something I'm proud of, but I find I miss the act of creation, the hours of sweat and frustration and the final, 'Aha!' when it all falls together. There's nothing like it. Afterwards, I'm usually sad for a few days."

"But at least you have the finished art to look at and appreciate— unless you sell it, of course."

Joanna shook her head.

"You've never sold anything?"

"Not yet."

"Well, that really makes us comrades in arms, doesn't it?" He said, raising his coffee. "Here's to success."

Joanna clinked her nearly empty glass against his, her eyes shining. "Success," she echoed.

"You want another coffee?"

"I'd better not. What time is it?"

Brian looked at his watch. "Nine-thirty."

"Oh, God, I've got to go. I told Erik I'd be home by ten."

"No problem," Brian said, masking his disappointment. The time had gone too damned fast. He signaled the waiter, making the universal motion for the check. It arrived moments later.

"How much do I owe you?" Joanna asked.

"Nothing. It's my treat. You can pay the next time, if you'd like."

"Okay, next time, it is."

Brian left cash on the table and the two of them put on their coats and headed for the door. Outside, the frigid air hit them like a slap in the face.

"My car's just around the corner. Can I give you a ride?"

Even though it was a relatively short walk, he didn't want the evening to end, not yet.

"Thanks. It's not too far. Straight down Fairfield to Beacon."

On Newbury, Joanna approached a sleek black late model Mercedes 500SL. The license plate read: ARTEEST. She clicked the keyless remote and the car chirped once, all the lights flashing. Brian held the door for her and then went around to the passenger side and got in. The interior, also black, had that rich smell of leather he loved. And it was spotless, not even a fleck of lint on the carpeting.

Joanna sensed his wonderment. "This was Erik's idea. I wanted a Volvo wagon."

"Nothing wrong with having a nice car," Brian replied, trying to ease her discomfort. "And it certainly goes nicely with what you're wearing."

Joanna grinned and shook her head. "I need to keep you around. You really know how to make me feel better."

"I do?"

She gazed at him tenderly. "Yes, you do."

As if recalling the lateness of the hour, Joanna inserted the key and started the engine. It growled with suppressed power, as only a big motor could. Brian had to admit he was just a tiny bit jealous, even if a Mercedes was not his style.

"So, where on Beacon do you live?"

"Three thirty-four on the Storrow Drive side."

Joanna glanced in the rearview, pulled the car out of the space, and sped toward Mass Avenue.

A Note from an Old Acquaintance

In the brief silence that followed, Brian wondered if he should ask the question uppermost in his mind. Would she consider it prying? And did he really want to know the answer? He decided he did.

"How did you meet your fiancé?"

Joanna seemed to measure her words before speaking. "I was a sophomore at Mass Art and Erik was called in to bid on some expansion plans they were considering at the time. I was on work-study and the administration selected me to show him around. He asked me out the next day."

"And the rest is history?"

Joanna nodded, negotiating the turn onto Fairfield. "You could say that. We've been engaged for about six months."

Brian tried to hide his reaction. Christ! Too late by a lousy six months. Up ahead, he spotted his building, suddenly regretting the turn in the conversation. Feeling like a prize fool, he stared out the windshield while she double-parked the Mercedes in front of 334 and turned on the hazard lights.

She turned to him, her expression a mixture of emotions.

"It's a lovely building," she said. "It suits you."

Brian nodded. "Of all the places I've lived since moving here, it's my favorite."

He turned to her then, their eyes locking. His heart thudded in his chest and his mouth turned to sand.

"It seems I can't help having a wonderful time with you."

"Me, too," she replied, her voice a near whisper.

She leaned toward him, ever so slightly, her eyes searing into his soul. Without knowing quite what compelled him to such reckless abandon, Brian kissed her. A soft moan issued from her throat, and she brought her left hand up, cupping the back of his head. The other caressed his cheek. Her lips were so gentle, so soft, yet they blazed with

101

an intensity that dwarfed the memory of his first furtive kisses with Laurie McCurry when he was twelve, and the thousands of kisses that had come after them, burning into his mind and heart with a quiet ferocity that belied its tenderness.

All too soon, it broke; and Brian pulled away, not wanting it to end, his mind and heart aflame with so many emotions he couldn't sort them out. Joanna's deep green eyes reflected these same feelings, yet in those vibrant emerald depths they grew crystal clear: joy, longing, lust, hope, and something else.... Was it fear? For Brian, it was the fear of another heartbreak, and the fear of never seeing this incredible woman again. He reached for her hand, feeling those long graceful fingers lace through his.

"You're trembling," he said, swallowing hard.

"So are you."

"I'd love to see you again, Joanna. Can I call you?"

She nodded, her eyes still locked with his. "I'd like that."

With the greatest reluctance, Brian opened the car door and climbed out.

"Drive safe."

Joanna smiled and nodded. "I'll talk to you soon."

Brian watched her drive off, waiting until her tail lights disappeared before going inside.

For the rest of the evening he went through the normal motions of his solitary life, realizing that up until that night at the Metropolis club, that life had been utterly meaningless.

10

By 9:45 THE TRAFFIC in the Westbound lanes of the Mass Pike had lightened, the rush hour long over, and Joanna found herself longing for the bumper-to-bumper snarl to which she'd become accustomed. At least it would give her more time to think. The problem was she didn't know what to think. She kept fiddling with the radio and the cassette player, trying to find something—anything to keep her mind from dwelling on Brian; but no matter what station she tuned in or which album she put on, her thoughts kept returning to him.

In Heaven's name, what had she done?

I let him kiss me. What was I thinking?

And that was just it, she wasn't thinking, at least not with her head. The thing of it was, she'd wanted him to kiss her, had wanted it from the moment she had looked into his eyes at Nick's party. The real irony was that she hadn't even intended to go to the party in the first place. Instead, she'd planned to spend the evening working in her studio. But it was during her afternoon meditation that something changed her mind. It was no magical revelation, no mysterious flash of insight, just a quiet certainty that she must be there.

It all came clear when Brian had asked her to dance. And it wasn't

103

that he was particularly handsome, either, not like Erik, whose dark male-model looks had turned her head so completely as a twenty-year-old. But there was something about him, something boyish and innocent, yet strong and assured. On the other hand, he wasn't ugly, either. She loved the way his lips curled sideways into that sweet smile, his wavy blonde hair, the way it curled around the backs of his ears, the slight dimple in his strong chin. But it was those eyes of his that had made her heart stutter in her chest. So steady, so blue and so...honest.

And he was funny, too.

Joanna giggled, recalling his leather jacket tango once again.

Yes, she'd wanted him to kiss her more than anything, had been afraid he would be too shy to do so. Yet, when he had, it overwhelmed her senses in ways that still defied description. She trembled at the memory, her fingers touching her lips, as if to recapture the feel of him.

What really thrilled and scared her all at once, however, were the acuity of his mind and the depth of his soul, his knowing what it truly meant to be an artist. Poor Erik, so consumed by the passions of his business and all that went with it, so assured in his dealings with Boston's powerbrokers, had no idea as to what it really meant to create something of beauty from the core of one's being. It really was like giving birth, your creations carrying a small part of yourself out into the world. Erik's buildings, so startling in their construction, so commanding in their presence, were merely testaments to his acumen, a reflection of his ability to hire the right people for the right jobs. He had no understanding of the creative mind.

Yet, she still loved him...didn't she?

She hadn't told Brian the whole story of how she and Erik had met. It was true she'd been asked to show him and his architects around, and it was equally true that he'd asked her out the next day, but only after pulling strings with the school to find out her number.

A Note from an Old Acquaintance

She'd been both annoyed and flattered that he'd gone to such lengths, yet she'd rebuffed him. But he persisted. Eventually, her resistance had broken down and she'd consented to a date. In spite of her tears and her dilemma, Joanna cracked a wistful smile, the memories of that night flooding her mind. Had it really been only six years ago? It seemed as if it happened a lifetime ago—and in someone else's life...

❊   ❊   ❊

...Joanna gazed at her reflection in the old cracked vanity mirror and sighed. She was a mess, a total freaking mess, and this date was a crazy idea, too. Her roommate, Marcia, thought she was nuts to have any doubts, foaming at the mouth over Erik and all of his "little presents" that arrived during the past week: flowers, candy, silly little dime-store baubles that made Joanna laugh, and more flowers.

Maybe she should call him and tell him that she wasn't feeling well. She sure didn't look all that great. Her hair was a frizzy rat's nest, her makeup looked as if a clown had applied it, and the dress, Marcia's so-called "Drop Dead" dress, clung to her in all the wrong places.

She looked again at the dozen red roses sitting in the vase next to the mirror. They'd arrived earlier that afternoon, the note saying: *Expect the unexpected—Erik.*

The smile those words brought to her lips belied her apprehension. He *was* sweet...*and* rich *and* handsome. So, why was she questioning it? Why didn't she just go with the flow? Was it the age difference? Joanna thought she was beyond that, but she couldn't help wondering what it might be like, years from now, if they stayed together. She shook her head again, this time at her own foolishness. Here she was thinking about the future and she couldn't even get her act together for one lousy date.

What time was it, anyway?

She stole another glance at the clock on the floor next to her futon. Even with the two burnt-out LEDs she could still tell it was—

5:15.

Crap. He would be here in fifteen minutes and she was a *mess*!

Relax, she thought. Remember your breathing. Everything will be fi—

The buzzer over the elevator blatted.

Joanna yelped, grabbed her lipstick and tried to steady her hands long enough to apply it.

"Joanna...?" Marcia called from the other end of the loft. "I think you might wanna check this out."

Joanna gave herself one last critical look, then moved through the beaded curtain separating her "bedroom" from the rest of the loft. She spotted her roommate across the two thousand square foot room staring out the bank of windows fronting Pittsburgh Street. The light filtering through decades of grime gave the room a dusty golden-red glow.

"What is it?" Joanna asked, frowning.

Marcia stabbed her finger toward the window, an excited expression on her narrow face.

Joanna started across the floor, neatly side-stepping the scattered piles of Marcia's clothing, her high heels clacking against the patchwork of ancient linoleum. She paused a moment near one of her new pieces, an idea flashing into her mind.

"Will you come on, already?" Marcia shouted.

Joanna reached the window, following her roommate's gaze toward the street below. A long Rolls Royce limousine idled at the curb, its flawless paint gleaming like a black mirror. Joanna's eyes widened.

"Oh, my...."

"I'll say one thing for him. He's sure got style."

"I can't go, Marsh, not like this!"

Joanna's roommate turned from the window and gave her friend a quick appraisal. "What are you talkin' about? You look bitchin'. And that dress...." Marcia licked her finger then reached behind her back, making a sizzling sound as her finger made contact with her ample derriere.

Joanna rolled her eyes. "Look at this!" she said, yanking at her auburn curls.

"Well, if you'd stopped workin' on that sculpture of yours a little earlier, I could have done somethin' with it."

The door buzzed again and Joanna moaned, her pulse rate accelerating.

"Calm down, calm down, you'll be fine. Here, let me...." Marcia reached over to a table piled with a jumble of cosmetics and pulled out a woven elastic band; then she arranged Joanna's hair in a loose bun atop her head. "There, perfect. Now *go*."

The buzzer squawked again and Joanna dashed to the elevator, pulling up the gate, scooting inside, and letting it fall back down with a loud crash. She stabbed the button for the first floor and closed her eyes, sending a silent prayer to Buddha for a measure of much-needed calm and poise.

The elevator motor groaned and creaked, and the car began its bumpy descent.

"Jo! Heads up!"

Joanna looked up the shaft and saw Marcia dropping her clutch purse. She caught it and laughed. Christ, if her head wasn't attached....

When the elevator reached the ground floor, Joanna spied the liveried driver waiting in the foyer, his finger poised to press the buzzer button again. He turned and gave her a courtly bow, then led the way out to the street.

Erik waited by the limousine's open rear door, an admiring smile on his chiseled face, every crease on his dark-blue Armani suit razor sharp. "You look so lovely this evening."

Joanna grinned, the anxiety leeching from her body. "I have my fashion consultant to thank for that," she said, looking up toward the third floor window. Marcia smiled and waved.

"Shall we?" Erik said, motioning toward the Rolls.

Joanna grinned again and climbed inside, the supple leather seat enveloping her with a quiet sigh. The all-black interior with its gleaming chrome and burled walnut accents exuded a mélange of beguiling odors: rich leather, a woodsy aromatic cologne, expensive single-malt whiskey and earthy pipe tobacco. Mostly, it smelled of money.

Erik settled into the seat beside her and Joanna's heart rate ratcheted up a notch. A moment later the limo pulled away from the curb with a quiet purr.

"So, where are we going?" she asked.

Erik locked eyes with her, dark pools that promised mystery and excitement. "Telling would spoil the surprise," he replied.

The limousine shot across the Congress Street Bridge onto Atlantic Avenue, wound its way past Fanueil Hall and entered the Callahan Tunnel. Traffic in the tunnel was heavy, but this didn't seem to faze Erik, who began asking her questions about her studies at Mass Art. The wonderful thing was, his eyes didn't glaze over when she told him. He actually seemed interested.

"So, what do you want to do when you graduate?" he asked.

"You mean what am I going to do for a living?"

He smiled. "I didn't say that."

"Probably teach."

"No fame and fortune?"

Joanna studied his face, trying to divine if the question was a face-tious one. She decided it wasn't.

"Well, fortune would be nice, but I'm not sure fame is everything it's cracked up to be. Besides, making one's name in the art world isn't that easy."

Erik chuckled. "You might be surprised. I saw some of your work at the school. Compared to everything else I saw there, I think you could go all the way, if you wanted."

Joanna felt a mixture of excitement and irritation, and wasn't sure why. Having a sophisticated and worldly man such as Erik saying things like that made her feel giddy. But surely he knew it wasn't like closing a business deal.

Outside the tunnel, Joanna realized they were heading for the airport.

"Okay, where *are* we going?"

"A favorite little spot I thought you might enjoy."

"Hmmm, and I guess I'll just have to be a good girl, and wait and see, won't I?" She gave him a coy grin, making him laugh.

Instead of taking the normal route into Logan, the driver guided the limo onto the surface streets. Soon, they arrived at a private hangar. A gleaming Gulfstream jet sat just inside the yawning doorway, the ground crew scurrying about making last-minute preparations.

"Oh, my God, this is—"

"—something you richly deserve."

Joanna started to say something else and thought better of it. It was just a date, right? Why not enjoy it?

The pilot emerged from the cockpit when they mounted the steps. He introduced himself and made sure Joanna and Erik were comfortable in the main cabin. "We should be at LaGuardia in a little under an hour," he said.

109

"How's the weather?" Erik asked.

"Smooth sailing, Mr. Ruby."

Erik nodded and the pilot disappeared back into the cockpit. Moments later, the engines fired up. In ten minutes they were airborne. Joanna watched the lights of the Boston skyline recede, wondering if this was all some heady dream, and any moment she would awaken in her seedy loft. Did she really deserve this? Did she really have anything in common with this man?

Joanna heard the sound of a cork popping and turned to see Erik pouring champagne into two crystal flutes. He placed the bottle back into the silver ice bucket and handed her one of the delicate glasses. He touched the rim of his against hers, eliciting a musical "ting."

"Here's to a wonderful evening with an enchanting lady."

Joanna felt her face grow warm and she quickly took a sip. The tiny bubbles tickled her nose and the dry sparkling wine glided down her throat, warming her stomach.

Forty minutes later the plane landed at LaGuardia, where another limousine, a Mercedes this time, whisked them into the city. Soon, they were pulling up to the front of an old brownstone in the West Fifties. The awning had no name, just a number: 21.

Once inside the brownstone, Joanna followed Erik and the lanky maitré d' up two flights of stairs, past various rooms crammed with chattering diners, stopping at a front room on the third floor. The brass plaque on the mahogany door read: Pete's Room. The maître d' opened it with a flourish and led the way. The elegant space looked to have been converted from a woman's dressing room, with painted cherubs on the nine-foot ceiling and heavy gold-brocade drapes framing the tall windows overlooking the street. The most surprising thing was there was only one intimate table for two in the center of the room, the white tablecloth, silver and glassware gleaming in the flickering candlelight.

A Note from an Old Acquaintance

The meal was delicious and meticulously served. Joanna even found it funny that every time she finished one of the little Melba toast slices they served, another would magically appear on her plate. She stuffed herself shamelessly.

Afterward, they decided to take a walk around the neighborhood, the limo following a discreet distance behind. The air had turned cooler and Joanna slipped her arm through Erik's.

"So, what do you want to be when *you* grow up?" she asked, a sly grin on her face.

Erik laughed. "You mean I'm not?"

"Oh, I still see the little boy in there somewhere."

His mood turned somber. "I want to build the greatest buildings in the world, buildings nobody will *ever* want to tear down."

"And that's important to you...."

Erik's eyes focused on a far away point. "You see that building on Park with the ring of colored lights near the top?"

Joanna spotted the forty-story building a couple of blocks away. Even at night she could discern its striking design: an unusual fusion of modern and rococo. "It's lovely."

"My father built it back in the Fifties when everyone else was throwing together these cookie-cutter glass and steel towers. Most of those are gone, now. He never settled for second best...."

Joanna felt his pride, and while it clashed with her Buddhist philosophy, she understood it and admired him for it. Still, this was a man who'd ordered steak tartare while she'd eaten salad and steamed vegetables. This was a man who dealt with powerbrokers and VIPs and she was just a kid who wanted to create her art and teach others the joys of the creative process. And while being with him thrilled her, it also made her feel like the proverbial fish out of water. As lovely and as wonderful as this date was, what kind of future could there be?

111

They were worlds apart. The only thing that made any sense was to tell him they shouldn't see each other again.

"Erik, I—" She stopped speaking, halting in her tracks, her eyes widening.

Erik frowned. "Are you okay?"

She looked at him then back toward the mouth of the alley they'd just passed. In a pool of jaundiced light from a flickering streetlamp, sat a young woman cradling a sleeping child. Both the woman and the child wore ragged, filthy clothes, but it was the haunted, desperate look in the girl's eyes that chilled Joanna.

"Oh, no.... She's just a kid." At the sound of Joanna's voice, the girl looked up, their eyes meeting for the briefest of moments; and in that look she saw hopes lost, dreams derailed, two lives poised on the abyss. Joanna turned to Eric. "We have to do something."

"Joanna, I don't know—"

"*Please*, we can't just leave them like this—not like this!"

He looked over at the woman and child, a range of conflicting emotions crossing his face. Finally, a long moment later, he nodded. "All right, wait here."

Erik approached the woman, who eyed him with a frightened wariness. He held up his hands then knelt in front of her and began speaking. Joanna strained to hear what was being said, but with the noise of passing traffic she couldn't make it out. Whatever he was saying had an effect. The girl visibly relaxed and a moment later, she nodded and allowed Erik to help her up. He looked toward the limo, giving the driver a signal. The Mercedes shot forward, screeching to a stop at the curb. The driver jumped out and held open the rear door.

The little boy had awakened and was rubbing his eyes, his head still resting on his mother's shoulder. He began sucking his thumb. He looked hungry.

A Note from an Old Acquaintance

As Erik eased them into the limo, the woman grabbed his hand, her thanks coming in a torrent of words and sobs. He squeezed her hand, rubbed the boy's head and closed the door. He turned to the driver.

"Take them to The Haven at Tenth and Forty-Second. Ask for Carla Montez. She runs the place. Tell her I want the woman and the boy taken in as a personal favor. Once you're sure they're settled come back and pick us up at the restaurant. Okay?"

"Sure thing, Mr. Ruby."

The driver climbed back into the Mercedes and sped off.

"Thank you," Joanna said. "Not many men would have done what you did."

"No? Well, I don't think I could ever refuse you anything, Joanna," he replied.

She smiled, a warmth suffusing her body.

"Where is he taking them? Is it a shelter?"

Erik nodded. "The building was my first project. My father thought it would be a good way to get my feet wet. His foundation, which I also manage, provides their annual budget."

Joanna looked into his eyes. In them she saw something more than the powerbroker and the little boy, something that dwarfed them both.

"I guess his heart was in the right place...like his son's."

She slipped her arm through his and leaned against him. They began strolling back toward the 21 Club....

    ❋   ❋   ❋

A horn honked, breaking Joanna out of her thoughts. She swerved back into her lane and wiped away the tears in her eyes. Where had that special part of Erik gone? Had it slowly slipped away, yet another

113

innocent victim of his unswerving ambition? Didn't he see it was driving them apart? Surely that sweetness lay buried in him somewhere still? Surely it was worth rescuing?

Her thoughts returned to Brian. No, she hadn't told him the whole story because she sensed, no she *knew*, it would have discouraged him, and she couldn't bear the thought of that, either.

What on earth was she going to do?

Flashing lights up ahead distracted her from her thoughts. The traffic around her began to slow. With a sinking feeling she realized there was an accident up ahead. A bad one.

"Oh, no," she mumbled, checking the clock. It was nearly 10:00. Time to call home. Joanna reached for the phone handset just as it rang, startling her. She snatched it up, pushed the SEND button and brought it to her ear.

"Hello?"

"Hi, babe, it's me."

"Hi, I was just reaching for the phone to call you. I'm on the Pike and it's all backed up. Looks like an accident."

"I tried you at the studio half an hour ago. Where were you?"

Joanna's mind scrambled for something to say, anything that would make sense.

"I finished early," she replied. "So, I decided to get some coffee on Newbury Street and ran into an old friend."

"Oh? Anyone I know?"

"No, just a classmate from Mass Art." How she hated it when he started asking questions like these. He had no reason to be so possessive, that is, until now....

"Ah, I see. So, what part of the Pike are you on?"

"I just passed exit 19."

"And how backed up is it?"

A Note from an Old Acquaintance

Joanna squinted through the windshield. "It's got to be at least another mile before I get to the accident scene. The traffic's just creeping along. They must have only one lane open."

Erik sighed. "All right, you won't be home for at least forty-five minutes. I'll be in my study, in any event."

"Everything okay?"

"Just the Wrightson building again. More revisions I need to go over. It never seems to end. I'll see you when you get here. Love you."

"I love you, too," she said, pushing the END button.

She replaced the phone onto its magnetic cradle, tears stinging her eyes again, her vision blurring. She'd lied about meeting Brian at Charley's, but that wasn't what was really bothering her. What had brought on her tears were those three little words she'd just spoken to her fiancé.

I love you.

She'd taken them for granted for so long; now they felt like lies, lies far worse than the one concerning her whereabouts.

The only thing that made any sense was to break this thing with Brian off, now, before it went any further. But she didn't know if she had the strength to do it. She certainly didn't want to do it. Why couldn't she have met Brian six years ago, instead of Erik, assuming her flighty twenty-year old brain would have recognized Brian for the treasure he was? She'd changed so much in all that time, and Erik hadn't. And what an awful thought that was.

Joanna reached for the tissue box in the glove compartment, the tears now flowing in earnest. She would meditate when she got home, that was the best thing. A quiet hour in front of Buddha would focus her mind and show her the true way of her heart. And whatever was revealed she would accept.

115

Calmer now, she dabbed her eyes and focused her attention on the road ahead. Traffic seemed to be moving a little faster, edging closer to the cluster of road flares and the collage of flashing lights. It took another twenty minutes before she came abreast of the accident scene. There were three vehicles involved, one of them a van. All were twisted and torn nearly beyond recognition. Three ambulances were parked nearby, their rear doors open. She stared, horrified, at four still forms lying together on the asphalt covered by yellow tarpaulins, one of them much shorter than the others.

A child.

Joanna turned her face away, trying to erase the images from her mind, knowing it to be a futile gesture. What her mother had always said now seemed truer than ever: "Enjoy the time you have, Joanna. Life is too short to miss anything."

Once past the accident, she pressed the accelerator and sped away, her mind and heart in turmoil.

❃   ❃   ❃

She arrived home just past eleven, easing the Mercedes into the three-car garage between Erik's Jaguar and his immaculate silver 1963 split-window Corvette. She punched the remote, lowering the garage door, locked the 500SL and walked through the side door into the kitchen. Soft indirect lighting gleamed off the granite counters. She placed her handbag on the countertop adjacent to the stainless steel Viking range, threw her coat over one of the chairs surrounding the steel and glass table in the breakfast nook, and headed into the main area of the house. She could tell the maids had been in today, as the usual daily clutter was missing.

Their home, which Erik had christened *Greycroft*, was a six thousand square-foot modern Victorian occupying a three-acre lot two miles from Newton Center. Not content with the mundane, Erik had demolished the lot's original structure—a forty-year-old colonial— hired the top residential architect and interior designer, telling each of them, "I want the new house to look as if it's been here for a hundred years, but with all the modern conveniences." The two men had outdone themselves, creating a showplace, every room an immaculate spread out of *Architectural Digest*. And while Joanna enjoyed the amenities, she often felt as if she were a guest in her own home.

True to his word, she found Erik hunched over rolls of blueprints in his study, a four hundred square-foot mahogany-paneled expanse. He looked up when she entered the room.

"Hi, sweetie," he said, yawning. "This project's a bear, let me tell you."

Joanna bent over him and kissed him on the cheek. "How bad is it?"

Ruby leaned back in his chair, tossing a pencil onto the blueprints. She noticed a yellow legal pad covered with the scrawl of his notations. "Old Man Wrightson read me the riot act today, telling me to get my act together or he was taking his business elsewhere." He shook his head, scowling. "I'm telling you, the man doesn't want to spend the money it takes to do things right."

"Not everyone does, Honey. Not like you. And it is his money."

"Well, you're right about that." He gave her a penetrating look. "Anyway, how was your day?"

She turned away from him. "It was okay. Lots of student meetings. And I'm really tired. I'm going to meditate for awhile."

Ruby nodded. "That's fine, but before you do, I want you to look this over."

He reached under the rolls of blueprints and pulled out a piece of poster board. Pasted to it, along with the requisite crop marks, fold lines and notations to the printer, was the layout for the front and back of a tri-fold brochure.

Joanna took it from him and stared at it. A moment passed before she realized what it was: the mailer Erik had hired Nick to design for her first show. She had to admit that Nick had done his usual terrific job. On the front was a picture of one of her more dramatic sculptures, a lighted sphere with fiber optic appendages.

The inside of the brochure was another matter. Nick had used a photo of her posing next to another one of her pieces. She was dressed in a black body suit and reclined on the floor, propped up on one elbow, with the other arm draped casually over a drawn-up knee. The photographer had captured her with what she now considered to be too much of a "come hither" look. Erik loved it, of course, had it blown up to nearly life size and hung in his office. At the top of the page was a headline reading:

JOANNA RICHMAN: AN EXCITING NEW FACE!

"Well, what do you think?" Ruby asked.

"How could you?" she said, tossing the layout onto the desk. "How could you do this? I told you— *I'm* not the show! Did you hear anything I said? Do you even care how I feel?"

He shot her an annoyed look. "Of course, I care."

"Then, why, Erik? Why are you using this—this cheesecake? It's degrading."

Ruby stood up, a vein throbbing in his temple. "It's *not* degrading. It's a terrific picture of a beautiful woman who just happens to be you. Something you've never been comfortable with. And I wish to hell I knew the reason why!"

"It doesn't matter."

118

"It sure as hell matters to me. I'm proud of you and I want to show you off."

"I don't want to be shown off. I want my art to speak for itself."

"It will, Joanna, it will, but the public loves a pretty face to go with its entertainment. It's just the way it is...."

Shaking her head, she moved toward the door. "You really don't understand, do you? My art's not 'entertainment.' It's a part of me."

She walked out, tears stinging her eyes once again, and ran up the stairs. Passing the master bedroom, she rushed to the end of the hall and entered her meditation room, slamming the door behind her. She left the light off and leaned back against the door, sobbing.

How could he be so stubborn? Couldn't he see what he was doing? Couldn't he see that to market her work in that way only cheapened it...and her? Why did he always have to try and get his way? It was almost as if he didn't care what she thought, that she was just another part of his business.

Joanna pushed that thought from her mind, wiped her eyes with the backs of her hands and stepped into the middle of the room, empty except for a large down pillow that sat facing a statue of the Buddha. She sat down on the pillow, placed herself in the lotus position and closed her eyes, letting the silence in the room calm her. She began her rhythmic breathing and called her mantra to mind.

A knock sounded at the door.

"Joanna, I'm sorry. Can we talk about this?"

Joanna opened her eyes, knowing that any attempt to meditate now was pointless. She rose to her feet went to the door and opened it. Erik stood at the threshold, looking contrite.

"Look," he said, "I'm a schmuck, I know it. I thought I knew better. I don't."

"No, you don't," she said.

Ruby took her hand. "Forgive me?"

Joanna nodded. "Yes."

Ruby took her in his arms and hugged her. "I'll tell Nick to change it, take out the photo, put in some more of your work. That okay?"

"Sure," she said, hugging him back. She held onto him so he wouldn't see the tears spring anew.

What on earth was she going to do?

11

BRIAN AWOKE SATURDAY MORNING more rested, more alive than he'd felt in a long time. The sun sparkled through the bare-limbed trees outside his windows, dappling the carpet with a kaleidoscope of light and shadow, and somewhere on the floor above him he heard a woman laugh. He smiled. Someone was having a little early morning fun. A glance at the clock told him it was just past 7:00. Time to face the day.

Rising, he threw on his robe, and went upstairs to retrieve his *Boston Globe* from the front stoop. He stood for a moment, struck by the beauty of the early morning light glinting off the windows of the ancient brownstones across the way. The air was warmer today, nearly in the forties, and birds twittered in the canopy of stately maples and lindens high overhead. It might not be spring yet, but the day seemed to hold the promise of something nearly as good.

Back downstairs, Brian toasted a bagel, spread it with cream cheese, poured himself a tall mug of fresh coffee and sat at his breakfast table, leafing through the paper. The hard news was the usual panoply of horrors, sprinkled with liberal doses of moralizing. Putting the front section aside, he turned to Arts & Entertainment, checking to see who might be playing at the Paradise or any of the other clubs he liked to frequent.

Nothing too interesting there, mostly a bunch of bands struggling through the last gasps of New Wave. And there wasn't anything special in the Movies section, either.

Turning the page, he read through the gallery listings, checking out the exhibitions.

So, Weller, interested in art now, are you?

"Can't imagine why," he said, taking a bite of his bagel, a big sloppy grin on his face.

He did find a number of listings of galleries at the eastern end of Newbury Street announcing new exhibitions starting that day. One of them, The Holliston Gallery, was hosting a show for Alexander DeLarge, an artist of the Photo-realism School. These were painters whose skills were so exacting and so refined they could paint a still life or a portrait that looked as real as any photo. Brian had always had tremendous respect for those who could draw or paint, his own artistic skills limited to stick figures and crude disembodied faces. The examples of Photo-realist paintings he'd seen in the past had fascinated him no end. Critics hated them, however, accusing the artists of being little better than commercial hacks best suited for billboards and movie posters. Brian thought the critics were fools. Anyone with half a brain could splatter paint on a canvas and call it art. Hell, even J. Fred Muggs—a precocious chimpanzee famous for his antics on *The Today Show* in the 1950s—had sold finger paintings looking very much like the canvases Jackson Pollock had painted on some of his better days.

On a whim, Brian decided to visit the gallery after putting in some time on the new book and a quick visit to the office, if for no other reason than to show his support for the artist.

After cleaning up his breakfast dishes and showering, Brian

brought out his Royal and got to work. The words came hard, though, his mind continually returning to Joanna's comments about his stories. She was so dead-on right that he found his admiration for her growing by the moment. The problem was, he was about halfway through the latest book and was coming to the realization that it was pointless to continue working on it. It was more of the same stuff he'd been collecting rejection slips on for the past five years. And did he really want *that* to continue? Did he really want to put in the titanic effort it took to finish a book only to have it end up in his dresser drawer, collecting dust along with the others?

He forced himself to re-read it from the beginning, resisting the urge to tweak it as he went along. Two hours later, after reaching the point where he'd left off, he realized the book was a failure. It had no heart. Sure, there was plenty of suspense and action, plenty of "red herrings," but in the end he didn't give a crap about what happened to anyone in the story. They were all interchangeable. Even his protagonist seemed bland and colorless to him now.

You can do better than this, Weller.

The problem was he didn't know what the hell to do.

It was just approaching noon, when he tossed the manuscript back in its box, threw on his leather jacket and walked to the office. He spent the next half an hour going over the books and checking supplies to see if they needed to order more videotape come Monday. Everything was in order, so he hit the street. He debated whether to stop for something to eat and decided against it. Time enough for food later.

The Holliston Gallery occupied the basement level of a redbrick Queen Anne row house located between Clarendon and Dartmouth Streets, and he almost passed it by, nestled as it was between an Indian restaurant and a bohemian style coffee house. Going inside, he was struck by the tranquility of the interior. Walls were a stark white, as were the freestanding partitions stationed at strategic points. Soft track lighting overhead highlighted each of the paintings without overwhelming them. Immediately inside the door was a poster set up on an easel. It depicted an example of the artist's work, the artist's name and the dates of the exhibition.

A slight woman in her fifties, with straight gray hair, approached him. "Welcome to Holliston Gallery. I'm Claire Holliston," she said, smiling. "Can I help you with anything?"

"Hi. I'm not sure, actually. I saw your notice in the paper this morning, and I thought I'd come by. I really love this style."

The woman's smile widened and she leaned closer to Brian. "It really goes against the grain nowadays, and that's something I've always enjoyed doing."

Brian chuckled, charmed by the woman's warmth and candor. She pointed toward the rear of the gallery. "There are refreshments in the back, coffee and pastries, and the artist is 'holding court.' He's a little full of himself, but he comes by it honestly."

Brian thanked the woman and began looking at the paintings. Every one was a dramatic tableau with chiaroscuro lighting, making the images look as if they were frame blow-ups from out of a motion picture. In fact, the artist had reinforced that impression by using the same Panavision-style wide-screen aspect ratio for most of the pieces on display. It was mesmerizing.

He worked his way down one wall to the back where he spotted the artist conversing with two patrons. The table with the refreshments stood nearby. Brian nodded to the artist, who watched him grab a blueberry Danish and fill a disposable plastic mug with coffee, all without missing a beat of his pontification. And while Brian could admire the man's facile way with pompous pronouncements, he only needed to hear a snippet of the conversation for him to agree with the gallery owner's opinion. The man *was* full himself.

He decided not to try and join the conversation and began examining the paintings on the other side of the gallery. Out of the corner of his eye, he caught sight of a couple entering the front door. They appeared to be in the midst of an argument. He was tall, with dark, almost black hair swept straight back and was dressed in an expensive-looking black and white herringbone blazer and black wool slacks. The woman was—Joanna!

Brian nearly choked on his Danish. Ducking behind one of the partitions, he pretended to look closely at one of the paintings, while keeping the other eye and both ears on Joanna and the man who could only be her fiancé. A flurry of mixed emotions rushed through him. A part of him wanted to stay and another wanted to duck out the back.

He stayed.

"...So, why don't you just go on to your office, Erik?" Joanna said. "You know that's where you'd rather be. You don't have to keep torturing yourself on my account."

"Fine, then. You want to keep popping into these little holes in the wall all day long, have at it. I've had my fill."

"Fine. Give my regards to Mr. Wrightson," she snapped.

Joanna's fiancé glared at her then shook his head. "I'll call you later."

Brian watched the man stalk out the door and vanish from sight. Joanna turned and sighed, her eyes downcast. For a moment, it looked as if she might follow her fiancé out the door, but then she straightened her shoulders and stepped up to one of the paintings, her expression intent.

He realized he still had a piece of soggy Danish in his mouth. So absorbed was he in watching Joanna that he'd forgotten to swallow it.

He took a sip of his coffee and watched her move closer to the spot where he stood.

She was even more adorable in the daylight. As before, she was dressed all in black, her hair a fiery halo around her head. She moved to the next painting, her brow knitting in concentration.

Brian drained his coffee, threw the empty cup and the remainder of the Danish into a trash basket and moved toward her, a smile forming on his lips.

"We're going to have to stop meeting like this."

She turned, her initial shock transforming into delight. "Brian! Oh, my God, what are you doing here?" she asked.

"I read about this exhibition in the paper, I thought I'd check it out."

Joanna squeezed his arm. "I'm so glad you did. I could use some cheering up."

"Well, then, you've come to the right guy."

She smiled up at him. "I know."

Brian felt as if he might float off the floor. Swallowing, he nodded toward one of the paintings. "So, what do you think of our friend's work?"

"His technique is excellent, but there's nothing of *him* in it."

Brian frowned and looked toward the painting. It showed a prostitute leaning against a brick wall a lit cigarette dangling from her mouth, the only lighting the red glow of a neon sign. The woman's expression was tired and forlorn.

"Look at the woman," Brian said, "look at her face. She looks as if she has no hope left in the world. Pretty powerful, wouldn't you say?"

Joanna peered closer, scrutinizing the face of the prostitute, which was only a small part of the picture, yet spoke volumes.

A Note from an Old Acquaintance

She turned to him with a new respect in her eyes. "You're right. I didn't see that."

"Every one of this artist's paintings has an element like that, something in it that's the real message. It reminds me of a painting I saw one day, years ago, as I passed the window of a gallery on Boylston. It was a landscape depicting this dark foreboding Victorian-style house atop a hill covered in wild grass and dotted with twisted Black Ash trees. Very dramatic. The title of the piece was 'Redwing.' For the life of me, I couldn't figure out why it was called that, until I looked closer. There, in the bottom right-hand corner, right above the artist's signature was a little red-winged blackbird perched on a stalk of wild grass. I've never forgotten it. It taught me always to look closer to find the truth of things and never be content with the obvious."

"What a wonderful story," she said.

Brian grinned. "Would you like to get some lunch?" he asked, after a moment. "All I've had since breakfast is half a lousy Danish, and I'm famished."

"I'd love to. How about the Indian place next door?"

Brian looked dubious.

"Come on, I hear they make a mean Tandoori."

After thanking the gallery owner and taking a couple of brochures, Brian and Joanna went next door to The Raj and sat at one of the tiny tables overlooking the street. As Joanna suggested, Brian ordered the Chicken Tandoori with rice, Nan bread and ice water. Joanna rattled off a list of dishes, whose names meant nothing to Brian. When the food came a few minutes later, he was surprised to see that none of the dishes Joanna ordered contained meat.

"No Tandoori for you? I thought you liked it."

"Erik loves it. I'm a vegetarian."

"Really? Why?"

"I'm a Buddhist. Buddhists by tradition and teaching are vegetarian. We don't believe in killing anything that contains a soul."

"A Buddhist from Long Island? Not too many of those, I would imagine."

"Now, you're making fun of me," she said, her eyes sparkling.

"I wouldn't dream of it. But I suspect your upbringing was slightly different."

"Jewish-American Princess through and through."

Brian laughed. "Somehow, I can't imagine you as a typical example of that breed. You're too—"

"I'm too...what?" she asked, raising a ginger eyebrow and stifling a grin.

"You're too grounded, and far too intelligent to be concerned about what color to paint your nails and how many parties you've been invited to. You make those women look like the caricatures they are."

Joanna reached across the table and grasped his hand, her thumb caressing his knuckles. "I can't believe no one's snatched you up, Mr. Weller." Her eyes locked onto his. "But I'm glad they haven't."

"Me, too," he said, suddenly thirsty.

For the rest of their meal, they talked about art and afterwards, they decided to visit more of the galleries along the street. It was growing dark by the time they left the last one.

"I should get going," she said. "Erik's meeting will be over soon."

"I had a wonderful time. I also learned a lot; you're a great teacher."

"Thank you," she replied. "It's easy when you have such a willing pupil. Will you walk me to my car?"

"My pleasure."

They began walking west on Newbury. The air had turned colder and the dense clouds overhead promised snowfall sometime during the coming night. As if reacting to the cold, Joanna slipped her arm through his and leaned against him. It made Brian feel ten feet tall, until he remembered that she was going home—to him.

When they came abreast of the Bookstore Café, Joanna stopped him. "Do you mind if I go inside for a moment?" she asked.

"Feeling literary?"

"In a way." She gave him a coy smile. "I'll be right out. I promise."

"I shall await my lady with bated breath," Brian said, giving her a mock bow. She laughed, gave him a peck on the cheek and disappeared into the store. She returned moments later carrying a plastic bag.

"Close your eyes," she said.

Brian gave her a look.

"I won't give it to you, if you don't."

"Give me what?"

"It's a surprise, silly."

Brian closed his eyes and felt Joanna slip something on his head.

"Okay, open up."

Brian opened his eyes and stared at himself in the store window. He was now wearing a black baseball cap with the word: WRITER embroidered in white Courier typeface.

He turned to Joanna, who had an expectant smile on her face. "Do you like it?" she asked.

Brian's heart swelled. "I love it."

Joanna came into his arms. "I saw it here yesterday when I was having lunch, and I thought of you. I couldn't resist getting it for you just now. You really like it?"

Brian nodded. "It's the sweetest thing anyone's done for me in a long time."

"A sweet hat for a sweet writer."

Brian laughed and they resumed their walk.

Joanna's Mercedes was parked near the corner of Exeter and New-bury. She opened the door and was about to get in, when she turned and kissed him. It was as soft and as urgent as the first one, and it left him breathless.

"I'd like for you to see my art, Brian. Your opinion would mean so much to me. Would you come by my studio Monday night?"

"I'd love to," he said.

"Great. Call me around six and I'll give you the directions." She reached into her handbag and took out a pen and another of her fiancé's cards. "This is my car phone," she said, scrawling the number on the back of the card, "in case you don't reach me at the studio. Just means I'm on my way. I hope you like my work."

"I can't imagine why I wouldn't."

She smiled, gave the bill of his new cap a playful tug then kissed the tip of his nose and climbed into the Mercedes. A moment later, she waved, pulled out into the street and sped away. He walked home and spent the rest of the evening in a pleasant daze.

12

ERIK RUBY STOOD AT the wet bar in the corner of his office and refilled his crystal tumbler with the dark, smoky Macallan single malt whiskey, allowing himself a congratulatory moment.

You pulled it off you son-of-a-bitch, you really pulled it off.

The meeting with Old Man Wrightson had lasted two hours longer than planned, but it had all been worth it. The old coot was in the bag, literally and figuratively. Since the last disastrous meeting, Ruby had done some digging and found out the older man had a weakness for the rare highland-made Scotch. Having the bottle of Macallan *1926* on-hand had helped to break the ice and smooth over the rough spots in the deal. It had also helped that all the revisions to the design had been reproduced in the models and artists' renderings, wowing the old man and his sycophantic entourage. Now, with the right palms greased down in Government Center, the construction on Wrightson Plaza would go forward, and Ruby & Associates would pocket a cool ten million in profits.

He turned from the bar and approached his desk, swaying in front of the enlarged photo of Joanna hanging on the wall, the same one he'd wanted to put into her mailer. How beautiful she looked in that picture. Why couldn't she understand how much it moved him—how much *she* moved him? What the hell was wrong with wanting to show her off, anyway? She was as much a work of art as anything she created.

Ruby shook his head, and lifted the tumbler of Scotch in a mock salute. "For you, Joanna.... All for you...."

He knocked back half of the fiery liquor in one gulp, grimacing.

His father would have understood. Ruby sneered and swallowed another mouthful of the Scotch, barely noticing the burn this time. Oh, yeah, the old bastard would have understood, all right. He would have tried to steal Joanna away from him, as he'd done with Carolyn.

The haze caused by the alcohol did nothing to dim the memory of the time he'd paid a surprise visit to his father's Fifth Avenue apartment, wanting to show off his acceptance into Yale, the old man's alma mater. Ruby had known something was amiss from the moment he'd let himself in the front door with his key. It was too quiet. Yet it wasn't. The farther he moved into the vast two-story penthouse, the more the alarm bells rang in his head and the hair stood up on the back of his neck. He climbed the plush carpeted stairway to the second floor, two steps at a time, stopping at the landing to listen. It was far less quiet up here. Moans, both male and female, emanated from the master bedroom at the end of the short hallway.

A part of him was embarrassed to have intruded upon his father's privacy. Another part of him resented his father for having a girlfriend so soon after what he'd done to his wife—Ruby's mother—in the divorce, yet the old man was someone he still loved and admired. Ruby turned to go; he had no business being there now.

"Oh, Lucius, fuck me! Fuck me, harder!"

His feet had frozen mid-step, a chill running up his spine.

A Note from an Old Acquaintance

That voice.... He knew that voice.

He crept nearer to the half-closed door and peered inside. There on the bed was his old man, Lucius Fulton Ruby III, eyes closed in ecstasy, razor-cut salt and pepper hair askew, grunting like a pig as his droopy old butt slammed the salami into Carolyn Duprée, Erik Ruby's curvy seventeen-year-old girlfriend. Her graceful tanned legs were wrapped around his father, her crimson-taloned fingers raking down his back, and she screamed his name over and over again with every brutal thrust. Her moans of pleasure and breathless endearments to his father were like knives in Ruby's heart. He wanted to kill them both. Instead, with tears flowing down his face, he left the apartment and went home to the smaller, less elegant one he shared with his mother. He said nothing to her; went to his room and brooded. It was bad enough seeing them together like that, but what really cut him to the quick was that he and Carolyn had gone out only the night before, and ended up in a make-out session on her living room couch. She'd pushed him away when he'd tried to go further, telling him that she wanted to wait for a "special moment" before they had sex the first time. The little bitch wanted to *wait*!

Sighing, he went back to the bar and poured himself more of the Macallan then walked back to his desk, picked up the phone and dialed. It was picked up on the second ring.

"Wunderkind Graphics."

"Burning the midnight oil, I see," Ruby said.

"Erik, is that you?" Nick asked.

"Of course it's me. Who the hell else would be calling you this late?"

"Are you all right? You sound like you're wasted."

"I *am* wasted. Sealed the deal with Wrightson. The old duffer is happy as a lark."

"You don't sound so happy," Nick said, his voice edged with concern.

"Why shouldn't I be? Closed a fifty million dollar deal with a good chunk of it destined for my pocket, I'm engaged to a beautiful woman who adores me, and I see your friend Weller everywhere I go."

"What? Wait a minute. What are you talking about? You're seeing Brian?"

Ruby took another sip of his drink and wiped his mouth with the sleeve of his cashmere jacket. "I don't know, maybe I'm losing my marbles, like my old man finally did, drooling away the rest of his days with a twenty-four hour nurse. I could've sworn I saw the guy in this gallery where I left Joanna today, hiding behind a partition. Crazy, huh?"

Nick's sigh sounded wheezy through the phone. "Listen. I'm sure it wasn't him. You've been sweating this deal for months. That kind of pressure's likely to do things to your head."

"Yeah, I can understand that, but why him?"

"Who knows? It doesn't matter."

"What if it *was* him, Nick, what am I supposed to think?"

"Coincidence, Erik. Just a fluke."

"There are no coincidences, old friend, just greater patterns yet to be divined."

"Well, last time I looked I wasn't Einstein, and neither were you. I think you'd better cork that bottle and go home to that beautiful fiancée. What do you say?"

Ruby shook his head and laughed. For once, Nick was talking sense. "When you're right, you're right."

"For once." Nick laughed then coughed.

"You don't sound so good yourself."

"Same old story, workin' my fingers to the bone."

134

A Note from an Old Acquaintance

"Oh, before I forget, those people from the Paragon Group call you?"

"Yeah, thanks for the referral. Looks like I'll be doing their annual reports."

"Glad to hear it."

"Anyway, Erik, just go home and relax. I'm sure everything's fine."

"Thanks, talk to you soon."

Ruby dropped the phone back onto the cradle and turned his gaze back to Joanna's photo, her smoldering eyes burning into his soul.

With a wordless cry, he hurled his tumbler against the wall, shattering it right below the picture frame. Rivulets of the expensive whiskey rolled down the wall, staining the Berber carpet.

"All for you...."

13

THE DRIVE INTO BOSTON from Newton was a slow, agonizing crawl. And while the plows had cleared the four inches of snow that had fallen the night before, her fellow drivers this morning seemed to want to take things slow and easy. Joanna glanced at the dashboard clock and frowned.

7:35.

Damn. If things didn't get moving soon, she'd be late for her eight o'clock class, not that her students couldn't handle things in her absence, but it galled her nonetheless, as if the latter part of her weekend hadn't been bad enough.

Erik had come home Saturday evening smelling of liquor and high on his deal with Wrightson. She'd tried to be happy for him, but the way he kept looking at her with those dark, hungry eyes of his had unsettled her. She knew what was coming. And a part of her wanted it, as she'd wanted his lovemaking in the past, so heated and passionate.

But something felt different this time. His passion seemed desperate, his caresses possessing an urgency that alarmed her. It took all her efforts to pretend that nothing had changed.

But everything had changed.

A Note from an Old Acquaintance

All during the act her thoughts had strayed to Brian. His soft lips, the firmness of his touch when he'd held her—God, she was turning into a romance novel cliché! And yet, it was true. She'd let herself fantasize that it wasn't Erik, but Brian making love to her. She felt a guilty rush of heat even now sitting in bumper-to-bumper traffic on the Mass Pike. What was she going to do?

And even though her heart's desire was clear to her now, she still felt torn. But that hadn't stopped her from spending all day Sunday cleaning her studio and arranging some of the new pieces in her display area. She wanted everything perfect for when Brian came over.

The traffic began to move and picked up speed. Joanna gave an inward sigh of relief. She would be on time for her class after all.

✿ ✿ ✿

By noon, with her morning classes and the Monday staff meeting behind her, she unlocked the door to her office and spent the next hour writing out student evaluations. This was the part of her job she hated, having to tell a student that he or she needed to improve or risk failure. Sometimes her comments bore fruit, other times they fell on deaf ears.

Her phone buzzed.

"This is Joanna."

"Excuse me, Professor," the receptionist said, "there's a delivery here for you."

"For me?" she said, frowning.

"Yes, ma'am."

It was a short walk from her tiny cubicle of an office to the reception desk near the front door. The receptionist, a chunky peroxide blonde with multiple piercings in one ear, the latest one in an endless line of front office personnel, and whose name she couldn't remember, pointed to a large white oblong box leaning against the wall.

Flowers.

Joanna shook her head. "Erik, you shouldn't have."

"Fight with your man?" the receptionist asked. "I always love it when me and my old man fight. Buys me a dozen long-stems regular as clockwork."

"Sounds like we have the same guy."

"Now, wouldn't that be a hoot?"

Joanna grinned, picked up the box and took it back to her office. Yes, regular as clockwork. That was Erik and his flower buying habits to a tee. And it was almost as if the young blonde had read her mind, as Erik always bought Joanna a dozen red long-stem roses whenever they had a disagreement. The box felt lighter than it should, though. Could he have gotten her something different? Unlikely.

Placing the box on her desk, she untied the yellow ribbon and pulled off the lid, spreading apart the tissue paper.

Inside was a single white rose, one of the loveliest she'd ever seen. Nestled among its leaves and thorns was the little envelope containing the obligatory card. She tore it open and read it:

> For *my favorite artist.*
> *A perfect rose for a perfect kiss.*
> —*Brian*

She felt a rush of heat to her face, a tightening in her throat. It was such a romantic gesture—so unexpected, so subtle, so...right. She pulled the flower from the box and brought it to her nose and inhaled its heady fragrance. It *was* a perfect rose. And the kiss....

Joanna trembled, recalling the taste of him. And then Erik's face blotted out that image, and her eyes flooded with tears. Placing the rose gently back into the box, she covered her face with her hands and let all the pent up emotions well up. The tears came unbidden; tears of joy and of despair, of hope and of desperation.

It took a full ten minutes for her to regain control of herself. Drying her eyes with a handful of Kleenex, she grabbed a vase off her shelf and dumped the bouquet of dried flowers it contained into her trash barrel then took it to the bathroom and filled it with water. Back in her office, she trimmed the stem and placed the rose in it, arranging the vase on the edge of her desk.

It was so noble and pure, so beautiful—and so fragile; she wondered how long it would last in this tight, windowless room, then realized it didn't matter. The gesture and the precious thought behind it would last forever.

She reached for the phone and punched in 411.

"City and listing, please."

Joanna cleared her throat. "Yes, can I have the number for Newbury Productions, please? I believe it's at 342 Newbury."

"Hold for the listing...."

A synthesized voice took the place of the operator. "The number is area code 617-555-0555."

Joanna jotted the number down, pressed the hang-up button and chewed her lip, her heart hammering against her ribs. She felt as giddy as a schoolgirl. Before she could change her mind, she punched in the numbers and waited. It was picked up on the second ring.

"Newbury Productions."

It was that honey-coated voice of his.

"Hello? This is Newbury Productions. Anyone there?"

"So, how's my favorite writer?" she asked.

His laughter was warm and inviting, immediately dispelling her nervousness.

"I'm well, but you're the last person I expected to call."

"Really?" she said, putting a coy edge to her voice. "The very last?"

He laughed again. "Did you like my little care package?"

"Yes, very much," she said, a lump in her throat. "It was very sweet of you. You didn't have to—"

"Yes, I did. But the hardest part was finding the rose that would measure up to that kiss."

Joanna's eyes grew moist again.

"Are you okay?" he asked when she didn't respond right away.

"I'm fine," she said, grabbing for the box of tissues again. "It's just you always know the perfect thing to say."

"It's easy when you have the perfect inspiration. As an artist, I'm sure you know how fickle the Muses can be."

"I do, indeed," she said, regaining control.

"So, how do I get to your studio?"

"Have you ever been to the Channel Club?"

"I practically used to haunt that place, and I have the hearing damage to prove it. Are you near it?"

She spent the next five minutes giving him the directions to her building on Melcher Street. "I'm on the top floor," she said. "The directions for the elevator are posted, but if you get into any trouble just holler. I'll hear you. See you at six."

They hung up a moment later and the butterflies returned to Joanna's stomach with a vengeance. In her heart, she knew this step was not a mistake, but she also knew in the deepest recesses of her being that there was no turning back.

14

BRIAN SLIPPED HIS SILVER '82 Celica into a space right behind Joanna's black 500SL, his front tire nudging the curb. Her directions had been perfect.

Alighting from the car, he scanned the neighborhood with a wary eye. The Fort Point Channel area was typical outmoded industrial: blocks of seedy multi-story warehouses awaiting gentrification or the wrecking ball, fronted desolate streets laid bare by the unremitting glare of peach-colored crime lights. The air was damp and colder here; and the wind, reeking of rotting garbage and the diesel fumes from nearby I-93, blew tattered sections of that day's *Boston Globe* past his feet. The already yellowed pages skittered away like frightened rats.

Across the way, jutting partway over the channel sat the Channel Club, its gargantuan parking lot nearly empty. Unusual for a Friday night. Either the bands on the bill were lousy that evening or the rumors he'd heard about the club being on its last legs were true.

He locked the Celica and walked into the building, a six-story pile of brick and limestone occupying half the block. It had a tired, shopworn appearance.

Inside was a long, narrow vestibule that smelled of mildew. His shoes echoed against cracked marble flooring coated with decades of grime, and he passed a wall full of tarnished mailboxes, some of them overstuffed with throw-aways and flyers, others empty and missing their doors. A bare sixty-watt bulb, hanging from the ceiling by a frayed cord, provided the only illumination. The elevator occupied the back wall. It was not what he'd expected. No sliding metal doors or articulated metal grate and no floor indicators. Just a single black Bakelite call button set into an ornate brass plate and a slatted wooden gate one needed to raise manually with a chain. Right now, it barred the way to a dark, empty shaft.

True to Joanna's word, he discovered the elevator instructions typed on a sheet of desiccated onionskin thumbtacked to a battered bulletin board; the faded letters were barely visible in the jaundiced light. Squinting, he took a moment to read them over.

Apparently, the elevator was so old the call button that brought the car to each floor was the only automated component of the system. The rest would be up to him, if this contraption were anything like the ones he'd seen as a kid.

Shrugging, he reached out and jabbed the call button. Somewhere, up on the roof, an electric motor kicked on, its deep whirring reverberating down the shaft. He saw the cables moving and a moment later the cast-iron counterweights shot past. Seconds later the inside of the elevator came into view, slowing as it braked to a stop level with the floor. Now came the tricky part. Inside the car there were no buttons, just a lever. Pulling it one way made the elevator ascend, pushing it the other way made it descend. What made it tricky was in knowing how *far* to push or pull it, as that governed the speed, as well.

Reaching for the loop of chain at the side of the elevator, he yanked it down, surprised by how little force it took to open what had to be a heavy gate. He stepped inside reached up and pulled it closed then grasped the brass lever. It felt cool, and silken smooth from years of anonymous hands operating it.

All right, Weller, don't kill yourself.

He gently pulled the lever toward him and was rewarded by the sound of the motor engaging with a loud clunk, followed by the whine of the rotors. The car began edging upward. Gaining confidence, he pulled back a little more and the car picked up speed.

That's it, just right.

He passed the second floor, seeing that it was a vast open space, interrupted only by the thick concrete support pillars spaced every thirty feet. Dusty windows at the far end let in anemic moonlight mixed with the garish peach glow of the crime lights.

Next came the third floor, then the fourth.

More grimy emptiness.

A part of him began to wonder if he'd get all the way to the top only to find more smudged windows and deserted rooms. Other than cheap rent, he couldn't fathom the attraction of a place like this.

He began to ease the lever back toward its neutral position when he approached the fifth floor. The car slowed, affording Brian a longer look. This level was not empty. Indeed, it seemed to hold all the furniture from all the other floors: oak desks and chairs, metal file cabinets and tables, all piled helter-skelter, no rhyme or reason, casting shadows that resembled deep-sea leviathans lying dead on a deserted beach.

He slowed the elevator further and gazed upward, seeing light from an interior source for the first time. Ah, he was in the right place. He brought the car to a stop level with the floor on the first try and raised the wooden gate. He gaped, amazed at what he saw.

From his vantage point, Joanna's studio appeared to encompass the entire floor. The same support pillars divided up the space, but instead of bare concrete they were painted varying shades of earth tones that

143

contrasted and complemented the varnished oak flooring stretching from wall to wall. Stainless steel halogen track lighting overhead created pools of white light separated by oases of shadow. It was dramatic, and it all served to draw the eyes to the most important aspect of the room: the art.

Brian eased into the studio, his eyes trying to take in everything they saw, his brain racing to make sense of it. Bright white partitions were set up at right angles on which hung sculptures made from some kind of diaphanous rainbow-colored material; they appeared to move, as if alive, resembling giant fabric jellyfish.

Another piece hung suspended from the ceiling: a large metallic sphere sprouting fiber-optic wires in precise swirling patterns. It was lit from within, each strand glowing with a different color. And the light pulsed in time to the hammer blows of his heart.

Moving further into the space he came upon another series of partitions supporting various diameters of ribbed ductwork and PVC piping, all painted a glossy black. The piece appeared both machine-like and organic. It was nothing less than a *tour de force*.

There were dozens more pieces of varying sizes and themes, and Brian felt as if he'd stumbled into a secret museum.

He rounded another corner and stopped short. Joanna, dressed in only a black bodysuit, sat cross-legged on a large white pillow in the middle of the floor in one of the pools of light, her auburn curls a flaming nimbus. Her arms rested on her knees palms up, middle fingers touching her thumbs. She appeared to be asleep, her breathing deep and regular. Somewhere in the back of his mind Brian knew this to be the Lotus position, a position used for meditation.

He studied her face, cataloging the features he found so enchanting, yet discovering new unseen nuances: the strong chin at odds with the soft contours of her face, the slightly off-center nose, the soft, moist lips that were neither thin nor overly full. All Brian could think about was this woman was as dazzling as her art.

He stared at her for what must have been a full five minutes before a tickle in his throat forced him to clear it. Joanna opened her eyes and smiled.

"Hi. I see you made it up the elevator in one piece," she said, her grin widening.

"Yes, but I was beginning to believe I was living in a *Twilight Zone* episode."

"Welcome to the dimension of imagination."

She laughed, rose to her feet in one fluid motion and came to him, taking him in her arms. Brian returned her embrace, willing time to stop.

"I missed you," she said.

"I missed you, too."

They moved apart and Joanna held onto his hand.

"So, what do you think of my studio, so far?"

"It's amazing, like a private museum. But the rest of the building's more like a tomb."

"You can blame Erik for that," she said, her smile disappearing. "He owns it."

She let go of Brian's hand and walked toward a chair, where she picked up an embroidered green silk kimono and wrapped it around herself. Brian couldn't help noticing her every sinuous curve and the way her hips swayed in that adorably provocative way. He'd been right about that cocktail dress she'd worn at the party; it had hidden every luscious contour of her body.

"He must do well for himself, if he can let a building like this lie fallow."

He watched Joanna tie off the kimono and move closer to him, his nose filling with the same heady perfume he'd come to associate indelibly with her. She was close enough that he could see the topaz flecks in the irises of her eyes.

"So, how about a tour?" she said, retaking his hand and squeezing it. "If this is the *Twilight Zone*, the show's just beginning."

For the next ten minutes Joanna walked him through the rest of her studio. Aside from the area where she displayed her finished pieces, there was also a partitioned space housing a fully equipped workshop that would have been the envy of any serious weekend hobbyist and not a few professionals. He recognized many of the brand names of the power tools as the same ones his father sold in his hardware store, and all of which hung from specialized hooks. Aside from these, there was a freestanding Craftsman hand tool cabinet on casters, a Dayton drill press bolted to the floor, a Makita table-saw, a Craftsman Mini-lathe, and a tank of Acetylene gas for welding.

"You know how to use all these?" Brian asked.

"Every one."

"I'm impressed. Rosie the Riveter's got nothing on you."

"Chauvinist," she said, mock-punching him on the shoulder. He overreacted, drawing a laugh from her.

Beyond the workshop lay the living quarters. This was also partitioned, but these walls rose higher, nearly reaching the ceiling fifteen feet above their heads. Inside, were a spotless kitchen with stainless steel appliances and granite counters adjoining a living room containing a glass-fronted entertainment center surrounded by a leather couch and two leather armchairs.

From there, she led him through an archway into the bedroom, where a thick futon rested on a low platform covered by a down comforter and various throw pillows of Indian origin. An authentic Persian rug lay on the floor beneath the platform and a small jade statue of a seated Buddha occupied an ebony plinth against the wall opposite the futon. The track lighting here was softer, more indirect, adding to the tranquil atmosphere. Through a door at the far end he spotted an immaculate bathroom, the walls, floor and glassed-in multi-headed shower stall sheathed in the same charcoal-gray granite as the counters in the kitchen.

"So, what do you think, now?" she said, the pride evident in her voice. He also detected a hint of apprehension, as if his opinion really mattered to her. The thought of that pleased him.

"I'm speechless, Joanna. It's wonderful.... It's like—" He stopped himself, hunting for the right word. "It's like a sanctuary...."

"You do understand," she said, her voice a near whisper.

"Yes."

She reached up and caressed his face, a questioning look in her eyes. He took her hand and kissed her palm. Her eyes closed and she inhaled sharply.

"You're trembling again," Brian said.

"You, too."

He kissed her then, feeling her melt against him. She moaned low in her throat and kissed him harder, her fingers raking down his back. She broke the kiss suddenly and rested her head against his chest.

"Just hold me," she said, breathless.

He encircled her with his arms, placing his chin on the top of her head. He breathed in the smell of her hair, recognizing the odor of lilacs. It felt so right like this, as if she'd always been a part of him.

"Are you okay?"

"No...."

"Do you want me to leave?" Brian asked.

Her arms tightened around him.

"No...."

He let out the breath he'd been holding and lifted her head by her chin. A lone tear traced a jagged course down her cheek.

"What is it, then? What's wrong?" he murmured.

"I don't know if I can do this, but I...." her lips quivered. "I don't want to lose you...."

"And I don't want to lose you, either. But I also don't want to be the cause of anything."

She shook her head. "You're not.... Please stay."

She kissed him again, first on his forehead, then the tip of his nose, and finally his lips, her mouth gentle and insistent—the sweetest of kisses. At that moment any lingering doubts left his mind forever.

He led her over to the futon and slipped the kimono off her shoulders. It fell to the floor, forgotten. Her eyes never left his while she peeled off the bodysuit like a second skin and tossed it aside, revealing a perfectly proportioned hourglass figure, her own skin like a smooth alabaster. A thick triangle of carrot-colored hair covered her pubic mound. She lay down on the futon, her eyes hungering for him.

Brian wasted no time shucking his clothes and joining her. She came to him, melding her body to his, her passion mounting as he kneaded her breasts in his soft, warm hands. He felt her nipples stiffen beneath his fingers, her breath a hot murmur in his ear.

"Oh, God," she said. "Don't stop doing that."

Inspired, he lowered his head to one of her breasts and flicked his tongue against the stiffened nipple. Her back arched in response, a low moan of pleasure escaping from her lips.

She rolled on top of him then, straddling one of his muscular legs and began to kiss his neck. Her fingers snaked through the thatch of dark hair that covered his chest and she ground her womanhood against his thigh. Brian groaned, and she moved lower, circling his navel with her tongue. He was already rock hard and wasn't at all sure how long he'd be able to hold out if she touched him there.

"Wait," he said.

She looked up at him.

"My turn."

She came into his arms again, giggling. He cupped her taut buttocks with his palms and kissed her deeply, his tongue dancing with hers.

She sighed and rolled onto her back, opening her legs.

"I want you," she whispered.

He mounted her, sliding home with no effort. She cried out, her voice echoing throughout the studio, as he began to thrust with an ever-increasing urgency. Her groans became louder and his low gasps of pleasure made for soft counterpoint.

He knew his moment of release fast approached and there was no way to hold back the tide. It washed over him and he arched his back, pushing into her. She cried out again, her legs crushing him against her even harder. A moment later the wave receded, leaving them both awash in a sea of ecstasy.

Brian looked down into Joanna's eyes, seeing the power of his feelings mirrored there. For the second time that night he willed time to stop, knowing it to be the foolish, futile thing it was, but nonetheless wanting this moment to go on and on and on....

❀   ❀   ❀

"What time is it?" Joanna asked.

Brian rolled over and picked up his watch off the floor, squinting to make out the dial. "Eight-fifteen."

Joanna nodded. She stood at the bedroom window, watching the planes taking off from Logan Airport, her arms holding the kimono closed around her, her expression unreadable.

He rose from the bed and joined her, wrapping his arms around her. She leaned her head back against his chest.

To the east, a jumbo jet lifted off a runway and banked sharply, heading toward Europe.

"I used to love watching planes taking off as a child," she said. "I'd always imagine myself on one of them, traveling to all sorts of exotic and wonderful places. Anywhere but Long Island."

"Was it really that bad?"

Joanna was silent for a moment. "I just didn't fit their mold," she said, caressing his arm. She gave it a tender squeeze and heaved a sigh. "We're going to have to get going soon."

"I know," he said.

She turned to him and gazed into his eyes. "Please tell me one thing, did you mean what you said? Do you really like my art?"

"I meant every word. It's brilliant. You should be exhibiting these pieces."

Joanna shook her head and walked back to the futon.

"Erik thinks so, too."

"Is that so bad?"

Joanna shot him a look. "My fiancé thinks he can solve everything with his checkbook. He thinks if he offers a gallery enough money they'll show anything."

"He's probably right."

"Which only makes it worse. I don't want it on those terms."

"But isn't the important thing to let people see your art? A sanctuary is one thing, Joanna, a mausoleum's another."

"Let's not talk about this anymore," she said, reaching for her bodysuit.

"Wait a minute. It's not really his money...is it?"

She sighed, shaking her head.

He went to her, taking her two hands in his. "Like I told you at the other night, I have a file cabinet full of rejections."

"Why? Why do you keep them?"

"As a reminder."

She frowned. "I don't understand."

"I keep them to remind me never to give up, that no matter what anyone says, I *know*, in here," he said, pointing to his heart, "that I'm true to my craft. Someday, someone's going to say, 'This is great, Brian, we want to publish it.' It's what keeps me going through anything and everything."

Joanna smiled. "And I believe you will."

"So, why don't you believe in yourself?"

"I do; but I want someone to say those words to me without Erik's thirty pieces of silver jingling in his pocket."

"Maybe I have a way for you to do just that," he said.

The idea had popped into his mind only moments before, surprising him with its audacity, as well as its simplicity.

"How?"

"Invite them here."

"What?"

"It's perfect, Joanna. You have a gallery right out there, all set up. All you need to do is get everyone here. Hire a caterer, a valet parking company—I'm sure for a few bucks they could use the Channel's parking lot, it's huge. Clean up that lobby, get someone to run that cranky old elevator and...presto, you've got yourself a show."

She stared at him, her eyes wide, the wheels turning. "Do you really think it could work?" she asked.

"Absolutely, but you've got to keep the faith, and you've got to be willing to take the risk. What do you think?"

"I think you're brilliant!" Joanna threw herself into Brian's arms, taking his face in her hands and kissing him. It was a full minute before they broke it. "You know what's really weird?" she said, catching her breath. "I wasn't even going to go to Nick's party, I was feeling so down about a lot of things, but I meditated that afternoon and when I was done I knew I had to go—I knew there was a reason I had to be there."

Brian kissed her forehead. "I normally don't go to those kinds of affairs, either. Can't dance to save my life."

"Could've fooled me," she said, grinning.

"Thanks. But seriously, it's funny how one little decision can change everything, isn't it?"

She nodded then grabbed his wrist and checked his watch. "Crap, we'd better get going. I told Erik I'd be home by 9:30."

They dressed quickly and Joanna took a few minutes to turn off all the lights before they headed to the elevator. Brian let her have the honors with the cantankerous old lift, not wanting to press his luck.

"How do you keep this place secure?" Brian asked when they reached the ground floor.

She smiled and pulled a barrel key from out of her handbag and inserted it into a small metal panel he hadn't noticed on his way in. With a twist of her hand the green LED turned red.

"I just activated all the motion sensors on the sixth floor, plus I deactivated the elevator. The only other ways in or out are the fire exits, and those are dead-bolted and tied into the alarm."

"Nice," he said, following her out onto the sidewalk.

He stopped dead in his tracks, his eyes bulging. "Oh, no! Damn it!"

"What, what is it?"

He pointed to his Celica, then turned and kicked a nearby signpost.

All four tires of his car had been slashed. And whoever had done it hadn't been content just to poke a hole and deflate them. They'd gutted them.

"Oh, God, Brian. I'm so sorry. This neighborhood isn't the best, but I've never seen anything like that happen before."

Brian nodded, regaining his composure. "What about your car?"

Joanna walked around the Mercedes, gasping when she came abreast of the driver's side door. Brian rushed to her side and surveyed the damage.

"Oh, man," he said, shaking his head.

The door had been keyed, and not just with random angry scratches. Two words were carved into the glossy black paint in crude four-inch high letters: RICH BICH!

Tears welled up in Joanna's eyes. "Erik's going to be so upset."

Brian placed his arm around her. She was trembling.

"Who would've done such a thing?" she asked. "It's as if they've been watching me—"

"Hey, now," he said, turning her to face him, "it's just a couple of stupid kids with nothing better to do. Besides, they probably thought bitch was easier to spell."

Joanna laughed in spite of her tears, and leaned her head against his. "Just hold me for a minute, okay?"

Brian enfolded her in his arms. Her breathing slowed and he felt her trembling subside after a few moments. "Are you going to be okay?" he asked.

She nodded, wiping her eyes. "I'll be fine. Can I give you a ride home?"

"If it's no trouble."

Joanna gave him a look. "Come on, get in the car."

They took a different route toward Back Bay, following Atlantic

Avenue, past Fanueil Hall, crowded even now with late shoppers and restaurant-goers.

What the hell was he going to do about his car? Without functioning wheels, how could he have it moved?

As if reading his mind, Joanna said, "Would you like to use my phone to call a tow truck?"

"I appreciate that, but I think I'll wait until morning. I'm going to have to find a place with a tilting flatbed truck. They can at least drag it up onto the bed on the rims." He shook his head, swearing under his breath.

"I'm really sorry about this. If you weren't visiting me...."

Brian turned from the window. "It's only a car, Joanna, and a rather unreliable one at that. As far as I'm concerned, I wouldn't trade the last three hours with you for a garage full of Ferraris..."

"...Or a 1963 split-window Corvette?"

"Not for a gaggle of them."

She laughed, her eyes shining. "There you go again, saying the most perfect thing."

He smiled. "It's what we writers do."

She brought his hand into her lap and held it while she drove with the other. They fell silent, leaving Brian to his thoughts. He'd wanted to say far more than his comment about the Ferraris, but was afraid of spoiling the moment. How do you tell a woman you've known for less than a week that you want to spend the rest of your life with her, that you can't imagine any kind of life without her in it? And how the hell do you tell a woman you love her when she was going home to her fiancé?

"Can I ask you something?" she said, breaking into his thoughts.

"Anything."

"Would you help me put my show together?"

A Note from an Old Acquaintance

"I'd love to, but do you think that's a good idea? I mean—"

"Don't worry about Erik. He's too busy to pay much attention. He'll just be happy I'm going along with his idea."

She fell silent again, her mood turning pensive. The sadness in her eyes lanced Brian's heart.

"You okay?"

Joanna nodded. "I'm fine. It's just that Erik doesn't understand what I go through with my art, what it means to me, not like you do. He thinks of it as my 'little hobby.' He'd be just as happy if I wanted to spend all my time going to parties and charming his clients. Maybe more so...."

"I'm sorry, Joanna."

She squeezed his hand. "You have nothing to be sorry about. You're kind and thoughtful and sweet."

Brian wasn't sure how to respond to that, or even if he should. "So the fact you're not wearing his ring has nothing to do with me?"

Joanna shook her head, a wistful smile turning up the corners of her mouth. "Erik won't let me wear it. He's afraid I'll fire it into one of my clay sculptures, or lose it. Truth is, I don't mind so much. Every time I put it on I feel like I'm on display, as if every envious eye in the room is glued to it."

Brian nodded.

"Anyway, about the show.... I'd love for you to look at the mailer Nick designed, maybe rewrite it."

"I'd be honored," he said, grateful to steer the conversation back toward safer ground.

"Great. I feel better about it already."

"How much lead time do you need for something like this?"

She thought for a moment. "At school, I'm flooded with invitations all the time. It's not unusual for these artists to send them out two weeks in advance of the events, sometimes less."

Brian nodded. It sounded reasonable. "If you can get me a photo-copy of your mailer this week, I'll turn it around as fast as I can. I'm sure Nick can find a printer and a mail house to get it out quick. Why don't we aim for March fifteenth, which I believe is a Friday. I can also check our files at the office for caterers and call around for some valet parking. Will that work for you?"

"Absolutely."

Brian looked out the window and realized they were now on Bea-con Street, just passing Clarendon. He'd be home soon.

"Are you sure your fiancé isn't going to want to put his stamp on this?"

Joanna shook her head. "No, he'll just write the checks."

A moment later, they pulled up in front of his apartment building. She turned to him and took his face in her hands and kissed him. "What time do you get off work?" she asked.

"It depends, sometimes not until late. The next couple of days are pretty hectic."

"Then why don't you call me on Thursday and let me know when you're leaving, and I'll bring the mailer and meet you here."

"Or you could just meet me at the office."

"Business wasn't the only thing I had in mind," she said, kissing him again.

"Ah, well, I guess I win the Doofus Award for that one, don't I?"

She laughed. "I'm sure you'll more than redeem yourself." She glanced at the clock, her mood shifting. "Damn, I need to go."

She gave him a quick peck on the tip of his nose and Brian took that as his cue. "I'll see you Thursday," he said.

As he had before, he watched her drive off before going inside.

After grabbing his mail, he checked his messages. There were a total of five, one from his mother. He replayed it twice, frowning.

A Note from an Old Acquaintance

"Hi, dear, sorry you're not home. Your father had a very interesting day at work. Call us when you get in, if it's not too late. Bye, Sweetie."

He glanced at his watch. It was just after 9:00. Not too late. He dialed their number, which was picked up on the third ring.

"Hello?"

"Hi, Mom."

"Oh, Brian, are you all right?"

"Why wouldn't I be?"

"Oh, don't mind me, I'm just getting senile."

Brian laughed. "You? Never. I just got your message. What happened with Dad?"

"I'll let him tell you, it's all a bit confusing to me."

The phone clunked when she put it down and Brian could imagine it resting on the flecked Formica counter in the kitchen. Through the phone, he could hear his mother yelling up the stairs for his father. A second later, the phone clicked when the extension was picked up.

"How you doing, Slugger?"

Brian grinned. It was the same greeting his father always used, ever since his little league days. Somehow, coming from the old man, it always sounded right. "I'm fine, Dad. Mom tells me you had an interesting day."

"You could say that," he said, turning serious. "Had some visitors over this past week from an investment group out of Columbus. They're looking to redevelop the entire downtown area, here, since we're pretty much a bedroom community. Pretty impressive plans, too. Got a lot of money behind them. They're interested in buying the store."

"Really?"

"They're talkin' about maybe two million for it. Lock, stock and barrel."

"Jesus, Dad—"

"Didn't think the old place was worth that much, did you?"

"No, I didn't."

"Well, aside from the land and the building, there's forty years of goodwill there. Your mother never wanted me to buy the place, thought renting was safer. Looks like an I-told-you-so's in order."

Brian laughed. "So what did you tell them?"

The older man chuckled. "Told them I'd give it 'due consideration.'"

"But sell the store? That place is your life."

"No, Brian. You and your mother are my life. Besides, it's not as if you're coming home to take over for me...."

This was a sore point between him and his father. While he loved playing in the aisles of Weller's Hardware as a child, had helped out after school when he grew older, and still relished the smell of fertilizer and machine oil, he could never buy into his father's dream.

"I'm sorry, Dad."

"Don't sweat it. You've got to follow your dreams, not mine. And I'm proud of you. You and your partner have done well for yourselves. And someday, if you're still writing, that'll come true, too."

A strange mixture of emotions arose in Brian: happiness that his father recognized and appreciated his ambitions and accomplishments, and sadness that the old man's dreams were dying.

"That means a lot to me."

"I know...."

"So, if you sell, what are you and Mom going to do?"

"Florida. Gettin' tired of shoveling the front walk every winter."

Brian smiled at the memory, and at the thought of his father in Bermuda shorts.

"Somehow, I can't picture you sitting on the beach with a Mai Tai."

"Nope, I'll just stick one of those fancy little umbrellas in my Michelob."

The older man laughed and Brian joined in.

"So, you going with anybody?" the older man asked.

"Mom put you up to that?"

His father laughed again. "So what else is new?"

"Actually, I've met someone pretty special, but I don't know if I want to talk about it."

"Afraid of jinxing it, aren't you?"

"How did you know?"

"You forget I used to be young once, too. What's her name?"

"Joanna."

"That's a beautiful name. Means 'Gift from God'."

"You surprise me, Dad," Brian said, grinning.

"I shouldn't. Who always won all those Trivial Pursuit games? Is she nice?"

Brian described her and how they met, and the older man's mood changed. "You be careful, Son. I won't tell you not to do what you're doing, because Lord knows I sowed a few wild oats in my own time, but you never know what a man will do when it comes to his woman."

"I love her, Dad. Never thought I'd hear myself say that after Julie, but it's there, it's real and I think she feels the same way."

"I'm happy for you, Brian. Just be careful, okay?"

"Okay."

"I'm not going to tell your mother about this, she'll have a cow, but anytime you want to talk, I'm here."

"Thanks, Dad, I love you."

"Love you, too. Take care of yourself. And get yourself down here one of these days, we miss you."

"Miss you, too."

They hung up a few minutes later and Brian realized that he should have asked his dad more about the people interested in the store. He'd gotten caught up in talking about Joanna. He'd try and call him in a day, or so.

Let's hope you didn't jinx this one, after all, Weller.

He shook his head, laughing to himself. It was a silly superstition, and one with which his father had also been intimately familiar. What was the old saying? Nothing new under the sun? It was all too true.

Grabbing a beer out of the fridge, he checked his schedule and saw that he had an 8:00 AM edit session. He decided to turn in early and save the writing for tomorrow. The problem was, he couldn't get Joanna out of his mind. Lying in his bed later, he kept replaying the evening over and over in his mind, savoring every moment.

He was in big, big trouble...and he wouldn't trade places with a living soul.

15

JOANNA WATCHED HER FIANCÉ stare at the two words carved into the side of her car and saw the blood rising in his cheeks.

RICH BICH!

In the stark fluorescent lighting inside their three-car garage, those childish letters seemed to glow with malicious glee. She'd fretted all the way home, wondering how Erik would take the news, and the sight of those awful words. Sometimes he could be so cool, the anger simmering under the surface for hours, before dissipating. At other times, especially when a deal turned sour, he would explode with rage, cursing God in his Heaven and the incompetency of fools. Fortunately, that anger was never directed at her, not like that, but it always disturbed her when he showed this side of himself.

Ruby's lips curled in contempt. "Those little low-life cretins couldn't even spell the word correctly." He turned his dark eyes to her. "So tell me again; what happened? Did you see anyone near the car?"

She sighed. "No, I didn't. When I left the studio, the words were already there. They could've been there for hours. I'm sorry."

Ruby sneered. "Not as sorry as I am."

"What do you mean?" she said, not liking the sound of that at all.

"Because it's my own damned fault," he snapped. He shook his head, his brow creased in annoyance. "And why is it, Joanna, when you have such a beautiful home, a home the majority of women would kill to live in, you feel the need to escape from it to that..." he waved his hand in a dismissive flick. "...bohemian retreat of yours? I'm beginning to think you'd rather be there than here with me."

The petulant tone in his voice angered Joanna, killing the stab of guilt his words engendered. "That's not true, and you know it. And I hardly see you when you're working on one of your deals."

"That's different."

"Really? How is it different?"

"That's what pays for all of this."

"So my work has no value?"

"Of course it does, but that's not the point. Your safety is. It was a mistake to put your studio in such an isolated place. That much is crystal clear. I should have sold that building a long time ago. Now it's time. You belong here with me...where you'll be safe."

"I'm not a china doll, Erik."

Her fiancé stared back at her with an implacable gaze, his mind made up. Joanna did her best to remain calm, but in spite of her outward tranquility, panic raced through her. She'd grown to love that funky space with its creaky old elevator and the freedom and independence it offered. It freed her creative spirit, too, allowing her ideas to flow without stricture or boundary. Even her meditations were deeper and more calming there. And then there was Brian and the love they'd shared only that evening. It was more than a sanctuary now.

"Please, don't," she said, hating the pleading tone in her voice. "I need that studio. Just as much as you need your office."

"Joanna, those punks could easily have waited around for you to leave. Did you even stop to think about that? What's more important, your art or your life?"

"They're *both* important...to me. And it's not as if anyone's stalking me. It's just some silly vandalism."

"Yes, of course, but surely you see my point, don't you?"

"Where will I do my work? There's no room at the school, and all your other properties are full."

Ruby's expression turned thoughtful. "There's enough room on the land, here. We'll build a new wing onto the house and put your studio in there. It'll be your space, just like Melcher Street."

"But that will take months. I can't just stop working!"

"Can we go into the house, now? It's cold out here."

Ruby turned and strode into the kitchen. Joanna followed, her heels clacking on the granite tile. She caught up with him in his study. "And what about my show, Erik? If I close my studio, I'll have no way to complete the pieces I need for it."

Ruby sat at his desk, and regarded her with a quizzical look. "What about it? You don't want my help—you said as much. Seems to me there *is* no show."

Joanna's jaw set. "What I said is that I didn't want you greasing some gallery owner's palms to *buy* me a show. But that doesn't mean we can't have one at my studio."

Ruby opened his mouth as if to offer a rebuke, his expression turning to one of amazement. "That's a very good idea...."

Joanna went to him and sat in his lap, encircling his neck with her arms. "So I actually do have a brain in my pretty little head?" she asked, batting her eyelids.

"One that's more than a match for mine," Ruby said, laughing. "But I'm still worried about you."

"Well, can't you just hire a security guard to watch over me?"

163

Ruby shook his head, his smile widening. "I can see you're going to have an answer for everything this evening, aren't you?"

"Hmmm, maybe." Joanna grinned.

"All right, I'll hold off on selling the building until after your show, and I'll look into hiring a guard."

"Promise?"

Ruby crossed his heart and held up his hand. "Promise."

Joanna kissed him on the nose, slipped off his lap, and headed for the door.

"Should I tell Nick to go ahead with the mailer?" he asked.

Joanna paused at the door, fighting a war inside her heart. She'd hated playing the manipulative little female, as she'd done just now. It was so against everything she believed. But she'd known it would work—and it had. And maybe that's why it felt so...sordid. On the other hand, her art and her ability to create it had been at stake, so perhaps this small misstep had been for the greater good. What about Brian...?

"Honey?" Ruby asked, breaking into her thoughts. "What about Nick?"

She sighed inwardly and decided to take the gamble. "I've asked Nick's friend, Brian Weller, to help me rewrite the mailer. He can work on it with Nick."

"Why him?"

"He's a writer," she said, her voice growing soft. "And he under-stands...."

She turned and left the room; and never saw the smile slip from her fiancé's face.

16

"MR. RUBY, YOU OKAY?"

Ruby turned from the view atop his latest project and spotted his construction foreman staring at him, his ruddy face clouded with concern. Ruby nodded. "I'm fine, Tommy."

"Well, just the same, sir, you wanna be careful about daydreamin' around here. There's only those cables for railings, and it's a long way down."

Indeed it was. Forty floors. And he knew better. A hard hat did little good if one walked off the end of a girder. The problem was he couldn't get this Weller character out of his head. It was silly, he knew it, but Joanna had knocked him for a loop when she'd dropped his name like a bomb last night. Her little flirtation at Nick's party was one thing, but why was she having anything to do with the guy, now? Could Nick have referred him? It stood to reason. After all, Nick's graphic design was great, but his writing was dull. Joanna's mailer deserved better. But was Weller the ticket? Maybe.... According to Nick, the guy was a "kick-ass writer," so perhaps it was only business for Joanna. Once Weller did his job and the show was over that would be that.

Except, he couldn't make himself believe that. He couldn't, because

165

of those six seemingly innocent words Joanna uttered before leaving the room: *"He's a writer, and he understands...."*

She said them the way a *lover* would, and no matter how much he tried to convince himself otherwise, the suspicions remained entrenched in his heart...festering.

Ruby turned to his foreman, who stood near the elevator going over the blueprints with a couple of his senior workers. "Hey, Tommy?"

The foreman looked up, his thick eyebrows arching. "Yes, sir?"

Ruby motioned for him to approach. The two other workers nodded and moved off. "What can I do for you, Mr. Ruby?" the foreman said, rolling the blueprints into a tight tube.

Ruby looked out over the Boston skyline, putting his thoughts in order. "You're the kind of guy that keeps his eyes and ears open, Tommy. You don't miss anything, and I like that."

"Thank you, sir, I appreciate that."

"I need a recommendation. You know anyone who does any private eye work? Someone good?"

The foreman frowned. "Yeah, matter of fact, I do. The guy's young and hungry, but he knows what he's doin'. You got a problem, Mr. Ruby?"

"Just a trifle, but I need someone discreet."

Tommy reached into his leather jacket, took out his wallet and extracted a gray-colored business card, which he handed to his boss. Ruby glanced at the card then slipped it into his jacket pocket.

"Cary's as discreet as they come. Did a great job with my cousin's divorce. He'll make your problem go away."

"That's comforting," Ruby said.

After finishing his inspection of the building site, Ruby drove his Jag back to Newbury Street. At his desk, he pulled out the card Tommy had given him and stared at it.

A Note from an Old Acquaintance

Mosley Investigations
Cary Mosley
617-555-2525

Did he really want to take this step? Did he really believe something more was going on than Joanna was letting on? He glanced toward her photo on the wall, his emotions welling.

"Damn it! This is NOT happening!" he shouted, pounding his fist onto his desk. The force of the blow knocked over a container of paper clips near the edge. He watched them patter to the floor, his mind grasping at straws.

He couldn't stand the thought of another man touching her—possessing her. Yet *not* knowing would be far worse. If she were sleeping with this Weller guy, he could deal with it. Just how, he didn't know, but given time he'd figure it out. He always did.

With Carolyn, his erstwhile girlfriend, the solution was easy. He gave her what she really wanted all along: a big payoff. He smiled even now, recalling her mad spending sprees, the cars, the clothes, the gambling losses, the drugs, and the quick descent into the mire of irreversible debt. She tried to get her act together, tried to snag another sugar daddy, but by then the word was out: she was damaged goods. Last he heard his little lost debutante was hooking for a greasy pimp who liked to use his fists.

The thought of anything like that happening to Joanna made him shiver. Carolyn was a shark, trolling for rich meat, and his father was too blind or too vain to see it. Joanna was far better than that, but that didn't mean she wasn't a woman. That didn't mean she was immune to temptation, not that Weller was a particularly tempting dish. He was just an average-looking guy. So, maybe he was just paranoid, maybe he was imagining all of it.

"But I'm not, am I, Joanna...." he said, staring again at her photo.

With a heavy sigh, Erik Ruby reached for the phone and dialed.

17

THE NEXT THREE DAYS passed in a schizophrenic jumble in Brian's mind, the time simultaneously racing and creeping by. When he had to concentrate on a client and a job, he'd check the clock and realize—with a shock—that three hours had passed. When his mind turned to Joanna, and this happened more often than not, seconds dragged on like minutes, minutes like hours. Fortunately, the edit suite was busy during that time, which meant he could lose himself in the tasks at hand.

By late Thursday afternoon, he was more than ready for the weekend...and for Joanna. Not only had she haunted his every waking moment, she'd invaded his dreams, as well, leading him on phantasmagoric journeys both spiritual and erotic. He awoke from them all awash in tears of joy and with a palpable longing for her that sustained and inspired him throughout the remainder of his day.

After his last client left it took every ounce of will and determination to go through the tedious routine of cleaning the suite and updating his logs when all he wanted to do was pick up the phone and call her. When he finally did, the studio line rang ten times before he gave up. He tried her car phone next and got the recording telling him the subscriber was not available. That was odd. Should he head home and call her from there, or try again? He opted to give it another shot. The studio line was answered on the second ring.

"Hello?"

"Hi. I tried you a couple of minutes ago and you didn't answer."

"Sorry," she said, sounding out of breath. "I was in my shop and the power tool I was using kept me from hearing it."

"Playing Rosie the Riveter again?"

"Yes," she said. "And you'd better be nice to me or I'll drill you a new one." She burst out laughing and Brian joined her, enjoying the sound of her laughter even more than the silly image her words evoked.

"How are you?" she said, after calming down. "I've really missed you, you know."

"And I've missed you. The last three days felt like three weeks."

"Me, too...."

"I'm just finishing up here, then I'm going to head home and jump in the shower."

"Why don't you wait for me?" she asked.

Brian grinned. "Only if you insist."

"Oh, I do, I do," she said, giggling.

"Well, I'll warn you, my ancient tub is a challenge."

"And I wouldn't have it any other way."

❀   ❀   ❀

They lay in each other's arms amid the tangle of his bedclothes, the afterglow of their marathon of lovemaking only now fading. Joanna shifted her weight, nuzzling his neck, a sigh escaping from her parted lips. She reached for his hand entwining it with hers.

"You have such wonderful hands, Brian, so strong yet so gentle."

He kissed her, caressing her jaw line. "I'm glad you appreciate them."

"I'd like to sketch them. May I?"

"Now? I thought we were going to look at your mailer."

She propped herself up on her elbows, looking down at him. "We can do that in a little bit. Come on, pretty please?"

She gave him a mock pout and he laughed. "All right, I know when I'm beaten."

Joanna smiled and climbed off the bed, going for the sketchbook and drawing pencils lying on the breakfast table next to her handbag. At least now he knew why she'd brought them.

Sitting cross-legged at the foot of the bed, she flipped to a blank page and then considered him for a moment. "Okay, now hold up your right hand, as if you're reaching for something."

"But that's the hand with the broken knuckle."

"I love that knuckle, it's so macho." She laughed at Brian's look of exasperation then turned serious. "Please, I really think it makes your hand unique."

Brian sighed and lifted his hand and Joanna began to draw, the only sound the scratching of her pencil against the paper. He loved the way she frowned in concentration, her lips pursing. He ached to kiss them.

After a few minutes, his arm began to tingle and throb.

"Can I move, now?"

"Not yet," she said, her pencil moving faster. "Okay, now turn it slightly to the left. That's it. Hold it there."

The sound of the pencil moving against the page grew more frenzied.

"Can I at least put on some clothes?"

"No, I like you just the way you are," she said, giving him a sly grin. "Now turn your hand a little to the right."

Brian sighed and did as he was told. After another few minutes she stopped drawing and smiled. "Okay, you can put your arm down."

He let out the breath he'd been holding and shook his arm to bring some of the feeling back into it. "Can I see?"

Joanna turned the sketchpad and Brian's eyes widened. There were a total of four views of his hand, showing it from every angle. She'd caught every nuance of it right down to the lines in his palm.

"My God, Joanna, it's exquisite. I had no idea you could draw like this."

"I do the abstract work because I love it, but I never would have graduated art school if I couldn't draw."

"An old art teacher of mine once told me that hands were the hardest things to draw correctly."

"He's right."

She put away the sketchpad and returned to the bed with a piece of art board. He saw that it was the paste-up of her mailer. He took it from her and looked it over. The copy was pretty weak, and he saw more than a few places where he could tweak it. It was Joanna's picture that grabbed his attention, however: the black bodysuit, the provocative pose, the smoldering look in her eyes—a look very much like one he'd seen earlier that night.

"Christ, this is a hell of a picture."

She groaned and fell over on the bed. "Not you, too."

"What did I say?"

"I've already been all through this with Erik," she snapped. "We're going to change it. Put in more pictures of my art."

"It's so striking, though. I can tell you without a shred of doubt that no one who gets this mailer as it is will ever forget it."

"I know. All they'll remember is *me*."

"Not such a bad thing in my book."

"God! You men are all alike."

She stood up and began putting on her clothes.

"Why are you so upset?"

"Because I thought you were different."

Brian was on his feet and by her side, taking her by the shoulders. She glared back at him in defiance.

"Hey, I *am* different," he said. "Look, it's a stunning picture, a real classic, but you're right it doesn't belong in this mailer. I just thought it was great because I'm so damned crazy about you."

Joanna's head snapped up. "What did you say?"

Brian looked shocked for a moment, then recovered, taking her face in his hands. "I love you, Joanna. I have from the first moment I laid eyes on you. And I hope to God I haven't scared the pants off you."

She trembled, her eyes filling with tears. "Oh, Brian, I love you, too." She kissed him then, her tongue jutting into his mouth. The longer it went on the more aroused Brian became. Suddenly, she began to laugh, breaking the kiss.

"Now what?" Brian said.

"You said you hoped you hadn't scared the pants off me."

Brian shook his head. "Yeah, so?"

"Well, as you can see, I'm still not wearing any."

Brian looked down and grinned. "So it would seem."

"So...what are you going to do about it?"

Brian tapped his chin. "Hmm, let me see...."

"Hey!" she said, giving him a playful punch on the shoulder.

"You want to play rough, do you? Well, I think it's time for the... tickle monster," he said, shifting his voice into a lower register.

A Note from an Old Acquaintance

"NOOO!" she squealed, running around the bed.

"You can run, but you can't hide from the tickle monster!"

He lunged across the bed, catching her around the waist and pulling her onto the mattress. She shrieked with laughter when Brian blew a raspberry against her belly. But instead of continuing the game, he reached up and caressed her face, placing a tender kiss on the tip of her nose. He gazed into her eyes, his mood turning serious. "What are we going to do, Joanna?"

She put a finger to his lips. "Ssssh," she said, her eyes moistening. "Let's not go there right now, okay? Let's just love each other."

She kissed him then, and he lost himself in her arms.

18

IN ERIK RUBY'S EYES, Cary Mosley was a walking set of contradictions, a man who shattered expectations and defied convention. When he entered Ruby's office on the dot for his nine o'clock appointment, he didn't walk, so much as glide—moving across the floor with the fluid grace and coiled power of a professional athlete. Reed thin, with broad shoulders, he was draped in an elegant dark-blue hand-tailored Brioni suit, immaculate white shirt, Harvard tie, ostrich leather shoes, and carried two thick manila file folders clutched in his left hand. And Cary Mosley was black, a deep shade of perfect ebony accented with rich highlights that shone as if he were carved from the purest obsidian. No, Cary Mosley wasn't Humphrey Bogart, but Ruby was impressed.

He stood and offered his hand. Mosley enveloped it in a grip made for a basketball player.

"Nice to meet you, Mr. Ruby," he said in a soft voice at odds with the rest of his persona. His smile revealed perfect pearl-white teeth and the crinkle of laugh lines around the eyes.

"I wish it could be under different circumstances," Ruby said, offering a rueful smile. "Please, have a seat."

A Note from an Old Acquaintance

Mosley folded himself into one of the leather chairs facing the desk and crossed his legs, placing the file folders onto his lap.

When Mosley was seated, Ruby eased back into his swivel chair and regarded him with a steady gaze. The black man met his stare with one of his own, his manner remaining calm and composed.

"Where should I start?" Ruby asked.

Mosley flipped open one of the files, pulling a Monte Blanc ballpoint from inside his jacket. "How about I give you what I have so far?"

Ruby arched a brow. "By all means."

"Brian Alden Weller was born in Nelsonville, Ohio, August 3rd, 1966, to Rita and Jefferson Weller. Father currently owns Weller's Hardware, also in Nelsonville. The business thrived for many years, but has recently fallen on hard times. There is currently tentative interest in buying the business, as well as the other businesses surrounding it, by an investment firm in Columbus intent on redeveloping the downtown area. The Nelsonville City Council is scheduled to vote on the proposal in about a month.

"As for Brian's childhood, idyllic, for the most part. And his schooling was average, though he showed an extremely high verbal aptitude on his SATs. Senior year of high school, he applied to five different colleges and was accepted into four of them. He matriculated at Emerson College and graduated with a BFA in film production. A year after graduating, he founded Newbury Productions with partner Robert Nolan, also an Emerson Graduate. Offices are located on the second floor of 342 Newbury Street. Company's profits have been modest, but steadily growing. This year looks to be their breakout—"

"Wait a minute," Ruby said. "They're not a public company, how do you know what their profits are?"

Mosley's cinnamon eyes twinkled. "Let's just say that a friendly banker is a friend indeed."

175

Ruby chuckled and motioned for him to continue.

"Though Brian trained as a filmmaker, and is Newbury Production's Director of Post-Production, it is plainly obvious to those who know him that becoming a published novelist is his true passion."

"But perhaps not his *only* one," Ruby said, his expression clouding.

Mosley closed the folder. "That's what I have, for now. If you hire me, I assure you I will find out everything you want to know, and then some...."

"Right. What's in the other folder?"

Mosley smiled and flipped open the second folder. "Erik Marcus Ruby was born May 2, 1954—"

Ruby bolted upright, a vein in his temple throbbing. "Wait a minute, what is this? You checked *me* out?"

Mosley held up a long-fingered hand. "Please, let me explain. I've been very successful, and one of the reasons for that success is because I do my homework—in every respect. My reputation depends upon my dealing with clients who don't hide anything from me. Even clients who don't intentionally hide things may neglect to reveal a vital piece of information that makes the critical difference in whether or not I reach the objective for which they've employed me.

"You're thinking about hiring me, Mr. Ruby, because you believe your fiancée is having an affair, and you want to get to the truth. It's consuming you, taking your mind off important things."

"That's true, but my past—my life—is my business, not yours."

"Of course, and everything in here is under the strictest confidence." Mosley handed over the file. Ruby took it and flipped through it, morbidly curious. "This is the only copy, and it's yours. I know all I need to know about you to know it would be a privilege working for you on this matter, as well as any others where I can be of value."

"So, I'm clean, as they say," Ruby said, a grin back on his face.

"Oh, there's the usual petty bureaucratic graft, but nothing that sets you apart from your peers, certainly nothing that would preclude my taking your case."

"And I intend to keep it that way."

"Of course. I will say this. Your hostile takeover of your father's company was a masterstroke. I'm just curious as to the why of it. You were his clear and uncontested heir apparent."

"Let's just say, his taste in women was his undoing...."

"Yes...." Mosley nodded. "Carolyn Duprée."

Ruby's smile dimmed. "You're good. Maybe too good."

The black man leaned forward in the chair, his manner turning grave. "As I told you, that file is the only copy, and you have my word that none of its contents will ever be revealed by me."

"Even if I tell you to take a hike?"

"Yes, but you won't."

Now Ruby was curious. "Really, and why is that?"

"Because you're a smart man who wants to leave nothing to chance, because you have a beautiful fiancée, whose affections may be turning elsewhere, because you have a growing business and you need someone to sweat the details, to watch for the things that fall between the cracks, someone to watch your back."

"And that someone is you?"

"Yes," Mosley said, sitting back in his chair. His eyes strayed to Joanna's picture. His reaction was subtle but Ruby noticed. A moment later, he turned back to face his prospective employer. "Mr. Ruby, I've worked for myself for quite a number of years, and I'm good at what I do, but I'm looking for a bigger challenge. Your business and my skills look to be a good match."

"One thing, and don't take this the wrong way, but you cut a rather distinctive figure," Ruby said, indicating Mosley's natty attire with a wave of his hand. "If you're going to follow my fiancée and Weller around, you don't exactly...blend in."

Mosley laughed. "When I was at Harvard, I had the privilege of being a member of the Hasty Pudding Theatricals. I can blend in anywhere. I might be that homeless derelict asleep on the park bench, the hotdog vendor on a street corner, a street musician outside the Arlington "T" station, or—"

"Or a security guard at my fiancée's studio?"

"Or a security guard at your fiancée's studio," Mosley repeated, his sly grin matching Ruby's.

"You're very persuasive, Mr. Mosley. And my foreman, Tommy Cervino recommended you highly. He told me you know what you're doing. But I'm also curious about something. You're no dime-store gumshoe. How could Tommy's cousin afford you?"

Mosley grinned. "Tommy's cousin did me a favor when my Ferrari was stolen in the North End a couple of years ago. He was working in the little trattoria where my girlfriend and I were dining. Took a liking to me, I guess. Said I reminded him of one of the Celtics."

"So, what happened with your car?"

"It was returned the next day...unharmed, not even a scratch. I gave him my card and told him to call me if he ever needed my help—on the house. When he suspected his wife was stepping out on him, he did."

"I like a man who keeps his promises," Ruby said, chuckling. "I assume Tommy's cousin received favorable terms in the divorce settlement as a result of your help?"

"My evidence was indisputable."

Ruby sighed and looked toward Joanna's photo. "No pictures. I won't have her degraded like that. I— I just need to know. What are your terms?"

"Two thousand per day, plus expenses."

Ruby nodded and reached into his desk. He pulled out a bound stack of crisp, new hundred dollar bills and tossed it to Mosley. "Here's ten thousand to start. If you need more, ask me." The black man glanced at the cash without reacting, then slipped it into his jacket pocket. That was good. Ruby didn't trust naked greed.

He stood and offered Mosley his hand. "If, during the course of your investigation, you discover them together. I want you to call me. Immediately."

"I wouldn't advise confrontation," Mosley said, shaking Ruby's hand. "Situations like that can get ugly."

"I appreciate that, but I'll take the risk."

"Okay, Mr. Ruby, it's your dime."

Mosley left moments later and Ruby sat down at his desk, his mind spinning. He couldn't believe he'd just hired a man to spy on Joanna, yet he'd done that very thing. Soon, he would know the truth, and there was an odd comfort in that thought, even though it might mean the worst.

One thing he was sure about: Mosley was the right man for the job, and maybe the right man for a more permanent position. That remained to be seen. He had to admire the guy's king-sized *cojones*, but he was a crackerjack salesman, too. And what he was selling was peace of mind. Time would tell if that would be the case. Time would tell....

19

JOANNA SIPPED FROM HER mug of herbal tea and turned her concentration back to her drawing. It was just before 8:00 and she'd been in her office since the school building opened at 5:45, leaving Erik snoring away in their bed. He'd come home late for the third night in a row, complaining about endless changes with his new building. And while she empathized with his plight, she was secretly glad he was too tired to initiate any intimacy.

Now, with her class beginning in a few minutes, she put the finishing touches on the idea for her new piece. It was something vastly different from her abstract machinery, something inspired by Brian. She smiled, remembering his "Tickle Monster" antics from the other night, her eyes finding the rose in its vase at the edge of her desk. It still flourished, showing only the barest of signs that it was beginning to die. A colleague advised her to put two aspirin tablets in the water, telling her it would keep the flower alive longer. She was right. The rose had opened, the petals spreading day by day into a glorious picture-book specimen.

A glance at the clock told her it was 8:00. Closing the sketchpad, she rose and tucked it under her arm, locking her office behind her. It was a quick walk down the corridor to her classroom.

"Good morning, everyone," she said, noting the glazed eyes on a few of her charges. No doubt a late night or two of partying to blame.

"Come on, now, it's a beautiful February morning, and we're going to do something a little different."

A couple of her students groaned. One of them, she recalled, was on her potential fail list. She wasn't going to let that spoil her mood, however. Moving to the side of the room, she dragged an easel front and center then propped her sketchpad onto it, flipping it open to the page she'd been working on. It was four views of two hands intertwined: a man's and a woman's.

"Oh, wow," a reed-thin girl with bright blue hair said, her kohl-rimmed eyes bulging.

"Great job, Teach," another added.

Joanna smiled, feeling a rush of pride. She'd taken the original four views of Brian's hand and redrawn them with her own hand in his. As before, every detail was lovingly portrayed. Her students were awestruck.

"Thank you," Joanna said. "Now that I have your undivided attention, this is your assignment. I want you to try and reproduce this with your clay."

The blue-haired girl looked as if she might choke.

"I know this is a quantum leap for most of you, but do the best you can. I promise not to grade you too harshly on this. It's mainly an exercise. And I'm going to do it right along with you."

"Then you'll need to remember what you always tell us, Teach," a longhaired boy said, grinning.

"Oh, and what's that?" Joanna said, stifling her own grin.

"ALWAYS KEEP YOUR CLAY AT THE PROPER HYDRATION!" the class sang out.

Joanna laughed. "Well, at least you've all learned something!"

The class erupted in a chorus of giggles and groans.

"Okay, then," Joanna said, clapping her hands, "let's get to work."

Two of the students brought out the clay, kept moist in a special container lined with a thick plastic bag. She had them distribute exactly three pounds to each student. A little more than necessary, perhaps, but it would give them a margin for error. She took her own glob of clay and began kneading it into the basic shape.

She'd decided to do the exercise last night when she realized that as well equipped as her studio was, she didn't own a kiln to fire the piece when it was completed. The school did. And turning it into a class project assuaged the morsel of guilt she felt using the school's kiln.

The clay felt moist and cool, and she loved the feeling of molding it, something she missed with her larger pieces. When it was done, she intended to put it on display as the centerpiece for her first show. Returning her thoughts to the task at hand, she started to hone the rough shape into the details that were burned into her mind.

"Feel free to come up and take closer looks at the sketches when you feel the need," she told the class. "The more details you can see in your mind, the more precisely your mind will direct your hands."

She looked down at her own piece and picked up one of the implements she'd laid out like a surgeon's tools.

This one's for you, my Sweet Writer.

❀   ❀   ❀

Wrightson was going to drive Ruby to drink. First it was the exterior sheathing on the building, changing it from black granite to red granite, then back to black. Then it was the flooring for the lobby. He'd recommended faux malachite, which wore better and looked exactly like the real thing, but Wrightson demanded the real deal, that is, until he was told it would cost over $300,000 and would be cracking inside a year from all the foot traffic. He couldn't fault the old guy for his taste, but he wished Wrightson would find something else to do, other than bother him with trivial details, details that piled on top of one another until they threatened to delay the project.

Ruby steered his Jaguar into the alley behind his building and rolled into his parking space, noting the dumpster had still not been emptied. He could see the old models for the building jutting out from under the lid. Damn sanitation department was the worst, although they couldn't hold a candle to New York for incompetence. At least the streets here were clean.

Up in his office, Ruby checked his messages and found one from Mosley.

"Hi, Mr. Ruby," he said between screeches of static. "Just wanted to give you an update. Please, give me a call when you get in."

Ruby switched off the machine, picked up the handset and dialed. The investigator picked up on the first ring. "Mosley, here."

"Anything new?"

There was a momentary squall of static and Mosley's voice dropped out.

"—ear me, Mr. Ruby?"

"Sorry, got a bunch of noise in my ear."

"I just passed an electrical substation. Happens sometimes."

Ruby chuckled. "I know what you mean. So, what have you got?"

"Our boy, Weller has stayed close to home and hearth, for the most part," Mosley said. "I've followed him back and forth from his apartment to his office several times over the last couple of days. And that's pretty much it. Of course, phone records might show they've been talking."

"Joanna told me he was helping her with the mailer for her show. He's got a legitimate reason to talk to her."

"What would you like me to do?"

"I want you—" The static squalled again and Ruby waited, his patience wearing thin.

"Sorry, thought I'd lost you," Mosley said when he came back on the line. "You were saying?"

"I was saying I want you to watch her studio," Ruby snapped. "Sorry, didn't mean to yell. I've got a lot going on and it's getting to me."

"No problem, sir. I'm on it. I'll swing over there, now."

"Okay, but hold off on the security guard gambit. She hasn't mentioned it again, and it might make her skittish if she suddenly sees you there large as life. If something's going to happen between her and Weller, I'd rather it happen sooner than later."

"You're the boss."

"One other thing. You're not driving the Ferrari, now, are you?"

"No, no," Mosley said, sounding amused. "That's my weekend car. This one's a five-year-old silver Ford Taurus sedan with a dent in the left front fender, a cranky car phone and a wheezy air conditioner. Precisely the kind of car everyone sees every day...and forgets."

Ruby grinned. "I like the way you think. Keep me posted."

He hung up and sat back in his chair. For the last few days Joanna had floated around the house as if she were on cloud nine. Nothing could dent her happy mood. He knew what that meant, and the implications of that knowledge grew like a cancer in his gut. What did she see in that penniless pissant writer, anyway? What could he offer her except uncertainty?

Enough! Mosley was right. All this *was* consuming him.

Soon, he'd have his answers and then he would have to come to grips with them. He still didn't know how he would handle it all and what he would do about Weller, but Ruby had a feeling Mosley would provide the spark of inspiration, whatever that might be. He just had to wait a little while longer.

They called patience a virtue. But that was a load of crap. It was purgatory for the soul. Nothing less.

Ruby forced his attention back to the Wrightson project. Now, this was something he could deal with. The old guy was tough, but Ruby understood tough. He didn't pretend to understand the world in which his fiancée moved, and it didn't matter. He just knew she belonged in his life. What was it about Joanna that enchanted and inspired him so? He stared at her picture and frowned. Sure, she was adorably beautiful, that was a given, but there was something else, something indefinable—something rare and precious....

He shook his head, a crafty smile curling his lips. If he could see this problem through, and his engagement survived it, he'd have the remainder of his life to unravel that little conundrum. And he could live with that just fine.

❀   ❀   ❀

The last several days had been a whirlwind of activity. With Bob shuttling between two simultaneous commercial shoots in studios across town from each other, Brian was left with the burden of running the business, as well as keeping a seamless workflow through the edit suite. It gave him little time for anything else, including Joanna.

Taking a break, he picked up the phone and called Nick.

"Hey little brother, how's it hanging?" the older man said in his characteristic wheeze.

"Busy as hell."

"And since when has that been a problem?" Nick laughed.

"Did you get the text changes on Joanna's mailer?"

"Sure did. Everything's cool. She signed off on the revised proof yesterday and it's in production. Should have it out to everybody right on time."

"Great. I'm sure she'll appreciate that."

There was a moment of silence before Nick coughed and resumed speaking. "Listen, kiddo, how about I spring for lunch today, or are you too freaking busy to eat?"

Brian chuckled. "No, not too busy for that."

"Good, then meet me at the Bookstore Café at 12:30."

"Why there?"

"'Cause I'm in an intellectual mood," he said.

"All right, Brainiac, I'll see you then."

He hung up and turned back to what he'd been doing: a quick tweak on a spot for a local muffler shop. The phone rang. Brian picked it up and wedged the handset between his jaw and shoulder, while he cued the tape decks to make the next cut.

"Newbury Productions," he said.

"That you, Slugger? You sound like one of those blow-dried announcers."

"Dad?" Brian straightened up and grabbed the phone from the hollow of his neck to keep it from falling. There was something in the old man's voice. "You okay?"

"Just a bit under the weather."

"Sorry to hear that, but I'm sure you didn't call me about that."

"No...," he said, with a heavy sigh. "Need a bit of advice from the other businessman in the family."

Normally, that line would have brought a smile to Brian's face, but there was no humor in his father's tone.

"What is it—what's wrong?"

"Looks like those fancy drinks at the beach are going to have to wait for a bit. That investment group pulled out."

"No.... Why? What happened?"

"The guy I was dealing with called me today and told me that a property in Columbus they'd previously scouted had reconsidered their offer and they were going to go with that. 'The Nelsonville Project,' as he put it, was being indefinitely postponed."

"I'm really sorry, Dad. I honestly don't know what advice I can give you. Seems to me it's out of our hands."

"Oh, I know that. It's just that your mother was really looking forward to getting out of here—me, too, the truth be told—and I haven't told her any of this yet."

Brian could understand that. His mother was the worrier of the family and sparing her reasons to worry was a habit for both men in the Weller family. "What about another buyer?"

"No other prospects. I've asked around. Well's run dry."

"How's business then?"

"That's the other thing your mother doesn't know. Aside from any seasonal doldrums, Home Depot opened a superstore about fifteen miles up the road a couple of years ago. Things have been drying up ever since, and there are loans I have to cover."

"To what extent?"

"Let's just say that the mortgages are mortgaged."

Brian exhaled, shaking his head. "What are you going to do?"

"I don't know. Muddle along for bit. Rob Peter to pay Paul. Gotten real good at that," he said with a dry chuckle. "I really wasn't under any illusions that the store was worth that much. It's the land; and the taxes are all paid up, thank God. Made sure of that. As a part of that larger project, it was pure gold. Now...."

Now, no one would want just that half-acre parcel Weller's Hardware sat on, flanked by the shuttered Bijou Theatre on one side and the flyblown shoe store on the other, not when the entire downtown area was in desperate need of a shot in the arm. For anyone to buy his father's store, it would be all or nothing.

They spoke for a few more minutes and hung up, with Brian feeling frustrated and angry that he couldn't help his father, or even offer much comfort. To have come to this point, after a lifetime of hard work, had to be eating the old man up inside.

Brian glanced at the clock; it was already a quarter past twelve. He needed to get going, if he was going to meet Nick on time. While he didn't have much of an appetite now, the walk and the fresh air might do him some good. At least he'd have a few moments to think. Maybe he would come up with something.

After making sure to alert one of the interns that he was out for lunch, he grabbed his jacket and left.

❀   ❀   ❀

The Bookstore Café occupied the first floor of a red brick building on the corner of Newbury and Clarendon. Brian walked in the door just after 12:30 and spotted Nick at a table in the back, nestled in the heart of the Mystery section. He had a half empty cappuccino in front of him. The dark circles under his eyes were deeper than usual.

Brian shook his hand and sat down. "You burning the candle at both ends, Nick?"

The older man rolled his eyes. "Tell me about it. Seems like all of a sudden all this work's come in. What makes it a bear is Cassie's not pulling her weight."

"Trouble in paradise?"

Nick snorted. "Now that's a funny one. I think the lady and I will soon have to reassess our partnership."

"Sorry to hear that."

Nick gave him a look. "Now I know you're being funny. She's done nothing but bad-mouth you since the party."

"I can't help that. She had the hots for me. I wasn't interested. I would've thought she'd have forgotten all about it, by now."

"So would I," Nick said, nodding, "but there you go. Anyway, enough about her. I just wanted to hang out with you for a bit. Take a breather and see how you're doing."

When he saw the look on Brian's face, he frowned. "What's up?"

Brian gave him a brief rundown of his conversation with his father, leaving out the dire financial details.

"Man, that's tough," Nick said, rubbing the stubble on his chin. "I remember my old man getting laid off when I was twelve. He sat around the house for months, driving my mother and the rest of us nuts. When the union finally called him, we threw a party."

Brian smiled at the images Nick's anecdote brought to mind.

"I just wish that I could do something for him," Brian said, shaking his head. "I'd lend him the money myself, assuming it would be anywhere near enough, but he'd never take it."

"That's my old man, to a tee. Charity just pissed him off."

Before Brian could offer a reply, a waitress approached the table and took their orders. Brian settled on a tuna sandwich and bottled water. Nick stuck with his coffee. When the waitress left, the older man continued. "I'm glad you told me, anyway. But, what I really want to know is how are *you*?"

Brian nodded, looking off toward the cover of a book on a nearby shelf that caught his eye. It appeared to be a romance, with a man and woman locked in a torrid embrace. Brian grinned. "I've never been better," he said, turning back to Nick. "Love life is great and so is business."

"Glad to hear that." He fell silent for a moment, as if searching his thoughts. "Listen, Brian, I really *am* glad everything's going well for you, but I got to tell you, you're worrying me."

Brian frowned. "Worrying you? Why?"

"Let's just say this business with Joanna isn't the smartest of moves," he said, looking uncomfortable.

Brian let out a long sigh. "You and my father should start a club."

"If he's anything like you, I'll bet he's a brainy old guy, and I'm sure he'll solve his problems, but I'm also sure he'd be the first one to tell you that sometimes we can be blind to what's best for us."

"And what's best for me, Nick?" Brian asked, not liking where this was going one bit.

Nick sipped his coffee then coughed. "Goddamn asthma. You know I look at you like my little brother, don't you? And I hate to see my little brother stepping into a minefield."

"I know what I'm doing."

"Do you? I don't think you have a frigging clue."

"What the hell is it to you, anyway?"

Nick looked down at his coffee.

"I asked you a question, Nick."

"Erik Ruby is a very old friend of mine. We went to college together."

Brian leaned forward with a worried frown. "Did he put you up to this? Does he know anything?"

Nick shook his head. "No to both those questions, or at least to the first one. I don't know what he knows; he tends to play things close to the vest, but you *both* mean a lot to me and I'm feeling the squeeze, here."

"So, I'm the one who's got to give?"

"Joanna's engaged to him, Brian. Are you forgetting that?"

"No I'm not. But I love her, and she loves me."

Nick's eyes widened. "She *told* you that?"

"Yes."

Nick's sigh turned to a wheeze and then a deep wracking cough. "Crap.... Sorry. This day's just getting better and better."

"Are you going to say anything to him?"

Nick's tired eyes bored into Brian's. "Like I said, I'm feeling the squeeze—and I don't much care for it."

Brian stared at the table, unsure how to react to Nick's words. Then it occurred to him that the truth was best.

"I can only speak for myself, but I've never felt this way about any woman I've ever known. Joanna and I connect on so many levels and in so many ways that I can't find the words to describe it, which is a little surprising, since—until now—words were my sole reason for living. That make any sense?"

Nick nodded solemnly. "More than you know, kiddo, more than you know.... I'll let you in on a little secret. Never told this to anyone, but when Erik first brought Joanna around, I fell for her like a ton of bricks. Those eyes and that *smile* of hers, and the way she giggles." He shook his head, fighting back his emotions. "Didn't know what the hell to do with myself. Couldn't say anything, sure as hell couldn't do anything about it. Couldn't sleep, couldn't eat, couldn't even fucking think straight."

The food arrived, but any appetite Brian had before was completely gone, his mind abuzz. "Jeez, Nick, I don't know what to say, I—"

"There's nothing to say. She was my best friend's girl.... She'll always be special to me, Brian, and she'll never know how I feel." Nick looked down at the dregs of his coffee, swirling its contents with his spoon. "You asked me if I'd say anything. I won't." He lifted his gaze

191

and Brian saw the pain etched into the deep lines at the corners of his mouth. "Looks as if we both have secrets to keep...."

"Excuse me, is everything okay?"

Brian looked up at the waitress, whose sweet round face registered concern. "Everything's fine, but I need to get back to my office. Would you wrap this up for me, please?"

The waitress smiled. "Sure, no problem." She scooped up the plate and took it behind the counter.

While he waited for her to return, Brian pulled out his wallet and left enough for Nick's coffee, his sandwich and a generous tip. Nick stared off toward the front of the store. It was an awkward moment and Brian wished he could melt through the floor. The waitress returned and Brian stood. Nick turned to him, a look of panic flashing across his features so quickly, Brian almost missed it.

"You have my word, Nick. She'll never know."

Nick offered a ghost of his cocky grin. "Thanks, *amigo*, I appreciate that. Be careful, okay? For the both of you...."

Brian nodded and left the restaurant, grateful for the blast of cold air when he reached the sidewalk.

Back in his office, he picked up the phone and checked the messages on his home answering machine. There was only one—from Joanna:

"Hey, gorgeous, just wanted to say hi and tell you how much I love you. God, it feels like forever since I've seen you.... Hope you miss me as much as I miss you." Her voice dropped half an octave. "I've also got another itch that needs scratching, too." She giggled and Brian smiled, his heart hammering. "Oh, Nick showed me the revised mailer yesterday, by the way. You really did such a wonderful job with it; I knew my sweet writer would come through for me.

"I also called the caterer and the valet parking people you recommended and everything's set up for the show. My God, I can't believe

A Note from an Old Acquaintance

I'm actually doing it. And it's all your fault! Seriously, I couldn't have done this without you, Brian. I'm so glad you've come into my life...in more ways than you can imagine....

"Oh, before I go, I wanted to let you know that I'm creating a special piece for you, but you'll just have to wait until the show to see it. Anyway, I've got a class. Call me tonight. I'll be at the studio. Love you."

For the first time since meeting Joanna, doubts crept into Brian's mind. Nick's confession had rocked him, but his echoing of his father's words had flipped a switch in his brain, making him question everything going on in his life.

Just as he'd told Nick with his own confession, he felt connected to her on multiple planes: physically, emotionally, intellectually and spiritually. The way he felt right now, he would marry her in a New York minute. Marry her and be happy. He smiled, imagining an entire lifetime with her, the wedding, anniversaries, birthdays, creating their art together, sharing each other's triumphs and tribulations—growing old together. A life—complete with a little curly-haired boy or girl not too far down the road. It was such a powerful and poignant vision that it made his heart ache with a bittersweet fusion of joy and pain. He could see it all with the vivid clarity of a storyteller's imagination, knowing that in some alternate universe it was playing out exactly that way.

Would she leave her fiancé—call off the wedding?

That was the real question, the one nagging the recesses of his mind no matter how hard he tried to block it out.

And even though she'd professed not to give a whit about the man's money, would she really give it all up for relative uncertainty? After all, anything could happen with his business. Anything involving the entertainment industry was at the whims and mercies of the marketplace. They were doing well today, but what about tomorrow?

And as confident as he was in his writing, who really knew when or even *if* that would ever pay off.

He wanted to believe she would give it all up, needed to believe it, but her reaction the other night when he tried to broach the subject of their future had been anything but encouraging. Maybe she simply loved the idea of being in love, but didn't want to take the risk of upsetting a comfortable life for the unknown. Maybe to her, Brian was simply a brief romantic interlude, a blip on her radar screen before—

Stop! If he kept thinking this way he would lose his freaking mind. He needed to talk to her, try to see how she really felt. Wasn't honesty between them the real basis for a strong foundation? Of course it was. But maybe it was too soon for that. Maybe he should play it cool, something his Dad always advised him to do when he'd started dating in high school. Good advice, to be sure, but hard as hell to put into practice.

He should at least wait until after her show, that would be the smart and decent thing to do. Let her have her moment in the sun. Once it was out of the way they could talk about that future, whatever it might entail.

He listened to her message again, reveling in the sound of her voice, especially when she alluded to her "itch." Brian had that itch, too, in spades. There were no doubts in that department. His desire for her was only exceeded by his love. And he sure wanted to be with her— every chance he got.

A glance at the clock told him a client would be arriving soon and it was time to prep the suite. He'd call her later. He needed to feel the warmth of her arms, the pleasures of her touch, and hear her murmurs of love. He knew all his doubts were built upon a quicksand of paranoia and the pain of a well-meaning friend. He knew all those doubts would disappear as soon as he gazed into the depths of those haunting emerald eyes.

20

PARKING AT JOANNA'S STUDIO was more difficult this evening, with cars overflowing from the Channel's parking lot and jamming both sides of the surrounding streets. It looked as if the club was hopping for a change and presaged what Joanna could expect the night of her show; at least he hoped she would have a good turnout.

One could never tell when sending out invitations. You had to go on the assumption that everyone invited would show up, knowing in your gut that at least twenty-five percent of them would fall out. Brian had labored over the guest list with her for an entire evening, could almost recite blocks of names by rote, so he knew the potential numbers could be huge. Aside from friends, family, colleagues and miscellaneous personages, they'd invited every major critic in the area. He'd even suggested a few from the New York media. It was a long shot, he'd told her, but you never knew. If one of them showed up and gave her a good review...well, the impact on her career would be incalculable.

Brian entered the lobby and noticed that the cleanup work had already begun. The marble floor, so begrimed from years of neglect, positively gleamed. The walls had been freshly painted and the mailboxes emptied, repaired and polished. The bare bulb still hung from the ceiling, but at least the wattage had been increased and the gloom dispelled.

He called down the elevator and rode up to the sixth floor. Joanna had her stereo on. He could hear it echoing down the shaft. Nearer the top, he recognized the tune as "The Party's Over" by Journey. He'd always loved that song and the album from which it came.

Exiting the elevator, he walked through her gallery and halted in his tracks. She was dancing in the middle of the floor dressed in her customary black bodysuit, her eyes closed, a beatific smile on her face. Brian watched her, spellbound. The way she moved her body with such grace and abandon never ceased to mesmerize him. He watched her until the music changed to another slower song a few moments later. The tune was "Who's Crying Now." Joanna stopped dancing, opened her eyes and raised her arms toward him, beckoning him.

He went to her, enfolding her into his arms, and they began moving to the soulful music. As always, time ceased to behave in the normal physical manner when he was with her. Instead, when he held her close, the warmth of her body suffusing his own, moments would elongate, stretching infinitely. And then, when least expected, the real world would intrude, snapping him back to reality, his enchanted mind registering that an entire block of time had elapsed.

They held onto each other, swaying to the music, long after the stereo had shut down, completely oblivious to anything but the rhythm of their hearts and the sound of their breath.

Joanna looked up at him, her eyes beseeching him. He kissed her long and lovingly, their lips melding to the point where he couldn't tell where hers ended and his began.

"I've missed you so much," she whispered. "I didn't think I could bear it any longer."

He put a finger to her lips, silencing her, then picked her up and carried her into the bedroom.

Once there they undressed each other slowly, lips kissing each new area of exposed flesh. Brian shivered with pleasure as her lips and tongue found that special place in the hollow of his neck, her hand caressing his inner thigh.

"Lie back," she said. "I want to make love to you."

And she did, paying notice to every part of him, her attentions teasing him inexorably towards his release. Just when it seemed as if he couldn't hold back any longer, she backed off.

"Don't stop, now!"

"Not so fast, big boy," she murmured, nuzzling his ear. "I'm having too much fun. Now it's your turn."

Brian smiled. "What did you have in mind, my lady?"

"Oh, I'm sure you'll think of something." She giggled softly.

She kissed him and rolled onto her back, beckoning him with her eyes.

Brian started at her toes, kissing each one in turn, marveling at their perfect shape and softness. He worked his way up the silken smoothness of her legs, pausing to nuzzle her pubic mound before moving on.

Joanna gasped, arching her back, as his tongue sought the recesses of her navel. She grabbed his hair with her hand and pushed his head lower.

"Now," she said, breathless. "I want it now."

He indulged her, reveling in the taste of her.

Her body thrashed against him, her cries growing more frenzied, ending in a long groan. She caressed the back of his neck, a sigh of contentment escaping her lips.

Brian raised himself above her and she moved beneath him allowing him entry. He began moving slowly, watching her pleasure build again, his own along with hers.

Their rhythms accelerated and when his release came, he collapsed onto her, feeling her arms wrap around him.

"I love you," she whispered.

"And I love you, too."

❀ ❀ ❀

Ruby had just crossed Mass Avenue and taken the on-ramp leading to the westbound lanes of the Mass Pike when Mosley's call came in. The car phone purred and he snatched it up, careful to keep abreast of the merging traffic. It was crawling at an agonizing pace, but at least it was moving.

"Yes?"

"Mr. Ruby? Our friend walked into your fiancée's studio about fifteen minutes ago."

"Why didn't you call me sooner?" Ruby said, his blood pressure rising.

"I apologize for that, sir. My car phone died, and it took me a while to find a public phone. There's not too many around this area."

That was true, but that little bit of information did nothing to alleviate Ruby's anger. "I just got on the Pike and the traffic's a bear. Go back to her studio and keep watch. If he leaves, assuming he hasn't already, get back to that phone and call me, right away."

"Yes, sir, will do."

"And remind me to buy you a new phone."

Ruby pushed the END button and slammed the handset back onto its cradle, swearing under his breath. Technology was a wonderful thing, until you really needed it. He wasn't angry with Mosley, more with himself for being so eager to leave the office when he did. If he'd tarried just a little longer, made just one more phone call, checked on one more detail, he'd be well on his way to the studio right now, instead of being stuck on the Pike going in the wrong damned direction!

Squinting, he scouted the road ahead. The angry red tail lights stretching to the horizon told the sad and sorry truth. And the worst of it was that the Allston-Brighton exit was at least two long, slow miles ahead. At least the eastbound lanes were moving. If he could get to that exit and turn around—

"Nuts to this," he said, swerving the car into the breakdown lane. "Time to see what this pile of British junk can really do."

Ruby tromped down on the gas and the Jag shot forward, racing by the stalled traffic to his left. A few drivers honked their ire at him when he passed. "Yeah, love you, too," he said, and mashed the accelerator to the floor.

He reached Melcher Street thirty minutes later, pulling into a parking space half a block from the building. He found Mosley's Taurus directly across from the front entrance. When he approached, the black man rolled down the window, regarding him with a casual expression.

"They're still inside," Mosley said. "His car is over there."

Ruby nodded, his eyes straying to Weller's dusty Toyota Celica and then to the building's top floor. The windows looked dark, but it was hard to tell in the glare of the neon tire sign flashing off and on. Still, not seeing her studio ablaze, as he was accustomed to finding it, made him uneasy.

"I still wouldn't advise walking in on them," Mosley warned.

Ruby lowered his gaze to the investigator, whose dark features glowed in the unforgiving glare of the crime lights. The black man's brow was furrowed with concern.

"I'll admit that a part of me doesn't want to go in there," Ruby said, "but it's the only way."

"You want me to stay?"

"Why?"

Mosley looked his employer in the eye. "To watch your back."

Ruby's edgy mood softened. "Sure, I appreciate that. Wish me luck." And with that, the older man turned and crossed the street, his eyes focused on the front door and whatever fate might have in store.

❊ ❊ ❊

Joanna sighed in her sleep, nuzzling her body closer to Brian's, her head resting in the crook of his arm. He leaned forward and nestled his face in the pillowy softness of her hair, the odor of lilacs filling his nose. With gentle movements, so as not wake her, he brushed her hair back from her face and gazed at her in repose. How girlish she looked, so adorably innocent, with those sparkling crimson curls and those big green eyes. And yet, how womanly and worldly she was, how grounded. After his old girlfriend's wild mood swings and maddening neuroses, Joanna's effervescence and razor-sharp mind were as refreshing as a cool oasis to a parched man in the desert. And that's just what he'd been until meeting her, a thirsty man staggering towards a mirage in an arid wasteland.

Joanna sighed again, throwing a curvy leg over him. Brian's heart swelled with contentment, along with the stirrings of desire. He thought about kissing her awake, watching those wondrous eyes flutter open, confused at first, then filling with joy, love, and smoldering heat.

But, no...not now, he thought. I just want to watch her. I just want to love her...like this.

He turned and eyed the clock on the low nightstand, noting there was still plenty of time. He then let his eyes roam the rest of the room, a room whose boundaries and furnishings had become so lovingly familiar—so much like a home.

Light from the glow of a neon sign on the roof of the building next door sliced through the half-open blinds, dappling the wooden floor and the Persian rug on which the futon rested; his eyes found the jade Buddha across the room sitting atop his polished ebony plinth. The statue sat bathed in an aura of pulsating crimson light, its happy grin shining with sparkling pink highlights. And while it was no doubt one of hundreds or even thousands made, the nameless artist who'd carved the statue had somehow managed to infuse the tiny face of this particular little guy with an extra measure of wisdom and joy. Brian smiled. Though this man's teachings were foreign to him, he nevertheless thought of him as a kindred spirit.

"Can I trust you to keep a secret, old friend?" he asked. "I could stay here forever...."

The little green Buddha remained mute, but from Brian's point of view across the room it seemed the statue's smile had widened. And was that a wink he saw or simply a flicker of neon in a carved jade eye?

He smiled again and turned back to Joanna, whose eyes were now open regarding him soberly.

"Hi there, sleepyhead," he said, kissing her.

She returned the kiss, her soft lips a quiet fire. A long, slender finger caressed circles on his abdomen.

"Be careful what you ask of the Buddha," she said, a sly grin exposing her perfect teeth. "You just might get it."

"And would that be so bad?"

"Mmmm, maybe not. Then you'd be my slave," she said, giggling.

"Or perhaps your model in residence?"

She raised herself on one elbow, her breasts grazing his chest. Her nipples were as hard as diamonds.

"Ooooh, you're much more versatile than that." She kissed his neck, eliciting a groan from deep within him.

From the bowels of the building came the sounds of the elevator gate sliding upward then crashing down.

Joanna started in his arms, as if jolted by a cattle prod. "Oh, my God, Erik's here!"

"What, how?"

Joanna bolted from the bed and began throwing on her clothes. "He's the only other person with a key. Get dressed! Hurry!"

Brian leaped from the bed and pulled on his shirt, then his pants, nearly toppling to the floor in his haste. Adrenaline made his entire body tremble. He wanted to believe that was all it was, but there was also an undercurrent of fear and the humiliation of being "caught."

The elevator began its upward course, the ancient motor clacking and clanking, whizzing and whirring, ticking and tocking, like an infernal clockwork symphony played by Morlocks.

"Where's the stairwell?" Brian asked, jamming his feet into his shoes.

If it was possible for Joanna to look more panicked, she did. "You can't go that way, they're alarmed. She grabbed him by the arm and led him out of the bedroom. Just outside the workshop doorway, she stopped and pointed. "Over there behind the artwork. He'll never look there."

"Why would he be looking at all?" Brian asked, his voice rising.

"Ssssh! Please go, now," she whispered, her eyes pleading with him.

Brian was about to protest, then realized it was pointless. He gave her hand a fleeting squeeze and headed into the exhibit section of the studio. A quick glance told him the elevator was nearly to their floor. He put on a burst of speed, ducked around one of the monolithic white partitions, and wedged himself into the shadows between two of Joanna's larger pieces.

Scant seconds later, the elevator stopped, and the door slid open, and then a single set of determined footsteps smacked across the wooden floor. The echoes made them sound like an army on the march. After a long, pregnant silence muffled voices reached his ears. He couldn't make out the words, but the emotions were plain enough.

He had to get out of there; his evening edit session couldn't be postponed, and he couldn't afford to be sitting there, crouching in the shadows like some luckless boob. He looked down to check the time and his breath caught in his throat.

Where was his watch?

❈ ❈ ❈

Ruby realized his mistake as soon as the gate to the elevator closed, sending a metallic clang echoing up the shaft. Damn it, there went the element of surprise. Of course, the crotchety old motor wouldn't be any quieter, either, so he gritted his teeth, grabbed the lever and pulled it, sending the lift upward.

What would he do, if by chance they hadn't heard, and were even now asleep in each other's arms? That image, at once so repugnant and so vivid, made his heart slam against his ribs and his breath come in short, angry gasps. He pulled the lever farther toward him, increasing the elevator's speed.

The third and fourth floors flew by in a blur, and he eased the lever forward, slowing it past the fifth floor, slow enough to see the mountains of discarded office furniture from decades past.

And then, as he'd done countless times before, he brought the elevator to a perfect stop on Joanna's floor. The track lighting was dimmed and shadows dominated, the only other light coming from Joanna's fiber-optic sphere. He stood stock-still and listened for a moment, hearing nothing, then lifted the gate and walked out onto the oak flooring, the heels of his hand-made Italian shoes clacking a cadence like tap shoes.

He found Joanna in her workshop, examining a piece of PVC piping, her back to the door. Beyond her, the bedroom lay swathed in darkness. Could Weller still be in there? Would he be that brazen? That stupid? Ruby stood in the doorway a moment longer, watching her. There was nothing about her manner or her dress to suggest anything, but still....

❀   ❀   ❀

Joanna watched Brian hide behind the partition for the piece she called "Helios 2," then rushed back into the bedroom. She did her best to smooth out the comforter on the futon and plump both of the pillows. Did that look okay? It would have to do. What on earth was Erik *doing* here, anyway? He usually called before coming to the studio.

She heard the elevator stop, and with a tiny moan of fear, she dashed into her workshop and picked up the first thing she saw, a piece of white PVC piping laying on her workbench.

Remember your breathing, she thought.

She heard his footsteps approach then stop. The seconds ticked off. How long was he going to just stand there and—

A Note from an Old Acquaintance

"Joanna?"

She turned, startled. "Erik! My God, you scared me."

Her fiancé smiled. "I'm sorry, my love. I was in the neighborhood and I wanted to see how you were doing. Surely you heard me coming up the elevator."

She shook her head, sighing. "You know how I am when I'm working. A bomb could go off."

"That's true enough." He nodded toward the piece of piping she was holding. "New idea?"

"No, at least nothing that's inspiring me," she said, putting the piece of pipe down on her workbench.

"That's too bad. Do you think you have what you need for the show?"

"I guess so," she said, starting to putter.

"Well, how about we take a little tour and you show me what you have in mind?"

"Can we do this another time? I'm really tired, and I've got at least another hour here."

"I'm tired, too, dear. Wrightson isn't the easiest client I've ever had. But since I'm here...."

Joanna sighed. "All right, but let me wash up, first, okay?"

She moved through the bedroom and Erik followed. In the bathroom, she snapped on the light and turned on the water, splashing it on her face. She noticed her hands trembling, but when she checked herself in the mirror, she saw only her face and nothing of the fear that raced her heart.

When she was through, she brushed past Erik, who stood partially blocking the doorway; he grabbed her arm. "What?" she asked, her eyes wide.

"I've missed you," he said, drawing her to him. It was something he'd done innumerable times, something that had always surprised and delighted her, to be swept into his embrace, smelling his after-shave, feeling his strength. Now it all felt wrong, and even his cologne was cloying.

"I missed you, too," she said, hugging him. It was then she noticed the faint glow on the nightstand.

Brian's watch!

"Are you okay?" Erik asked. "You're trembling."

Joanna pulled away from him. "I'm fine, just tired, like I said. Let's go look at the art."

She took his hand and led him out into the studio where her pieces were arranged.

❄   ❄   ❄

Ruby's mind was not on the art. They walked past each piece and Joanna made comments, but they went in one ear and out the other. Where the hell was Weller? He couldn't have taken the stairs, so he had to be here, somewhere. Unless Mosley was wrong, unless Weller had left while the investigator was searching for a stupid pay phone. But what about his car? The car was still here.

"Erik did you hear me?"

Ruby's eyes snapped to Joanna, who was staring at him, frowning. "Sorry, I was thinking about the building."

"I'm glad my art is so important to you," she said, glaring. "Why am I wasting my time? I've still got work I need to do."

Ruby shook his head. Maybe this whole thing was a mistake. Mosley did warn him that confrontation was ill advised, and he'd been prepared for it, though not this kind.

"You're right. I'm sorry. I'll see you at home."

A Note from an Old Acquaintance

He turned and walked to the elevator, his anger rising. He felt like a blithering idiot and that was something he could never abide.

❀   ❀   ❀

When Brian heard the whine of the elevator, he stepped out from behind the partition. Joanna stared at him with wide eyes then threw her arms around him.

"I really thought he was going to find you," she said, sobbing against his shoulder. "And when I saw your watch on the nightstand, I nearly had a heart attack!"

"It's okay, it's okay," he said, but the doubts he'd felt earlier raised their ugly heads. They walked back into the bedroom arm in arm, and Brian retrieved his watch. Joanna moved to the window and stared out through the blinds, clearly agitated.

"Listen," Brian said, the words catching in his throat, "maybe we should lay low for awhile, at least until after your show."

Joanna whirled to face him, her lips trembling. "What! What are you talking about? You *have* to come!"

"It's not that I don't want to. I do...more than anything. But with your fiancé there it's just asking for trouble."

"He doesn't know about us!"

"Can you be sure of that, after what just happened?"

A look of guilty panic flitted across her features. "I told him you were helping me work on the mailer. He has no reason to think otherwise."

"So, he knows who I am?"

Joanna nodded.

"Sweetheart, he has every reason to think otherwise. You're a young, vital, passionate woman, and if I were your fiancé, I'd worry, too. As much as I want to come, I think it's just a bad idea. It'll be like shoving his face in a pile of crap."

"Well, I'm glad you're so considerate of his feelings. What about mine!"

"I don't care about his feelings. I care about you and your show, and I don't want to be the cause of any scene that ruins it."

Joanna's eyes filled with tears. "But I need you there, Brian. You're my rock."

Brian sighed. How could he argue with that? He reached for her and she shrugged him off, her body stiffening. "Why don't you just go," she said. "You got what you came for, anyway."

"What the hell is that supposed to mean?"

Joanna glared at him. "You're a man, figure it out."

Brian checked his temper, knowing her words were borne out of pain.

"Don't you ever think that. You know I'm not that kind of man."

"No? You waited until after we made love to tell me you're abandoning me just when I need you the most!"

Brian shook his head. "I'll admit my timing stinks, but I've been struggling with this for days. I'm not abandoning you, Joanna, please try and understand."

She hugged herself, her expression like that of a lost little girl. "I do understand. You're afraid of Erik. I just thought you cared more about me than yourself."

"Hey! That's not fair, and you know it. I'm not afraid of him. I'm afraid for you."

He moved closer to her, but she turned away and wouldn't meet his eyes. "I love you, Joanna. Please don't take it this way."

"Just leave...."

"Please...don't do this."

A Note from an Old Acquaintance

"I want you to leave, *now.*" She turned and pushed him away. "GET OUT!"

The last two words reverberated off the walls, punching him in the gut. Feeling powerless and seeing no other way, he left the bedroom and called the elevator. Waiting for it was agony. When he closed the gate and reached for the lever, he heard her sobs echoing through the studio and blinked back tears of his own. It felt as if a vital part of him had been cut out and left bleeding on the ground.

Brilliant move, Weller. You should have just sucked it up and gone to the show. Screw her fiancé. How could facing him be any worse than this?

Outside, he was only mildly relieved to see that his car was untouched. He got in, started the engine, made a U-turn and headed home. With every second that elapsed and every foot of ground he covered, he felt as if a little more of his soul were dying—piece by agonizing piece. He wanted to go back, almost made U-turns in the middle of busy intersections several times, but stopped himself. She would never listen to reason or apologies right now.

Only a little time would give him that chance.

And only if she truly loved him, as much as he loved her.

The bitter irony was that she'd accused him of being selfish, when all he'd wanted to do was spare her embarrassment and give her art the shot it deserved. And the critics they'd invited would only give her one shot.

Now this.

He slammed the steering wheel till his hand ached, cursing everyone he could think of, including her fiancé. It couldn't end like this, it just couldn't. He wouldn't let it. But the one thing he didn't know how to do was fix the unfixable.

❀   ❀   ❀

"You're fired," Ruby said, to a stunned Cary Mosley.

The black man gaped at him through the open car window. "He's *in* there," he replied.

"No, he's—" Ruby stopped speaking when he saw Mosley's expression change from stunned surprise to a wary watchfulness.

"Look."

Ruby turned in time to see Weller emerge from the building, get into his Toyota, pull a screeching U-turn and speed off. Ruby turned back to Mosley, feeling twice the idiot he'd been before. "I'll never doubt you again," he said. "Meet me at my office tomorrow afternoon. It's time we discussed your future in more detail."

21

RUBY PILOTED HIS JAGUAR through the traffic on the Mass Pike, expertly weaving in and around the slower cars. He glanced at Joanna, feeling a swell of pride. God, she looked stunning tonight. She wore a black cocktail dress with her hair piled up in that way he'd always loved, just the right amount of makeup and a minimum of jewelry, only the one-and-a-half carat diamond earrings he'd given her a few hours earlier in honor of her first show. He caught a gleam of them in the oncoming headlights from the westbound traffic. They were as flawless as Joanna.

The only fly in the ointment was the fact that she'd been so down the last few days, moping around the house as if nothing mattered. He hated seeing her like that, even though he was secretly glad. It meant only one thing: a certain would-be-writer was out of the picture. Ruby had done his best to hide his glee and played the attentive, solicitous husband-to-be, anticipating every shift in her moods. It seemed to have worked.

"Excited?"

She turned and gave him a wan smile. "Yes.... Nervous, too."

"Stop worrying, you'll be fine. Wait until you see the building, they'll be agog before they even get upstairs."

She looked at him and nodded. "I'm sure it'll be lovely." She turned and stared out the passenger window, lost in thought.

Ruby gripped the wheel, his knuckles turning white. He wanted to make Weller pay for the pain he'd caused her—and him. Oh, yes, most certainly for that. But that would have to wait for another time. Tonight was Joanna's night, and he intended for it to go off without a hitch. The one detail that nagged at his mind was Joanna's new piece, the one she'd been so secretive about. She wouldn't tell him anything about it, wouldn't even let him see it in progress, telling him only that it was unlike anything she'd ever done. Even now it sat under a black cloth, set off from all her other pieces, waiting for its unveiling at the height of the show. He hated surprises.

"What time is it?" Joanna said.

Ruby glanced at his Rolex. "Five-thirty. No one's arriving until seven. There's plenty of time."

"Plenty of time," she echoed.

He frowned, glancing at her for the umpteenth time.

The car passed under Mass Avenue, entering the long tunnel. He moved over into the right-hand lane, watching for the South Station exit, an uneasy feeling squirming in his gut.

❀ ❀ ❀

There was still plenty of time for Brian to show up, Joanna thought. God, she'd been such a bitch, had realized it the moment she'd heard him descending in the elevator that night. She'd wanted to call him back, had run to the empty shaft, to no avail; it was too late.

Silly stupid pride!

That's all it had been. Of course, she understood why he'd been hesitant to attend her show. He'd wanted to spare her any chance that something would go wrong. And to think she'd accused him of callously using her body. For the millionth time since that night, Joanna held back the tide of her tears, not wanting Erik to see how upset she really was. That he knew something was wrong was obvious. She'd made up a story about her sister being ill to cover the real reason. It seemed to mollify him.

To his credit he'd been sweet as could be and the diamond earrings were beautiful, but she didn't want them, and only wore them to make him happy. She would gladly trade them without a moment's remorse for the chance to tell Brian how sorry she was and how much she loved him. She'd picked up the phone so many times she'd lost count, had dialed his number only to hang up before the first ring, her heart in her throat. What if he rejected her totally? What if he was waiting until after her show to call the whole thing off? She couldn't bear that thought.

Her nerves were raw to the point where even her meditations didn't help. She'd wanted this show so badly, and now it was all she could do to show up and go through the motions, something she'd promised herself she would do. No matter what.

And she'd made herself another promise.

If, after the show, she and Brian could patch things up, she intended to leave Erik.

There, she'd allowed herself to think the unthinkable.

While a small part of her still had feelings for her fiancé, she knew in her heart it was over. With Brian, she felt as if she'd always known him, felt connected to him in so many ways both subtle and profound.

Soul mates....

That was the phrase her mind had struggled to recall over the last few days. It described her feelings and intuitions to a tee. She wanted to be with Brian for the rest of her life...if he would have her.

Bill Walker

The car exited the Pike at South Station and made the loop onto Atlantic Avenue. When they turned onto Summer Street and crossed the bridge over the channel, Joanna leaned forward in her seat, stunned. The building, her building, looked as if it were lit up like a Christmas tree, with large searchlights aiming up at the structure from all sides. More lights, positioned on the roof, shot bright white beams of light skyward.

"Erik, what did you do?"

Her fiancé grinned. "Called in a few favors. Didn't I tell you they'd be blown away?" He laughed, pleased with himself.

They drew up to the front of the building and a valet parking attendant in a crisp starched uniform opened her door and then Erik's. He handed Erik a ticket, climbed into the Jag and drove off toward the Channel's parking lot.

Erik held out his arm and Joanna slid hers into his, hesitating for only the briefest of moments.

"Let's show them how it's done," he said, and walked her toward the entrance.

❄   ❄   ❄

Brian paced the floor of his apartment, his eyes darting to the clock radio so often he'd begun to wonder if it had stopped.

6:05.

In less than an hour Joanna's show would start...without him.

Stop it, Weller. You keep thinking like this, you'll go nuts!

The problem was he couldn't stop thinking about Joanna, the show, and the mess the other night had become. And the more he thought about that night, the more he kicked himself for not giving in to his instincts and going back.

214

Still 6:05.

Maybe the stupid thing *had* stopped. Too bad he couldn't turn it back. That would solve a lot of problems. Sitting on his bed, Brian picked up his guitar and began strumming a few chords, only to put it back on its stand. At other times, the instrument was both therapy and inspiration; now it barely distracted him.

6:06.

Stop it! Just stop it, now.

He tried to imagine what she was doing at that very moment. In his mind's eye, he saw her walking through the studio making sure everything was in place, the caterer setting out food and drink and—

—her fiancé gloating.

Brian ground his teeth, seething. Whether the man knew anything about what was going on, or not, he'd won by default. He'd won because Brian had tried to do the right thing, only to have it blow up in his face. He'd wanted to give Joanna some space, a little time to figure things out. Had resisted every urge to call her and do whatever it took to make amends. Now, here he was climbing the walls and missing what he hoped would be a night of triumph for the woman he loved.

Well, enough was enough.

He stood up and began pulling off the clothes he'd worn all day. If he hurried, he could take a quick shower, get dressed and get down there. He'd miss maybe twenty minutes, but that was fine. He went to his dresser where the invitation sat propped up against his mirror. It had arrived a couple of days ago, and he'd kept it, because he couldn't bear the thought of throwing it away—throwing her away.

With his resolve more firmly entrenched, he hurried into the bathroom and turned on the water, groaning with pleasure as the hot spray needled into his back.

Twenty minutes later, he was behind the wheel of his Celica, racing down Boylston Street, one hand on the wheel, and the other trying to comb his scraggly hair and straighten his tie. His mood plummeted when he spotted the snarl of traffic at Tremont Street. He glanced at the clock.

6:40.

At this rate, he'd be lucky if he got there at all.

❋   ❋   ❋

For a while, at least, Joanna was able to lose herself in the last-minute preparations for the show. Some of the larger pieces needed relighting and some had to be repositioned when changing the lights proved inadequate. She'd taken Brian's advice and redesigned the layout for her partitions and artwork, so as to make the arriving guests move through an informal maze, thereby forcing them to view her art before coming into the main area where the food and drinks were set up.

"Think of it this way," he'd said. "Every hotel-casino in the world makes you walk through its casino to get to anything else in the complex. This way, by the time your guests get to the food, their appetites will be whetted in more than one respect."

That had made her laugh at the time, as she'd had one or two other appetites in mind, but his advice, as always, was sound and much appreciated.

Looking up at the ceiling, she spotted a pulley that looked as if it needed tightening and she grabbed her stepladder and a pair of vise-grips from out of her shop.

"Do you need a hand?" Erik asked.

"I'm okay," she replied, kicking off her heels and climbing the ladder. She reached up and gave the bolt holding the pulley another couple of twists then retightened the nut. She plucked the wire to test its tautness and nodded. That should do it.

When she reached the floor, she turned and saw Erik standing by the new piece, staring at the black cloth, a bemused look on his face.

He couldn't suspect anything, could he? If he did, wouldn't he have said something, flown off the handle, as he so often did when something about his business went awry? Perhaps it was just the mere fact she was keeping it under wraps that bothered him, having never done this in the past. Time would tell, once the cloth was removed and everyone had a chance to view it. She was excited about that, as she'd never been about any of her other work. It had turned out perfectly, firing in the kiln with no ill effects. She'd then debated what color glaze to use, deciding on just a satin clear coat. Anything else would have looked unnatural. With just the dark gray of the clay, and the hint of gloss, it resembled something carved out of rock.

"Excuse me, Ma'am?"

Joanna turned to find the caterer, a woman in her late thirties, holding out a tray of assorted hors d'oeuvres.

"Oh, these look wonderful," Joanna said.

The woman cracked a proud smile. "Would you like to try any of them?"

"Oh, God," she said, patting her stomach. "I don't think I could eat a bite right now, but thank you."

"I understand, Ma'am. And by the way, my crew and I think your artwork is terrific."

Now it was Joanna's turn to smile. "Thank you, that's so sweet of you. Let's hope the critics think so, too."

The woman nodded. "Oh, I expect they will."

Joanna watched the woman walk back to the kitchen area, feeling a sense of calm stealing over her. This was going to work. Brian was right. Brian....

A pang of longing rushed through her when she glanced toward the new piece. His presence was all she needed to make the evening complete.

Please come, Brian, please come....

❀   ❀   ❀

"Do you read me, sir? Over," Mosley asked, his voice squawking into Ruby's ear. He lifted his arm and spoke into the microphone attached to his wrist.

"Yes, I do, but how do I turn the volume down on this damned thing?"

"It's on the cuff band, next to the microphone. Over."

Ruby rolled his eyes and made the adjustment. He still felt a little foolish wearing the radio, with the wires snaking up his back and down his left arm. The power pack felt unnaturally heavy and warm in the small of his back and the earpiece itched like hell, too, but Mosley had insisted that this was the best way to stay in touch. With all the people they expected, it seemed like a good idea at the time.

"How am I reading, now? Over."

"Ah, that's better," Ruby said. "Stay alert and let me know the moment he shows, that is, if he has the nerve."

"Will do. Over."

"Erik, who are you talking to?"

Ruby looked up to find Joanna standing in the doorway. "Just the security guard. Nothing to worry about. You okay?"

She nodded. "But I can't get used to you speaking into your wrist like that. I keep thinking the President's coming."

"Well, you never know." Ruby smiled, in spite of his fiancée's unintended sarcasm.

"I think we should put on a little music, what do you think?" she asked, frowning.

"Good idea. Not too loud, though."

She nodded again, looking distracted. He wanted to tell her everything would be fine, but he knew she wouldn't really hear him in her present state.

And everything would be fine, especially with the new information Mosley had dug up on Weller's background. An idea had formed in his mind overnight and Ruby knew it would work. If Weller showed, he'd use it. If not...then all was well, regardless.

Grinning, Ruby picked up an hors d'oeuvre off one of the trays lying on the counter and popped it into his mouth, earning a disapproving frown from the caterer. Ruby glared back at her, and she turned away.

He took another hors d'oeuvre and walked out into the main room, his mind now focused on the show.

❀   ❀   ❀

Once past Tremont, the traffic began moving faster, surprising Brian. Perhaps there'd been an accident somewhere in the theatre district, causing the gridlock with Boylston. Who knew? In any event, he found his nerves winding even tighter. Would Joanna be glad to see him, or would she have him thrown out on his behind?

And in spite of his professed lack of fear of her fiancé, he was curious to take the measure of the man Joanna intended to marry to see if he could discern just what it was that had attracted her in the first place, other than his power. Brian's mother had always said women were attracted to that in spite of themselves, and he tended to believe it, which only made it all the more amazing that he'd even been able to compete on the same field as the guy. Then again, Joanna was no ordinary female.

After another minor glitch in the traffic that delayed him an additional five minutes, he turned onto Summer Street just as his clock struck 7:15. It took a moment for his eyes to register what it saw up ahead, and when they did, he gaped.

Joanna's building was bathed in white-hot beams from strategically placed searchlights, making it look like a scene out of an old German propaganda film.

Turning onto Melcher, he joined a line of cars waiting for the valet. A small knot of guests climbed the steps and disappeared into the entryway. Brian's pulse quickened. It looked as if the turnout was going to be nothing at all to worry about.

After a few more minutes, his car drew abreast of the entrance and the driver's side door was opened by one of the valets.

"Good evening, sir," the valet said, handing him a ticket.

Brian nodded his thanks and went inside, passing a tall, well-dressed black man guarding the door. The one new thing he noticed in the lobby was the brushed aluminum hemispherical chandelier that had replaced the bare bulb, its subtle indirect light the final tasteful touch.

The elevator was ascending, ferrying the latest load of guests to the sixth floor. He waited, joined by six other couples moments later. He listened to their eager chatter, trying to discern if any of them were the critics they'd invited. Nothing he heard was revealing, except he did glean a sense of anticipation. Brian crossed his fingers.

The elevator started down, and the crowd quieted, thirteen pairs of eyes gazing upward. A moment later, the elevator slid into view and came to rest. The operator, a young woman in a uniform similar to the valets, opened the gate and motioned everyone inside. The gate was closed, the lever pulled, and up they went.

The first surprise came when passing the second floor. The entire expanse was Ferrari red: floor, walls, windows and support pillars. The light spilling in through the windows, augmented by hidden red lights, gave the space a look right out of Dante.

"Oh, wow," one of his fellow passengers said.

"Reminds me of one of my hangovers," another added, and everyone laughed, the mood turning festive.

The next floor carried on the same theme, this time in vibrant blue. The third floor was green and the fourth yellow. The final surprise came at the fifth: a stunning purple, with no sign of the hundreds of chairs, file cabinets and desks. It must have taken hours of someone's backbreaking labor to remove them all, not to mention painting and lighting the floors. To Brian's mind, Joanna's show was off to a tremendous start.

The elevator slowed when they moved through the fifth floor, coming to rest at the sixth with only the faintest of bumps. Brian was impressed, since he'd never quite gotten the hang of stopping the blasted thing without shaking his guts. The crowd pressed forward when the operator pulled on the chain, opening the gate.

His fellow passengers seemed hesitant to leave the car, until he realized it wasn't hesitancy, so much as awe.

Just as he'd advised, Joanna had arranged the partitions so that anyone exiting the elevator would be guided through a maze of exhibits. The first was her fiber-optic sphere, the lights pulsating nearly in time to the New Age music droning through the sound system.

And though he was familiar with most of the pieces on display, he walked along with the group, gauging their reactions and listening to their comments. He noticed one of them, a tall gray-haired man dressed in a black suit, pull out a notebook and jot a few notes. Bingo. Here was one of the critics. He resisted the urge to say something to the man and moved on. Up ahead, the crowd thickened and Brian smiled. This was the kind of traffic jam he could deal with.

22

THE GUESTS HAD BEGUN arriving just after 7:00 and Joanna forgot her nerves in the rush of greeting them and making each one feel at home. The waiters, a good half-dozen of them, began circulating with the trays of hors d'oeuvres and flutes of champagne. The room filled quickly and everyone with whom she shook hands buzzed with excitement about her art. She watched as some of them took food and champagne and headed back through the maze to take another look.

She tried keeping her attention on the end of the maze, hoping to see Brian, but the size of the crowd and the people constantly vying for her attention made it nearly impossible for her to do that. She fought back a wave of sadness and turned her attention to a middle-aged woman who'd just asked her a question about where she got her ideas. She smiled, remembering her first date with Brian.

"Well," she said, "the obvious answer would be from me, but that wouldn't be entirely accurate...."

❋   ❋   ❋

After viewing all her art, Brian moved into the main room. He spotted Joanna in the midst of a horde of well-wishers, and felt a rush of desire and pride. She looked so beautiful in her black dress, so excited and happy, too, as well she should. With a glimmer of recognition, Brian noticed the tall, dark-haired man dressed in a navy-blue Armani suit standing off to her side.

Erik Ruby. Joanna's fiancé.

Brian grabbed a flute of champagne off a tray and took a sip, turning to avoid any chance of eye contact with the man, now that he'd picked him out of the crowd. The champagne was dry and smooth, and no doubt expensive. A range of emotions swept through him, jealousy and envy being the most prominent. The man had that chiseled GQ look that always made him feel inadequate. He fought that, knowing that if looks were all that mattered to Joanna there would never have been anything between them.

He saw some of the guests moving back into the maze and decided to follow them. If there was going to be a confrontation—and he really had no doubt there would be—he wanted to wait until after Joanna unveiled her new piece.

Moments later, surrounded once again by Joanna's art, Brian found himself standing beside the critic he'd spotted earlier. The man studied a series of rock-like pieces, each suspended by a thin, nearly invisible filament. The title, printed on a card mounted to a black wire-framed stand, was *Islands*.

"Interesting piece," Brian said.

The man glanced at him and smiled. "Very," he said. "Are you with the media?"

Brian hesitated. If he said yes, would the man open up to him, or would he be more honest with an outsider? Brian decided to stick to the truth.

"I'm a writer, but I'm not affiliated."

"Ah," the man said, relaxing. "I had my fill of that years ago.

A Note from an Old Acquaintance

Nothing like a steady paycheck, especially when you've got two kids in college." He stuck out his hand. "Jason Forster, *New York Times.*"

Brian shook the man's hand, barely able to contain his excitement. His suggestion to send invitations to the New York media had borne fruit. "Brian Weller. You're a long way from home, Mr. Forster."

"Please, call me Jason. I'm from the area, actually. Grew up in Natick. My wife and I were planning to visit when the invitation showed up. Thought it was a great opportunity to take our little trip on the paper's dime."

"Has it been worth it?" Brian asked.

The critic turned back to the piece they'd both been admiring. "This artist has a real understanding of form and space. You see the way she's suspended the components, each on separate planes? It emphasizes the theme of isolation in three dimensions. Yet the entire effect is one of harmony. To answer your question, however; yes, very much so."

Brian nodded, feeling a genuine respect for the man. He'd always wondered about critics in general, whether they really knew what they were talking about or had excelled in slinging the B.S. in school, parlaying that dubious skill into a cushy career.

"I'm sure the artist will appreciate that very much."

"Do you know her?"

Careful, Weller.

"We've met once or twice at other shows."

The critic nodded and they moved on to another piece. Before either one of them could comment about it, the music cut off and a voice came over the sound system.

"Excuse me everyone, may I have your attention? Please make your way back to the main area for an announcement."

The music came back on and the critic turned to Brian. "What do you suppose that means?"

"I hear she's going to unveil a special piece she created just for this show, supposed to be a stylistic departure."

The critic smiled. "Well, then, let's see what there is to see." He indicated for Brian to lead the way.

❋ ❋ ❋

Ruby watched everyone filter back into the room and waited until the last few stragglers gathered in the loose semi-circle that formed around him and Joanna before raising the wireless microphone back up to his lips.

"Friends, colleagues, students, and members of the press, I want to thank you all for coming from the bottom of my heart. You have no idea how much Joanna and I appreciate your loyalty and your patronage. When I first met this wonderful lady, she was barely twenty and only just testing her artistic wings. I'm proud to say, that in my humble, non-artistic opinion, she's more than ready to leave the nest."

There was sharp applause mixed with a few exclamations of affirmation. Joanna beamed, and Ruby's heart raced.

"So, without further ado, I want to introduce the lady of the moment...Joanna Richman."

The room erupted, and Joanna stepped forward, taking the microphone from her fiancé. She mouthed a "Thank you," faced the crowd and waited for the applause to die down.

"Thank you, everyone," she said, her husky contralto commanding everyone's attention.

"As I try to teach all of my students, an artist's life is not an easy one. You will be constantly called upon to balance the forces of your creative lives with those of your day-to-day existence—always striving to find a way to let your art flourish while making your way in a world that values mediocrity over substance. And when I've taught them all I know, I leave them with one last thought: Never compromise your vision and *never* give up."

"You tell 'em, Teach!" a young voice piped up.

"My favorite critic," Joanna said, pointing out the blushing young man. The crowd laughed and Joanna joined them. When they quieted, she continued.

"I'm so happy and so grateful that you've joined us here tonight. And to commemorate this occasion, I've created a special work of art. It's a departure for me, and comes from a part of me only recently awakened. I hope you see it the same way I do. I—"

Joanna's voice trailed off, her eyes widening in shock. The gathered crowd grew restless, muttering amongst themselves, and Ruby frowned. What the hell was going on? He stepped toward her, his words of comfort dying in his throat. Despite Mosley's warning only moments before, he was still unprepared for what he saw. It was *him*; that bastard Weller was here!

❀ ❀ ❀

Oh, my God, he's here! He's here!

The rest of the words of her speech had flown from her mind the moment her eyes had found Brian in the crowd. He smiled, his eyes shining with pride. He raised the champagne flute he was holding in salute, his lips mouthing the words, "I love you."

Her eyes filled with tears, this time tears of joy. She wanted to run to him, take him in her arms and never let him go.

Suddenly aware of the buzz in the room, Joanna cleared her throat. "Excuse me, I'm just a trifle nervous."

The crowd relaxed, some of them chuckling.

227

"Now...where was I?" she said, cracking a sly grin.

"You were about to whip it out," someone quipped.

The crowd laughed, relaxing more.

"So I was," Joanna said, her smile lighting up the room. She reached for the black cloth. "The title of this piece is, *Communion*."

With a deft yank of her arm, the cloth came away. There was an audible gasp from the crowd. They began applauding and Joanna finally allowed the tears to flow.

❄   ❄   ❄

Brian's heart lurched in his chest when the cloth covering Joanna's new piece was pulled away. He pressed forward with the crowd, one eye on Erik Ruby and the other on the remarkable work she'd created. It stood on a solid four-foot pedestal of varnished mahogany and was a life-sized representation of two hands, a man and a woman's, their fingers intertwined. The detail was exquisite and the effect nothing short of astounding. Even more astounding, the hands were his and Joanna's. It left him breathless.

He wanted to move closer, but the crowd kept him from being able to advance more than a couple of feet. He caught Joanna's eye and nodded his approval. She was crying, but he could tell it was from happiness. She covered her mouth with her hands and nodded back to him.

"You were right," a voice said behind him.

Brian turned to find Jason Forster at his elbow.

"I was?"

"Oh, yes. It's definitely something totally different than the other pieces. And it's terrific. She's a major talent. Please tell your friend that she's going to get very prominent mention in *The Times* this week." The critic winked, patted him on the shoulder, then melted into the crowd. Brian felt a strange mix of emotions. It was obvious he'd never fooled the critic for a moment, but it was just as obvious that Joanna's art had spoken volumes. And the man was deeply impressed.

Coming out of his reverie, Brian looked for Joanna, seeing the crowd once again surrounding her, her fiancé standing at her side. The man smiled and nodded in response to something someone was telling him, but his cold eyes were locked onto Brian, boring into him.

All right, pal, I'm not hiding from you now.

Brian moved through the crowd, gently pushing past people until he'd made his way to where Joanna stood. He was just behind a middle-aged couple gushing over her art. Brian held Ruby's gaze, refusing to look away, refusing to let the man intimidate him.

When Ruby turned to speak to another guest, Brian shifted his attention to Joanna. She looked at him, her eyes shining. "Hello, Brian, it's so nice to see you again. Thank you so much for coming." She held out her hand and Brian took it.

He immediately saw Ruby's eyes flick from their handshake to the new piece on its pedestal nearby, the light of understanding dawning in his eyes. The older man's face flushed anew with anger.

"Erik, this is Brian Weller, Nick Simon's friend."

Joanna's fiancé tore his eyes away from *Communion* and offered his hand. Brian took it. It felt cold and clammy.

"Ah, yes.... Thank you for coming, Mr. Weller," Ruby said, his voice oily smooth. "We're so glad you could find the time."

The man's grip became vise-like. Brian kept his expression neutral and applied his own pressure in return, the two of them fighting a silent battle for supremacy. The barest of frowns crossed Joanna's face and she said, "Erik, why don't you get Mr. Weller another drink. He's out of champagne."

The man turned sharply toward Joanna, looking as if he might offer a stinging rebuke. Instead, he smiled, the pressure on Brian's hand abating. "Certainly, my dear, we wouldn't want our guest to go thirsty, now would we?"

He let go of Brian's hand and marched off into the crowd, headed for the kitchen.

"You look so beautiful tonight," Brian said.

Joanna reached for his hand, caressing it. "Oh, Brian, I can't tell you how sorry I am about how I acted the other night. Can you ever forgive me?"

"There's nothing to forgive, Sweetheart."

Her smile was radiant. "What do you think of *Communion*?"

"It's one of the most beautiful things I've ever seen, and certainly the greatest compliment anyone's ever paid me. I'm humbled."

"And you humble me," she replied. "Every time I look in your eyes. I'm so glad you're here."

For the briefest of moments, there was no one else in the room but the two of them.

"I wouldn't have missed this for anything," he said. "And I've got some good news for you, too." He leaned closer to her. "See that gray-haired gentlemen dressed in black over there by the dessert table?"

Joanna followed his gaze and nodded.

"That is none other than Jason Forster...from *The New York Times*."

"You're kidding! My God, you were right."

Brian grinned, enjoying the moment. "But that's not all. We had an interesting conversation, especially after you unveiled *Communion*."

She gave him a puzzled look.

"Sweetheart, he all but told me he's going to give you a rave review. He said for me to tell you to expect 'very prominent mention this week.'"

Joanna's hand flew to her mouth. "Brian, Jason Forster's their head critic. He only reviews the names. Do you know what this means?" She was trembling.

Brian nodded, squeezing her hand. "Means you're a name now, too."

"Oh, my God! I can't believe this. I don't know what I would have done without your help; you've been so wonderful."

"I'm glad you feel that way, but it's your talent, not mine. You did it."

She started to reply, when Brian spotted Erik Ruby returning with a flute of champagne.

I wonder if I should worry about drinking it.

"You're fiancé's coming back. And he knows."

"What? How?"

"If you'd seen the look on his face when he saw us shake hands...."

She gasped. "*Communion.*"

"Right."

Brian let go of her hand and took a step back, as Ruby rejoined them. He handed Brian the champagne, his eyes once again darting to *Communion* before coming to rest back on him.

"So, Mr...uh, Weller, is it?"

"That's right."

"What is it you do? Are you with the press?"

"Me? No, I'm a filmmaker and a novelist."

He caught Joanna out of the corner of his eye signaling him to be careful. She then let herself be led off by someone she knew.

"Filmmaker, eh? That must be a hard business," Ruby said.

"It has its moments."

"I imagine it does. I can also imagine that it's feast or famine—a bit like the hardware business. One day everything's fine and the next...."

Brian felt a crawling sensation at the base of his spine. "We've learned to roll with the punches, Mr. Ruby."

"Please, my father was Mr. Ruby."

"Erik, then."

"Still, one never knows if one might be out on the street from one day to the next. Am I right?"

Ruby's smile reached every part of his face, except his eyes.

The crawling sensation flashed into a white-hot anger Brian barely managed to hold in check. Somehow Ruby knew about his father's deal. What else did he know? And did he have something to do with that deal going bad? He didn't see how, but just the same, his father's words echoed in his mind:

"...you never know what a man will do when it comes to his woman."

"I'm sure we'll be just fine, Erik. As I said, my partner and I roll with the punches." Now it was his turn. "And by the way, please congratulate Ms. Richman on her show and especially this new work. It's a masterpiece. One can tell it comes from a very special place in her heart."

Ruby glared at him. "Yes, I'm sure it is a special place, but Joanna is also a practical woman. She knows her limits."

"Really? I don't think she has any limits, not where her talent is concerned, anyway. As for the rest of her life, well, needs can change...."

"Yes, indeed they can."

It was time for Brian to leave. There was no more point to this verbal jousting. "Please tell Ms. Richman that I had a wonderful time and that I wish her well with her career."

"Going so soon?"

"Unfortunately, yes. I have an early edit session tomorrow."

"Well, it was very illuminating to meet you, Brian. I'm sure we'll be seeing each other soon."

Brian ignored the veiled threat and retraced his way back through the maze, but not before he caught Joanna's eye. She nodded her understanding and winked at him, the hint of a smile gracing her lips.

Outside, he handed over his ticket to the valet and waited for his car, his thoughts on Joanna's fiancé. The next move was Ruby's. He only hoped that whatever happened would not cause Joanna any pain. That he knew he could not bear.

❋　❋　❋

Ruby watched the silent exchange between Joanna and Weller, his temper seething. His patience was at an end. When the younger man left, he made his way into the studio's bedroom, and spoke into the microphone on his wrist. "Did you hear any of that, Mosley?"

"Yes, sir, I did. Over."

"Good. I want you to bring him to my office at nine."

"What if he refuses?"

"I don't think he will." Ruby filled Mosley in on the plan he'd been formulating and the black man chuckled.

"I'll have him there, Mr. Ruby. No problem. Over."

Ruby lowered his arm, shot his cuffs and gave a quick check to his surroundings. No one had heard a word. Making his way out to the main room, he rejoined Joanna, who was holding court with a few of her friends, students and colleagues from the school. He leaned close to her.

"Something's come up. I'm going to have to go to the office in a little bit. I shouldn't be too late."

"That's okay," she said, nodding. "I can handle the cleanup here. Thanks for letting me know."

Ruby swallowed his anger, giving her a loving look. It was only the thought of what was to come when he had Brian Weller in front of him once again that kept him from losing it completely. He'd have that pleasure in about an hour and a half. He couldn't wait.

23

BRIAN PULLED THE CELICA into the Danker & Donohue garage and climbed out, leaving the car running. The attendant loped over and climbed in, giving him the high sign.

"Take it easy, Jimmy," Brian said.

The attendant cracked a snaggle-toothed grin. "Sure thing, Brian. And any time you want your old job back, you just let us know. The boys miss you."

"You never know," Brian said, shooting him a salute.

It was a running joke between the two of them. For nearly a year, not long after he and Bob had started their company, Brian had moonlighted as the night manager at the garage. He didn't miss the late nights, but at least while he'd worked there they'd let him park for free, and the job had given him the chance to do some writing when things slowed up in the wee hours.

Out on Newbury, Brian ducked into Bauer Wines and bought his usual six-pack of Samuel Adams, its heft a familiar comfort. He joked with Howie for a few minutes then headed out again, fighting the urge to cross the street and check the office, knowing it was fine. It was his nerves that were not. All the way home, he kept thinking of his conversation with Ruby, and what the man's veiled words really meant.

Maybe I'm just jumping to conclusions. Yeah, and maybe pigs could fly.

Ruby knew something he shouldn't and that was all there was to it. He shook his head and picked up his pace. The temperature had dropped another few degrees, and the wind cut through his jacket, chilling him.

He paused at the light at Fairfield and Beacon and dug for his keys. Freeing them from the confines of his pocket, he stepped off the curb and froze. A red Ferrari 328 sat idling next to the side entrance of his building, white plumes of exhaust billowing from the twin pipes. Leaning against the car, dressed in an immaculate dark-blue suit was the same black man he'd seen guarding the door to Joanna's building. The man regarded him coolly, inclining his head in a casual greeting.

Brian crossed the street and approached, his nerves tingling.

"Good evening, Mr. Weller," the black man said. "I trust you enjoyed Ms. Richman's show."

"Ruby send you to ask me that?" Brian said, placing his key in the side door lock.

"Mr. Ruby is concerned."

Brian pulled the key from the lock and turned. The black man wasn't smiling now. "Oh, really? And why would he be concerned about little old me?"

"I think you know, but let's just say family ties are important to him, just as I'm sure they're important to you."

Brian's patience ended. "You know, Mr...."

"Mosley. Cary Mosley."

"Right. It's cold out here and I've had a long day. Tell your boss he should mind his own business."

"That's just what he's doing, Mr. Weller...."

I walked right into that one, didn't I, Brian thought. "Okay, what does he want?"

"I'm not at liberty to say. However, he would like to see you in his office at your earliest convenience."

"Now?"

The black man remained silent, his eyes boring into him. Brian felt tendrils of fear creeping up his back. Mosley seemed to sense his unease and cracked an easy grin. "Don't worry, Mr. Weller, after you hear what Mr. Ruby has to say, I'll be bringing you back here—safe and sound. Promise." He held up his hand in a Boy Scout salute.

"What if I still say no thanks?"

"That's your prerogative. I'll leave and the matter remains unresolved."

"And just how does your boss expect to 'resolve' it?"

"I'm not at liberty to say."

A part of him wanted to send Ruby's errand-boy packing, while another part—the curious writer—had an overwhelming desire to know what the older man had in mind. It would probably be a complete waste of time, but there was no way he could go inside now and put it out of his mind. Not where Joanna was concerned.

The smile was back on the black man's face, as if Mosley already knew his decision.

Brian shook his head, resigned. "All right. Let's go."

Mosley held open the door and Brian climbed into the Italian car, jarring his back when he dropped into a bucket seat lower down than his body expected. He placed his six-pack of Samuel Adams on the floor between his feet and belted himself in. Looking out the windshield, it felt as if he were seated right on the asphalt. Mosley walked around to the driver's side and climbed in. A moment later, they shot out onto Beacon, then hung a left on Gloucester, the Ferrari tearing through the turns without even screeching the tires.

Brian watched Mosley shift gears with an effortless ease and felt a pang of envy. "The investigation business must be lucrative," Brian said. "That is the reason Ruby hired you, isn't it?"

Mosley grinned. "I'm not at—"

"—liberty to say, I know." Brian sighed. "What *can* you say?"

The black man's smile disappeared. "That after tonight both yours and Mr. Ruby's problems will be solved."

"But I don't have a problem," Brian said.

"We all have problems, Mr. Weller."

Mosley was silent for the rest of the short ride to Newbury Street. They parked in the alley behind Ruby's brownstone and took the cramped elevator to the top floor. Brian's stomach fluttered, betraying his nervousness. He squared his jaw, refusing to show any sign of it to Mosley.

When the elevator door opened, the black man led the way. Brian was impressed with the space. It took up most of the top floor with a large plate-glass window affording a stunning view of Newbury Street. The furnishings were sparse and modern looking, which contrasted well with the otherwise Victorian appointments: high ceilings and wide, ornate moulding and mahogany wainscoting. A fireplace was set in one wall. He looked above it, his heart nearly stopping. There, blown up to life size, hung the picture of Joanna, the one they'd pulled from her invitation.

"Have a seat," the black man said, indicating a leather armchair facing the steel and glass desk. Brian took one more look around then sat down. The chair, butter soft, gave under his weight with a gentle wheeze, the odor of leather and saddle soap reaching his nostrils.

"When's your boss arriving?" Brian asked.

"Oh, he'll be here in good time, Mr. Weller. In the meantime, would you like a drink?" Mosley indicated the well-stocked wet bar near the plate-glass window.

"And I thought this was B.Y.O.B.," Brian said, pulling out one of the Samuel Adams. "Want one?"

"Not while I'm working, I'm afraid."

"Ah, too bad." Brian twisted off the cap and took a long draw, making a show of really appreciating the hops-laden brew. It was all a mask to cover the deep-seated unease gnawing at his guts.

Still, the smooth, cool liquid seemed to calm him and clear his head a bit. He glanced at the clock on the desk, a modernistic Lucite LCD affair. Even though the numbers were reversed, he could tell it was nearly 9:00.

The elevator began to whine, and Brian's body tensed.

Calm down, Weller.

A few moments later Ruby strolled into the room, carrying a manila folder, looking relaxed and on top of the world. Brian hated him more at that moment than he'd ever hated anyone in his life.

The older man took a seat in the swivel chair behind the desk and regarded Brian for a long, silent moment, before turning to Mosley.

"Pour me a Macallan, won't you, Mr. Mosley?"

The black man complied, handing the tumbler of Scotch to Ruby, who sipped it and sighed, his eyes moving to gaze at Joanna's picture. Brian couldn't help stealing glances of his own. Ruby smiled.

"Quite a shot, isn't it? Draws your eye right to it. I can't tell you how long it took to get it right. Hours. By the time we were done Joanna wanted to kill me, but—as you can see—it was worth it."

Brian sat up straighter in the chair. "The problem is, Ruby, you can't see it for what it is. She's nothing like that picture."

"And you would know her better than I?"

Ruby swiveled in the chair and stared up at the photo. "When I first saw her, she was barely out of her teens, yet I could see the woman she was becoming. Before that day I was totally consumed by my ambition. All I could think about was the next deal and the money and power it would bring. But from the moment I laid eyes on her, I realized my ambition meant nothing without her. All I had accomplished up to that moment turned to ashes."

Brian stared past Ruby, focusing on Joanna's face. He understood that feeling all too well. Almost from the moment he'd met Joanna, he found himself drawing inspiration from her.

Ruby turned from the picture, his expression hardening. "And then you show up," he said. "I could tell something was different about her from that first night at the party. There was a sparkle in her eyes that was never there for me. I wanted to deny the obvious, but I couldn't. So, I hired Mr. Mosley to watch the two of you."

Brian knuckles turned white on the beer bottle. "I figured as much."

"You didn't think I was just going to let her go her merry way, did you?"

"She's her own person, Ruby, not an extension of you. You don't *own* her."

Ruby stood, a bemused expression on his chiseled face. Rounding the desk, he reached out and straightened Joanna's picture with a self-satisfied nod. He then took the chair next to Brian, leaning toward him like a close friend offering secrets. Brian caught a whiff of his Aramis cologne.

"Let me be honest with you, Mr. Weller," he said, his eyes, losing their hard, cunning edge, his voice growing softer. "I know how you feel about her, I really do. She does something to a man's soul. You've felt it, too; and she's not even aware of it. Do you realize that? She has no earthly idea of the effect she has on men like you and me, which is precisely what makes her so devastating.

"I saw how she affected Nick, and he's always believed that I don't know about that. But I do know. I saw it in his eyes. I saw *her* in his eyes. I see her in your eyes, too, Mr. Weller." He paused, his voice taking on an edge. "Joanna and I have a destiny to fulfill, and I will never allow you nor anyone else to alter it."

"What makes you think she wants to stay with you?"

"And what makes you think she wants to live in squalor?"

Faced with the older man's unbridled arrogance, Brian fought to keep his cool. "What do you want, then? You want me to stay away from her?"

"Do you really believe you can?" Ruby asked, the corners of his mouth curling in a knowing smile.

Ruby was right, damn him. Brian looked toward Mosley, whose expression was that of a man who'd blundered into the wrong hotel room. "How about pouring me some of what your boss is drinking?" he asked.

Ruby nodded and Mosley went to the bar, poured the Macallan and handed the tumbler to Brian. He took a sip, the fiery liquid burning down to his stomach.

"So, what's the point of bringing me here?"

Ruby reached for the folder and brought it onto his lap. It was thick with various forms and papers. "As I said, I had Mr. Mosley watching you and Joanna. I also had him look into your background. I know everything there is to know about you, Mr. Weller, and then some." Ruby glanced at Mosley, who offered a proud smile. "Because of that, I also know about the situation with your father."

"Which is none of your business," Brian said, his head beginning to throb from the whiskey.

241

"That is going to change."

"What's that supposed to mean?"

"What did your father tell you?" Ruby said, ignoring the question.

"That things are tough and his deal fell through." Brian hated even admitting that much, but if Ruby was telling the truth, he wasn't revealing anything the older man didn't already know.

"I'm sure he didn't want to worry you, but the truth is much worse. He owes hundreds of thousands to three separate banking institutions, and they are all *this* close," Ruby held his index finger and thumb about half an inch apart, "...to foreclosing. Your father's a nice, decent man, Mr. Weller, and he's worked hard all his life. All he's wanted to do is provide a future for his family."

It was just like his Dad to soft-pedal the worst of things. It was one of his only faults. And hearing the unvarnished truth of the situation made Brian heartsick. He drained the rest of the whiskey and set the empty tumbler on Ruby's desk. "So, why tell me all this?"

"Because I envy you."

In spite of the headache, Brian frowned. "You envy *me*? Why?"

"Because my father was a vain and selfish man whose philosophy of fatherhood extended to making sure the boarding schools I attended, from the age of seven, were well endowed. But that's not why you're here."

Here it comes, Weller.

"I'm a businessman, first and foremost, so I'm going to put this in concrete terms, though Joanna deserves better. I'm willing to pay down your father's debts. *All* of them. He'll then be free to sell the store, or keep it and run it as long as he's able. That's up to him, but this sordid business with Joanna ends tonight."

Brian's anger boiled over. "So, you think you can just buy me off? Is that it? That everyone has their price?"

"Everyone does, Mr. Weller, but some are bought more cheaply than others."

"You're right about one thing, Joanna *does* deserve better."

Ruby's jaw clenched, and the coldness returned to his eyes. "I'll ignore that, for the moment." He reached into the folder, brought out a sheaf of papers and handed them to Brian. "This is a deal memo outlining our agreement. If all the points meet with your approval, sign it, and I'll have my attorneys draw up the final papers for your signature."

Brian stared at the papers, wanting to tear them to shreds. "You just expect me to sign this?"

"Sign it and help your father."

"And abandon Joanna."

"SHE'S NOT YOURS TO ABANDON!" Ruby shouted, his face reddening. Mosley stood, looking wary, and Ruby waved him back. "I'm sorry, Mr. Weller. As you can see, I'm on the edge, here. Let me add some incentives for you to think about. If you refuse this deal, the gloves will be off. I'm already negotiating with your father's banks. I'll put your parents on the streets, Mr. Weller; don't even think that I won't.

"You also will never have another private moment with Joanna ever again. I'll see to that. I'm selling her building and moving her studio to our home.

"Finally, if you foolishly persist, I've made overtures to your landlord about buying 342 Newbury Street. I assure you, he *will* sell. Where will you and your partner go, when I pull your lease?"

"You can't do that!"

"I've done it before...."

It was all Brian could do to keep from wrapping his hands around this bastard's neck. He forced himself to remain outwardly calm.

"How does it feel walking a tightrope, Ruby?"

The other man frowned.

"How does it feel knowing you have to watch yourself every moment lest the mask slip from your true face?"

Sadness crept into Ruby's eyes for a brief moment, replaced almost instantly by the familiar piercing glitter. "A lot better than knowing you've sacrificed your father's love and security for another man's fiancée," he replied.

Brian collapsed back into the leather chair, fighting back the emotions threatening to overwhelm him. He picked up the papers. "What else?"

"You're going to call Joanna now, while she's still at the studio, and tell her you're breaking it off. And then you'll leave town, for good. I promise you I'll leave your partner alone, whether I purchase the building, or not."

Brian's head throbbed, but that pain was nothing compared to the agony caused by his utter powerlessness, and the prospect of losing Joanna forever. But what choice did he have? His father needed the help Ruby was offering, help he wouldn't get from anyone else, and Ruby knew that.

Brian sighed. "I can't leave right away, I've got loose ends to tie up, and not the least of which is getting Bob to buy me out. It's not something we were planning on."

Ruby nodded. "You'll have thirty days. That's time enough to settle your affairs. I will also put my end of things in motion." He pointed a manicured finger at Brian. "One last thing. You are to have no contact with Joanna, whatsoever. If she calls you, you hang up. If she writes you letters, you're to leave them unanswered. If she tries to see you at your office or apartment, you turn her away. Is that understood?"

Brian nodded, looking away to hide his rage and hopelessness.

Ruby turned to Mosley. "Bring him the cordless phone," he said, pointing across the room toward the wet bar. The black man rose to his feet, grabbed the phone off its cradle and handed it to Brian.

It felt like a weapon in his hand.

"I assume you know the number well enough," Ruby said.

Brian stared at Joanna's picture one last time, trying to find a way out—any way that would not mean disaster.

I hope you'll forgive me someday, Sweetheart. Lord knows I don't know if I'll ever forgive myself.

Brian lifted the phone, his hands shaking. He dialed the number that was now tattooed across his heart. Ruby picked up the extension and for a fleeting moment Brian was ready to throw it all to the wind and tell him to go to the devil—the deal was off—but there was too much at stake. He cleared his throat and swallowed the bile backing up from his stomach.

The phone rang half a dozen times before it was picked up.

"Hello?"

In the background Brian heard the sounds of people cleaning up after the show, clinking glassware, babbling voices and laughter.

"Hello, hello, anyone there?"

Ruby's eyes narrowed and he mouthed, "Do it—now!"

"Hi," Brian managed to choke out.

The sound of his voice had an immediate effect.

"Hi, Sweetie!" Joanna giggled. "You'll have to excuse me, but I think I've had just a little bit too much champagne," she giggled again, "and I'm feeling rather proud of myself. I'm so sorry you couldn't stay, Brian. I miss you so much; you know that?

"And wasn't everything wonderful tonight? My God, I'm still walking on clouds. Everyone was just gushing about my art, especially *Communion*. This show's been everything I've ever dreamed about, and I owe it all to you and your brilliant idea. I still can't believe *The New York Times* came, too! I'm giddy and scared to death all at the same time." She paused, catching her breath. "And I'm talking too much, too, aren't I? I'm not letting my sweet writer get a word in edge-wise."

"You deserve it, Joanna...all of it."

She was silent for a moment. "Something's wrong, isn't it?" she said, her voice taking on a tone of concern mixed with apprehension.

"Yeah...."

Ruby glowered at him.

"What is it, my love? Whatever it is, we can weather it. Together. I'm going to leave him, Brian. I decided that tonight. It's over."

Brian squeezed his eyes shut, biting his lips, a lone tear escaping from the corner of his left eye. The sound of Ruby's hand slapping the chair's armrest, made him open them. The man was trembling with rage.

Hope you have a heart attack, you bas—

"Brian, are you there? Please tell me what's wrong."

"Uhh, I don't know how to say this...."

"What?"

"We need to stop seeing each other, Joanna."

There was stunned silence on the other end of the line. And when she finally spoke, Brian heard the quaver in her voice. It was a knife through his heart. "What? W—what are you saying?"

"You need to give your marriage a chance."

"I don't *want* to marry him! I want to marry *you!*" She paused and then she asked the question he was dreading. "Do you love me, Brian? Tell me that, at least."

"It was unfair of me to come between you and your—"

"Please tell me the truth, Brian," she repeated, her voice cracking.

Brian shook his head. Nothing was worth this. Nothing! He beat the arm of the chair with his fist.

"Tell me, please. You owe me that much. I just need to know if you—if you really love me." The catch in her voice made him want to die.

God, I can't say it!

"No.... I—I don't," he said.

"I don't believe you!" she cried. "How can you say that to me? How can you say that after all that's happened between us, after all we've shared? Why are you doing this?"

"I'm leaving town, I just didn't think it was fair to lead you on anymore."

She was openly sobbing now. "Why are you doing this?"

He bit his finger, drawing blood. "I—I'm sorry, Joanna, for everything."

"BRIANNNN!"

He pushed the talk button ending the call then threw the phone into the fireplace, shattering it.

Her final scream had come through Ruby's extension. The older man gently replaced the phone onto its cradle then clapped his hands together in a slow, measured applause. "Bravo, Mr. Weller, bravo. I especially loved the part about needing to give our marriage a chance. You're a far more talented writer than I ever gave you credit for."

Brian shot to his feet, jabbing a finger in Ruby's direction. "You keep your word! You keep it, or so help me I'll—"

Ruby raised his hand, cutting him off. "I have a lot invested in Joanna, Mr. Weller. Rest assured I'll take care of my end, as long as you take care of yours." He rose to his feet. "And, now it's time for me to be the caring husband-to-be, anointing her wounds and giving her much needed comfort. Soon, she'll come to understand that I have her best interests at heart. I always have."

Brian's eyes bored into Ruby's. "Just so you don't fool yourself, Ruby. You don't understand her, you never have. To you, she's some precious jewel to hoard and hide from prying eyes, something only for your enjoyment. But she's a living, breathing intelligent woman, filled with complications and passions you can't control. Someday she'll realize what you truly are...and what you've done. It may not be today, or tomorrow, but someday that mask is going to slip."

Ruby met his gaze, the sadness returning. "You're probably right, Mr. Weller. The only solace I can take away from all this is that it won't be because of you."

❀　❀　❀

Joanna sat on the floor, her hand still on the phone, wanting it to ring, praying for it to ring. Tears coursed down her face, smearing her makeup, not that she cared. She'd tried to call him back, first at his home, then at his office. She'd left messages in both places, pleading for him to call her. If he hadn't been in either of those places, from where had he been calling? Or was he just refusing to pick up the phone? The thought of that made her heart ache so much she doubled over.

"No, no, no," she whimpered.

The caterer and her crew had given her wide berth, uncomfortable in seeing Joanna go from being on top of the world to the depths of despair. She looked up, squinting through the tears clouding her eyes.

Where had they gone?

Her thoughts boomeranged back to Brian. Something was bothering him, she could tell from the moment he'd spoken. What could it be that was so bad he would break off their relationship and not tell

A Note from an Old Acquaintance

her the reason? Could it be that he'd been using her all along and had started feeling guilty?

No, it couldn't be that. She refused to believe that.

But the thought persisted, nonetheless, making her remember the first boy she'd loved at twelve, how he'd kissed her and bragged about it to every boy in school. She'd wanted to die, had stayed home for three days, refusing to leave her room.

Oh, Brian, you couldn't be like him! You're too sensitive and caring for that. Oh, God, she loved him.

And now...she had nothing.

Nothing, except her art.

She walked aimlessly through her maze looking at each piece, trying to remember what it was that had inspired her to create it. Surely they were worthy inspirations. But every piece now drew a blank. Back in the main room, she approached *Communion*, her lips quivering as the tears threatened to flow anew. She caressed it, feeling every bump and vein in Brian's hand. She knew it so well, as well as her own.

"Oh, my sweet writer, why did you do this?"

She didn't want to believe the love he'd professed was a lie. All a lie. It couldn't be true! But when she'd pressed the point, when she'd begged him to tell her the truth, he'd said: *"No...I don't."*

Joanna's hand shook, first from the pain in her heart and then from blind, overpowering rage.

"NO!" she cried, pushing over the mahogany pedestal supporting *Communion*. The artwork toppled to the floor, shattering into several pieces.

Joanna stood there, trembling in shock, the anger forgotten as a wave of remorse overwhelmed her. This was all she had left of Brian, of the love she was sure he'd felt. All that was left, and now it lay shattered like the pieces of her heart.

She dropped to her knees, fumbling to put the pieces back togeth-er, tears dropping to the polished wooden floor like rain.

They wouldn't go back together!

There were too many fragments.

And then the hopelessness of it all raced through her body and she threw back her head and screamed.

"NOOOOOOOO!"

Her cries of agony echoed throughout the deserted building, throughout all the cleaned and painted floors now darkened and awaiting the return of the dust.

24

As HE'D PROMISED, MOSLEY dropped Brian at his front door just after 10:00, offering a few useless platitudes before roaring off in his Ferrari. Brian didn't hear a word the man said, as the evening's events kept running through his brain in a continuous loop. He wanted to turn them off, at least for a while. In his present state, however, sleep would be impossible; but he still had the remainder of his six-pack of beer. They were warm, but he didn't care.

Once inside his apartment, he sat on the carpeted floor with the lights off, his back against the door, and opened one beer after another, draining them. He just wanted to be stinking drunk. Maybe then everything would feel right.

Because none of it did.

With just three simple words, he'd destroyed the most important person in his life, traded her love for his father's financial security. At least he hoped he had. Brian squeezed his eyes shut, tears streaming down his cheeks. Ruby had known that Brian would never let his father and mother suffer the horrors and indignities of destitution, not when saving them was attainable by a mere stroke of the pen. It was a Hobson's choice of the highest order.

And the price?

"Please forgive me, Joanna...."

He was leaving her with a man who'd professed to love her, bared his soul in a way few men would. Yet Brian doubted Ruby really knew the true meaning of the word, and he would never understand her in the way Brian did, for it was a connection that went far beyond the needs of the flesh.

There had to be a way to put all this right, but how? Would Ruby really do the things he'd threatened if Brian reneged? Of course he would. Brian had no doubt. Everything he'd threatened was perfectly legal and utterly devastating. Yet, as much as Brian despised the man, he also believed Ruby would make good on his end of the deal. A businessman to the end.

His dad would have a thing or two to say about a man like Ruby. Dad....

Brian went to the phone intending to call him then noticed the blinking light on his answering machine.

Joanna.

It had to be.

He eased himself onto the loveseat next to the answering machine and pressed the PLAY button, steeling himself. The tape rewound, taking far longer than usual. The machine clicked to a stop then began to play. At first, there was nothing but the hiss of the tape. Then Joanna began to speak. Her voice sounded as velvety soft as it always did, but Brian could hear the anguish behind the words.

"Brian? Are you there? If you are, please pick up.... I'm going to try you at the office, but if you get this message first, please call me back." She paused a moment, then sighed. "I don't know what happened tonight to make you say what you did, but I wish you would trust me enough to let me help you.

A Note from an Old Acquaintance

"I meant what I said about leaving Erik. He's been good to me, but he doesn't understand; he doesn't have the soul of an artist, as you do.... I love you, Brian, with all of my heart, and I want to spend the rest of my life with you. Please know that. And please also know that there's nothing on this earth that is so bad that you can't tell me what it is. You're worth more to me than anything, even my art.

"In the short time we've known each other I've really come to believe that everyone has a soul mate, but so many people go through life never finding theirs. But I found you. You've touched the very core of me. You're my soul mate, Brian, and you always will be. Please, please, please call me back and *talk* to me. I love you...."

Brian went to hit the erase button. His finger hovered over it, but he couldn't bring himself to press it. Couldn't destroy the only tangible thing he had left from her. And even if he did, he knew that he'd never be able to erase her words from his mind or his heart.

Soul mates.

As clichéd and overused as that term had become in the culture at large, Brian believed in it. He also believed Joanna was right about the two of them. They *were* soul mates. But it didn't change the facts, didn't change what he'd agreed to do.

Brian picked up the phone and dialed his parent's number. It was late, but not too late.

"Hello?"

"Dad?"

"Hey, Big Guy. How are you?"

Brian fought back a wave of sadness, his eyes tearing up again. "I'm still in one piece, I think."

There was a brief silence on the line. "You okay, Brian?"

"You just called me 'Big Guy.' You remember when you started calling me that?"

253

The older man chuckled. "Sure do. You were about six years old and your mother and I had called you 'Little Guy' since you were toddling around in your diapers. You got real angry that day, stomping your little foot, saying: 'I'm NOT a little guy. I'm a Big Guy!' And except for a few slips of the tongue, we've called you Big Guy ever since."

The memory of his younger self, coupled with all that had happened that evening, brought his wall of self-control crashing down. "I'm not feeling so big right now, Dad."

"Hey, hey, now, what's happened?"

"I'm not sure if I can tell you, or even if I should."

"It's your lady friend. Am I right?"

"Yeah...."

"You can tell me anything, you know that."

Brian sighed. "Someone very dear to me said the same thing tonight. And I betrayed her. I told her I didn't love her...and I do...more than I can say...."

"Take a minute and catch your breath. And then I want you to tell me everything. Okay?"

"Okay."

"Your mother's upstairs asleep, so it's just the two of us, man to man."

"Thanks, Dad."

"You kidding? That's what dads are for. Someday you'll be in my spot, God willing, and then you'll know."

Brian took a deep breath and told his father everything that had happened since meeting Joanna, ending with what had occurred that night. When he finished, the older man remained silent for a moment.

"Son, I won't tell you what you did was right or wrong, because I know no matter what I say you're going to beat yourself up over this for a long time, maybe the rest of your life. But that man is evil for making you do that. And because of what he's done, I'm not going to accept his money."

Brian sat up straight, suddenly sober. "You *have* to take it, Dad! If I back out of this, he'll ruin us all."

"All the more reason, I should refuse. There comes a time, son, when a man's got to take a stand."

Panic flashed through Brian. He fought it, forcing his voice to remain steady. "Is that what you're going to tell Mom when the banks foreclose and they take your business and your home? This is a way out, for the both of you. Let me at least have this. If I can't have Joanna, at least let me help the two of you."

The old man was silent again, for longer this time. "You think he'll really come through? Been let down a lot, lately."

"If you knew Joanna the way I do, you'd know the answer to that."

The old man sighed. "Truth is, that man's going to do what he's going to do, regardless. I'm sure the banks will be only too happy to take his money, even if I jump up and down and hold my breath 'til my face turns blue. And if he doesn't, we're no worse off than we were. I'm sorry, Brian," he said, his voice choking with emotion. "Sorry, for you and your lady, and for not trusting you with the truth."

"That's okay, Dad."

"No, it's not, but I'm proud of you. Someday your Joanna will find out what you've done and she'll love you all the more for it."

"You don't know how much I need to believe that."

"Believe it, Son. And hold it close to your heart."

"Could you use some help in the store? I think I'm going to need a job."

"What, you suddenly get a hankering for the smell of machine oil and fertilizer?"

Brian laughed. "I don't know if I'd put it quite that way."

"Well, you're the writer in the family."

"And I don't know if I'll ever write another word."

"Sure you will. I know you. You were scribbling stories and shoving them into our hands when you were ten."

Brian grinned. "Sorry about that."

"Sorry for what? Most of them were pretty darn good. And you've only gotten better. Your time will come."

"Maybe, but even if Ruby wasn't making me leave, I need to get away from here. Everything about this town, every brick and stone, reminds me of her. And if I stay, I won't be able to stay away from her."

"I know what you're going through. Believe me. You want to come and set with us a spell, you know your mother and I will be glad to have you. And there's a few stories I can tell you during those lazy afternoons when the store's empty that might teach you a thing or two."

Brian chuckled. "My dad the sage."

"Just because I'm old doesn't mean I haven't lived."

"I know...."

"Not yet, you don't. But you will. And one more thing. You may not be with her, but she'll always be with you, in your heart. Use that, Son, use it and create the kind of art she'd be proud of. I know you can do it."

"I appreciate that, even if I don't quite believe it right now. Anyway, I'll let you know my flight info as soon as I make the reservations."

"What about your car?"

"I'll either store it or sell it, along with the stuff in my apartment. That old jalopy's not getting any younger."

"Neither are the rest of us," his father said.

"It'll be good to see the both of you."

"The pleasure's all ours, Big Guy. Love you."

"Love you, too."

Brian hung up the phone and smiled. "You really are a sage, Dad."

❀   ❀   ❀

Despite their "agreement," Brian kept seeing Mosley everywhere he went: when he left his apartment in the morning, watching the office from across the street, or sitting at a nearby table in the restaurant where he was having lunch or dinner. After a week of this Brian had had enough. He called Ruby, not at all surprised that the man took his call immediately.

"Mr. Weller, to what do I owe the pleasure?"

His tone was light-hearted, smug. Brian resisted the urge to smash the phone.

"I want you to call off your guy," Brian said.

"Ah, well, Mr. Mosley is simply looking after my interests. He's funny that way."

"Yeah? Well, I'm not laughing. You want me gone in three weeks, you'd better tell him to back off."

"Have you broken the news to your partner?"

Brian's mouth turned into a tight line. "I'm doing that today, as soon as he gets back from his shoot."

"Do that. We wouldn't want all this to be last-minute." He paused for a moment. "Oh, by the way, Joanna's doing fine, getting right back to her routine. Just thought you might be concerned."

Brian's temper turned from a simmer to a low boil. He held himself back, not wanting to give the older man one ounce of satisfaction.

"Believe it or not, Ruby, I'm glad to hear that. She means more to me than you'll ever know."

The older man was silent for a moment. "I actually do believe you, Mr. Weller."

"Just tell Mosley to go and find something else to do. All right?"

"Very well, Mr. Weller, just be aware that the clock is ticking...."

Brian spent the rest of the day negotiating a long-term storage deal with Danker & Donohue for his Celica. He didn't want the hassle of trying to sell it just now and depending upon where he ended up settling, he might need it.

He also called his landlord.

The man was less than thrilled to learn that Brian was leaving with the lease period only half over, but was mollified somewhat when told that Brian would undertake the job of subletting it. It was one more task added to a list that kept getting longer and longer.

Then there was Bob.

He arrived back at the office at 4:00, pounding up the stairs in a frenzy of last-minute details from the shoot that day. Brian did his best to quiet the butterflies in his stomach, cornering Bob in the conference room. To his credit, his partner took the news well. Brian didn't want to tell Bob the truth, so he told his partner that his father was ill and needed help with his business. It was a lie, but a plausible one.

Over the next three weeks, he never heard another word from Joanna. A part of him was deeply hurt that she'd given up so easily; while another part was relieved she hadn't shown up at the office or his apartment, something he would have done.

As it was, he'd been a nervous wreck every time the phone rang, either at home or the office. He'd started screening his calls, just in case, hating himself, but he couldn't take the chance. He knew his heart too well. If he'd seen or spoken with Joanna, he would have broken down, told her everything, and then God only knew what would've happened.

Perhaps, as Ruby had said, she was doing fine. Conceivably he'd played the part of the caring fiancé so well that she'd already put Brian behind her. Written him off. He didn't want to believe that, but her silence spoke volumes.

By April fifteenth, all his preparations were completed and he sat on the front stoop waiting for his ride to the airport with only his suitcase and his guitar. Not much to show for the seven years he'd lived in Boston since starting college.

He spotted Bob's Honda approaching from down the block and met him at the curb. Bob waved and popped the trunk. Brian wasted no time putting in his luggage and slamming it closed. He turned, and gave 334 Beacon one last look. He'd miss this place. So much had happened there, so many words written—and two hearts broken.

Shaking his head, he climbed into the car and Bob pulled away from the curb, taking the left at Gloucester and then another at Marlborough. Soon they were on Storrow Drive, braving the mid-afternoon crush of traffic.

"You going to be okay?" Bob asked.

Brian turned from the window where he'd been reading the sign advertising the adjacent apartment complex:

IF YOU LIVED HERE YOU'D BE HOME NOW.

"I'm fine. Looking forward to seeing my folks. Been awhile."

"You give them my best. And please tell your dad that I'm pulling for him. I always enjoyed his company."

Brian nodded, feeling like a heel. He'd hated telling that lie. But that one paled in comparison to the one he'd told Joanna.

"He'll appreciate that. He's always had a tremendous respect for you."

Bob smiled and nodded. "Thanks for telling me that." Bob slapped the steering wheel, shaking his head. "Damn, I almost forgot."

"What?" Brian said, frowning.

"Someone called the office looking for you yesterday. Someone named Joanna."

Every hair on Brian's body stood up. "What? What did she say?"

"She wanted to know if you'd left town yet. I told her you were flying out today. She thanked me and hung up."

"That was all?"

"Yeah, she definitely seemed agitated."

Brian sat back in the seat, a wave of emotions racing through him: joy that Ruby had lied and she'd not simply given up, and fear. Fear for his parents, for himself...and for Joanna.

"She's the one you met at Nick's party, isn't she? The curly redhead Debbie was so high on?"

"Yeah."

"She seems like a sweet lady."

"Sweet is an inadequate word for her."

Bob gave his friend a look and returned his attention to the road. They were silent for the rest of the ride to Logan.

At the Delta terminal, Bob threw the car into park, ignoring the disapproving glare of the State Trooper eyeing the flow of traffic. He fetched suitcase out of the trunk and placed it on the sidewalk. Brian held the guitar.

"You take care of yourself, you hear?" Bob said, grasping Brian's shoulder. "And anytime you want to come back, you let me know. The door's always open."

"Thanks, I appreciate that, and your understanding."

Bob snorted. "Come on, your family's got to come first."

Brian nodded then stole a glance at his watch.

Bob noticed. "You better get going."

"Right. Give Debbie my best."

Grabbing up the suitcase and the guitar, he headed into the terminal, joining the check-in line. It wasn't too long, thankfully. The downside was it gave him time to think.

She hadn't given up. And she'd probably called at a time she knew he wouldn't be there, trying to find out anything she could. Again, it was something he would have done were the shoe on the other foot. It meant only one thing: she was headed for the airport. But how would she know where to find him?

Brian fought back a wave of regret. While he wanted to see her again with all of his being, he knew if he did he would never leave.

At the ticket counter, Brian gave the woman his ticket and suitcase.

"You're going to have to check that guitar," she said.

"I called up about this the other day, this will fit in the overhead."

"I don't know about that."

"Listen, ma'am, this guitar is a 1961 SG/Les Paul and is older than I am. It won't take getting banged around."

Maybe it was the way he'd said that, or the look in his eyes, either way, the woman relented, handing back his ticket, along with his boarding pass.

"Have a good flight," she said.

He nodded and headed toward the gates.

❀   ❀   ❀

Joanna gunned the Mercedes through the Callahan tunnel, for once grateful that she'd gone along with Erik's choice in automobiles. The powerful German car easily passed the other vehicles with power to spare. The fact that she'd crossed the double line, risking a ticket, didn't even faze her.

Ever since getting off the phone with Brian's partner, she'd been calling the airlines trying to find out what plane Brian was flying out on. Thankfully, there were only so many flights to Columbus, Ohio, narrowing down the task considerably. The problem was finding someone willing to reveal whether or not he was on a specific flight. The break came at six o'clock this morning. She'd found a sympathetic older woman, telling her that she'd had a fight with her fiancé and had broken off their engagement. Could she please tell her the flight number Brian was on so she could run to the airport and beg his forgiveness?

It had worked like a charm.

Now, she had less than half an hour until his plane left and the traffic had slowed to a crawl just past the tollbooths.

"No, please, not this," she said.

Joanna tried calming herself with her breathing exercises, and when that didn't work began jabbing the horn and shouting, joining the cacophony around her.

For her, the last month had been a living hell, trying to hide her feelings from Erik and desperately trying to find some way of reaching Brian. She knew he was avoiding her, but in the deepest regions of her heart she knew it wasn't because he wanted to. And that tenuous knowledge buoyed her, and made her all the more determined to learn what had happened. She'd given up trying to call him at home, and she'd tried driving by the office and his apartment several times, to no avail. Somehow she'd always missed him.

A horn honked behind her, bringing her back to the present. The traffic had begun to move, though it took another ten minutes to get into the airport. She passed two crumpled cars that had collided, nearly blocking the entrance. It figured.

Pressing the accelerator once more, Joanna sped up the ramp to the departure level, watching for the Delta terminal. She spotted it up ahead and nosed the car into a spot near the curb. The car would probably be towed, but she didn't care.

A quick glance at the clock confirmed her worst fears.

Twelve minutes until departure.

Turning off the engine, she got out and ran into the terminal, ignoring the angry shouts of a State Trooper. Inside, she paused to confirm the gate his plane was departing from—the last one at the end of the terminal—then ran down to the security checkpoint. There were a dozen people waiting to get through, but when her eyes found the sign, her heart sank.

TICKETED PASSENGERS ONLY BEYOND THIS POINT.

"You're not getting away this easy, Brian," she said, turning and dashing back up into the terminal. The only area of the counter that didn't have a wait was First Class. She ran up, breathless. The middle-aged black woman behind the counter regarded her with a bored expression.

"May I help you?"

"I need a ticket," Joanna said, pulling out her credit card and sliding it toward the woman.

"Destination?"

"The Columbus flight."

"I'm sorry, Ma'am, that flight's sold out, and it's nearly departure time."

"I just need a ticket to get past security. I don't care where it's going. There's someone on that flight I have to see...before it's too late."

The black woman's jaded expression softened. "Your boyfriend?"

Joanna nodded, her eyes filling with tears. "Yes, please."

"Okay, honey, how about Boise, Idaho? That sound good?"

"It sounds wonderful," she said, laughing through her tears.

The black woman's fingers flew over the keyboard. "I'm just givin' you any old seats, Honey, so it'll be spittin' outta here in just a second. In the meantime, let me run your card."

The black woman slid the credit card through the card reader and handed it back to Joanna, just as the ticket printer started chattering. A moment later the woman ripped it out, slapping it into Joanna's waiting hands.

"I hope you make it, dear."

"Thank you," she said and ran off back toward the security check-point.

The line for security was longer than it was before. She craned her neck trying to get a glimpse of his gate, but it was below a rise in the corridor and she couldn't see past the halfway point.

Six minutes left.

One of the Security officers, a swarthy man in a too-tight uniform nodded to her. "Your purse, ma'am."

God, she was so stupid.

Joanna threw her purse onto the conveyer and walked through the metal detector.

BEEEP!

Four minutes!

No!

Frantic, Joanna pulled off her two bracelets, dumping them into the proffered plastic tray. The swarthy security man watched her, his jaw moving in a lazy circle as he chewed his gum.

She went through again.

A Note from an Old Acquaintance

BEEEP!

Her necklace!

She tore it off, breaking the catch.

The small diamond skittered off across the floor, and she slammed the chain into the tray then went back through the detector.

Nothing....

She let go of the breath she'd been holding and glanced at the clock.

Two minutes!

She was going to make it!

She ran.

She ran past dozens of passengers coming off flights through two opposing gates, nearly colliding with a cluster of chatty flight attendants. She yelled back her apologies and put on another burst of speed.

The gate was just up ahead. It was...

...empty.

No, please, no!

She reached the desk, startling the gate attendant, a bottle blonde with too much makeup and round owlish glasses.

"Has it left?" Joanna said.

The woman gave her a sour look. "It's just pushing back now. Where were you during boarding call?"

Joanna's lips quivered, her shoulders sagging.

"Oh, God, no...."

Her eyes darted to the plate glass window, spotting the tail of the plane reversing from the gate.

She ran to the glass, moving with the plane, her eyes searching every one of its tiny windows. If she could somehow see him, maybe she could draw his attention. She'd hop around like a madwoman if she had to, she didn't care. If somehow he saw her, he'd know...

...that she really loved him.

Please, please see me, Brian!

Where *was* he?

Was he seated on the other side of the plane?

The airliner turned, the windows catching the glint of the sun, now making it impossible for her to see anything, or anyone, behind them.

"No, no, no...."

The plane moved farther and farther from the gate. A moment later it stopped. The driver of the truck pushing back the plane jumped out and disconnected the long metal arm from the airliner's front wheel strut then hopped back into the low-slung vehicle and drove off.

The plane began taxiing forward, slowly at first, and then picked up speed.

She placed her hand on the window and watched as the plane moved inexorably out of sight, the tears blurring her vision.

"Goodbye, my sweet writer...."

2006

25

"LADIES AND GENTLEMEN, WE'VE begun our final approach into the Boston area. Please fasten your seatbelts, raise your tray-tables and seatbacks into the upright position and turn off any laptop computers and portable electronic games and devices until the plane has reached the gate...."

Brian drained the last of his Evian and threw it into the plastic bag held open by the flight attendant, a slim brunette in her early forties. She smiled.

"Hope your flight was okay, Mr. Weller, it's been an honor to meet you. And thanks again for the autograph. My husband will be thrilled. He's read every one of your books."

Brian returned her smile. "You're more than welcome. And please tell him I appreciate his loyalty."

The flight attendant nodded and moved past him. Brian lifted the table back into its upright position, turning the catch to lock it in place. He glanced out the window, spotting Deer Island passing below the plane. He stifled a yawn and checked his watch.

Nearly 1:30.

It wouldn't be long, now.

A Note from an Old Acquaintance

He'd been traveling for nearly twelve hours, counting the interminable layover in Houston.

Now he knew why they called it the "Red-Eye." His own eyes felt as if someone had ground sand into them. He'd tried, unsuccessfully, to sleep on the plane, but as in times past all it got him was a throbbing ache in his temples and the feeling he'd been steamrolled twice over.

He leaned his head back against the seat and watched the Boston skyline glide by. Ancient brick and brownstone landmarks sat nestled among sleek glass towers, proud and unbowed by age. Even from a distance he could sense the city's racing pulse, its eager headlong rush into the twenty-first century. Yet, in so many ways, it remained as he remembered it: a small town playing dress up in big city clothes. And that was why he loved it, its lack of pretension and its cosmopolitan flair, its stuffy conventions and its contradictions, all thrown together into a patchwork quilt of close-knit neighborhoods rich in diverse ethnic flavors. Brian smiled, feeling a pang of nostalgia for the golden city of his youth.

And then there was Joanna.

They'd managed to speak a couple of times a week in the time leading up to his departure and the conversations were friendly and easy, her musical laughter ringing in his mind even now. But she never once asked him what had happened, and that both comforted and disturbed him. Perhaps she was feeling her way, too nervous to ask the most burning questions in her mind for fear of putting him off. He could understand that—all too well. All during those conversations his mind kept replaying the events leading up to his leaving Boston, her final desperate scream echoing in his mind.

It still sent a chill up his spine and made his heart ache with guilt and shame. His father had been right; he'd beaten himself up over it for all these years. Brian sighed as another, more poignant ache washed over him. The old man had been such a pillar of support in those first few weeks back home in Nelsonville. It was hard to believe he'd been dead for nearly a decade, his mother following her husband three years later.

Maybe now, he'd be able to find some measure of peace. Maybe Joanna had truly forgiven him.

He'd find out soon enough....

The plane landed moments later and Brian stared out the window while the airliner taxied into position at the gate. It was the same terminal from which he'd departed fifteen years before, now completely renovated inside and out, as was the rest of Logan. He almost didn't recognize it.

When the door opened, Brian stood waiting with his carry-on. He was the first out, striding up the Jetway, his mind a jumble of emotions. Inside the terminal, he took a moment to get his bearings then struck out toward Baggage Claim.

"Excuse me, Mr. Weller?"

Brian stopped and turned, spotting a tall man in his early twenties dressed in a Brooks Brothers blazer and tie, standing near the desk. The young man stepped forward, offering his hand.

"Gerald Pomeroy, Mr. Weller. I work for Kevin Romano."

Brian took the younger man's hand, surprised at the strength of his grip. "Nice to meet you, Gerald. Anything new from my publicist extraordinaire?"

Either Gerald had no sense of humor or was too intent on making a good impression to acknowledge the light humor. "He wanted me to help you get settled. I'll also be accompanying you during your signings. We're all set with your first one at the Prudential tomorrow. Where are you staying?"

"Park Plaza."

Gerald nodded. "Great hotel. How about I pick you up there around 10:30 and we'll drive over?"

They began walking toward Baggage Claim, the earnest young man keeping up a steady banter.

"Do you have any other bags?" he asked, indicating the suit bag.

"Just one more."

They made their way downstairs to the baggage carousels and waited nearly ten minutes before the one designated for his flight began turning.

Gerald nodded. "I'll get my car and meet you outside. It's a blue Ford Explorer."

The younger man disappeared through the sliding glass doors, leaving Brian to his thoughts. His bag showed up moments later.

Outside, the November chill cut through Brian's light jacket, making him wish he'd worn the heavier one he'd packed. He looked up a moment later, spotting Gerald's SUV threading its way through the airport traffic. It pulled up to the curb and Brian signaled the younger man to stay put then stowed the bag into the rear seat and climbed in.

The ride into Boston proper was faster than he'd anticipated, with Gerald taking the new Ted Williams Tunnel into the now underground Central Artery. Brian had read about the "Big Dig" for years, thinking it was all lunacy. But here they were zooming through the gleaming tunnel at a time of day where it would have been bumper-to-bumper in the old days.

They reached the hotel at 2:45.

After thanking Gerald and retrieving his bags, Brian entered the lobby and approached the front desk. The clerk, a balding man in his late thirties did a mild double take, a sure sign he'd been recognized, something to which Brian had never grown accustomed.

"Good afternoon, Mr. Weller. I trust you had a good flight."

"Well, I got here in one piece, at least," Brian said, cracking a grin.

"And we've got to be thankful for that," the clerk replied, looking down at his computer screen, his fingers dancing on the keys. "I've got you set for the Presidential Suite, it's on the Penthouse level—"

"Can I have something lower down? Just a bit superstitious."

The clerk nodded. "Certainly, Mr. Weller. Let me see what else we have available."

"As long as it's non-smoking."

"All our rooms are, sir."

While the clerk did a check for available rooms, Brian glanced around the lobby, noticing a couple of other people from his flight, including the flight attendant to whom he'd given his autograph. He caught her eye and smiled.

"Mr. Weller, I have a room on the second floor. It's not a great view, but it's comfortable."

"That'll be fine."

Ten minutes later, Brian opened the door to room 264. It was large, about fifteen by twenty, with a king-sized bed and a clean, spacious bathroom. And while the view wasn't much, the room had a homey feel that soothed his frayed nerves. He'd had enough of "Presidential Suites" to last a lifetime.

Pulling out his cell phone, he checked for messages. Then he dialed the number for the school.

"Boston Art School."

"Professor Richman, please."

"She's in class, sir, would you like voice mail?"

His first impulse was to say no and hang up. He resisted that urge. "Sure," he said.

A Note from an Old Acquaintance

There were a series of clicks and then he heard her voice: "Hi, this is Professor Richman. I'm either in class or off campus. Please leave a message and I'll return your call as soon as possible. If this is about setting up an evaluation meeting, please leave me at least three choices for dates and times and I'll schedule the one that works best. Thank you."

BEEEP.

"Hi, Joanna, it's Brian. Just got in to the hotel. It's been so long that I'd forgotten how close it is to Newbury Street and your school. Hope all is well. I'll see you in a couple of hours."

He hung up, feeling a bout of butterflies coming on. He had to be nuts to do this. What did he hope to accomplish except to open old wounds?

And what to do with himself over the next two hours?

He debated calling the front desk and putting in a wake-up call for 4:00, but visions of some idiot clerk going on break and forgetting to have his relief make the call ran through his mind. He could see himself waking at 6:00 groggy, disoriented and devastated.

No, the best thing to do was to stay awake.

Grabbing his suitcase, he threw it onto the bed, opened it and withdrew his russet-brown leather A-2, an expensive and authentic reproduction of the bomber-style jackets worn by the Army Air Corps during World War II. He always loved its dashing look with the colorful squadron patch on the left breast and his name embossed on a leather tag sewn above it, plus the heavy horsehide made it one of the warmest jackets he'd ever owned. He pulled it on and left the room, taking the stairs into the lobby and out onto Arlington Street.

Time for some Starbucks coffee. Maybe then he'd be able to keep a clear head for the evening ahead.

❋   ❋   ❋

273

"Okay, everyone, that's it for today," Joanna said. "Remember to have your fall projects in to me by the end of next week."

There were a few of the requisite groans from the class, but most of her students took it in stride, packing up their tools and books and exiting the class, laughing and chattering about the upcoming Thanksgiving break. Joanna smiled. Some things never changed, except that her students looked more and more like babies every year, more like her son, Zack. Of course what that really meant was something she preferred not to contemplate.

Turning out the lights, Joanna locked the classroom and headed to her office. Inside, she saw the blinking light on her phone indicating active voice mail. She dialed the access number and put the phone on speaker. The first one was from Erik. As usual, he sounded rushed and annoyed.

"Hi, Honey. I'll be home late. Got another meeting with the inspectors. I'll really be glad when this building's done. Don't wait up for me."

Joanna frowned. There'd been a lot of these meetings, as of late, not that she was all that disturbed by them. It was also convenient in that she wouldn't have to make any excuses about being out with Brian.

The next message was from Zack telling her that he was also staying late at school to finish up the sets on the play and would she pick him up at eight. She made a mental note to tell Brian. There were three messages left: two from students, the last one from Brian. She listened to it and smiled, her eyes moving to the white rose sitting in its fluted cobalt blue vase atop her bookcase—nearly identical to the one he'd given her so many years ago. She'd purchased it on a sentimental whim, as a reminder of him; and even now, gazing at its unsullied perfection, it evoked a bittersweet pang.

A Note from an Old Acquaintance

Was she being a fool for doing this, for having contacted him after all these years? As much as she wanted to see him again, there was a tiny part of her that wanted to run—take the back stairs and escape. But even the thought of standing him up was something she could not bear. Hadn't he had enough pain in his life already, losing a son and a wife?

Joanna glanced at the photo of her son on the desk, its tarnished silver frame shining dully. It was like looking into a mirror, his curly red hair, big green eyes, and that winning smile. He was going to break hearts someday, if he wasn't already. And looking at his image now nearly broke hers.

Keep my little boy safe, she prayed.

Sighing, she looked at the clock. It was nearly 4:00. In half an hour she would be walking down those stairs into the lobby and there he'd be. She hoped he wouldn't be disappointed. She didn't think she'd changed all that much, but now on the cusp of forty, she wasn't the starry-eyed kid she'd been when they'd last seen each other, and she'd never lost the last ten pounds she'd gained from her pregnancy with Zack. Funny thing was, those extra pounds really hadn't bothered her that much, until today.

Shaking her head to rid her mind of those kinds of thoughts, she spent the next twenty minutes updating her class notes and checking her evaluations schedule. Then, as the clock reached 4:25 she touched up her lipstick, straightened her skirt, grabbed her handbag, and left her office, nearly forgetting to turn off the lights and lock the door.

Get a grip on yourself, girl...

...Yeah, fat chance.

Feeling a little giddy, Joanna marched past the receptionist and pushed through the glass door. She started down the steps and stopped dead in her tracks.

Brian waited at the bottom of the stairs, leaning on the baluster. It reminded her of that scene in *Gone With The Wind* when the camera got its first larger-than-life look at Clark Gable.

God, he looked so handsome standing there in his bomber jacket and gabardine slacks, the dark wine-red western boots adding a rakish flair. He seemed taller, somehow, and broader in the shoulders, as if he'd been working out; and his face had that chiseled, sinewy look some of the luckier men acquired when they aged. The final nostalgic touch sat on his head, looking as crisp and new as the day she'd bought it for him: the black "WRITER" baseball cap.

Brian smiled and stood up straight. "So, how's my favorite professor?"

She rushed down the remainder of the steps and flew into his embrace, feeling the taut strength of his arms enfolding her. The familiar woodsy aroma of his cologne filled her nostrils, washing away the past fifteen years, as if they'd never existed.

"Hello, my sweet writer," she said.

❀　❀　❀

Ruby led a contingent of city inspectors through the thirtieth floor, a dour group of identical-looking men in hardhats and dark suits. Each of them held a clipboard, which they consulted frequently, asking pointed questions and making notations. It was a rite of passage Ruby endured countless times over the years for every building he'd ever constructed. And he'd never gotten used to it, or their humorless demeanor.

Twenty floors to go.

They'd been at it for most of the afternoon, and he had to hand it to the bastards. They were thorough.

A Note from an Old Acquaintance

"Mr. Ruby?" one of them pointed to an electrical outlet.

"Yes?"

He walked over and bent down to examine what the inspector was showing him. It was damaged. Something heavy had smashed into it. Probably one of the little hand operated hydraulic forklifts that were used all over the building to move materials around.

"No problem, we'll replace that."

His cell phone throbbed against his waist and he moved over to one of windows overlooking downtown Boston. It was a breathtaking view.

"Excuse me," he said, pulling it from its clip. "Yes."

"Our pigeon's come home to roost," Mosley said, his voice sounding as if he were standing next to him.

Ruby's features clouded. "Tell me."

"I tracked him from the airport. He's staying at the Park Plaza. Couldn't get the room number."

"What else?"

"He met the lady in the lobby of the school. She seemed rather glad to see him."

Ruby watched one of the inspectors shake his head and mark down something on his clipboard. Damn them. This was going to take half the night.

"Sir, are you there?" Mosley asked. "Do you want me to stay with them?"

"Yes, but don't let them see you."

Ruby hung up, his jumbled thoughts stoking the flames of his anger.

What to do, what to do? The situation with Weller had drastically changed. Instead of the struggling would-be writer he'd known fifteen years before, the man had become internationally famous; and he had to admit Weller's literary stature astounded him. He'd even read one of his earlier books out of curiosity, finding it strangely compelling, though it galled him whenever he saw Joanna reading one, the man's smiling face staring out from the back of the dust jacket. That very stature and the attendant monetary rewards also precluded a repeat of his previous strategy.

He was not about to lose Joanna, not for a second time. There had to be a way to make Weller back off. He just needed to find it. And patience where his wife was concerned had become a rarefied commodity.

He rejoined the inspectors, who had gathered at the elevators, ready to ascend to the thirty-first floor. Only nineteen left. Putting on a smile he didn't feel, he keyed open the freight elevator and waved the inspectors inside.

You won't take her from me again, Weller.

You won't!

26

WITH NEARLY AN HOUR and a half to go before their dinner reservations, Joanna and Brian decided to take a stroll up Newbury Street and check out their old haunts. The Indian restaurant where they'd eaten lunch so many years before was now Italian, and most of the little galleries had changed hands—probably several times over—but the one thing that hadn't changed was their enthusiasm over seeing what other artists had created and their mutual respect for each other's opinion.

Joanna had taken his hand when they'd emerged from her building and had not relinquished it. That was more than okay with Brian. It felt so natural that it didn't even register with him, at first. And when it did, the surge of adrenaline made him feel giddy.

"What else would you like to do?" she asked after they'd exited the last gallery.

Brian thought about it for a moment, staring up at the street sign at the corner. It read: Fairfield. He smiled. "I'd like to see my old apartment."

Joanna returned his smile. "I'd like that, too."

While they strolled the quarter mile to Beacon Street, the memories of that night in Ruby's office rose in his mind, sobering him. Joanna sensed the shift in his mood.

"You okay?" she said.

He looked down at her, the dark thoughts dissolving. She looked wonderful. When she'd first appeared at the top of the stairs, he'd been a little disoriented, expecting to see her hair piled on top of her head, as he remembered it. It was still as red and curly as ever, but had been cut into a modern variation of a Twenties-style bob that flattered the soft contours of her face.

"I'm fine, now," he said. "Just a little fried from my flight."

She shook her head. "I can't stand flying. It really makes me nervous."

"You? Nervous? Never."

She punched his shoulder and they both laughed. A moment later, they came to the corner of Fairfield and Beacon. Brian's old building stood diagonally across from them, and it looked exactly the same, as he expected it would.

"Want to go and see if anyone's home?" she asked.

Brian stared at the building, feeling the years drop away. "No... that's okay. Don't want to bother anyone." He checked his watch and saw that it was 5:45. "We should get going, anyway."

She nodded and they headed east on Beacon, toward Charles Street.

The HUNGRY I, a favorite neighborhood haunt since the late Seventies, occupied one of the old brick row houses at the foot of Beacon Hill, the main dining room residing on the basement level. Brian took Joanna's hand and helped her down the steps, barely avoiding the heavy granite lintel over his head.

Inside, soft candlelight cast a warm glow, and he saw that only a few of the tables were occupied, being still early for the fashionable set. The place looked different, yet the same. It must have been the

A Note from an Old Acquaintance

chocolate-colored walls and the old prints hanging from them that strayed from his memory, but the basic layout remained unchanged.

They were met by the host and led to a table near the front of the building. It struck Brian, when he helped Joanna with her coat, that it was the very table he'd imagined them occupying. The host handed them menus, recited the specials, and then left them alone.

"This is lovely," Joanna said.

"Promise you won't think I'm a sentimental old fool?"

She gave him a scolding look. "I'd never think that. Why would you even say it?"

Brian shrugged. "I don't know. It's just that this was one of the places I was planning to take you...back then."

Her expression turned wistful. "I'm glad we're here now."

"I just hope the food's still good. Is there anything you can eat?"

Joanna opened the menu and studied it; Brian did the same.

He didn't expect to see the Wiener Schnitzel he used to love still on the menu, and it wasn't. However, there was a chicken dish that didn't sound half bad.

"Actually, there is," she said. "Stewed pumpkins."

Brian tried to hide his reaction, and Joanna laughed. "Come on, where's your open mind?"

"I think I left it in L.A," he replied, grinning.

"Now you're being silly."

"And it's one of the things you love about me."

"Yes, it is...," she said, staring at him.

"Can I get you two something to drink?"

Brian looked up to see the waiter. "I think we're ready to order, if that's okay."

"No problem," the waiter said, brandishing his pencil and pad.

Brian let Joanna order her pumpkin dish and then sent a silent

281

prayer to the food gods and ordered the rolled, stuffed chicken. The waiter walked away a moment later, leaving an awkward silence. Joanna stared at the burning candle, her expression unreadable.

"You know, you look terrific," he said, giving voice to his innermost thoughts. "The vegetarian diet and your meditations are obviously doing wonders for you, because your skin is flawless."

"Thank you," she said, blushing. "Staying out of the sun helps, too, especially for us redheads."

"I'm sorry, I'm embarrassing you."

"No, you're not. I was just thinking."

"What about?"

"My son."

"Everything okay?"

Joanna nodded. "He's staying late at school. I actually have to pick him up around eight."

"No problem. I'll make sure we get you out of here on time."

"No, please don't think I don't want to be here, I do, but...."

"But what?"

"I think I told you he's doing the sets for his school play, and that means he's always climbing up in that rigging. Every time I think about what could happ—" She stopped herself, her eyes welling up.

Brian covered her hand with his. "Hey, if he's anything like his mom, and I'll bet he is, he'll be fine."

Joanna smiled, dabbing at her eyes. "Thank you. You still know the perfect thing to say."

"Do you have a picture of him?"

Joanna reached into her purse, extracted her wallet and pulled out a laminated photo then handed it to Brian.

"It's his school photo from last year."

Brian held it closer to the candle and smiled. The boy was Joanna's spitting image, the big eyes, curly hair and radiant smile, but the features had a masculine look that made them his own.

"Handsome boy," he said, handing it back. "And he certainly takes after his pretty mother."

"Thank you," she said, replacing everything back into her purse. "My husband adores him, but I think deep down he's always been bothered that Zack shows no physical resemblance to him."

Brian hid his reaction at the mention of Joanna's husband, not wanting her to see that he resented the man's intrusion, however fleeting. Joanna saw the look, misinterpreting it. "Oh, God, I'm sorry, Brian. I didn't think— Your son...." She bit her lip and Brian felt a rush of emotions. She looked so vulnerable.

"It's okay."

"Do you have a picture of him?"

He nodded and pulled it out of his wallet and handed it to her. She stared at it and he could see her hand trembling.

"Oh, my...."

"People said he looked just like me. They would always stop us in the street, remarking on it. And the little guy loved to dress just like me, too. It got so I'd get him dressed first in the morning, then match my wardrobe to his. The little guy got such a kick out of that. That's what I called him, 'Little Guy.' And he called me...Big G—"

Brian stopped talking as the pain and loss overwhelmed him. Joanna gripped his hands in hers, her own eyes tearing.

"Forgive me, Brian, I didn't mean to stir all this up."

Brian squeezed her hands in return. "Nothing to forgive. I'm dealing with it. A little more each day."

"I don't mean to pry, but what happened? All I know is what I heard on the news...about the accident."

Brian nodded.

"Joey had a disease called Neimann-Pick Type C. It's a very rare genetic disorder where the body doesn't metabolize cholesterol, so it builds up in the brain. Most kids die from it by their early teens.

"Penny was the carrier, something we only found out after he was born, and she blamed herself for it. She began drinking and taking sedatives, anything to blot out the pain she was feeling. I had no idea where she was getting the pills. And I tried my best to help her.

"They were on their way back from Joey's doctor and she ran a light. She was all doped up and shouldn't have been driving at all. She'd even neglected to belt Joey into his car seat properly, something she never would have done under normal circumstances. He was thrown from the car and died instantly. Penny...well...."

Joanna stared at him, the horror his life had become reflected in those beautiful eyes. And he hated himself for it.

The food came a moment later, granting them a reprieve. They spent a few moments eating in silence.

"How's yours?" she asked.

"Not too bad. And you?"

"Delicious. Want a taste?"

"Sure, why not. I think I brought some of that open mind with me, after all."

Joanna grinned then skewered a piece of the pumpkin onto her fork and held it out. Brian leaned forward and took the proffered morsel with his mouth, his eyes locked with hers.

He chewed it, his expression turning thoughtful. Joanna watched him, her mouth curling into a sly grin.

"Well?"

"I'm not sure what I was expecting, but it's not bad. Sort of like zucchini, at least the way the chef's prepared it. Want to switch?"

Joanna shot him a look of mock horror. "Not on your life."

Brian chuckled, happy that the grim mood from a few moments before was dispelled. When he smiled again, Joanna frowned. "What?"

"I was just thinking about the night we met."

Joanna's expression softened. "I think about that night a lot, too. What made you smile just now?"

"That I almost didn't work up the nerve to ask you to dance. It took me nearly half an hour, you know."

"I didn't know that," she said, her eyes twinkling in the candlelight.

"You looked so wonderful out there, so free and uninhibited that I wanted to be a part of that, too."

Joanna nodded, suddenly pensive. "Erik doesn't care much for dancing these days."

And there he was again, barging into their time together. "Well, I can't think of anyone else I'd rather go dancing with. Want to go? I'm ready, if you are. And I promise I'll only break a couple of your toes."

Joanna laughed. "You're teasing me, now."

"Only a little."

"And I'm tempted, but...."

"I know...."

Joanna took a sip of her water, regarding him with a look he couldn't interpret. "Are you looking forward to the signings or are they just business to you?"

"You always did ask pointed questions," he said, breathing an inward sigh of relief that the conversation was veering onto safer ground. "And I wouldn't have it any other way." He took another bite of his chicken and washed it down with a sip of water, considering her question. "I really enjoy meeting my readers. I never get tired of hearing how much they love the stories I've told them. If I didn't have that I'd feel I was writing in a vacuum. That doesn't sound egotistical, does it?"

Joanna shook her head. "Not at all. And you can count me as one of your loyal fans, too. I thought *A Nest of Vipers* was terrific. And I'll bet you're already deep into the next one."

Brian looked up and out the oblong street-level windows, watching pairs of legs walking by. He debated for about ten seconds whether to tell her the truth, then realized he had no choice. He owed her at least that much honesty, even if he couldn't bring himself to tell her the real truth about what had happened between them.

Brian looked back at her and shook his head, letting out the breath he'd been holding. "I haven't been able to write a word since finishing *Vipers*, Joanna, and even completing that book was a Herculean task. I don't know what I'm going to do...."

She leaned forward and rested her hand on his arm, giving it a squeeze. "I was so proud of you when your first book came out. And the ones that came after got better and better. You deserve everything you've achieved."

"Sometimes I wonder about that. So much seems as if it depended upon luck."

"I know.... I was lucky to meet you," she said.

Again, he looked into her eyes, finding himself losing momentary track of time. She spoke again, breaking the magic spell.

"I've had dry periods with my art that really scared me, but I managed to get through them. Of course, I've never had anything happen to me, like what's happened to you, so I'm sure my advice and words of encouragement must sound hollow to you."

Brian squeezed her hand in return. "Nothing you say will ever sound hollow to me."

Before she could reply, Brian heard a series of musical tones that sounded like the melody from the Harry Potter films.

Joanna started. "My phone." She reached into her purse and pulled out a flip phone, opened it and put it to her ear. "Hello?"

She listened a moment then replied. "So, you think you might be done a little early?"

"You need to go?" Brian said.

Joanna raised a finger, shaking her head.

"Okay, Honey, if you want to hang out with your friends for awhile, that's fine. I'll still be there at the same time. See you then. Love you."

She closed the phone and looked thoughtful. "He's turning fifteen tomorrow, and since we both have the day off, were going to do whatever he wants to do."

"Sounds like a plan to me."

"God, I still can't believe he's in high school. Seems like yesterday I was changing his diapers every two seconds." She laughed.

"Oh, I had my fill of that, too, that's for sure," Brian said, remembering his poopy diaper days with Joey.

"I just had a thought. Would you mind if I brought Zack to your signing tomorrow? He's a real big fan of yours, too. In fact, he says he wants to be a writer someday. He's pretty talented."

"I'd be honored if you would. I'd like to meet him. Has he written anything?"

"Just some short stories. I think they're pretty good, but I'm just his mother." She gave Brian a smile and a shrug.

"Tell you what. Have him e-mail me the best story he's got. Tell him I'd be happy to read it over tonight and offer any pointers I can."

"You don't have to do that, Brian."

"I want to. I wish I'd had someone help me along earlier in my career. Might have saved me a lot of time, assuming I would have been smart enough to listen. And I have a feeling your Zack is one on-the-ball kid. Like his mom. And I promise...only encouragement."

Joanna beamed. "He'll be thrilled."

"If you two have the time, I'll even spring for a birthday lunch, that way he and I can talk a bit. How's that?"

"It's a date."

The rest of the meal was consumed with more small talk, the main question that hung between them remaining unspoken.

After coffee for Brian and herbal tea for Joanna, Brian paid the bill and they left, heading back towards his hotel.

The air had turned colder, but Brian didn't even feel it. Instead, as they strolled back down Charles Street toward the Public Garden and the Commons, Brian fought a war inside his heart.

He was still in love with Joanna, maybe always had been, but those feelings had been suppressed, put on a shelf like a favorite toy, only to be discovered years later and appreciated in a new light.

Watching her now, while she walked beside him, he wanted to laugh with joy and cry in anguish. The anguish seemed to be winning. All those years wasted, years he could have spent with her, had he not folded like a bad poker hand. His father had believed he'd done the right thing, but many times, like now, he wondered if he had. That Joanna bore no ill feelings was obvious, but was she happy now? He'd wanted so much to ask her that, pin her down—get to the truth. But what if that truth ran counter to his innermost wants and needs? What if she was truly happy? Could he live with that?

"Do you mind if we cut through the Gardens?" Joanna asked, when they reached the corner of Beacon and Charles.

"Sure," Brian replied, hating the catch in his voice.

They struck out across Beacon through a break in the traffic and that's when his inner alarm went off, the emotions of the past few moments replaced by a chill colder than the night surrounding them.

They were being followed.

Brian was sure of it. He'd had inklings of it from almost the moment he'd met Joanna at the school, but had shoved them to the back of his mind, only wanting to revel in the joy of seeing her again. Now, as they made their way past the lagoon where the swan boats plied the waters of spring, he knew someone was behind them dogging their every move.

He'd learned the skill five years ago, while conducting research on a novel about snipers he'd been writing at the time. And it had been a difficult one to master. He could almost liken it to Joanna's meditations, the opening of the mind, tuning oneself into one's surroundings.

Joanna slipped her arm around him, hugging him close. He turned, and she smiled up at him; it also gave him the chance to peer behind him.

There he was, fifty feet back, strolling along as if he had no place in particular to go.

And it didn't fit. Not at 7:45 at night.

They emerged from the Public Gardens onto Arlington Street and walked toward the hotel. Joanna slowed when they came abreast of the hotel's side entrance, a questioning look in her eyes.

"I'll walk you to your car," Brian said.

Joanna smiled and slipped her arm through his. She led him to a parking garage behind the hotel, handing a ticket to one of the attendants.

Brian looked for their tail, but the man seemed to have melted into the night. He was out there; Brian knew it. The question was what would happen next, after Joanna left? Whatever it was, he was ready for it.

Joanna's car arrived a few moments later, a black Volvo SUV. Brian laughed and Joanna frowned. "What?"

"Looks like you finally got your Volvo."

Joanna smiled, looking relieved. "My husband saw the light, a rare occasion, to be sure."

She came to him then, hugging him. "I've so enjoyed this evening, Brian. You can't know how much. I wish we could have done it sooner."

Brian nodded. "Me, too. Guess neither one of us was really ready for it, until now."

"Guess not," she replied, gazing into his eyes.

It was an awkward moment. He wanted to kiss her, and almost did, but held himself back, afraid to spoil the moment. And maybe more than a little afraid that it wouldn't.

"I'll see you tomorrow, okay?"

"I'm looking forward to it. I'll tell the store to expect you. That way you won't have to wait in line."

"My God, I didn't even think of that. You must get mobbed at these things."

"You could say that," he said, nodding, a twinkle in his eye. "It goes with the territory, and as I said earlier, I really love it."

She squeezed his hand, kissed him on the cheek and got into her car. Brian closed the door and watched her drive off down Stuart Street. At the end of the block she turned the corner and was gone from sight.

He walked back to the hotel, his emotions welling up within him. He fought back the tide until he reached his room where it all came crashing down upon him.

He sat on the bed, covering his face with his hands. It had been a terrible idea to come. And yet it was a wonderful one, too. Joanna had been everything he'd expected her to be...and more. She'd barely aged and yet possessed the self-assuredness that only came with maturity. He didn't think it could be possible to love her more than he had so many years ago, but he did. And that was what made it so wonderful and so terrible.

Brian went into the bathroom and threw cold water on his face. God, he was so tired, yet his body was all wound up. The man who'd been following them—he was sure it was the same black man who worked for Ruby back in 1991. What was his name...Moser? Mosley! That was it. He looked older and heavier, but he'd walked with the same confident stride. So, Ruby knew he was back. Well, that was fine. Let him stew in his vitriol, let him choke on it. Ruby had nothing to offer him now, and no control over his actions or desires.

Feeling the walls closing in, Brian put on his leather jacket and left the room. Outside the hotel, he walked up Arlington, grabbed a latté at the Starbucks just as it was closing then strolled back on Newbury, checking out the merchandise in some of the store windows. A moment later he found himself standing across the street from Joanna's school, a five-story red brick building in the Georgian style.

Lights were illuminated in a few of the windows on the upper floors, and he wondered which one was Joanna's classroom. He imagined himself a fly on the wall during one of her classes, watching her take command, hearing the enthusiasm in her voice as she outlined a new concept, and feeling the thrill of seeing understanding dawn in those bright young eyes.

Brian smiled. This woman was a rare jewel, indeed.

"All right, Ruby. You want another round, you've got one."

27

JOANNA REACHED THE GROUNDS of Newton High School just after 8:00, pulling the Volvo into a space near the curb with a clear view of the entrance. Zack was nowhere in sight, and she almost got out to go look for him, but decided against it. He was at the age where he didn't want his mother making a spectacle of herself over him. She shook her head, feeling a pang of nostalgia for the little boy who wouldn't leave the house without a "Big Hug" from Mommy. She'd wait. He'd be along any moment.

She kept her eyes on the door, her thoughts turning to her evening with Brian. She'd been so apprehensive, had been from the moment she'd first e-mailed him weeks ago. She recalled something he'd said in his first reply that had haunted her ever since.

I've often thought about you over the years, wondering what you were doing at a given moment, and if you were happy.

And that was the thing. She hadn't been happy, not for a long time. Yes, she had Zack and her art, two things that were very dear to her, but once their son was born, Erik had withdrawn into his world of deals and seemed to care less about her from day to day. Sometimes she wondered if he was even aware that she occupied any space in his life.

292

A Note from an Old Acquaintance

And now she could just kick herself. After all these years of wondering, promising herself over and over again, she'd chickened out, had left the one burning question in her mind unasked.

What happened, Brian? Why did you leave me?

And there it was again.

It had hung in the recesses of her mind all throughout their dinner. She'd started to ask it half a dozen times and stopped herself, feeling the moment wasn't right. And then the opportunity was all but lost when the conversation turned to his family. God, how could she be so insensitive to give voice to her worries about Zack, when his own son—

Joanna bit back the tears. How much she wanted to go to him now, comfort him, tell him that everything would be all right. But would it? How could she say something like that with her own life in a shambles?

Something out of the corner of her eye made her look toward the entrance to the school.

It was Zack. He moved toward the car with that loping gate that tugged at her heart, reminding her once again that her boy was growing up. He saw the car and picked up his pace.

She sat up straighter and checked herself in the rearview mirror. Nothing looked amiss. Her eyes were clear.

Zack opened the door and climbed in.

"Hi, Mom," he said, smiling.

Joanna ruffled the curls on his head. "Hi, Sweetie."

The boy squirmed in his seat. "Mom, come on...."

"Zack, there's no one here but us."

He looked around, saw that she was right then cracked a shy grin. He leaned over and gave her a hug. "Is that better?" he asked.

"Yes."

Joanna threw the car into gear and headed down the street.

"So, how was your day?"

"Okay," he said, staring out the windshield.

"Just okay?"

The boy nodded and Joanna rolled her eyes. Teenagers! Masters of the monosyllabic.

"Are you excited about turning fifteen tomorrow?"

Zack smiled. "Yeah."

"Well, I've got a surprise for you."

He turned to his mother, a quizzical look on his adorable face.

"How would you like to meet Brian Weller?"

The boy's eyes widened. "You kidding me, Mom?"

Joanna crossed her heart. "I kid you not. He's an old— friend of mine," she said, her heart pounding. She'd almost said *old flame*. "And he's going to be signing his books at the Prudential Center tomorrow. Thought you might like to go. Of course, if you're not interested...."

"Awesome! How did you find out about this?"

"Like I said, Brian's an old friend. We had dinner tonight."

"Cool."

Joanna laughed. Everything was either awesome or cool at this age. "I told him you were a writer, too."

The boy looked horrified. "No, Mom, you didn't!"

"What's wrong with that? You are aren't you?"

"Yeah, but he's like the greatest. I'm just a kid."

"And so was he...once. He told me a story a long time ago about how he used to write stories as a boy. And how much he loved telling stories. You feel that way, too, don't you?"

Zack nodded.

"Well, don't be angry, but he's offered to read one of your stories. All you need to do is e-mail it to him tonight."

A Note from an Old Acquaintance

Zack didn't say anything, but Joanna saw the gleam of excitement in his eyes.

"Do you have one in mind?"

The boy nodded. "Yeah, I do. It's the one I finished last week. I feel really good about it."

"So, you're not mad?"

Zack shook his head. "Nah, not really. I was just kind of blown away, is all. I hope he likes it."

Joanna patted his thigh. "If I'm any judge of talent, I'm sure he will."

They arrived home at 8:30, pulling the car into the garage. Joanna frowned, noticing the split-window Corvette was missing. Erik drove it infrequently, always concerned about the mileage, and he almost never did so at night.

Inside, she checked her voice mail then remembered Brian's offer. She grabbed a pen and paper and jotted down his e-mail address.

"Zack?" she called out.

When she got no answer she walked to the back of the house, finding him in his bedroom already at his computer, waiting for it to boot up. She stood in the doorway, watching his intent expression and feeling a rush of pride, love...and sadness. He looked so like his father, just now. She also noticed his room was neater than usual. The bed was made, covered with his version of a bedspread: a huge black flag. In the center was a white arm holding a bleeding red heart that resembled a hand grenade. Next to it emblazoned in red block type were the words: GREEN DAY. His guitar rested on top of the bed. When he wasn't writing he was playing. He practically slept with that guitar. She shook her head, wanting to cry and smile at the same time.

"Hey," she said.

Zack turned, an excited look in his eyes. "You really think he'll like my story, Mom?"

"I'm positive."

"What about Dad?"

She knew what that question meant. And it brought back an ugly memory from a vicious fight she and Erik had over Zack attending a special writer's camp the previous summer. She'd given in and the boy had stayed home. Another time her husband had gotten his way. Well, no more. No more disappointments.

"You let me worry about your father, okay?"

She entered the room and handed him the note. The boy glanced at it then opened up his AOL account, bringing up a blank e-mail document. He began typing, his fingers a blur. Joanna was amazed by his speed. With her it was a wonder she managed with one finger. In a moment, he was done writing. He attached his story and was about to hit the SEND button.

"Wait," she said, "I want to add a PS...."

❈   ❈   ❈

Brian took his second shower of the day, trying to relax, but even the hot luxurious spray failed to take the edge off his case of nerves. Turning off the water, he toweled himself dry and put on a white terry-cloth robe with the hotel's logo embroidered onto the breast pocket and left the bathroom. He went to the desk where his laptop sat glowing. The little mailbox flag was blinking.

There were two e-mails, one from AOL and one from an AOL member named "MadZack." Brian smiled. Joanna's boy.

He double-clicked on it, opening it up.

November 10, 2006

Dear Mr. Weller:

A Note from an Old Acquaintance

My Mom told me that you were willing to take a look at one of my stories. I really want you to know how much I appreciate that. Just hope it doesn't bore you too much. I also wanted to thank you for inviting us to your signing tomorrow. I'm really looking forward to that, as I think Mom is, too. I can tell she really thinks the world of you. That makes two of us. Thanks again.

Sincerely,

Zack Ruby

PS—Just wanted to wish my favorite writer a good night.

Joanna

Brian downloaded the story and brought it up onto the screen. The first thing he noticed was that Zack knew proper format. That was something so many aspiring writers either assumed they knew or didn't care to learn. Good for you, kid. He wished he could print it out, as he'd learned long ago that the eye missed things on the screen that they picked up in a hardcopy printout. Couldn't be helped. He scrolled down and began to read. Twenty minutes later he sat back, letting out the breath he'd been holding. He shook his head, awed. This kid was good, so good that Brian knew he'd be selling his stories to the top markets very soon, if not already.

This story, in particular, a tale about a boy trying to relate to his distant father, really rang with truth, anguish and beauty. It was the kind of writing that would have the critics falling all over themselves. Brian suspected it was more than a little autobiographical and it brought on a wave of sadness. Although he had the best of relationships with his own father, Brian could feel the loneliness and despair coming through this boy's words and that was a major accomplishment. And it humbled him.

Brian brought up his AOL account and replied to Zack's e-mail.

Dear Zack:

I just read your story and wanted to let you know I'm looking forward to talking to you about it. I just realized I've been up for nearly twenty-four hours, so rest is what these tired old bones need. See you tomorrow.

Best,

Brian

PS—And good night to my favorite professor.

❊   ❊   ❊

The 1963 split-window Corvette rocketed through the night, its powerful V-8 engine roaring.

Twelve hours.

He'd been with those inspectors for twelve hours and they still weren't finished. And the list of repairs and changes that needed to be made to the building to meet code filled a sheaf of papers that rivaled a phone book in thickness. And there were still ten floors left. Fortunately, he had another week before they would return, giving him time to check out those floors himself and beat the bastards to the punch.

Ruby downshifted the Corvette, barely slowing to take a sharp turn. The building was only part of his problems. He still didn't know what to do about Weller. The file with all the old surveillance, background information and their signed agreement still resided in the locked file cabinet at home, but all of it was meaningless, now that Weller was going back on his word. That was the real crux of the issue. With every deal he'd ever made, Ruby toed the line, delivered the goods—kept his word. Now, the one deal that meant more to him than all the others was going up in smoke. Weller was back, he was rich and famous, and there wasn't a damn thing Ruby could do to stop him—at least, nothing legal. And he'd be damned if he'd let Weller push him over that line, not when he'd spent his whole life building his impeccable reputation. Ruby cursed and struck the wheel with the flat of his palm. There had to be a way....

He arrived home just after 9:00, relieved to see Joanna's car in the garage. He'd known it was going to be there, as Mosley had reported her departure from the Stuart Street garage moments after she'd driven off.

Inside the house, he saw that Joanna had already gone upstairs, the light from their bedroom spilling out into the upper hallway. Ruby walked to the back of the house, finding his son typing away at his computer.

"Hi," he said.

The boy turned and smiled. "Hi, Dad. Long day."

"You're not kidding," he said, moving into the room. He sat on the boy's bed, moving the guitar out of the way, frowning at the Green Day flag. Kids never changed, always the rebels.

"So, tomorrow's the big day, eh, Chief?"

"Yeah," the boy said, resuming his typing.

"Wait, hold up on that for a minute."

Zack turned and regarded his father, a questioning look on his face.

"How would you like to check out the building with me tomorrow? I know you've been wanting to see it, so how 'bout it?"

Ruby could see a battle going on behind the boy's eyes.

"What is it?"

"Well, Mom and I are going into town tomorrow to a book signing. She's introducing me to Brian Weller. He's taking us to lunch afterward."

Ruby felt his entire body grow cold.

"How nice of him," he said. "Maybe I should go talk to your mother."

"I think she's meditating."

Ruby stood and went to the door. "Oh, I think she'll want to talk about this."

He marched through the house, his anger mounting. The door to her meditation room was closed. He hesitated for only the briefest of moments then threw open the door. It banged against the wall, putting a dent in the sheetrock.

Joanna sat on the floor in the lotus position, the glow of a candle the only light in the room. She opened her eyes, studying her husband with a calm gaze. Her serenity only angered him more.

"What is this? Going to a book signing tomorrow? You knew I wanted to take Zack to the building."

"And you know how much he wants to be a writer, Erik. He can see the building anytime. This is a great opportunity for him."

"Opportunity for what? To get his hopes up, just so someone can rub his face in the dirt someday because he's not good enough?"

"He *is* good. And you'd know that if you bothered to read any of what he's written."

"I'm sure he's got talent, but it's a waste of time, Joanna. People like Weller are a rare commodity."

"I'm glad you see it that way," she replied, the hint of a smile on her face.

Ruby glowered. "That's not what I meant."

"I know what you meant."

"Then why encourage him to think he can make any kind of decent living from it?"

Joanna rose to her feet in a fluid move and met her husband's glare with one of her own. "Money isn't everything." She started to leave the room and Ruby barred the door with his arm.

"Money isn't everything, eh?"

"Let me by, please."

"Where would you be without everything I've given you? Living off your precious art?"

Joanna's eyes narrowed. "I make good money off my commissions."

Ruby snorted. "Enough to live like this?"

"The trouble is you think I wanted all this. You wanted it, Erik, not me! You spent the days and nights holed up in your office sweating over your deals because you wanted it! Now, let me by."

She pushed his arm away from the doorframe and stalked out. Ruby's slow burn turned white-hot. He followed her into the bedroom, his eyes scanning the thousand square feet of rare antiques, including the mahogany four-poster bed on its riser at the far end. The room, as usual, was neat as a pin, marred only by the sight of Joanna's street clothes tossed casually onto the bed. He found her in the bathroom seated in front of her vanity.

"Maybe you didn't want all this, Dear, but you're certainly used to it, aren't you? Or would you rather still be living in that illegal loft I found you in when you were a student?"

Joanna closed her eyes, sighing. She opened them and stared back at her husband's reflection. "Do you really want me to answer that question?"

He hated it when she backed him into a corner like this. Well, this time he wasn't backing down.

He leaned forward, grasping her shoulders. "Maybe you'd better," he said. "Because I'm reaching the end of my rope."

"You're hurting me!"

301

Ruby let go of her. "Well?"

"I'm tired, Erik. It's been a long day and I want Zack's birthday to be the one he wants."

Ruby ground his teeth. "Sure, why shouldn't it be? Lord knows he'd rather spend it with you than me."

"That's not what I meant."

"Isn't it? You think anyone's going to give a damn about your precious Brian Weller in fifty years? I'm making a mark on this city."

Joanna slapped her hand on the vanity. "You leave him out of this."

"Oh? I've struck a nerve, have I?"

She stood and wheeled on him. "He's a caring, sensitive man, which is more than I can say for you. Your son needs your understanding, not a guided tour of your accomplishments!"

"I'm doing the best I can. And what's wrong with what I've accomplished?"

"Nothing and everything! They're glass and steel, Erik! You've got a flesh and blood boy down there who's been trying to reach you for years! All he wants is his father to love him and know that his needs and desires are important."

"I DO LOVE HIM!"

"THEN SHOW IT!"

God help him, he wanted to hit her, just reach back and slam his fist into that face—the face he'd adored all these years—and which now gazed back at him with such loathing and contempt. His hands balled into fists and his entire body shook. Then, all at once, the anger fled, leaving him feeling drained and hollow.

"I'm going downstairs to the office. There are some things I still need to do."

He walked out of the bedroom with Joanna at his heels.

A Note from an Old Acquaintance

She remained at the top of the stairs, watching him descend.

"That's fine, Erik, go and escape like you always do! Go play with your blueprints and whatever it is you keep in that locked file cabinet of yours and ignore what's really important!"

She kept yelling, but Ruby tuned it out, finally cutting her off with the slam of his office door. He sat in the dark, trying to sort everything out in his mind. A part of him knew she was right, the part of him that felt panic every time he tried to talk to his son. He was so much like his mother, yet there was a deeper part of the boy that frightened Ruby, an extraordinary intuition, as if Zack could see right through to the core of him. It was so simple when he was five years old, so easy to bring a smile to that tiny face. Now, he just didn't know what to do or say.

Now there was true irony for you.

Here he was, a man who could and did deal with titans, men who could break him if he wasn't on his toes at all times, brought to his knees by the knowing look from a pair of young limpid green eyes.

Ruby shook his head. Joanna was wrong. He *did* love the boy. How could he not?

Weller was poisoning her heart and mind once more; and except for one brief blip all those years ago, they'd been happy since he'd left town...hadn't they? Now, it was all turning sour.

Now, Weller was taking the boy from him, too!

Ruby slammed his fist onto his desk, his entire body trembling with rage. What was he going to do?

❀　❀　❀

Zack's fingers flew over the keys, the words poring out onto the screen. The new story promised to be even better than the one he'd sent to Mr.

303

Weller. The faster he typed, the faster the words came, almost fast enough to drown out the sound of his parents screaming at each other....

Almost....

The words kept coming...along with the tears.

28

THE PHONE RANG, AND Brian grabbed for it on the nightstand, almost knocking it to the floor.

"Hello," he said in a voice thick with sleep.

"Good morning, Mr. Weller, this is your wake-up call."

"Thank you."

Brian replaced the phone onto its cradle and sat up, groaning. He'd finally dropped off sometime after midnight. His body was still on California time and felt as if a tribe of pygmies had trampled it. A glance at the clock told him it was just after 9:00. At least the call had come on time.

Climbing out of the bed, Brian went through his stretching routine. The problem was the older he got the longer it took to work out the kinks. After finishing with the stretching, he went through his isometrics, his muscles fairly singing by the time he finished ten minutes later. He then turned on his cell phone and checked his messages. There was one from Kevin, telling him about a talk show appearance he wanted to book for him back in New York.

The other was from Joanna.

"Hi, Brian. Just wanted to tell you I had a wonderful time at dinner last night. Can't wait to see you in your element. Zack is all excited, too. See you soon. Bye."

Brian smiled. He couldn't wait, either. It was strange, though. She'd sounded cheerful, but there'd been an undercurrent to the sound of her voice that bothered him. That, coupled with the remnants of the dream he'd been awakened from, made for an unexplainable disquietude.

The dream was the oddest thing. He was having dinner with Joanna at the HUNGRY I, just as they had the prior evening, but this time they weren't alone. Penny was at the table, too, looking as beautiful as he remembered her. The two women were chattering away, the best of friends, and he was sitting there feeling left out. But the strangest, and most ironic thing was the dream didn't seem all that odd. Knowing each woman as well as he did, he was sure they would have been fast friends, were it not for the nature of his relationship with the both of them. Perhaps it was because they were similar in lots of ways.

Brian shook his head, filing that thought away. It would be good fodder for a book, at some point. He took a quick shower, dressed in a pair of khaki slacks, a chambray shirt and his boots, then grabbed his flight jacket and the laptop and left the room.

Downstairs, Brian went to the front desk. The woman working behind it, a strawberry blonde in her early twenties, looked up and gave him a perky smile. "Good morning, may I help you?"

"I was wondering if I could ask you a favor."

The young woman nodded. "Sure."

"Would it be possible for me to print out a short document of mine?"

The woman frowned. "We don't normally do something like that."

Someone from the back room called out to her. "Uh, Judy?"

Brian looked over her shoulder, spotting an older man beckoning her. "Excuse me," she said, going over to him. Brian watched the man whisper something to her. Her body language immediately changed. Brian knew what was coming.

The young woman hurried back to the desk. "I'm so sorry, Mr. Weller, I—I didn't recognize you."

Brian held up his hand. "It's quite all right, believe me," he said, feeling embarrassed for the girl. "I really don't expect special treatment."

The young woman shook her head. "No, no, it's not that. It's just we're always worried about viruses. My manager said you can plug into our printer, if you wish."

"I appreciate that, but I know what you mean about viruses. Tell you what. If you have a spare CD I'll burn my document onto it and your manager can check it. I know it'll be fine."

The woman looked relieved. "I'm sure it will. Would you like us to hold the printout for you?"

"Well, I have a signing I'm going to in about an hour. Could you have someone bring it to me in the restaurant?"

She nodded. "I'll bring it myself."

Brian smiled. "Thanks. And tell your manager I appreciate it very much."

While the young woman went in search of a burnable CD, Brian turned on the laptop and reopened Zack's story. Then resaved it on the desktop. The woman returned a moment later and Brian proceeded to copy the story, handing the burned disk back to the woman. Thanking her again, he shut off the computer and headed to the restaurant.

To his disappointment, he discovered it was a buffet. He took a moment to scope out the food, feeling a little queasy when he spied the mound of bacon swimming in pools of partially coagulated grease.

Maybe Joanna had something with her vegetarian diet, after all. It certainly sounded more appetizing than this looked. Instead of his usual large breakfast, he opted for a bagel with cream cheese, along with some much-needed coffee, and took a seat in a booth toward the back of the restaurant. In spite of getting nearly nine hours sleep, he still felt disoriented.

He was also nervous.

He'd been through hundreds of signings over the years and had always handled them with reasonable aplomb, enjoying them. Now, he found he could barely choke down his bagel, his stomach doing flip-flops like a kid about to take his driver's test. Of course, most of this was because he knew Joanna was coming. But the lion's share of his nerves was because he wasn't sure how he would handle meeting her son. A thought kept nagging at the back of his mind, one he didn't want to acknowledge, but which refused to be ignored. Hopefully, it would all come clear when he and the boy had a chance to talk. And then he would need to speak to Joanna.

He looked up to see the strawberry blonde from the front desk crossing the floor toward him. She smiled and handed the pages to him.

"Sorry, again, Mr. Weller," she said.

"No problem."

She turned and left, and Brian took the opportunity to reread the hard copy, making some mental notes about the boy's style. It was every bit as powerful and moving as it had been the night before, perhaps even more so in the cold light of day. And while he now noticed a few very minor errors, the kind of errors beginning writers made, the boy had a huge talent. So many would-be writers turned out perfect prose that left one cold. This kid wielded words like weapons.

His cell phone rang.

A Note from an Old Acquaintance

"Hello?"

"Hey, Captain, how's tricks?"

Brian smiled. "I'm just fine, Kevin. How're things with you?"

"Good, good. Just wanted to see how my boy, Gerald's treating you. You all ready for this morning?"

"Gerald's a good kid. Seems to be on top of things. And, yes, I'm as ready as I'll ever be."

"Glad to hear it. Anyway, just wanted to run something by you. Since we're thinking about doing that talk show, how would you like to do a couple of additional signings in the Big Apple? Some of the stores there have been hearing about your little Boston jaunt—"

"Oh? I wonder how that rumor got started?"

Kevin Romano laughed. "Guilty as charged. So, anyway, Brentano's, the big one in Manhattan, wants to host you early next week. It's about two days after your last one there in Boston, so it makes no sense for you to fly back to L.A., only to turn right around and come back here. What do you think?"

Brian sighed. "Well of course I'm flattered. That particular Brentano's was always one of my favorites, but can we wait a day, or two? See how things go?"

"Sure...sure thing. They'll kick and scream a bit 'cause they want to start blasting this all over the radio and newspapers, but I'll tell them you're considering it. You take care of yourself and have some fun."

"Thanks, Kev."

He closed the phone and put it back into his shirt pocket, feeling guilty. The truth was Brian didn't know if he even wanted to go through with any of the signings beyond that day's. Joanna was so close, yet so far, and he didn't know if he could endure being so near to her for the rest of the week, not with his feelings for her blossoming anew. Maybe what he should do was call Kevin back and tell him that he needed to get back to L.A., that his agent called about an urgent meeting at Universal and to please cancel everything.

He almost did it—almost....

But the forces that made him want to run were the same ones compelling him to stay, because there was a part of him that never wanted to leave. There was nothing left for him in L.A. He hated all the schmoozy lunches and phoney-baloney friendships that faded into oblivion the moment you were no longer the "flavor-of-the-month." Aside from Joanna, there were lots of things about New England that stirred his blood. Still a Yankee at heart, and that's all there was to it.

His cell phone rang again and he looked at the number, frowning. Who was this? He flipped open the phone and brought it his ear.

"Mr. Weller? It's Gerald—Gerald Pomeroy."

"Hi, Gerald. What can I do for you?"

"I'm outside, sir, it's time to go."

Brian looked at his watch and rolled his eyes.

"Sorry, Gerald, got caught up in reminiscing. I'll be right out."

He put the phone away, paid his bill, and grabbed his jacket and computer. At the front desk he asked the strawberry blonde to hold the laptop for him then headed outside.

Gerald's Ford Explorer sat rumbling at the curb, plumes of exhaust wafting upward in the chilly air. The young man waved and Brian went round to the passenger side and climbed in. The car smelled of cinnamon.

"Kevin wants to get a few pictures before things get started. The photographer should be set up and waiting."

"No problem," Brian said. "I'm ready for anything."

The ride to the Prudential Center was short and sweet. Gerald pulled his Explorer down into the garage off Huntington, parking near a service elevator. A stocky balding man in a green jacket with a Barnes

& Noble badge pinned to his lapel stood next to the elevator doors. He raised a Motorola radiophone to his mouth and spoke into it. It squawked back a moment later, followed by a squall of static.

Brian and Gerald exited the car and the man approached.

"Hi, Mr. Weller, I'm Jim. Everyone's waiting upstairs. It looks like we're going to have quite a crowd."

Brian nodded. "I have a friend of mine, who's bringing her son. Could you have them escorted in when they arrive?"

"Absolutely, just give me their names."

Brian told him and the man wrote it all down on a small pad he'd produced from inside his jacket. When they took the elevator up to the store level he realized how different the Prudential Center was from what he remembered. Everything had changed, plus it had mushroomed into a complex that stretched from Boylston Street to the north to Huntington Avenue on the south.

Jim led Brian and Gerald through a series of service entrances that felt like an endless labyrinth, finally reaching the store through its loading dock.

The store itself was impressive, almost intimidating. Two floors of shelves packed with books of every variety, and both floors several thousand square feet in size. A group of employees met them on the second floor near the front entrance. Through the plate-glass windows Brian saw a line of about twenty-five people. Behind them, a nervous-looking employee guarded the escalators leading down to the arcade. That meant there were more people waiting below. A lot more.

The manager, a harried man in his thirties, stepped forward and introduced himself and the half-dozen others. Brian did his best to remember their names, but gave up trying, thankful they wore their badges.

Next came the pictures, one with all the employees together and

311

then ones with each of them individually. Brian played the good sport, hugging the women and shaking hands with the men.

Afterward, the manager led him to a table in the back. Brian's eyes widened. Next to the table was a pallet's worth of books.

"I hope this is okay, Mr. Weller," the manager said, noticing Brian's reaction.

"Everything's fine. I just hope we sell them all."

"You kidding? I hope we have enough."

Brian laughed and took his place at the table.

Eat your heart out Stephen King.

His cell phone rang again. He was going to have to remember to shut it off once things got going.

"Hello?"

"So we meet again."

Brian's stomach lurched. It was Ruby.

"How did you get my number?"

"You should know by now that I have my sources."

"So, you're Mr. Big, so what? What do you want?"

"I want you to do your business, Mr. Weller, and go back to L.A., where you belong. I want you to leave Joanna alone, and I especially don't want you filling my son's head with any pie-in-the-sky dreams."

Brian felt a rush of anger for Joanna, and particularly for Zack.

"You have a problem with your wife? Take it up with her. As for your son, I would think you'd want to encourage his talent. He could be great someday."

The man was silent for a moment.

"Don't push me, Weller. You may be a hotshot writer, but you're still a punk to me. Leave my family alone."

Ruby hung up and Brian fought the urge to call the man back. But that was pointless. What would he do, challenge Ruby to a duel with black powder pistols at twenty paces? Brian laughed at the absurdity of that image, which served to take the edge off his anger. But there was also an undercurrent of fear he couldn't dislodge. Ruby sounded desperate. Had to be if he was calling out of the blue like this. And because of that Brian wondered to what lengths the man would now go to protect what he thought was in danger. The implications weren't pretty.

Before Brian could ponder it further, the store manager opened the front doors of the store, letting in the first twenty-five people in line.

The onslaught had begun, but Brian knew this was nothing compared to what might be just over the horizon.

29

"WHAT TIME IS IT, Mom?" Zack asked, drumming his fingers on the Volvo's dashboard.

Joanna glanced over at him, trying not to let him see her smile. "You asked me that five minutes ago."

The boy sighed, and adjusted himself in the seat, trying to find a comfortable position. "I hate these seats."

"Never bothered you before."

Zack turned to his mother and stuck out his tongue. They both laughed. "Guess I must be nervous," he said.

Joanna reached over and gave his shoulder an affectionate squeeze. "There's nothing to be nervous about. Brian's a nice man. You'll like him. And I'm very sure he'll like you."

"I know that, but will he like my stuff?"

Joanna moved the Volvo into the right-hand lanes. The Prudential exit lay a mile ahead.

"We're almost there," she said. "Just relax. I'm sure he'll like what you've done. You're a terrific writer."

The boy gave his mother one of his patented looks. "I appreciate that, but you're just—"

A Note from an Old Acquaintance

"I know— I'm just your mom."

Zack smiled again and turned his attention to the passenger window. They were just emerging from the exit when they spotted the news vans and the crowd milling around outside the Barnes & Noble.

"Oh, wow," Zack said, his eyes widening.

"Looks like we're going to be having a late lunch," Joanna commented.

It took them nearly fifteen minutes to find parking, finally opting for the Danker & Donohue garage on Newbury. They walked the quarter mile to the store.

The boy's expression turned melancholy when he saw the crowd up close. It looked even bigger. Joanna tugged his sleeve, motioning toward the escalator. "You need to trust your mom," she said.

Leading the way, she and Zack wormed their way up to the front of the crowd. A bookstore employee, a heavy-set man in a green jacket standing behind a velvet rope, regarded her with a weary look. "Ma'am," he said, "you'll have to go back to the end of the line. Mr. Weller's informed us that he'll sign books for everyone, or until we run out. And that's looking more and more likely."

Joanna squinted at the man's badge. It read "Jim."

"Jim, did Mr. Weller by chance let you know a couple of friends of his were coming by?"

The man's hard expression immediately melted away, replaced by a sheepish grin. "You must be Joanna and Zack," he said. "My apologies."

He turned and waved to someone up on the second level. A skinny kid with too much hair gel in his spiked locks raced down the escalator.

The younger man shook his head in amazement. "Is this something else, or what?"

"It's something, all right. Listen, Harv, these two people are friends of Brian Weller. He's asked us to have them escorted in."

The younger man straightened up. "Sure thing." He turned to Joanna and Zack. "Follow me."

Joanna grabbed her son's hand and the two of them followed the young man up the escalator. The line broke at the door, where several employees, one with an attendance counter, were letting people in a few at a time. Joanna realized Zack still held onto her hand, something he'd stopped doing when he was eight years old. His grip was tight. God, he really *was* nervous. She looked at him. His eyes were intent and purposeful, showing nothing of what he must be feeling. She was so proud of him.

Once inside, the young man led them to the back of the store. There were about fifteen people lined up in front of the table where Brian sat. He was signing books as fast as the store employees handed them to him. But he appeared at ease, smiling at the middle-aged woman at the head of the line. She could just hear the tail end of what he was telling her.

"...and please tell your husband that I appreciate his loyalty and that I hope he feels better soon."

Brian looked over at Joanna and winked at her then resumed signing. The young man named Harv, leaned over and spoke into Joanna's ear. "Would you like anything to drink?"

"No, thank you. Zack?"

The boy shook his head without taking his eyes off Brian.

"No problem," Harv said. "We have a couple of chairs set up over there behind Mr. Weller," he said, pointing them out. "Make yourselves at home."

"Thank you, Harv," Joanna said.

She nodded to Zack, and the two of them walked behind the table, scooting around what was left of a serious stack of books. She had no idea how many they'd started with, but the man at the door was right. There looked to be far fewer books than people wanting copies. She hoped there wouldn't be any problems for Brian.

She turned to Zack and watched him. He was so absorbed by what Brian was doing, his wide eyes taking everything in. She'd known that he was a fan of Brian's work for a long time, at first concerned that his young mind was reading such hard-hitting adult fare. But her unease had dissipated when she'd come to realize that her son saw life for what it really was. It had frightened her that a boy so young could see the intricacies of life so clearly, and yet it had filled her with pride and awe when she'd read the stories he'd written. So mature, so filled with honest emotion, especially the latest one. It made her cry, for it was Zack's eloquent way of trying to reach his father, and it had fallen on deaf ears.

Joanna felt her face flush and she turned away from her son, blinking back the tears. Erik was so consumed by his ambition that he didn't see what was slipping through his fingers. She'd even tried to get him to read Zack's last story, had watched him as he'd started it, but he'd soon complained of being tired and put the pages on his nightstand, where they remained for days, until she'd put them away.

Erik Ruby was afraid of his son.

He was afraid of losing him and afraid of truly knowing him. She just wished she knew why. What was it that drove that wedge between them?

She shook her head and watched Brian stand for a photograph with a heavyset man who'd brought his own camera. He placed his arm around the man as if they were old friends, mugging for one picture, then taking another, more serious one, one she was sure the anonymous man would treasure. It was clear Brian reveled in making contact with his readers, just as he'd said. Her heart went out to him when thoughts of his personal tragedies ran through her mind. She had doubts about her own abilities to handle anything close to what had happened to him; and she prayed she would never have to find out how real those doubts might be.

Another hour went by, with Brian turning to her several times, mouthing, "Are you okay?" and "Sorry about this."

She smiled back each and every time, not wanting him to think she was in the least bit uncomfortable or bored. And the truth was, she wasn't. It was so pleasant and so easy just being near him.

The pile of books grew smaller and smaller. Several times, store employees would come from the front, survey the inventory, frown and shake their heads then return to the waiting crowd.

When there were perhaps two-dozen copies left, a balding man whom she assumed was the store manager approached the table, knelt down and had a whispered conference with Brian. The man looked worried. Brian placed his arm on the man's shoulder and spoke to him and Joanna saw the manager relax. The two of them stood up and shook hands and the manager trotted off toward the front of the store.

Brian turned and came over to where Joanna and Zack were seated. They stood up and Brian hugged Joanna then stuck out his hand to Zack.

"Hi, Zack, I'm Brian. Your mom's told me so much about you that I already feel we're old friends."

The boy cracked a shy smile and shook Brian's hand. "It's an honor to meet you, Mr. Weller," he said.

Brian smiled. "Please, call me Brian. My dad was Mr. Weller."

Zack's smile widened.

"What just happened?" Joanna asked, nodding in the direction the manager had gone.

Brian shook his head. "It would seem my publicist is more of a powerhouse than I give him credit for. As you can see, we've run out of books and the manager told me there are at least two hundred people still waiting."

"What are you going to do?"

"I told him I'd be happy to return before leaving town and sign any books that people pay for over the course of the week."

"That's so nice of you," Joanna said.

Brian shrugged then nodded toward the few people still waiting at the table. "They're worth it. Every one of them. It's the least I can do for what they've done for me."

Joanna nodded, feeling a rush of emotions. She knew exactly what he meant.

"I should finish up here and then we can go. I'm starved. Any place good around here?"

"There's a Cheesecake Factory across the way. How's that?"

"Sounds wonderful. Will they have something for you?"

"Oh, I'm sure I'll manage," she said.

Brian grinned and returned to the table, where he quickly signed the remaining books. The manager returned from the front and shook Brian's hand again. "I appreciate your willingness to come back, I really do. There were some pretty irate people out there, just now, but they took that news pretty well."

"I'm glad," Brian said. "When do you think you'll have the books?"

"Probably in about three days. It'll take that long to get them from the central warehouse in Jersey."

"Great. I've got four more gigs over the next week. How about I come back the morning of the seventeenth. I'll have a few hours before my flight leaves to tie all this up."

"That's perfect," the manager said. "The front is pretty clear or would you prefer us to take you out the back way?"

"The front's fine. My friends and I are going to grab a bite to eat. Thank you so much for having me."

Brian grabbed his leather jacket and the three of them headed toward the front of the store, the manager leading the way. The last of the crowd had melted away and Joanna was relieved they didn't have to run a gauntlet to get to the restaurant. She realized she was ravenous.

They took the escalator down, crossed the Huntington Arcade and entered the Cheesecake Factory. It was crowded, as it always tended to be. Getting a table anytime soon didn't look promising. But when Brian headed for the hostess, Joanna saw the young woman look at him with a wide-eyed expression and she relaxed. How tempting it must be to take advantage of worldwide recognition. Brian spoke to the young woman then came back over to them.

"They can have a table for us in ten minutes. That okay with you guys?"

Joanna nodded. "That's record time for them," she said, grinning.

Brian laughed then frowned when his cell phone rang.

"Excuse me," he said, pulling it from his pocket and flipped it open.

"Yes?" He listened for a moment then laughed. He pulled the phone away from his face and turned to Joanna. "My publicist. He's giving himself a hernia from patting himself on the back." Joanna and Zack laughed, and Brian went back to his conversation. "Yes, Kevin, you're the best, but let's hope these little Mom and Pops don't get mobbed like this. I can handle the big ones. Just don't want to see these little bookstores get trashed. Okay? All right, talk to you later."

He put away his phone and chuckled. "I really think he's as blown away by this as I am."

"But surely this isn't the first time something like this has happened to you," Joanna said.

"No, but the book's been out for a while now. This kind of reception is highly unusual."

"Well, you're an unusual man."

Brian laughed. "Coming from you, I'll take that as a compliment."

She touched him on the arm. "You'd better."

The hostess approached. "Your table's ready, Mr. Weller."

The three of them followed the hostess to a secluded booth in the rear of the restaurant.

"Is this okay?" the hostess asked, looking nervous.

"It's perfect. Thank you."

She smiled, passed out the menus and left.

The three of them sat and got comfortable. The waitress appeared moments later. "May I bring you some drinks?"

"You know, I think we're ready to order," Brian said, "unless you two need a moment."

"I think we know what we want. Zack?"

The boy nodded and the three of them ordered.

When the waitress left, Brian turned to the boy. "So, aside from writing, what do you like to do, Zack?"

The boy shrugged. "I like to play guitar."

Joanna saw Brian's reaction, a combination of shock and delight.

"Really?" Brian said. "Who's your favorite band?"

"Green Day."

"He blasts that 'Idiot' album day and night. Drives us crazy," Joanna said.

Zack smiled devilishly.

Brian laughed. "Well, maybe you won't believe this, but they're my current favorite, too, though I still love all my old favorites, like Hendrix and Cream."

Zack perked up. "Those guys are totally killer."

"In fact, I saw Green Day in L.A. not too long ago, during their 'American Idiot' tour. Got to jam with Billie Joe backstage."

"Whoa, really? How cool. Did he let you play one of his Juniors?"

"Sure did, the Fifty-six sunburst single-cut. The one he calls 'Floyd.' Light as a feather, too."

"Wow. I really want one of those. The new one's really suck."

"Zack!" Joanna said, looking horrified.

The boy shot his mother a guilty smile. "Sorry, Mom."

She shook her head and rolled her eyes at Brian, as if to say "Kids!"

"I know what it is for me, but what is it about playing guitar that does it for you?"

Zack leaned forward. "It's like therapy, you know? I can be sitting there trying to write something and it just won't come, not for anything. Yet, when I pick up my guitar and start wailing, it's like my mind switches into another realm, you know? It recharges me. Usually, after a little while, the words start coming again. Then I can't stop them. The chicks dig it, too." The boy laughed.

"Exactly," Brian said, grinning. "How long have you been playing?"

"Four years."

"If you've been at it that long you'll stick with it. And it'll be your best friend."

The food arrived then and the three of them took a few moments to satisfy their immediate hunger before Brian spoke again.

"I reread your story this morning, Zack."

The boy put his fork down, his attention riveted on Brian. "I've got to tell you honestly that you have a real gift. You have the ability to put the reader right into the hearts and minds of your characters, and that is one of the few things no one can teach."

A Note from an Old Acquaintance

"You really liked it?" Zack asked.

Joanna's heart hammered in her chest.

"Liked it? I was humbled by it, Zack. Now, there were a very few things that you'll need to be aware of as far as grammar and style, but these are technical issues. Someday they'll be second nature to you. The important thing is to keep writing...and reading—everything you can."

"You really think it's that good, Brian?" Joanna asked.

He turned and regarded her with a tender smile. "He's got the heart and soul of a true artist. And his mastery of the craft at this age is amazing. He just needs to keep at it. Not let anything distract him from that goal. If that's what he really wants."

"It is," Zack said. "It's what I really want."

"Good. Now, if you'd like, we can take a closer look at what I was talking about. You game?"

"Sure!" the boy said.

Brian pulled the printout of the story from his jacket pocket and began going over it, showing Zack how he could revise it.

While Joanna watched the two of them together, she came to a realization, one that had nagged at the back of her mind for the last several weeks, since she'd first e-mailed Brian.

She was still in love with him.

Irrevocably and completely in love with him.

She felt a mixture of both joy and sadness, neither one of them winning the battle for supremacy in her heart. What was she going to do, now that the dies of their lives were so irreversibly cast? She thought of the old movie she'd seen on TV recently, *Same Time Next Year* with Alan Alda and Ellen Burstyn. It was a beautiful story about two lovers, married to others, who met every year at the same resort to continue their love affair and share the joys and sorrows of each other's lives.

Could she lead a second life like that? She didn't know, but a part of her wanted to try—anything to keep this wonderful man as a part of her life.

"...so, it's really that simple," Brian said. "Point of view is the most important tool you've got."

"I get it," the boy said, grinning. He turned to his mother. "Mom, I've got to go...." He indicated the area where the restrooms lay.

She got the message and nodded.

"Excuse me," Zack said, rising.

After he left the table, Joanna covered Brian's hand with hers. "You don't know how much I appreciate your helping him. It means the world to him...and to me."

Brian caressed her hand, then looked off the way the boy had gone. "Please forgive me for asking this, but I have to know. The guitar playing, the writing.... Is he mine, Joanna?"

Her eyes widened. "Oh, Brian.... No...."

He nodded and the look of disappointment that crossed his face nearly broke her heart. "I—I was pregnant with him when I met you. I didn't find out I was until after you were gone."

"How can you be sure he isn't?"

Joanna looked down at the table. "My husband had a cancer scare a few years ago. They did a lot of tests. He didn't think one more little blood test would be noticed."

"Paternity?"

She nodded.

"So, for all those years...before that...."

"I believed he was yours."

He let out a sigh. "How did you feel when you found out he wasn't?"

"That I'd lost you again," she said, her voice nearly a whisper. "I wanted to call you back then, so many times.... But I was scared. I left him, Brian.... I moved back in with Marcia—right after you left Boston. But when I started getting sick every morning—"

"You went back...."

"Yes."

Brian's eyes locked with hers. There was so much more she wanted to say...and so much she needed to know. Why, then, was she afraid to ask the one question burning in her heart?

She wasn't going to cry.

She *wasn't*.

"You know, if my little Joey had lived, I'd want him to be just like Zack.... Joanna...I—" He looked past her shoulder. "He's coming back."

She let go of his hand and shifted in her seat, smiling when Zack rejoined them.

Did he see the guilt on her face?

If he did, her son was smart enough not to let on. Joanna looked to Brian and saw that he showed nothing of the emotions that had gone through him moments before. He smiled warmly at Zack. Joanna relaxed.

"Well, I say we should have a little toast," Brian said, raising his glass of Evian. "May the future never disappoint us."

For the rest of the meal Brian entertained them with stories of the various celebrities he knew and their secret kinks and quirks. Joanna couldn't remember laughing so hard. Afterwards, outside the restaurant, there was a moment of awkwardness, as if neither Brian nor Joanna knew what to do next. Zack broke the silence.

"Mom, why don't you take Mr. Weller back to his hotel?"

Joanna rolled her eyes, feeling foolish. "Of course. Can we give you a lift, good sir?"

Brian bowed low with a flourish and said, "I would be most honored, milady." His upper-crust British accent was dead-on.

The three of them laughed and began walking toward the street. Zack hung back. "I'll see you later, Mom, okay?"

"Wait a minute, where are you going?"

"I thought I'd take the 'T' and meet Dad at the building. You know he's been dying to show me around."

"But you're only fifteen and I don't think—"

"Mom, my friends and I have been taking the 'T' for years. I'll be fine. Okay?"

She saw his determination and that subtle pleading look that begged her not to embarrass him in front of Brian. She sighed. "All right, but be careful."

Zack nodded and turned to Brian. "Thank you again, Mr. Weller. I really appreciate all your advice and your faith in me."

Brian met the boy's gaze and smiled. "It's Brian, and you just keep writing, okay? Don't ever give up, and you'll make it."

The boy grinned and loped off through the arcade.

Neither Brian nor Joanna said much during the ride to the Park Plaza. For once the traffic was light and she found her anxiety growing by the moment. Except for the few other bookstore signings Brian had scheduled, he would soon be leaving town, their time together nearly at an end. The thought of that made her feel as if she might burst into tears at any moment. She fought back wave after wave of emotions, and it took every bit of her will to put on a neutral face. Five minutes later, they pulled into a parking spot adjacent to the hotel.

She turned and found Brian staring at her, smiling warmly. "Kind of feels like a first date, doesn't it?"

"Yes, it does," she said, letting out the breath she'd been holding, her smile matching his. She took his hand, their fingers interlacing.

A Note from an Old Acquaintance

"I'm so glad you came back, Brian.... I—I've missed you...." She looked at him again, lips trembling, her vision blurring with a rush of tears.

Brian's eyes grew sad. "Please don't, Joanna, it's okay—"

Before he could go on, and before she could change her mind, she kissed him. His warm, soft lips melded with hers and Joanna felt as if she might faint, her entire body floating on a pillow of air. Brian pulled away first, the expressions on his face a mixture of guilt and passion.

"I'm sorry," Joanna said. "It's still too soon, isn't it?"

"No, it's not that. I mean, it's—" He shook his head.

"What is it, Brian? Please, tell me."

"I loved Penny, I really did, but—"

And suddenly a part of her didn't want to know whatever it was he was about to reveal. "You don't have to say this now," she said, feeling the tears coming on again.

"Yes, I do. I should have fought for you back then, Joanna, with all my might. I should have fought for you. And I didn't. Instead, I folded my tent and slunk out of town, leaving you...hurting you. And I've never forgiven myself."

Joanna's heart beat like a jackhammer, her throat as tight as a drum. She could hardly breath. "What are you saying?"

"I've said too much already."

She took his face in her hands. "Wait a minute. There's something I need to say, too. I'm *still* in love with you. It's why I e-mailed you after so many years, because you've never been far from my thoughts, and I needed to know if what I felt was really true, or just a fantasy. I finally realized how real my feelings were when I saw you and Zack working on his story, I knew it then without a particle of doubt. And nothing you say now about the past will ever change that."

His eyes grew sad. "Yes, it will."

"Please, tell me what happened. I can't bear it any longer."

He turned and stared out across Arlington Street.

"Please...." she repeated.

He turned back to face her and retook her hand. "You remember, on the phone, when I told you I didn't love you?"

She nodded, remembering that awful moment as if it had just happened. "I was so devastated, Brian. I wanted to hate you. I really did, but I couldn't. I just couldn't understand why it was happening. And you just hung up without listening to me. Whatever it was I would have stood by you."

"But that's the point, Joanna, you couldn't."

She frowned. "What do you mean?"

"Joanna, please believe me now when I tell you that I've loved you from the very first moment I saw you at the club that night and I've never stopped. Never.... All through my life with Penny, you were there in the background, inspiring me, sustaining me. Your belief in me back then is what's made me the writer I am today." He paused, and Joanna held her breath. "What I told you that night was a lie, a filthy, despicable lie. And I told it because I had no choice."

"But, why?"

Brian sighed and shook his head. "After I left your show, your husband sent his errand-boy, Mosley, to follow me home and bring me to his office. Once I was there, he showed me the file he'd put together on me. There were things in there about me that even I'd forgotten about. One of the things it revealed was that my father was on the verge of financial ruin; he owed a total of nearly three-quarters of a million dollars to three different banks.

"Your husband gave me a choice there and then: If I agreed to break it off with you and leave town...he would pay off all my parents' debts, free and clear. If I refused, not only would I never see you again, he would leave my parents to the sharks and ruin me and my partner in the bargain." Brian paused, fighting his emotions. "I couldn't let my parents lose everything they'd spent their entire lives working for. I—I just couldn't. When I told you that I didn't love you, I was calling you from his office. He was listening to every word we said."

Joanna's mind had gone blank. This couldn't be true. It couldn't!

She shook her head, wrapping her arms around herself. "No, no, no," she said. "He wouldn't do something like that. Erik's a ruthless businessman and that's something I've always known. But this? Please tell me this isn't true."

"I wish it wasn't," Brian said.

She began to cry, the tears welling out of her eyes the size of small pearls. "I—I need to go— I just really need to go. I'm sorry, Brian, but this is all just too much."

Brian exited the car and barely closed the door when she sped away, the screech of her tires echoing between the buildings.

30

RUBY STOOD AT THE windows of his new corner office on the penthouse level—the only completed interior space in all the building's fifty floors—his dark eyes transfixed by the panoramic view of downtown Boston. Sun glinted off the distant State House dome, and mid-afternoon crowds teemed in nearby Fanueil Hall. From this sweeping vantage point he felt the thrumming pulse of the city—a city he was transforming building by building—brick by brick.

Bricks....

His eye's flicked to the red-brick expanse of Government Center, dominated by the hulking poured-concrete behemoth of City Hall; his lips curled in a knowing smirk. He still marveled at the incredible amount of graft necessary to gain the height restriction variance, the greedy manicured paws outstretched without hesitation or humility. Yet he'd paid it all, gladly, his sleek thousand-foot tower of glass—Ruby Plaza—now standing as mute testament to his master plan. And it was only the beginning.

His recent meeting with the Mayor and the City Planning Committee had yielded the opportunity of a lifetime: the complete transformation of Government Center, a project of immense proportions worth billions, and potentially the crowning glory of his career. The bids were in—the final decision due any day.

Like a proud eagle staring down from its aerie, he watched and calculated, the heady promise of the future stretching out before him. The thrill of it all made his blood sing.

Ruby turned from the view and eyed the décor again, nodding his approval. The massive desk, the last of the Chris Hembree pieces, arrived that very afternoon, and the designer had followed his installation instructions to the letter. It was perfect, looking as if it had always resided there. Still, Ruby missed the Victorian ambiance of his old Newbury Street office, but he'd outgrown it, emotionally, as well as in size and scope. This is where he belonged, now, amongst handcrafted furnishings of polished steel, aluminum, and beveled glass—at the top of his game. The old things would have been out of place.

There was only one holdover.

He glanced at the framed life-sized photo of Joanna now hanging on the wall opposite the desk. The photo still stirred him as it did when he first saw the transparency lying on the photographer's light table so many years before. It would always have that effect on him, even when she no longer looked this way.

"All for you, Joanna...."

He turned, hearing a sound at the doorway.

"Hi, Dad," Zack said, smiling shyly.

The boy moved into the room, his eyes wide at the sight of his father's grand inner sanctum.

Ruby grinned and walked over to his son, giving him a bear hug. "So you decided to come and visit your old man, after all?"

"Yeah," the boy replied.

"I'm glad. Happy birthday, Son."

"Thanks. This office is really awesome, Dad."

"Glad you like it. It's a bit lonely right now, but that'll change soon enough, when everyone moves over from the old building. Already have half the floors rented, too."

Zack nodded and took a seat in one of the chairs, propping his feet on the glass coffee table.

"Zack," Ruby said, pointing at his son's feet.

The boy removed them from the table, looking guilty.

"Your mother parking the car?"

"No. She didn't come."

Ruby frowned. "She didn't come? How did you get here?"

"Took the 'T'."

"You took what? At your age?"

The boy rolled his eyes. "Dad, it's fine. Like I told Mom, I've been doing it for years."

"Then where is she, Zack?"

The boy's expression turned sad. "She took Mr. Weller back to his hotel."

Ruby froze, his mind scrambling to control the fury racing through him. "Zack, why don't you hang out here for a moment. There are some sodas in the fridge at the wet bar. I need to go check on something, okay? Then we'll take a little tour, if you like."

"Okay, Dad."

Ruby crossed the floor and strode out the door, closing it behind him. In the hallway, he pulled out his cell phone and pressed the STAR key.

"Please state the command," a synthesized voice intoned.

"Name dial," he replied.

"Please state the name."

"Joanna."

"Did you say...Joanna?"

A Note from an Old Acquaintance

"Yes."

"Joanna...connecting."

The phone rang once.

"Hi, this is Joanna. If you've reached this message—"

Ruby pushed the END key, his anger growing. She could have forgotten to turn it on. He'd lost count of how many times she'd neglected to do that over the years. Then again, it also could mean she didn't want to be disturbed....

He gripped the phone, his knuckles whitening. He wanted to crush it in his bare hands, almost as much as he wanted to crush Weller.

Calm down, calm down. Keep it cool. There's a better way....

The next number he punched in manually. Mosley answered in record time.

"Good afternoon, Mr. Ruby. What can I do for you?"

As always, the black man's voice had a calming effect.

"It's time to end this thing, Mr. Mosley. I want you to bring Mr. Weller to the building in an hour. And if my wife's with him, bring her, too."

"Understood, Sir. And should he resist?"

"Then do whatever you need to do to persuade him. But I don't want him hurt. Clear?"

"Yes, sir."

Ruby closed the phone, feeling a weight lifting from him. He had no idea how he'd feel later, but for now his conscience was clear. One way or another, it was ending tonight.

❀   ❀   ❀

Joanna raced down the Mass Pike, heedless of both the speed limit and her fellow travelers. She kept checking the rearview to see if any state

333

police cruisers might be dogging her, making ready to pull her over. There was only the normal traffic.

She was a mess. What little makeup she wore was streaked and smeared on her face, the tracks of her tears clearly visible.

But inside she felt worse. She still couldn't believe what Brian had told her. It was so monstrous, so evil. That the man she'd lived with for nearly half her life, the father of her child, could have hidden this side of him from her for all these years....

It *had* to be a lie.

But what if it wasn't?

Would he be so heartless and cruel as to make up a story like that after all he'd been through? And hadn't he also confessed his love for her?

Where was the truth?

Could it have been in front of her eyes all this time?

She slammed her hand against the wheel. "No, no, NO!"

Joanna's tears sprang anew and she used the back of her hand to wipe her eyes. She needed to keep calm. She needed to get home. She needed to find the truth.

And she knew just where it lay.

The house was dark when she arrived, which meant that Erik and Zack were still at the building. She screeched to a stop in the driveway, grabbed her keys and threw open the door.

Inside, she punched in the code deactivating the alarm then raced to her husband's office, going right to the file cabinet. It was a formidable one, made from thick powder-coated steel and designed to withstand a five thousand degree fire for nearly an hour. It had taken four men to move it into the house. All his important papers resided in it...and maybe something else.

She tried the drawers. They wouldn't budge, not even the slightest play.

A Note from an Old Acquaintance

At his desk she threw open the drawers, her hands scattering the contents onto the floor.

The key! Where's the key?

Nothing....

She started to cry again, then stopped.

The studio....

She ran back the way she'd come, passing through the kitchen into the new wing, stopping at the steel door to her studio. She fumbled the keys, her hands slick with nervous sweat. With a growl of anger, she fitted the correct key and yanked the door open. It slammed against the wall, the hollow boom echoing in the room.

Inside was a replica of the studio she'd had in Fort Point Channel, minus the living quarters and kitchen. But all the tools remained, plus some new ones. She went to the drills, selecting a large AC-powered Makita. It was heavier and bulkier than their cordless brethren and had a second handle near the chuck, in addition to the standard pistol grip. It was the only one that had a prayer of getting through that lock. With the drill in-hand, she grabbed a set of diamond-tipped bits, her safety glasses, and returned the way she'd come.

Back in Erik's office, she uncoiled the drill's power cord and plugged it into the outlet behind the desk. She flipped the motor direction switch to counter-clockwise, grabbed the chuck with her left hand and pulled the trigger, loosening it just enough for her to insert the half-inch bit she'd chosen. She then switched the motor direction back to clockwise and pulled the trigger again. The drill made a loud ratcheting noise when the bit locked into place.

She was ready.

She slipped on the safety glasses, placed the end of the bit onto the lock housing just above the top drawer and bared her teeth. "Let's see what there is to see."

335

She pulled the trigger and the drill whined. Smoke began pouring from the shallow depression the bit chewed into the lock's carbide steel. In spite of the power of the drill, it looked as if it was going to be slow going. She stopped, adjusted the torque switch to its maximum, placed it back on the lock and restarted the drill, redoubling her pressure.

The bit screamed when it tore through the metal of the lock, bits of corkscrewed steel spewing from the hole and pattering against her safety glasses. The room began to reek of hot metal.

"Come on, come on!"

The drill bit sank a little further.

Yes! It was going to work!

Two minutes later, the drill pushed forward with a sudden jerk. The lock was gone.

Joanna yanked the drill free of the hole and threw it down onto her husband's swivel chair, ripped off her safety glasses then pulled open the top drawer.

She found Brian's file near the back. Unlike the other obsessively neat files surrounding it, the dark blue folder was thick with papers shoved in every which way, as if someone had been looking through it in a hurry. She brought it to the desk, turned on the green-shaded banker's light and began examining its contents. There were reams of information about every aspect of Brian's life and that of his parents, all in cold black and white type, just as he'd described them.

And there was one more thing.

Lying at the bottom of the file folder was the agreement between her husband and Brian. Three typewritten pages spelling out just how little she was valued as a person. To her husband, she was nothing more than a commodity to be bought and sold.

A cold anger built inside her. Erik had known about her and Brian all along—and never said a word—never dared to confront her. He'd just sat back and watched, watched and waited, until he could spring his scheming little trap, a trap that nearly ruined a man's life.

And hers.

Tucking Brian's file under her arm, Joanna went upstairs and peeled off the clothes she'd been wearing and changed into black jeans and a black silk blouse. She'd always loved wearing black, thought it complemented her white skin and red hair. It also simplified a life fraught with stress and ambition. Now, it signified something else, something more funereal.

Downstairs she lingered at the front door, wondering if she would ever return there. Could she ever sleep in her bed again knowing what she now knew about Erik? And what about Zack? Could she allow him to be influenced by such a man? Joanna felt a stab of fear. He was with Erik now. She knew he would never deliberately harm their son. She was sure of that. But what about the subtle things, the things he showed the boy by example? What was Zack learning from that?

No. She couldn't allow that. She needed to act.

Joanna returned to her car, placing the file on the passenger seat. She turned the key and the engine caught. The dashboard, with its dazzling displays sprang to life, glowing like a Christmas tree. She checked the gas gauge and then the dashboard clock. It was almost 5:00. She closed her eyes and took several deep breaths.

You can do this. You *have* to do this.

For Zack....

For Brian....

And for you....

She opened her eyes and threw the car into reverse.

It was time to go take back her life.

31

IT HAD BEEN A mistake to come back.

That was the thought that wouldn't be denied, wouldn't be rationalized away to some innocuous comfort zone inside his mind. It kept reverberating, growing louder and louder. So, instead of finding peace and the closure he'd sought when he'd returned to Boston, all he'd done was hurt the woman he'd loved for nearly half of his life. Hurt her a *second* time. And he really couldn't decide which sin was worse: the lie he'd told her all those years ago, when he'd said he'd never loved her, or telling her the unvarnished truth now?

Brian sighed and shook his head, recalling the rush of tears welling from those shattering green eyes, that look of anguish, a look he'd put there because he couldn't keep his damned mouth shut. When they'd pulled up in the car and he'd had made his little joke about it feeling like a first date, he'd been trying to avoid thinking that moment might be the last time he would ever see Joanna. That and the thought of going on with the rest of his tour and then leaving town had overwhelmed him. And that was when she'd kissed him. Those tender lips had seared his heart, obliterating his self-control, and he'd just blurted it all out without any kind of preamble, without even *trying* to soften the blow.

A Note from an Old Acquaintance

You idiot!

It was obvious he handled the lives of his characters far better than he handled his own, and those of the people he supposedly loved and cared about. At least in the pages of his books he had more control. At least there, he could rewrite his mistakes.

Brian shook his head in disgust and stood, the muscles of his legs aching in protest. He'd been sitting too long. Maybe he'd take a shower and get something to eat, if he could stomach it. Then he'd try and call Joanna. He had her home number, though he'd never used it before. And he didn't give a damn if Ruby was there, either. He'd tell the bastard to shove it and put his wife on the phone. Brian smiled at the image his thought evoked, knowing it was a futile one, at best. Even if Ruby didn't hang up on him, what made him sure Joanna wouldn't? Damn, he'd really screwed everything up.

A knock came at the door—loud and insistent.

"Yeah, who is it?"

"Cary Mosley," came the muffled reply.

Even though alarm bells were ringing in his head, Brian went to the door and opened it.

"Good evening to you, Mr. Weller," Mosley said. "May I come in?"

Brian opened the door wider and stepped aside. "I was wondering when you'd show up."

Mosley walked into the room and moved to the window, peering out through the curtains. He'd turned gray around the temples, and there were a few lines around the cinnamon-colored eyes, but his manner of dress had not changed a bit—still natty and expensive.

"Not much of a view for a world famous author."

"No, but it suits me," Brian said. "So, to what do I owe the pleasure?"

Mosley was silent for a moment, as if he hadn't heard, then he said: "My wife, Althea, is big fan of your books. She says they're the only ones that ring true, the only ones with honest emotion.... We were both sorry to hear about your wife."

Brian was touched by the sincerity in the black man's voice. "Thank you, I appreciate that."

Mosley turned from the window, his expression troubled. "He really does love her, you know."

"Why are you telling me this?"

"Because I think he's on the brink of doing something rash and I don't want to see him go down in flames."

"Even if he deserves it?" Brian asked, moving to the desk and shutting down his laptop.

Mosley shook his head. "No. He does a lot of good with his money. He helped your father."

"You were there, Mosley. Did I really have a choice?"

"No, you didn't."

"And I also imagine you're here because of some self-interest on your part, as well?"

"*Touché*, Mr. Weller."

"Well, it's nice to know no one's perfect." Brian slipped the Mac-Book into a zippered case. "So, why are you here?"

"He wants to see you."

"I kind of figured that, but I'll be gone in a couple of days. Not much point, is there?"

"Mr. Ruby doesn't see it that way."

"And how does he 'see it'?"

"That you're a perennial problem in search of a solution."

Brian laughed. "Good one, Mosley, you should be doing stand-up. I'll bet he thinks he's found that solution, too."

"That's what I'm afraid of."

"Then go back and tell your boss that you missed me, that I was out."

"I'm sorry, I can't."

"Is this the moment the snub-nosed thirty-eight makes its appearance?"

Mosley's grin was wan. "I have a permit, but choose not to carry. I am a black belt, however."

"Ah, well, I'd hate to see you muss those clothes," Brian said, grabbing his A2 flight jacket off the bed. "Let's go see your boss."

❊　　❊　　❊

The Mass Pike was a parking lot.

Cars crept forward at a pace that would have made a snail feel like Speedy Gonzalez. Brake lights flared like angry eyes and horns blared, making Joanna want to scream. She tried to keep her mind focused, tried not to let her nerves get the better of her.

She glanced at the clock. It was 5:15. Time to call Erik.

She pulled her cell phone from her handbag and punched in his number.

"Hello, Dear," he said.

His voice was silky-smooth, as if nothing was amiss. In years past the sound of it would have made her knees weak; now, it just hardened her resolve.

"Hi. Is Zack with you?"

"Yes, and we've been having a nice father-son experience. Can't say I was happy that he came here on his own, however."

A flash of guilt shot through Joanna. She fought it. "My friend needed a ride."

There was a brief silence. "So I heard."

"I'm coming to pick Zack up. We need to talk."

"You're right about that. We do...."

She didn't like the sound of that. Not at all.

"Let me speak to Zack."

She heard Erik say something she couldn't make out and then Zack came on the line.

"Hi, Mom."

"Hi, Sweetie. You okay?"

"Sure. Dad's been showing me all around. Everything's so huge, you know? We're going up on the roof next."

"You be careful and stay away from the edge."

"Ah, Mom, I'm not an idiot."

She smiled. "Of course, you're not. But I'm sure it's windy up there. Just be careful, okay?"

"Okay," he said, pausing. "Thanks for taking me today. It was really cool meeting Mr. Weller."

Joanna smiled. "I'm glad. He really thinks you're on your way."

"Yeah," her son replied. She could tell from the sound of his voice that he was still trying to get used to that idea.

"He's more than just an old friend, isn't he?"

Joanna nearly fumbled the phone. Where on earth was this coming from? "I'm not sure how to answer that, Sweetheart. It's complicated."

"It's okay, Mom, Dad's out of the room. I saw the way you and Mr. Weller look at each other. Like I said, I'm not an idiot."

Joanna felt herself losing control again, tears stinging her eyes. "Honey, we shouldn't be talking about this. Not now."

"I—I just want you to be happy, Mom. You haven't been for a long time."

Tears clouded her eyes, making it hard to see the road, which now looked like a smear of red light through the windshield. She wiped her eyes and steadied herself.

"That doesn't matter, Zack. All your father and I want is what's best for you."

The boy was silent for a moment. What he said next pulled the rug out from under her. "I'd rather you and Dad live apart than have you slowly killing each other's spirits, like you have been."

Oh, God, what had she done to deserve such a wonderful, insightful boy? Any other kid his age would have made the same observations about her and Brian and hated them both for it. And she wasn't sure this wasn't worse in some way. He was much too young to be so mature.

"Zack, I—"

"He's coming back. I love you, Mom."

"I love you, too, Baby."

The phone went dead and Joanna tossed it back into her handbag. She gripped the wheel and cursed both her husband and the traffic.

◈   ◈   ◈

Mosley's cell phone rang five minutes after they pulled away from the hotel in the black man's silver F430. Mosley pulled a sleek ultra-thin model from inside his jacket, glanced at the number on the display then brought it to his ear.

"Yes, sir. We're on our way.... Okay."

The black man handed the phone over to Brian and shifted gears, the Ferrari's eight-cylinder engine responding with a throaty rumble.

"Yes?" Brian said.

"Well, it looks as if it's going to be old home week. My boy is here and I just got off the phone with Joanna. Seems she's real anxious to see me, too."

"Zack is there? Ruby, are you out of your mind?"

"I've never been more sane, Mr. Weller. It's time my son learned how things really work, not how they do in books."

Ruby hung up and Brian handed the cell phone back to Mosley.

"He's got Zack there with him?" Mosley asked.

Brian nodded. "And apparently Joanna's on her way there, as well."

The black man let out a sigh, shaking his head. "Sometimes I wonder about this job."

Brian gave him a look, but said nothing.

Ruby's new fifty-story monstrosity of steel and glass occupied a full block of State Street real estate in downtown Boston. Brian managed a glimpse of the top right before Mosley piloted the Ferrari into the basement parking area. Round and round they went, descending level after empty level, until they came to the private parking area. An articulated metal grate blocked their way. Mosley reached up to a remote and pushed the button. The grate began to ascend, rattling in its frame as it rose. When it was high enough to let the Ferrari slip through, Mosley gunned the engine and the car rocketed forward, coming to a stop in front of a bank of six elevators. Only one other car occupied a space.

Ruby's Jaguar.

Brian was the first to exit the car. He pushed the elevator button and waited; Mosley joined him. A moment later, one of the elevators opened and the two of them entered. The interior was spacious, like those used in hospitals, but lacked the second set of doors.

"I assume you know where we're going," Brian said.

Mosley nodded and punched the button for the fiftieth floor. The elevator accelerated upward, floor indicators snapping on and off in rapid succession, synchronized with the toll of an electronic bell. It slowed when it passed the fortieth floor, but not enough to prevent Brian from feeling as if his stomach was rising up his throat.

Easing to a stop, the elevator doors hissed open. Mosley strode out and Brian followed. The floor was only partially completed, with steel studs, wiring conduits, and plumbing still visible in places not yet covered by drywall. Buzzing fluorescent fixtures hung askew from chains and silver foil ductwork crisscrossed overhead. The air reeked of paint, adhesives, and the chalky odor of the plasterboard. The only sounds were their feet crinkling the thick plastic tarps, which covered the pristine charcoal gray carpeting.

Mosley led the way toward a set of double doors at the end of the hall. When they drew closer, Brian saw the name affixed to the polished mahogany in three-inch brass Art Deco-style letters: ERIK RUBY.

Mosley opened the door and motioned Brian inside. Somehow, even knowing Ruby and his expensive tastes did nothing to prepare him for the majesty of the space, at least two thousand square feet of ultra-modern luxury with two adjacent walls of floor to ceiling plate glass. The only object that was no surprise was Joanna's life-size portrait dominating the wall opposite the desk. The chair behind the desk was empty.

"So, where is he?" Brian asked.

Mosley had gone directly to the wet bar and poured two tumblers of single-malt scotch. He handed one to Brian. "I believe he's showing young Zack around. He'll be here soon enough."

Brian sipped the scotch. "Just like death and taxes."

❃   ❃   ❃

The blue lights began flashing just as Joanna turned onto State Street. Erik's building stood a mere five hundred feet ahead.

"Not now!" she said, easing the Volvo over to the curb. The police cruiser pulled up about twenty feet behind her and stopped. She tried looking in the rearview, but the cop had his brights on, which made seeing anything behind her impossible.

"Creep."

It was a full minute before she heard the cruiser's doors open, followed by a burst of radio static. She grabbed her handbag, rummaging for her wallet. The knock at her window, a sharp rapping sound, startled her. She looked up and a flashlight snapped on, blinding her.

"Please roll down your window, Ma'am," the officer said.

She pushed the button for the window and it slid down. A blast of icy air blew into the car, making her shiver.

"License and registration, please."

She handed them over. "What did I do, officer?"

The cop didn't answer. She forced herself to relax. After all, her husband was right down the street. He would keep for another few minutes.

❀ ❀ ❀

Brian went to the window and looked out over the view of Government Center and Beacon Hill. Beyond that, due west, was Newton. And from here Charlestown was a mere stone's throw. A man could get used to a view like this. Problem was, a view like this might give one delusions of grandeur. Make one think he was above it all, like—

"Mr. Weller, welcome to Ruby Plaza."

Startled, Brian turned to see Ruby and Zack standing in the doorway. The older man had his arm around the boy, who looked happy and relaxed.

A Note from an Old Acquaintance

Ruby patted his son on the back and moved toward the bar, where Mosley had a scotch waiting for him. Zack smiled and nodded to Brian then sat down on one of the spindly leather and steel chairs, picked up an *Architectural Digest* off the glass coffee table and began flipping through it.

"So, Mr. Weller, it would seem that old problems don't stay solved," Ruby said, moving from the bar to the chair behind his desk. He sat down heavily and regarded Brian with a hooded gaze.

He's already a few sheets to the wind, Brian thought.

"What is it going to take to make you go away for good?" Ruby asked.

The scotch had given Brian a pleasant buzz, it also made him feel bolder and more reckless than he might have felt otherwise. "How about single-shot black powder pistols at twenty paces?" he asked.

Ruby chortled. "Tempting, but I was thinking of something a bit more prosaic."

"It always comes down to money for you, doesn't it, Ruby? Every man has his price."

"Of course," Ruby grinned, draining the whiskey. He held up the empty tumbler. "Mosley, a little more of this, if you please."

The black man brought over the bottle of Macallan and poured a couple of jigger's worth into Ruby's tumbler. When he turned, Mosley gave Brian a look, as if to say, "Watch yourself."

"So, what is it going to take?" Ruby asked again.

"Let's just say my price is a bit steeper than it used to be. I don't think even *you* can afford it."

"DON'T FUCK WITH ME, WELLER!"

Brian heard the magazine Zack was holding hit the floor with a loud slap. He glanced toward the boy, who stared at his father with saucer eyes. Mosley, still standing by the bar, had gone rigid, look-

347

ing very much like the department store mannequin he resembled.

Ruby leaned forward in his chair, the springs squeaking in the silence following his outburst. His face had a blotchy appearance, but it was the blazing eyes that gave Brian pause. They were the eyes of a man poised on the edge of sanity.

❀   ❀   ❀

"Please sign here, Ma'am," the cop said, handing her the ticket book. She scrawled her name and handed it back. He tore off the original and handed it to her, keeping the carbon in his book. "Your court date and notice to appear are at the bottom. Failure to appear will result in suspension of your license. Is everything clear, Ma'am?"

Joanna nodded. "Yes, officer."

"Very good, Ma'am. And please try and remember to come to a complete stop before making a right turn."

She waited until the officer returned to his cruiser and drove away before she pulled away from the curb, gunning the Volvo. She covered the last five hundred feet to Erik's building in seconds. The tires screeched when she made the left and headed down into the underground parking, the SUV's suspension jouncing as it rolled over a speed bump. She skidded to a stop in front of the elevators, tumbled out of the car at a dead run, clutching the file against her chest. Her finger jabbed the elevator call button.

She scanned the floor indicators, noting that all of the elevators were at the top. One started moving. The numbers descended with agonizing slowness.

"Hurry up, hurry up," she muttered.

Moments later the elevator at the far end slid open and she dashed into it, hitting the button for the top floor. She watched the floor indicators with mounting dread. Until this moment, the confrontation with her husband had seemed inevitable, her anger like a force of nature. But now, as the floors ticked off one by one, her unease grew, doubts assailed her. She re-opened the file and stared at the agreement again, her eyes riveting on Brian's and her husband's signatures. The doubts became fleeting shadows. Her anger returned....

❀   ❀   ❀

"Why did you come back, anyway?" Ruby asked, his anger ebbing to a low simmer. "You gave me your word."

Brian didn't know what to say. In practical, concrete terms Ruby was right. He *had* given his word; but how do you explain fifteen years of regret? How do you explain the pain and guilt from two broken hearts?

"You wouldn't understand," Brian said.

"Try me."

Brian met Ruby's gaze. "I came back because my life had reached the point where I didn't know if I could go on any longer. Because I've been in love with Joanna for nearly half my life, and because our 'deal,' as you put it, was entered into under what I would delicately call 'dubious circumstances.'"

Ruby's laugh held no humor. "You certainly took the money quick enough, didn't you? As for the contract, my attorneys will tell me it's ironclad, and you've breached it."

"Fine, you want the money back? No problem. I'll have twice the original amount wired into your account tomorrow. Will that make you happy?"

Ruby shot to his feet, slapping the desk with the flat of his palm. "It's not the money, punk, it's Joanna! You were never supposed to see her again. Ever! THAT was the damned deal!" Ruby knocked back the rest of his scotch and slammed the tumbler down onto his desk, his eyes locked on Brian. "Look at you, the hotshot writer with your fancy words. You filled my wife's head with them fifteen years ago, now you're doing the same thing with my boy."

"No, he's not, Dad."

Ruby silenced the boy with a glare and moved out from behind the desk. "I want you to leave them both the hell alone."

"You seem to be forgetting something," Brian said. "Joanna contacted *me*."

Ruby sneered. "Yeah, I know all about that. But nobody told you to reply, did they? And nobody told you to get on a plane and fly three thousand miles to make whoopee, *did they?*" He moved closer to Brian, his expression oozing contempt. "And what kind of man are you, anyway? Out chasing skirts, declaring your undying love for another man's wife, when your wife's corpse is barely fucking cold. Just what the hell kind of goddamned low-life are you?"

There was no conscious decision to move on Brian's part. One moment, he was sitting there, listening to Ruby's bitter invective and the next he was on his feet, his hands wrapped around the older man's throat.

"MR. WELLER! DAD! NO!" Zack screamed.

Like a flash of black lightning, Mosley was between them, pushing Brian back. "Take it easy," he said in a low voice. "He's not worth it."

Brian's eyes were still locked onto Ruby's, but at the sound of Mosley's gentle, insistent voice, the anger left him. "You're right, he's not," Brian replied, backing off. Ruby rubbed his throat, but the smile of contempt had grown wider and Brian felt his anger rising again. "You know, Ruby, I can understand why you said what you said. Maybe, I would have said the same thing. But what I don't understand is why Joanna's stayed with you all these years. What did she see in you?"

"Why don't you let *me* answer that?"

Every man in the room turned toward the door where Joanna stood, clutching a file folder against her chest, righteous anger burning in her eyes. It took a moment for Brian to realize the significance of that manila folder. It was the same file Ruby had shown him all those years ago—it *had* to be. And somehow she'd found it.

When Zack saw his mother, he ran to her and hugged her. She shook with emotion and Brian's anger toward Erik Ruby rose another notch.

Joanna let go of her son and stepped forward. She held up the file. "I know everything, Erik. How you bartered for me like one of your buildings. Do I have such little value to you that you would do such a thing? How dare you! How dare you turn me into one of your deals!"

The man's smile faltered. "How dare you betray me! How could you be with *him*?" He jerked his head toward Brian.

Joanna turned her gaze to the floor, her body trembling. "I'm not going to make excuses. Nothing I say will ever excuse what I did." She raised her head, her eyes defiant. "But I also won't apologize for falling in love with a man who truly loves *me*, a man who when faced with a choice of giving me up and helping his family or pursuing me and losing everything—chose to do the right thing." She looked to Brian and smiled. In that one moment, Brian loved her more than he'd ever loved her. He returned her smile with one of his own.

Joanna turned back to her husband. "You could have come to me, Erik. You could have said that you knew and that you were hurt and that you loved me with all of your heart, and could we try and work this out? You could have said all those things. And I would have listened...."

"But, instead, you turned us into a business transaction. And you waited. You waited for the perfect moment you knew would break our hearts. And I'll never forgive you for it.

"We're finished, Erik. I'm leaving—for good this time. I don't know what I'll do, where I'll go, but I'm going. And Zack is going with me."

Ruby took a step forward, his eyes wide. "NO! You won't take my son. You have no idea what I've gone through, what I had to do."

"But I do know," she said holding up the file again. "Zack is nothing like you, and I won't have him growing up to be anything like you. You want to know what I saw in you? I fell in love with a man who once went out of his way to help a young girl and her child. That man died somewhere along the way, and I was too blind to see it."

Ruby stared at the floor, his body shaking. When he raised his head a moment later, Brian saw a cold anger in the man's eyes.

"But I did everything for you, Joanna. All for you...."

Ruby's words hung in the air. Zack looked from his father to his mother, his lips trembling.

Joanna shook her head. "No you didn't, Erik. You did it all for *her*," she said, pointing toward her photo on the wall. "And that woman is nothing but a shadow—a ghost. You created her that day at the photographer's studio, hung her on the wall, and put all your hopes, desires and dreams into her, made her come alive. But I'm not her, Erik—I'm *not* Galatea. I'm Joanna—just Joanna, and I don't love you anymore."

The room was as quiet as a grave. Brian watched Ruby, wondering what the older man would do, but he simply stared at his wife and then at her picture on the wall, his expression unreadable.

He opened his mouth to speak. "Joanna—"

The phone rang, startling everyone. It rang two more times before Mosley walked over and picked it up.

"Ruby and Associates.... Yes, sir, I'll tell him." Mosley held the phone to his chest. "It's the mayor."

Ruby's entire demeanor changed. "Put him on the speaker."

When Mosley hesitated, Ruby reached over and stabbed the speaker button. "Good evening, sir."

"Erik, I knew you'd be working late, and I wanted to be the one to give you the news. The Government Center Project is yours. The council vote was unanimous."

Ruby closed his eyes and exhaled, as if a great weight had lifted from his shoulders. "Thank you, sir. You don't know how much this means to me. I'll make the city proud."

"Never had any doubts. Now, if you can tear yourself away from that office and that pretty wife of yours, a few of us are meeting at the club for drinks. I'd be pleased if you would join us."

"I'd be honored."

"Great. We'll see you there in twenty minutes."

The phone went dead and Ruby stared at it, a sardonic smile curling his lips. "I've been waiting nearly ten years for that call," he said, shaking his head. "It would seem some dreams are meant to be, after all...."

Then, as if reaching a decision, he straightened his spine and walked toward his wife. He passed her and stood gazing up at her photo. "We could have shared that dream, Joanna, but you've made your choice, haven't you?" He paused, his jaw clenching. "I'll be home later to pack some things. I'll be staying at the club until my living quarters are ready here. My attorney will also be in touch. I'd suggest one for you, but that would clearly be a conflict."

Brian was stunned, and if Joanna's open-mouthed expression was any gauge, so was she.

"I—I'm sorry, Erik," she said.

Ruby turned from the photo. "A little late for that, now, don't you think? I just hope Mr. Weller's pockets are deep. You're going to need it."

"There's nothing you have that I want," Joanna said, meeting his piercing gaze with one her own.

Ruby nodded, the confident smirk back on his face. "We'll see, won't we?" He turned to Zack, clasping the boy on the shoulders. "I'm sorry you had to see all this, Chief. But I want to make it up to you. How would you like to come with me and meet the Mayor? Another birthday treat. What do you say?"

The boy stared at his father, his expression a mixture of incredulity and sadness. "No, Dad," he said, shaking his head. "I'm staying with Mom."

Ruby's grin disappeared. "Very well." He marched over to one of the built-in cabinets and pulled out his overcoat, folding it over his arm, then walked back to Joanna's photo. His eyes betrayed a fleeting moment of pain and longing before disappearing behind the familiar mask. "Mr. Mosley?"

"Yes, sir?"

"Before you go home to that lovely wife of yours, I'll need you to take this down. Store it with the rest of the outgoing trash. It's time we got rid of the shadows and the ghosts...." He turned and gave everyone a curt nod and left the room. Mosley followed him, his features etched with concern.

Joanna ran to Brian, collapsing into his arms.

"When I walked in, and saw you two fighting like that, I thought I was going to lose you again! And now everything's changed. Why do I still feel so awful?" She cried against his shoulder, and he nestled her head in the hollow of his neck. The warmth of her suffused his body.

"It's never easy closing a chapter of your life," Brian said. He tilted her chin so he could look into those beautiful tear-clouded eyes. "But I promise you—you'll never lose me again, Joanna. Never again."

Seven Months Later...

"Is it much farther?" Zack asked, breaking the long silence between them.

"You mean, 'Are we there yet?'" Joanna said with a sly grin.

"Please tell me I never said that."

Joanna chuckled. "Oh, you were one of the worst offenders. Annoying, but cute."

Zack grinned and turned his head to watch the passing New Hampshire scenery. "I'm glad he's finally back. I hope it's for good this time."

His mother gave his thigh a loving pat. "It's for good."

Ever since they'd left Boston earlier that afternoon, Zack watched his mother's excitement grow. She'd been a nervous wreck the night before with all the packing, and spent way more time in the bathroom that morning fussing with her hair and makeup; but he had to admit she looked beautiful in her new summer dress.

Brian—he still found himself wanting to call him Mr. Weller—had been really great during all the months it took for his parents' divorce to wind its way through the courts, calling from Los Angeles every night and giving her the moral support she needed, and helping him with his writing. All of Brian's guidance paid off just last month, the day his first story appeared in the June issue of *Harper's*. Even his dad was impressed, proudly showing off the magazine to all of his bigwig friends.

"The turnoff's just ahead," Joanna said.

"Are you sure?"

"If I'm not we're going to end up in the lake. That's it up ahead."

Zack's eyes widened. He didn't know what he'd expected, but Lake Sunapee was a lot bigger than he'd ever imagined.

"Are we going to live up here?" he asked.

"Just until the new townhouse is ready. This will be our weekend retreat."

"Cool."

Joanna slowed the SUV and made a right turn onto a street paralleling the lake. Moments later, she eased the car to a halt in front of a two-story crescent-shaped modern, set on a low rock promontory jutting out into the lake.

The outer curve of the house, mostly windows, faced the lake and the long dock dominating the small cove. At the end of the dock, Zack spotted a sleek all-mahogany 1940s-style inboard speedboat. A lone figure knelt by the craft, snapping on a weatherproof cover over the cockpit and windscreen.

Joanna spotted the man and turned to Zack. "Do I look okay?"

She looked so comically worried that Zack wanted to laugh. Instead, he gave her arm a gentle squeeze. "You look really pretty, Mom."

Her face lit up. "Thanks, sweetie," she said, kissing him on the cheek. "Now, be sure to put the gift someplace special, okay? I'll leave it to your sharp artistic eye."

Zack gave her a "thumbs-up," and grabbed the heavy box by his feet. Joanna ruffled his hair and they both climbed out of the SUV. She hesitated a moment, watching the man work on the boat and then started toward him. Something made him stand and look her way. Even at that distance Zack saw the dramatic change in the man's demeanor.

"So, how's my favorite professor?" Brian called out.

Zack heard his mother giggle and then she took off running, pounding down the dock and launching into Brian's arms.

For a second, Zack was afraid they'd both tumble into the lake, but Brian held her and swung her around. Her laughter echoed across the water.

Grinning, Zack hefted the box and walked into the house. It took him a moment to get his bearings then he passed through the foyer into the living room. He nixed both the fireplace mantel and the glass coffee table in front of the couch. Then he spotted the teakwood table in the dining area and gave a satisfied nod. Perfect. He placed the box on the table.

Through the plate glass window, he saw Brian and his mother standing at the end of the dock, their arms around one another, heads touching, watching the sun beginning its descent toward the mountains beyond the lake's western shore.

Smiling again, he opened the box and lifted out the sculpture, placing it in the middle of the table, turning it to catch the light just so.

It was breathtaking.

Two hands, a man's and a woman's, lovingly intertwined, every bump and line rendered in flawless detail.

And even though he'd placed them on that table mere seconds before, he knew within the deepest regions of his heart those loving hands would remain together... forever....

Ms. Joanna Eleanor Richman

and

Mr. Brian Alden Weller

request the pleasure of your company
at their marriage
Saturday, the seventh of July
Two thousand and seven
at seven o'clock in the evening

Woodhaven

New London, New Hampshire

Acknowledgments

I would like to thank the following people for their invaluable contributions to the creation of this book:

Elizabeth Klungness for her deft guiding hand and sage editorial advice.

Serenity Richards for her keen typograhical eye, and for attempting to kill my excess commas.

John Devine, Refrerence Librarian at the Boston Public Library, for answering all my questions and for making me realize how much I miss Boston.

Liz Trupin-Pulli, my agent, for never losing faith.

Mike Kupka for translating my still life concept into wondrous reality.

Howie Rubin of Bauer Wines, oenophile extraordinaire.